This book cleverly marries the world of higher education intrigue, politics and wicked problems with those of the outside world and they come together beautifully. It made me smile, it made me reflect and it definitely gave me food for thought.

Jo Peat,
University of Roehampton

This book is both a very good read and a deeply thoughtful critique of the use and misuse of "quality" as a concept in UK higher education.

Tony McCulloch,
University College London

A satisfying, immersive, page turning mystery that also asks important questions about how we share and assess knowledge - at university but also more generally.

Professor Julie Hall,
London Metropolitan University

Fascinating, this book is an engaging novel and exploration of issues in higher education combined. This sounds like it can't be achieved, yet here it is. I found myself agreeing with the protagonists' discussions throughout the story. There are passages of pure romantic charm interspersed with agonies of second guessing.

Peter Gossman,
University of Worcester.

Who Stole Quality?

a university campus tale

Charlie Rondeau

MAPLE
PUBLISHERS

Who Stole Quality?

Author: Charlie Rondeau

Copyright © Charlie Rondeau (2024)

The right of Charlie Rondeau to be identified as author of this work has been asserted by the author in accordance with section 77 and 78 of the Copyright, Designs and Patents Act 1988.

First Published in 2024

ISBN 978-1-83538-069-7 (Paperback)
978-1-83538-070-3 (E-Book)

Book Cover Design and Book Layout by:
White Magic Studios
www.whitemagicstudios.co.uk

Published by:
Maple Publishers
Fairbourne Drive, Atterbury,
Milton Keynes,
MK10 9RG, UK
www.maplepublishers.com

A CIP catalogue record for this title is available from the British Library.

All rights reserved. No part of this book may be reproduced or translated by any form or by any means, electronic or mechanical, including photocopying, recording or by any information storage and retrieval system without written permission from the author.

The book is a work of fiction. Unless otherwise indicated, all the names, characters, places and incidents are either the product of the author's imagination or used in a fictitious manner. Any resemblance to actual people living or dead, events or locales is entirely coincidental, and the Publisher hereby disclaims any responsibility for them.

Prologue

What better place to look for examples of quality than on a university campus. Would any group of committed university lecturers not pursue quality in all aspects of their work - in their teaching; in their research; and in their publications? If they were lucky they might get to unite all three and produce a virtuous circle of activities. If they were unlucky they might have to imitate the person who tries to spin several plates at the same time. In which case, the quality may suffer, but it would be unlikely to dampen their desire to do the best they could in the circumstances.

This is a story about the pursuit of quality in a UK university environment. The policies and practices that feature are real. Readers already familiar with them will, no doubt, have their own interpretations as to their meaning and significance. The named institutions, agencies, and authors are also real, but all the unnamed institutions, scenarios, and characters are fictitious.

The book is written in the form of a novel, but by someone who is more used to academic writing conventions, not literary genres. There is a whodunnit here, but not one likely to bother the likes of a Rebus or a Wexford. Not traditional Crime Fiction, then. But things do need solving (or, perhaps better, re-solving). That said, maybe it is just a simple Romance.

The action takes place over a fifteen year period. Perhaps that qualifies it as Historical Drama, but it is very recent history. Certainly, it is no *War and Peace,* except as a metaphor for the turbulence experienced by the main characters, and as a reference to the university as a battleground of ideas.

Note on educational acronyms

The characters in this tale, on occasion, use some of the commonly accepted acronyms and abbreviations in circulation at the time.

QAA: The Quality Assurance Agency for Higher Education. The agency charged with reviewing the quality of learning and teaching in UK universities.

HEA: The Higher Education Academy. A national professional body, aimed at enhancing and recognising the value and status of learning and teaching in UK universities.

RAE: The Research Assessment Exercise. The national process whereby the quality of UK university research was evaluated between 1986 and 2008.

REF: The Research Excellence Framework. The replacement for the RAE, with an enhanced emphasis on the the impact of UK university research outside of academia.

FE: Further Education. A commonly used abbreviation for post-16 UK colleges which focus - but not exclusively - on vocational education and training courses, usually below - but not exclusively - degree-level.

HE: Higher Education. A commonly used abbreviation for the degree courses run by - but not exclusively - UK universities.

NSSE: The National Survey of Student Engagement. A survey used in American universities to judge the on-going quality of student participation and engagement in learning activities.

NSS: The National Student Survey. A summative survey used in UK universities to judge the overall quality of undergraduates' experiences of their degree courses.

For Graham, Patricia and Alfred

'When *I* use a word,' Humpty Dumpty said in rather a scornful tone, 'it means just what I choose it to mean - neither more nor less.

'The question is,' said Alice, 'whether you can make words mean so many different things.

'The question is,' said Humpty Dumpty, 'which is to be master - that's all.'

Lewis Carroll, *Through The Looking Glass*, Chapter 6

Part One

Paranoia

"Would she stick to a story, if they had one?"

(Dec 15th 2000 - Jan 14th 2001)

Chapter 1

It was the last day of term. Dr. Jack Lowell looked across the campus from the window of his third floor office. It was 4pm and the sun was setting behind a thick blanket of grey cloud. Jack had two things on his mind. He had received an email at lunchtime telling him that his article on totemic metaphors in urban environments had been accepted for publication, subject to minor changes. This would be his third peer-reviewed article to appear in an international journal. The news also meant he would feel more relaxed about discussing its contents in the paper he was due to present at a conference the following week. But it was unlikely that this academic success would register with his senior colleagues, and he let this gnaw away at him as the campus darkened.

The other thing on Jack's mind was whether his lover, Dr. Charlotte Rudolph, was going to ring him. It was around this time on a Friday afternoon they would sometimes meet - to walk, talk, and have sex. Jack had been hoping the phone wouldn't ring. He knew the relationship had to stop, but as he looked down at the phone he began willing it to ring. Lotte's mental state was a worry. He had watched her face change whenever there was even a hint that they might not be able see each other. Perhaps the right moment would just happen. He had been seeing Angela Salaman from the English Department for the last month and the feelings of guilt were becoming overbearing. At least the two women were very different which made it easier to split them in his head.

***

Across the other side of the campus, Dr. Charlotte Rudolph was looking out of her office window. From her second floor vantage point she could see the steady stream of staff and a few leftover students leaving the campus in the direction of town. This was the end of her fourth term at the university and she smiled as she thought about the kind words her students had said to her at the end of the seminar she had just returned from. She loved her students, and spent a good deal of her time thinking about how to make her classes interesting for them. But she was also aware how this was deflecting her attention away from her non-existent research profile.

Lotte had other things on her mind. She knew that her abusive husband was going to be late home that evening because the art college where he worked was having an end of term party. His college was twenty-five miles from their home, and because he would have been drinking, the need for him to catch a train would mean he was unlikely to appear before nine o'clock. It was always fifty-fifty whether the drinking would put him in a good or bad mood. She thought about Jack Lowell. She felt safe with him and the sex felt shared, nothing like the aggressive acts of domination she was often subjected to by her husband. She looked up at the clock on her office wall - 4.37. Her eyes then darted to the telephone, willing it to ring. She had the prospect before her of spending a few hours in that warm space with Jack, or a drive home to her house, where the clock on the living room wall would begin its count down to the sound of the key turning in the front door. It was no good, she had to ring Jack.

***

'Hello Jack, it's Lotte. I was wondering if you'd like a wander along the river into town?'

'And I was just wondering if you were going to ring. That'd be nice. I'll shut up shop and be over in ten minutes.'

Jack was relieved to hear Lotte's voice. The slight movement in his groin hastened his coat donning and confirmed to him that he had no choice in the matter of seeing Lotte. He also knew that Angela was away at a writing retreat and wouldn't be back in town until late in the evening. As he left his building he looked up to see whose lights were still on. The ground floor was in darkness; only seminar rooms there. Psychology, second floor, Sociology, third floor and History, fourth floor. Just a couple of lights on in the History Department, and one in Psychology: the office of his friend, Roger Fergusson. He walked briskly across campus, pleased to see it emptying, making it unlikely that he would see any of Angela's colleagues. Lotte was waiting by the entrance to the Philosophy Department, wearing her dark red coat and silk scarf, and she smiled as he approached.

They began walking towards town. Lotte motioned to lock her arm under his, but Jack was quick to remind her about such an obvious sign of affection in public. They continued their stroll in silence. A little way along the road into town a footpath branched off to the right, leading down to the river. This was the path they always took and as they approached the banks of the river Lotte broke the silence by asking Jack if he remembered the first time they had strolled along by the river.

That stroll had been six months earlier on a balmy June evening. It was also the first evening they had sex, in a secluded wood out of town, when it became obvious that neither of them wanted to drive back to their homes. Throughout the summer they looked for other secluded places. Jack became aware that Lotte was aroused when the chosen spots had more than a hint of the forbidden - like a cemetery. He loved the sense of adventure, but once he started piecing together the story of Lotte's abusive relationship with her husband, he also began wondering if there was something deeper going on.

It was cold down by the river, but warming up in a pub was not an option: it was likely they would be greeted by some of their colleagues enjoying an end of term drink. Instead, Jack checked that the coast was clear and then passed his arm around Lotte's waist. He motioned to have her lean against a large tree just off the path and began snuggling his nose into her neck. The combination of her silk scarf and warm neck was intoxicating, and he licked her ear lobe. She began undoing the bottom two buttons of his coat before gently slipping both her hands behind his lower back. 'Fancy a workout at the gym?' she whispered.

'That'd be nice.'

Lotte's question was code for having sex in the storage area above the old gym. This was a long room which stretched across the length of the gym ceiling. It contained a collection of old gym equipment and discarded office furniture. A few months back Lotte had overheard one of the porters explaining to a new recruit that there was a spare key to the door of this storage space at the end of the small shelf which rang along the top of the door. She had enjoyed enticing Jack to take advantage of the opportunity it presented. He was magnetically attracted to the cocktail of excitement and fear. Waiting for her invite was part of the attraction.

As they approached the building Jack looked up at the windows of the offices which were at one end. Ground floor, the University Admissions team; second floor, the Staff Development team; and third floor - the same floor where the storage area was - the Quality team. There was one office light on and it belonged to the Head of Quality, Dr. Richard McGiffen. His window blind was down, but you could work out from the shadows that there were two people standing in the room. Richard often worked late. 'I see Dickie Mac is still at it,' Jack said.

'Sad fuck.'

'There are two of them up there. Perhaps he's got his lover in there, and he's using a quality manual to guide him.' Jack and Richard were friends, but he felt comfortable saying it.

'His idea of sex is to photocopy some quality assurance data, roll it up, and stick it up his arse.'

They didn't need to go anywhere near Richard's room because there was a staircase at the other end of the building and the key was kept on that side. The seminar rooms were bound to be empty at this time, and seeing them all in darkness confirmed this. The small sign on the door read 'Storage Room OG3.2'. Lotte turned the key. Once inside, Jack took a deep breath, relieved that they were safely inside but also to take in the comforting smell of old furniture and rubber mats. Lotte initiated proceedings by locking their fingers together and rubbing her nose against his. This was a ritual they always performed before having sex. What followed was as explosive as ever. But then, suddenly, there was a loud thumping noise, then another, followed by one more. 'What the hell was that?' Jack whispered.

'Don't worry about it.'

They both knew it wouldn't be one of the porters, because they were creatures of habit and never began their rounds of the campus before 7.30 each evening.

'But I am worried,' Jack said. 'That was a loud noise.'

'It came from the other side of the building. McFuckface would have heard it and gone to investigate.'

Jack was comforted by the thought that if they did leave the room they were bound to bump into Richard, so best they stayed put. He didn't have any time to mull over any other options because Lotte beckoned him back towards her. Some ten minutes later and exhausted by the sex, they lay on the small piles of yoga mats, as they always did. Lotte was the first to speak: 'Will I see you over Christmas, Jack?'

'That might be tricky. I've got that conference next week and when I get back I need to visit my parents.'

Jack's parents were both ill, with cancers, and Lotte knew this.

'But you could come back after a few days, couldn't you?'

Jack pondered the question before answering: 'They'll probably expect me to stay over for Christmas. You could come to the conference with me; if you want?'

'You know I can't do that, even though I'd love to.'

'How about you ring me at home and see if I'm there?'

Jack looked at his watch. It was now 6.47 and time for them to go. He didn't want to leave anything to chance, even though he knew the porters never came to this building first. 'We need to get going,' he whispered.

'Can we just hold hands for another ten minutes?'

Without waiting for an answer, Lotte placed her head on Jack's chest. From past experience he knew that more sex was likely to follow, but he was also anxious that she might begin speaking about their relationship. After a couple of minutes he broke the silence: 'Come on, I don't want to take any chances; I love it up here.'

'I'd like to see the look on the porter's face if he saw us leaving the room.'

'Not going to happen,' Jack said.

His instant response became the cue for both of them to tidy themselves up, shut the door, and return the key to its place.

As they made their way to the car park, they passed the library, which still had all of its lights on. A postgraduate student was coming down the steps. She shouted out: 'Happy Christmas and New Year, Dr Lowell. I doubt I'll see you again until the new year, so have a good one.'

Jack acknowledged the greeting, and shouted back: '2001 already!'

Lotte enquired as to why he didn't seem bothered they had been seen together.

'We're just walking to the car park together, aren't we?'

'Yes, after having had sex above the old gym.'

Jack pondered the remark; her mischievousness was always attractive, if a little dangerous at times.

They waved goodbye to each other across the tops of their cars which were some distance apart in the almost empty car park. Jack was relieved that he would be returning to the comfort of his flat, where he could lock the door and put his feet up. As he drove off, he steadily turned up the volume dial on the car stereo as he picked up speed: Bryan Adams, *Reckless* album. But it was not long before his mind was turning back to the thumping noise he had heard earlier. He thought about going back to see if there was any evidence as to what it was. He decided against it. What would he say to anyone who saw him: 'I heard a noise an hour ago when I was in a storage room and I've come back to see what it was?'

Chapter 2

Dr. Jack Lowell was 36 years old. He had worked at the University for just over five years. Previous to that he had worked part-time in a couple of other universities, just for a few hours a week. It was a relief when he was finally offered a full-time permanent academic post at his present institution. The post was in the Sociology Department, the subject of first degree, master's, and PhD. His PhD was on the significance of linear time in Marxist thought, but when he realised how crowded the field of Marxist studies already was, he switched his research interest to the work of the French sociologist Emile Durkheim, after having taught an undergraduate course on the founding fathers of sociology. It was there that he realised that a radical reinterpretation of Durkheim's work was underway and that he might be better off joining that small band wagon rather than the juggernaut which Marxist studies had become.

Jack enjoyed his teaching, particularly on the master's programme, and he was supervising two PhD students. He had imagined that he would be more research-active than he actually was by this point in his career, but he was finding it difficult to secure a big research grant - one from which he could buy himself out of some of his undergraduate teaching. The University was a former polytechnic and was one of the first to be granted university status after the 1992 Higher Education Act - the Act which enabled a wider range of institutions to apply for university status. The University was gaining a good reputation for its research output, but Jack had his sights set on a job in pre-1992 university, one where he imagined he would be able to devote more of his time to his research interests.

There was another reason that Jack wanted out from his present post. His research reputation needed a boost by being successful in the Research Assessment Exercise - the national process by which the quality of university research was measured. Although the University took part in the exercise, it was in a limited capacity, and Jack was convinced that the internal panel of his peers - who judged which work should go forward - was shunning him. He would be the first to admit that his research output was nowhere near prolific, but he was developing a reputation and his work was being cited by other academics. If that panel would just support him a little more it could just be the impetus he needed, and it might also help him secure that big research grant.

Jack had reserved a good deal of contempt for one particular research panel member: Dr. Ralph Smythe, the Director of Research at the University. From Jack's checking, Smythe's own research output appeared to amount to one peer-reviewed journal article and a small number of professional consultancy documents. He hadn't written a single book and didn't appear to have secured any large research funds.

Jack's only one-to-one with Ralph Smythe hadn't gone well. Whenever he thought about that meeting he could only see Smythe's fountain pen casually striking out bits of his CV as irrelevant. Jack had reconciled himself to his fate by concluding that your face had to fit. He didn't consider himself to have a chip on his shoulder, but he was from a working-class background, and his overarching assessment of the situation was that this contemptible representative of the Oxbridge elite just had it in for him - unconsciously, perhaps.

He regularly trawled the higher education job adverts, while continuing to enjoy his teaching. He tried to interest his undergraduate students in research processes by looking for ways to link his own research with his teaching. Sometimes he would stop a lecture and ask his audience of undergraduates how they might go about solving a problem. If some of them took the bait he would then proceed to ask them how valid and reliable they thought their knowledge gathering techniques might be, and how useful any results might be for various official bodies, including the government of the day. Depending on their reaction he might then say that he would continue the discussion in the upcoming seminar. It was clear that his students enjoyed his approach and it was not long before this came to the attention of the Quality Officer, Dr. Richard McGiffen. Richard had asked Jack if he would run a workshop for all the academics at the University on innovative ways to link research and teaching. The first one was not well attended, but Richard was keen that the workshop should become an annual staff development event, and soon after that Richard and Jack struck up a friendship.

***

Dr. Charlotte Rudolph always imagined she would become some kind of teacher. Her father was German and had taught Philosophy for many years at a German university, before meeting her mother. Her mother's degree was in German and they had met while she was on a postgraduate exchange programme in the university where her father taught. He was fifteen years her senior and they decided it would be easier for him to secure a university post in England, while her mother looked to secure a permanent post as a secondary school teacher on the outskirts of London. Their relationship was tempestuous from the start. Her mother had a strict Catholic upbringing, which they endlessly argued about, and the abusive hold her father had over her mother was apparent throughout Lotte's childhood.

Lotte's first degree was in Philosophy, but she then opted for a master's in Women's Studies. She went on to complete her PhD on the subject of splits in the radical feminist separatist movement. While she was undertaking her research she won a scholarship and with the money she spent a year at the University of California, in Berkeley, interviewing radical feminists on their enlightenment trajectories. While in the United States she began envying the freedom that tenured academics seemed to have - in their teaching styles, pursuing their own research interests, and in their freedom of speech. By comparison, the UK seem like an academic straitjacket, with its emerging limitations on how you must teach; how research must be linked with specific departmental objectives; and how you increasingly needed to demonstrate some kind of corporate allegiance. She often asked herself why universities needed to be corporations, but hadn't ever looked into it. Some of her concerns had been prompted by her father's stories about the increasing need to steer research in particular directions if you wanted to be a successful academic, but also by having seen her mother openly cry after a visit from a group of Ofsted school inspectors. By comparison, there seemed to be much more trust in professionals in the United States.

After returning from the United States, Lotte taught part-time in a local college, and on an adult education evening class course, while she wrote up her PhD. It was at the adult education centre that she met her future husband. He was also running a course there, on the History of Art, and she instantly fell under his spell, as he outlined over coffee-breaks how Art was able to transform people from the inside out. Each week she would look forward to the coffee-breaks, which grew into dinners and days out at museums. He was eleven years older and she looked up to him. Although she hadn't entertained the idea of marriage, she accepted his proposal after eighteen months of dating. Her only stipulation was that she keep her maiden name. It was a few months into their marriage that the abuse started. With the benefit of hindsight she knew she should have been quicker to see his fits of temper for what they really were. But, at the time, and in textbook fashion, he always explained them away as part of his artistic temperament, and she had, somewhat naively, accepted that.

Lotte was shocked and delighted when she got a full-time post at the University. She hadn't long completed her PhD, and she was still only 26 years old. The interview panel had been impressed with her knowledge of both philosophy and feminism, and asked if she could start immediately. For the first few months she could feel a little skip in her step every time she made her way from the car park to her office. She had no great aspiration to become a research-focused academic and the interview panel had made it clear to her that her main responsibility would be to teach first-year undergraduates. She was delighted to hear that and immersed herself in preparing her classes. She knew she would be required to become research-active at some point, because of the University's aspirations. And for that purpose, she had composed a paragraph in her head, should she ever need to outline a research proposal. Her father was an expert on the 19th century philosopher Fredrick Nietzsche, and she had written an undergraduate dissertation on his work. She was well aware of the feminist backlash against Nietzsche - because of some of his comments on women - but she also knew that there was a small, but growing, literature base, arguing that his philosophy *was* in keeping with many feminist principles.

Lotte enjoyed working in the Philosophy Department. Her colleagues didn't spend much time together, and seemed quite cut-off from the rest of the University. It suited her because she didn't feel the need to socialise, and she knew it angered her husband every time she mentioned University get-togethers and possible attendance at University events. She also liked the fact that many of her colleagues in the Department had nothing but contempt for the quality agenda which was sweeping across the campus. The Department had a reputation for not showing its face at staff development events aimed at enhancing professional practice. She would often overhear colleagues running down people who worked in the staff development and quality teams, with comments like: 'what do they know about teaching philosophy or undertaking research?' And those comments were in keeping with what she thought about the inspectors who had made her mother cry. But the Philosophy Department *was* holding a trump card: they had done far better than anyone expected in the last Research Assessment Exercise, which had helped to enhance the University's reputation.

Chapter 3

Jack was enjoying his morning coffee in bed, part of his Saturday morning ritual, but before long he was combing through the papers in his shoulder bag. Somewhere in there had to be the letter giving details of the arrival arrangements for the conference where he was due to present his paper the following week. Frustrated about not being able to find it, he reconciled himself to the fact that he would have to return to his office on campus. This was only a three-mile drive, and, had it not been the middle of winter, he would have made the journey by bike. Before he left his flat, he phoned Angela Salaman to see if she would like a coffee in town. She lived ten minutes from campus so there was every prospect that she would accept the offer. She said she would meet him in an hour, at the coffee shop where they had meet several times before.

As he pulled into the University car park, Jack could sense that something wasn't right. There were far too many cars there for a Saturday morning, particularly given that term had finished. He wondered if the usual parking restrictions had been lifted because something was going on in town. Then he saw two police cars, parked in the corner. Just as he was locking his car door, he saw Dr. Norman Thornhill, a colleague from the History Department, who was moving quickly towards him. His shoulder length hair was bouncing as he walked, and his tweed jacket and corduroy trousers completed what Jack considered to be his weekend look. They had little in common, but had become friends after discussions about how the purpose and role of universities had changed over the years. Norman's Oxford DPhil had been on the moral foundations of the work of Cardinal Newman and Jack had often used Norman's ideas in his workshops on teaching and learning. As soon as he was in earshot, Norman blurted out: 'It's unbelievable, isn't it?'

'What is?'

'Haven't you heard, Jack? Richard McGiffen is dead.'

'What do you mean? How?'

Norman proceeded to relay the emerging story: Richard McGiffen had been discovered on the second floor of his building, at the foot of the stairs which led up to his office on the third floor; the porter had found the blood-stained body, around eight o'clock the previous evening; the police had cordoned off the whole area, and officers were moving in and around the building which housed the old gym.

Jack was taken aback, but not so much that he didn't start thinking about his own movements the previous evening. He had probably been no more than one hundred feet from where he imagined Richard had met his demise. He thanked Norman for telling him the grim news, and explained that he needed to be alone to take it all in. He walked back to his car, but decided to head into town. He was not yet late for his meeting with Angela, and he decided that he wanted her company.

Angela was sitting at their favourite two-person table. 'Hey, that was lucky, I got our table,' she said, as he approached her.

'Brilliant. I'm sorry I'm a bit late. My trip to campus was more eventful than I expected.' He thought it best to get the coffees before he said anything else.

Angela was a part-time lecturer, and only taught on one course at the university - on the 19th century novel - while she completed her PhD. Somewhat paradoxically, her PhD thesis was on the significance of breaking form in the postmodern novel, but she had often explained to her non-university friends that beggars can't be choosers, and that you were lucky if you got to teach on courses that directly related to your research.

After a little bit of coaxing, Jack repeated the story that Norman Thornhill had given him thirty minutes earlier. He extended the story slightly to explain that Richard had been the Quality Officer at the University, and that they had been friends. Angela had little idea what a Quality Officer did, but didn't say anything. She rested her hand on Jack's knee at the point he mentioned their friendship. When Jack paused she said she would be happy to stay with him if that would help. Jack decided that it would help, and after finishing their coffees they went back to his flat. They ended up laying on his bed for most of the afternoon, gentling caressing each other. Half of him hoped that she might initiate something more, but when she didn't, he decided she might think less of him if he made any wrong moves. Darkness began to surround them, and around five o'clock she said that she was due to meet up with some friends for dinner.

Jack spent the evening in darkness, feeling guilty that his thoughts kept returning to what the police were uncovering, rather than mourning his friend. He was sure that nobody had seen him go up to the storage room with Lotte. He always checked that the coast was clear, and given that the building was well used it wouldn't be unusual for two academics to be seen entering it. But this was different. What if somebody had noticed, and they had already told the police? His thoughts whirled around, but not so fast that each one could not be processed. He decided, categorically, that he would have to tell the police about his tryst with Lotte; at least that he had been in the building with her. Or perhaps he could say that it was just him in the building. But what if Lotte was interviewed? Lotte, Lotte; what was she going to do? Would she stick to a story, if they had one?

One thing that Jack was clear about were the thumping noises he had heard from the storage room: that was definitely Richard falling down the stairs. But was he pushed; was it an accident; and who was that person in Richard's room? No doubt about that, he would have to tell the police about the mystery person. But would he be able to pull that off, convincingly?: He was pretty sure that second person was his friend, Roger Fergusson; mainly judging from the height of the silhouette. He could say that he was some distance from the building, heading to the library, and that he just glanced over. But what was actually wrong with saying that he was having sex with Lotte? The answer to that question was obvious: her husband, and Angela. And what about Gracia, the postgraduate student, who had shouted to him from the steps of the library. What if she had already stepped forward and told the police who she had seen on the evening of the murder. Murder? Surely, it was an accident. If it was an accident then nothing needed to be said.

Jack was calmed by his final thought, but not for long, because all the other thoughts returned and he went through them all again, and again, each time trying to carefully process them, in order to close off the possibility of being implicated in Richard's death. But what if people concluded that he might be the perpetrator? Eventually, he hauled himself off to bed, only for the processing to begin again.

Chapter 4

Lotte looked forward to Saturday mornings, when she would drive the ten miles to the market in the town closest to her village. It was a good place to take stock of the week's events and she enjoyed the small-talk in and around the stalls. The market was quiet during the winter months, but none of that mattered. She was relieved to have left the house before her husband had got up. He hadn't come home until 11pm the previous evening, by which time she had gone to bed. She had listened carefully to his usual moves: shoes hitting the wooden floor, the toilet flushing, his teeth cleaning ritual, and finally his watch meeting the bedside table. As he moved around the place she imitated deep sleep. Within ten minutes he began snoring. This was a good sign, because the more drunk he was the more he snored. He was at his most abusive when he was slightly drunk, but she had learnt not to take anything for granted; the anger switch was easily flipped.

As she wandered around the market her mind was mainly on Jack and the storage room above the old gym. She saw her head approach his chest; the comforting smell of his skin; and how his raised heartbeat had relaxed her. She thought about his gentleness while they were having sex, but also how she wished he would let himself go a bit more. Her mind moved to the public places they'd had sex, and how easy it was to tease him about his nervousness. Jack was very much work in progress, except she had made little progress in understanding what lay behind his desire to spend so much time in his own space. Except, of course, his obvious concerns about her husband, although he'd never actually said anything. But, maybe, they were her *own* concerns. They'd never discussed him, so perhaps this was the next step.

She needed to cut short her trip because she was going out with her husband at midday. She stopped to buy sandwiches from the artisan bread stall so they could have a picnic lunch in the car. They were due at an art exhibition being staged by a friend. She was sure he would be in a good mood in the car, and at his gregarious best amongst his friends.

It was a pleasant afternoon, which culminated in the suggestion that the two of them stay over for the night at a friend's house. A group of them had planned a trip into central London the following day and it would be much easier if they all headed into town from the Underground station, which was close to the couple's house. But around 7pm Lotte explained to the female host that she was pre-menstrual and that she would prefer to go home. Within a few minutes a simple plan was agreed: Lotte would drive home and her husband would get the train back from Paddington Station the following afternoon.

***

Lotte enjoyed making scrambled eggs and toast on a Sunday morning. The weather was cold, but the sun was shining through the kitchen window as she watched the birds pecking at the food she always provided. She was busy with thoughts about how she might get to spend some time with Jack on this fortuitous day. Around 11am she finally picked up the phone, having convinced herself that she could persuade him they should meet up. She let the phone ring for some time before putting down the receiver. He must be there she thought, so five minutes later she tried again. Then again, another five minutes later. She had tried this tactic before: Jack always picked up in the end.

After ringing Jack on and off for nearly an hour, Lotte decided there was nothing for it: she was going to drive to his flat. She had been there on a couple of occasions, but they had agreed that it was not a good place to meet in case her husband found out the address. On the drive over she began increasingly winding her self up about why Jack had not answered the phone, but then calming herself down by the prospect of being in his arms. Perhaps this would be the right moment to discuss her husband with him, but in his flat? As she approached his flat she hit the steering wheel hard: was Jack seeing someone else; perhaps he didn't realise how much he meant to her; perhaps she wasn't smart enough for him? And what would be the point in leaving her husband if she didn't have Jack?

She parked close to Jack's flat, composed herself, then strode purposefully to the front entrance of his block. She paused for a moment and then pushed hard on his buzzer. 'Hello Jack, it's Lotte.'

He buzzed her in and within a few minutes she was approaching his door, which he had already opened.

'I just don't understand you sometimes, Jack.'

'Sorry Lotte, I'm just really depressed about what has happened.'

'Well!' she shouted. 'What *has* happened?'

'Richard...Richard McGiffen is dead.'

'What!'

Jack motioned for them to sit down on the sofa, where their conversation quickly turned to the question of whether they should go to the police.

'But what do we know?' Lotte said. 'Other than the fact we heard some thumping noises. That doesn't prove anything.'

'But we did see that person in his office. And that's got to be significant.'

Lotte could sense that Jack's real concern was to say something to the police in order to alleviate some of his misplaced guilt. But this was certainly not the time for her husband to find out that she'd be on the campus with Jack.

'But we don't know who that person was, Jack?'

'Well, we certainly need to think about this. We can't just leave it.'

Lotte motioned to hold Jack's hand, but, in response, he put both hands on his head. She rubbed her hand on his thigh, which made him lower his head closer to his knees.

'Don't you want me here, Jack?'

'Lotte, It's not that, I just need to think things through.'

'You do still want us though, don't you...Jack?'

'I just need to be on my own for a while. Can we take a break, Lotte?'

There. He'd said it.

'Are you seeing someone else?'

Lotte had been desperate to ask this question before and now she'd just blurted it out.

'What do you mean by *seeing*?'

There. The confirmation.

'Who is she? Do you love her? What's she like in bed?'

'It's not like that. She's very sweet.'

'Lame, you mean? I bet she doesn't do I what I do?'

'Can we not talk about this now?'

She pushed him against the back of the sofa, and put her knees either side of his thighs. He tried to move her away from her, but she started beating her fists against his arms. He raised them in case she hit his face, which enabled her to keep beating.

Lotte looked down on Jack, angry that he looked like a pathetic rag doll.

'Please, stop!' Jack yelled, as he began crying.

Lotte fell to the floor, banging the carpet with her fists. Jack got up and positioned the two of them so they were lying side by side, and then nestled his face into the base of her neck. After around fifteen minutes, Jack started to stand up, picking her up as he rose. He cuddled her as they walked to his bed. They lay there, caressing each other for the next two hours. As the room darkened, Lotte whispered in Jack's ear that she needed to get going. They gently hugged by the front door, kissed each other on the cheek, but said nothing.

***

Lotte's husband arrived back at their home around seven o'clock, a good hour after she had arrived home from Jack's flat. He was in a good mood and told her the news about plans for an exhibition of his own work. To celebrate, they went out for a pizza, where they chatted about what he might put in the exhibition. She offered suggestions which he said he would consider. She was pleased he only had two glasses of wine. He was exhausted when they got home and went off to bed early. When she joined him, he kissed her on the cheek and cuddled up to her. As she drifted off to sleep, she decided that this new woman in Jack's life was no match for her: he just needed to be shown more clearly what she could offer him.

Chapter 5

Jack lay in bed on Monday morning, inspecting his arms. It looked like they were covered in bruises all the way up to his shoulders. This was the evidence he needed. There was no need to see Lotte anymore. In his head he could see a huge throbbing vein on her neck as her fist came down on him. He wondered if she regretted her violent outburst, but then realised that he was thinking about her again. His mind wandered back to why he had started seeing Angela Salaman. She was safe and predictable. Lotte was the opposite. He was magnetically attracted to Lotte, the wild horse, running in and out of his life, but her marriage worried him, and so did the bruises he sometimes saw on *her* arms. It was definitely time to focus on Angela, but, knowing that he needed to prepare for his conference, he decided against ringing her that morning.

By the time he was dressed, Jack had resolved to tell the police that he *had* seen someone in Richard's office, but couldn't offer a description because of the blinds and his distance from the building when he had looked up. He had enough time to do it because his conference was only a 90-minute train journey away, in Birmingham, and he wouldn't be presenting his paper until the following morning. Everything in place, he thought, except that conference letter, which he realised he hadn't collected from his office on Saturday morning. After breakfast, he drove back to campus, thinking he would first find the conference letter, then walk to the police station in town.

In the car, he rehearsed what he was going to say to the police: that he had seen Richard's office light on; that there were two people in there; that he couldn't make out who the second person was; perhaps neither of them were Richard. He liked the final comment because it looked like he was adding useful information into the mix. If they asked him about what he was doing near the building, he would now say that he was going to one of the seminar rooms at the other end because he was sure he had left something in one of the rooms. As soon as he pictured himself climbing the stairs to the seminar room on the third floor he panicked that Lotte might tell the police something different, but he comforted himself by the thought of her husband, knowing she wouldn't risk him finding out.

Jack found the conference letter, but just as he was locking up his office door, out popped Dr. Marion Barton from the room next door, his colleague from the Sociology Department. Marion taught courses on the sociology of law, specialising in social justice. She had undertaken her PhD, part-time, while working at the University, on the subject of police policy and practice in the 1980s. She was also a qualified solicitor and was often consulted by the University Solicitor's Office.

'Hello Jack. I thought that was you. I suppose you know everything?'

Jack confirmed that he did know everything, but was then taken aback when Marion said that the police had been interviewing their colleague, Dr Roger Fergusson, from the Psychology Department.

Jack and Roger had been good friends for some time. Their friendship began after a heated argument, when Jack had stated that he considered Psychology a conservative and reactionary discipline. Roger had countered by arguing that the more psychoanalytically-minded psychologists were far more radical than the majority of sociologists. Roger taught a course on the work of Sigmund Freud and they had subsequently spent many an hour discussing Freud's challenge to mainstream psychology. Roger's PhD research was on the use of clinical terms in cultural contexts, including classroom settings, and he always attended Jack's workshops on teaching and learning for academic staff.

Jack was anxious for Roger, but still consumed by how he might, himself, be implicated in Richard's death. 'Really, Marion? What's that all about?' He asked his question, hoping his guilt complex wasn't written all over his face. Marion explained that Roger had told her about the earlier meeting in Jack's office and that he'd then had a blazing row in Richard's office. Jack knew that Roger was going over to see Richard because he had come to see him first, in order to take some advice. Jack had not put two-and-two together, because the meeting between Roger and Richard had been scheduled for 4pm. Could Roger have been there two hours later; maybe he went back, and that's when the real argument started? Marion went on to explain that Roger had voluntarily gone to the police, in the hope that he might eliminate himself from their enquires. She said he had been nervous because he knew he would have to admit that there had been an argument, and this might implicate him in some way.

'Is Roger all right?' Jack asked.

'Yes, I spoke to him on the phone. The police told him they would be in touch if they needed any more information.'

He thanked Marion, and then made a hasty retreat, using the conference as his excuse. As he walked back across campus he reflected on the current situation. Roger had been to see Jack because he wanted to make it clear that he intended to confront Richard about what he considered to be the poor advice Richard had offered for the impending visit to the Psychology Department by The Quality Assurance Agency for Higher Education - the body who review the quality of teaching in UK universities. That visit had not gone well, and the Department had received the lowest score so far for any of the University's departments - 20 out of a possible score of 24. Roger had taken it particularly badly, having played a major role in amassing the necessary documentation for the visit. And Jack had agreed that it probably would be a good idea to have it out with Richard.

Jack considered it preposterous that Roger might consider killing Richard, but what if things had got heated and Roger had accidentally pushed Richard down the stairs? Jack comforted himself by hearing the words that his mother often used: it'll all come out in the wash. Indeed it would, he thought. He also thought that surely he was now in the clear, because there was no longer a mystery man. What would be the point of telling his story to the police? It wouldn't add anything. He had heard the thumps all right, but surely it must be clear to the police by now that Richard had fallen down the stairs. And how would *he* know what initiated the fall? That's a job for forensic science. Except for the timings. Jack knew he had seen the two people behind the office blind a little after 6pm. That must be relevant. Perhaps there had been another visitor to Richard's office, after Roger? The Psychology Department had only just received its low score in the review, so perhaps a queue of people had been to see Richard that day? Jack also knew that the thumps must have occurred a little after 6.30pm. But what if the police wanted precision? 'I was preoccupied and couldn't be sure' just wasn't going to cut it.

By the time that Jack had got back to his car, he was clear that this was not the time to go to the police. He needed to get more information from Roger, but he wasn't sure exactly what. He would just have to hope that Roger would start up a conversation, which he might then surreptitiously steer in appropriate directions. He comforted himself again, this time by the thought that at least he'd had the accidental good sense to go on to campus before going to the police, and also by the thought that he would be away for the next two nights at the conference.

Chapter 6

Lotte was at home, thinking about Christmas, about how the last two had turned violent. It was possible she would be able to engineer spending time with her parents, but that often didn't go well either, because of her poor relationship with her father. It was no good suggesting that they go to her husband's parents, because she knew they didn't like her. But staying at home was just not on. She had promised herself 'never again' last January 1st, and had assumed that she would have left the marital home by now. But here was another year gone and she hadn't been able to make the move. And last summer had brought so much promise. Where did those months go, and where had Jack gone? With Jack came a brighter future, but it was not all his fault. She knew she had to leave the marital home of her own accord. Was this the real reason why Jack was acting so strangely? Was he disappointed that she was still living with a violent man? It was clear to her that Jack had no idea how to handle the bruises he had seen on her arms. It was also clear that the weekend had been uneventful, so what excuse would she have to leave her husband at this moment?

Was she actually hoping her husband would abuse her in the coming week, giving her the excuse to leave? She hated admitting to herself that she had wished this before, and she also hated admitting to herself that she lacked the courage to just get up and go each time. She had developed a wide range of coping strategies, but had often reflected on how they acted against her. She then reminded herself that she was a rational person, jumped up, and decided to make some coffee. As she left the dinning room, she glanced across at the birthday card her husband had bought her. No mention of her birthday from Jack, she thought; she remembered telling him when it was.

There was no reason for either of them to be out of the house. Lotte's husband was beginning his exhibition curation in the studio. At lunchtime, in the kitchen, he became annoyed about the amount of coffee in the cupboards compared to tea. The bickering escalated throughout the afternoon. Early evening, Lotte ended up with more bruises. This time with one around the eye. He was always careful not to harm Lotte's face, but a misplaced punch had accidentally caught her on the eye. He withdrew immediately. Lotte retreated to the bedroom to recover, and heard nothing from him that evening. He slept that night in the studio on a camp bed. Nice birthday, she thought, before turning over to go to sleep.

Lotte was up early the next morning, hoping she could slip out of the house before seeing her husband. He was up because she could see that the studio door was open, but he said nothing as she made her way to the front door. She shouted down the corridor that she was going to the supermarket. She was actually planning to see the only friend she had confided in, Carol Morgan. They had become friends when they were both students on the master's course in Women's Studies, a friendship which continued when Carol got a part-time job locally in a solicitor's office and began volunteering at a nearby women's refuge. Carol had suggested several times to Lotte that she should consider moving into a refuge, partly because of her own positive experience several years before. Carol was twenty years older than Lotte, and although she looked up to her, Lotte had made it clear that there was no way she would contemplate going into a refuge.

The sun was bright as Lotte drove to meet Carol. She tapped the steering wheel as she listened to Nina Simone's greatest hits on the CD player. She dropped her sunglasses down her nose and looked in the rearview mirror, to check that the concealer was doing its job. She stopped at a telephone box by the side of the road to see if Carol was available for coffee.

They agreed to meet at a nearby garden centre. When she pulled into the car park she could see the place was busier than she was expecting. Christmas decorations were for sale around the entrance, along with a row of Christmas trees. The sight stirred a mixture of emotions, but she brushed them aside as she strode to the coffee shop, which was in a separate, but connected building. As soon as she opened the door she was greeted by the comforting smell of coffee. Carol was already there and she waved at Lotte from a table on the opposite side of the room. The fact that Lotte was still wearing her sunglasses meant that no small talk was required.

At that table in the garden centre cafe, Operation Remove Lotte was put in motion. Lotte would move in with Carol and her partner. Carol would keep occasional watch on the marital home and if her husband drove off in his car, Lotte would get the signal to move in and quickly collect as many of her belongings as she could. Knowing that Lotte's husband would suspect where she might be, Carol would ring him and explain the situation. Carol had nothing but contempt for him and if he even dropped a hint that he was going to come and get Lotte, she was clear that she would threaten to phone the police, *and* definitely phone the Principal of his college. Carol knew he would not be that worried about the police because he would know how to allay any fears they might have. But the Principal: He *would* be concerned about that.

Carol had been planning for this eventuality for some time, but would only have initiated proceedings on Lotte's request. Lotte hated the thought that Carol would phone the Principal. She knew how much her husband loved his work and how mortified he would be. She also knew it could result in an almighty eruption of anger, which might get her friend hurt, as well as herself.

Chapter 7

Jack arrived back home from his conference on Wednesday evening. He was looking forward to buying a takeaway and relaxing in front of the TV, but he was also mulling over what he needed to say to Roger Fergusson. He couldn't wait until after Christmas. He had the perfect excuse to ring him: that he had heard from Marion about the police interview, but it had taken him so long to make contact because of his conference paper.

Just after ten o'clock the next morning Jack made the call. 'Hello Roger; it's Jack. Sorry to phone you at home, but I was worried about you and wanted to know how you were.'

'It's nice of you to call, Jack. I suppose you know I went to the police? It was very pleasant, and they seemed happy with what I told them. I was hoping they were going to say I was eliminated from their enquires, but instead they said they'd be in touch if they needed to be, and they would prefer it if I stayed at home over the Christmas period. That freaked me a bit, but on reflection, what else were they going to say.'

'Indeed. Marion told me that the meeting you had with Richard had been explosive. I thought it might be.' They both laughed nervously. 'How long were you with Richard?'

'Now *you're* sounding like the police. I guess it was a couple of hours.'

'Blimey. I thought you were just going to say your piece and get out of there.'

Roger went on to explain that this had been his plan, but they had ended up going through all the reasons why Psychology had dropped so many points in the visit by the Quality Assurance Agency. Richard said he was pleased that the course management had been praised, and that he could see why some aspects of the teaching and learning regime had been criticised. This was the red-rag-to-a-bull comment, from which the heated argument had began. Jack keep fishing to see how he could get back to the crucial issue of timings, but there was no obvious way to do it. Roger was concerned to get a reconfirmation from Jack that there *was* a sound case to be had against Richard: that it was, indeed, Richard's poor advice on how to handle the teaching and learning questions that resulted in the Department's poor score.

Once the phone conversation had come to its natural end, they both wished each other a happy Christmas break. Jack was already pretty sure that the person he saw behind the blinds in Richard's room *was* Roger, but now he had the confirmation. He was also sure he had not heard any raised voices while he was in the storage room with Lotte, indicating that their argument must have finished by that point. He was also pretty clear that Roger had nothing to do with Richard's fall, other than the fact he had obviously put Richard in an agitated state. Perhaps Richard had a heart attack? It'll all come out in the wash, he thought, again. For the time being Jack could see no reason to go to the police. If he heard that the police wanted to reinterview

Roger that would naturally change things. But had he conveyed any guilt feelings to Roger? Was Roger now suspicious of *him*?

Jack lay on his sofa thinking everything through again, but this time he kept coming back to the thought that perhaps *he* had caused Richard's death, by winding up Roger.

Chapter 8

Carol and her partner, Marjorie Hayworth, had spent a good part of the last three days reassuring Lotte that everything was going to be okay. Margie worked at a local further education college as an admissions advisor, directing students to courses and study support opportunities. She was only three years older than Lotte, but they had never struck up much of a friendship. Lotte put this down to a kind of sibling rivalry between the two of them with regard to Carol's attention. But since Lotte had moved in, Margie had been extremely kind, perhaps privately acknowledging that Carol needed to put her arms around Lotte at this crucial time. While appreciating all the kindness, Lotte remained anxious that her husband would come knocking at the front door.

A letter from her husband arrived on the fourth day, which Lotte's eyes darted all over to check what threats were contained therein. There were none, just apologies and reminders about good times, and at statement at the end that he was happy for her to stay at Carol's over Christmas. Carol demanded to read the letter but dismissed it before she had even got through the first page: 'You are not to reply to this, Lotte.'

'But if I don't reply he'll get angry and probably come round here.'

'And I'll be waiting for him.'

The letter was left on the kitchen table, and commented on every time one of them caught sight of it.

Carol and Margie made it clear to Lotte that one of them would always be in the house with her, but on Lotte's insistence, both women went Christmas shopping on Saturday morning. As soon as they left the house Lotte rehearsed once more what she would say to Jack, if she could get him to answer his phone. She felt she had nothing to lose by phoning him. She looked at her watch and decided that this would be a good time to ring - Saturday lunchtime.

Jack picked up the phone, assuming it was one of his parents.

'Hello Jack, it's Lotte.'

'Hi Lotte. You know you don't have to say your name; I know it's you.'

'I'd really appreciate your advice, Jack.'

She had thought this would be the right way to start the conversation, but his last comment put her on edge.

'Of course.'

'I've left him, and I need to think about where I'm going to live.'

She spoke calmly, and without emotion.

'Where are you now?'

'I'm at a friend's house. Do you think we could meet up for a coffee?'

Jack explained that he was just about to leave to visit his parents, but agreed that a meeting would be a good idea.

'Look,' Jack said, 'I could come up from Brighton next Tuesday. What about we meet in London?'

'That would be lovely.'

Lotte was disappointed that it wouldn't be sooner, but at least a date was fixed and it would be something to look forward to.

'Where shall we meet?' Jack asked.

'How about in the restaurant at the Victoria and Albert Museum?'

Lotte liked the V and A, mainly because she knew her husband didn't. In her head, she could hear him saying that it wasn't contemporary enough. Because of that, as an act of defiance, she became even more attached to the place. She had often imagined wandering around the museum rooms with Jack. They agreed to meet on the steps outside at midday, or just inside if it was cold or wet.

Lotte smiled to herself, pleased with how well the phone call had gone, and that she now had a positive focus. But, alone in the house, she began reflecting on Jack's tone, repeating his sentences in her head, each time with a different emphasis. She thought of Scorsese's Travis Bickell, talking to himself in the mirror. Still, the ball was now in her court. She began preparing some lecture notes. After a few minutes her eye was drawn to the opened notepad where she had jotted down some ideas for an academic paper, on Nietzsche and Feminism. She placed a book over the notepad, but then started thinking about how she would love to tell her father that she had presented a conference paper on Nietzsche.

***

Jack was looking forward to the train journey up from Brighton to London; meeting up with Lotte once he was there was another matter. As he entered Brighton Station he took a deep breath, to take in the smell of coffee and pastries. He recalled that sense of adventure when his parents first trusted him to make the journey up to London on his own. He looked up at the train announcement boards above the platform entrances. There was something lyrical about the familiar order of the train stations to London, and he rehearsed the order several times over in his head.

His train was going to be late so he bought a coffee and a *pain au raison*. As he sat, he took stock of his visit to his parents. It had followed a familiar pattern: pleasant childhood thoughts on the journey down, which slowly turned sour when he failed to connect with them in actual conversation. He had no idea how to talk about their illnesses, and by the time he went to bed on the first night he was feeling the usual mix of anxiety and guilt.

As he drank his coffee at the station, he reflected on the previous evening, and his brother, who had joined the family for dinner. His brother was a builder, who had left school without any qualifications, and still lived close to the family home. These facts always heightened his sense of estrangement from the family, which was made worse by never having been able to adequately explain to his brother or his parents what exactly he did all day. Being the first person from his extended family to attend university, none of them understood his decision. He knew he was the black sheep of the family, and he had reconciled himself to the jokes, partly because he agreed with them. Before dinner, his mother couldn't resist making her usual announcement that Jack was going to give a lecture on why the dinner might not be good for them. He jumped to thinking about when his dad had seen a local job advert for a Biology teacher which he thought might suit him. He smiled to himself, but then started to become niggled by 'black sheep', because of its implied racism, but also because it sounded like political correctness gone mad.

The train announcement brought his stream of thoughts to a close and once settled in his seat he began rehearsing the information he needed to elicit from Lotte. He was adamant that this must not be an amorous occasion, but his mind soon became transfixed by the thought that she might now be willing to speak to the police about Richard. If she had left her husband why shouldn't she? And what if they ended up in another heated row about Angela, with Lotte threatening to go to the police in order to have a hold over him? As the train pulled into East Croydon he realised he didn't have long to get his script straight. He concluded that the key thing was to keep their conversation on the subject of Lotte's accommodation, and to make sure that no emotional buttons were pressed.

As the train pulled into Victoria his mind turned to the Victoria and Albert Museum. He'd never been there before, and he felt on the back foot.

***

Lotte's train was approaching Paddington Station. She was feeling quietly confident. She smelt her wrist to see if she could smell what Jack did. She felt sure that their conversation would naturally move from her accommodation needs to their relationship. For the moment, she was quite happy living with Carol and Marjorie, so she rehearsed some reasons for needing to move out: that the house was small; her husband might come round; she didn't want to impose. As the train was pulling into Paddington Station the thought crossed her mind that Jack might not turn up. She consciously dismissed the thought and strode quickly down the platform, towards the Underground.

Lotte arrived at the steps of the museum just a few minutes after midday, but she didn't have much time to become anxious because Jack arrived within ten minutes. She was relieved to see him, and smiled as he approached. They gently let their faces touch, and ducked a little to feel each other's necks. Jack followed Lotte, through the museum shop, down the corridors which made their way around the museum's quadrant, and into the restaurant. 'It's lovely, isn't it?' she said, as she moved towards one of small tables against the large circular wall. Jack looked up at the large circular chandeliers, feeling a little intimidated about how comfortable Lotte appeared to be.

The place was busy, but there were a few spare tables and chairs. Lotte liked to get a table in the central area of the restaurant, and preferred to be against the wall. She had spend many an hour here, drinking coffee and writing philosophical quotations on the back of the art postcards she routinely bought in the museum shop.

'I've never been here before,' Jack said. 'This room is really great.'

So as not to lose their place, Lotte agreed to get the lunch and coffee while Jack guarded the table. He said he would be happy with any salad items, and some bread. Jack was vegetarian so she decided to stick with salad items for both of them. As they began eating, he initiated proceedings: 'So, what are your thoughts about what you want to do?'

'I'm not sure. I don't know whether it would be a good idea to move further away.'

'What's this?' Jack said, as he pointed his fork at one of the salad items.

'You know what couscous is, you idiot.'

'Do I?...Do you think your husband will come after you? Would you consider going back to him?'

'You sound like you want me to go back to him, Jack?'

'No, no, I was just thinking that you must have lots of thoughts going round in your head at the moment. It wouldn't be unusual to be thinking all sorts of things.'

'Jack, do you think we have a future? I mean, I would understand if you didn't want to see me any more. I can see that things are difficult for you, too.'

'Of course I want to see you, Lotte. It's just a difficult time, isn't it?'

'Have you told your new girlfriend about me? Is she telling you not to see me? Is that it?'

'That couscous is nice; good choice...No, I haven't seen her for over a week. You know I've been away. And anyway, she's not my girlfriend...I'm still thrown by Richard's death. I feel really disorientated.'

'Are you sure you're not just saying that to avoid me?'

'No, of course not...So, you know this place well?'

Lotte looked Jack in the eyes, then immediately down at their table.

After finishing their coffees they walked out of the restaurant, at which point Lotte admitted defeat to herself, and suggested they part company. Jack was keen to escape the fraught situation and suggested that it might be for the best.

'Shall we just accept that it's a bad time for both of us at the moment,' Jack said, trying to bring things to a close reasonably amicably.

Lotte looked down at the floor, but not before producing a faint smile, to indicate that she agreed. She walked back towards the restaurant, while Jack departed in the opposite direction.

***

Jack had a restless night wondering about how angry Lotte might now be and whether this might prompt her to go to the police.

Lotte lay in bed wondering if she should leave things for a while, but ended up plotting again, about what needed to be done to remove this new woman on the block.

***

The next morning Jack said his goodbyes to his parents, letting them know he would be back on Christmas Eve. He spent the drive home convinced he needed to see Lotte again, to assess the situation. He couldn't leave things hanging like this over Christmas and the New Year. When he got back to his flat he paced up and down his front room, trying to process the various permutations of his predicament. The phone rang. He watched it, thinking that it wouldn't be his parents, so it must be either Angela or Lotte. Whichever one it was, it would be a good idea to speak to them.

'Hi Jack.'

It was Angela.

'I was just wondering if you were back and fancied a coffee?'

'Hi Angela. That's funny, I was just about to ring you. I've just this minute got back to the flat. Why don't you come over here?'

'Sure; about an hour's time?'

Jack paced up and down again, before quickly tidying the place for Angela's arrival. She arrived as planned and they sat drinking coffee, in silence. Angela broke the silence: 'Would you rather be on your own at the moment, Jack?'

'It's not that Angela. I just don't think I'm good company at the moment.'

'But if our relationship is going somewhere, surely we need to support each other in such moments?'

'You're a sweetheart, Angela. I'm just a bit low.'

'I don't want to pressurise you Jack, but a little bit of affection would be nice.'

'Sorry.'

'I was expecting a little bit more back from you, Jack. It really sounds like you would rather we didn't see each other anymore.'

'I'll probably bounce back. I'm going back to my parents for Christmas. They'd really like me to be there.'

'Okay, it's your decision, Jack.'

Sensing Angela's discomfort, Jack suggested they lie down on his bed.

'I don't think that's a good idea, Jack.'

They both accepted that the final words for the day had been uttered, and shortly after Angela was on her way.

As she was leaving, Jack said: 'Do you want me to ring you after Christmas?'

'If you want.'

Jack hated what had just happened with Angela, but he did have the option to ring her at anytime. He was also nervous again about Lotte. What if she was now really angry with him, and she *really had* left her husband? She was now a loose cannon. He went to bed that evening having decided that if the phone rang the following day he would definitely pick it up, whoever it was.

***

Lotte spent the evening having a heart-to-heart with Carol. She had been in no mood to talk, but when Carol suggested that some mid-term planning was required, she agreed, out of loyalty. Lotte hadn't ever said much about Jack, only that she enjoyed his company. She said it again, only for Carol to warn her that it wouldn't be a good idea to leave the arms of one man and go straight into the arms of another. Carol was well aware of the hold that Lotte's husband had over her, and advised her that a crucial turning point had been reached, and that it really wouldn't be good to backslide, not now, particularly after she had been so brave.

'But what if he comes round here? I don't want to put you through that, Carol. It's not fair on you.'

'Bring it on. He needs to be told what a brute he really is, Lotte.'

Carol was sure that Lotte's husband would not want a confrontation with her. And Lotte was sure that this was why he had dismissed Carol in the past, as a cranky and bitter woman, and that Lotte shouldn't be wasting her time with her.

The two of them finished their conversation, with Carol reassuring Lotte that she could stay as long as she wanted, and that she could talk about anything at any time. Carol said she had discussed Christmas with her partner, and both of them had agreed that they would be delighted if Lotte agreed to join them for the festivities.

Lotte went to bed reassured on all fronts, except about Jack. Should she just give up on him? Was it her fault that their relationship had deteriorated? She lay awake with the uncomfortable thoughts. At around four in the morning, she decided that there wasn't anything to be lost by another phone call to Jack the following morning.

Chapter 9

As she washed the breakfast things, Lotte watched Carol and Margie through the kitchen window. They were going down to the shed at the end of the garden to retrieve the Christmas decorations. She smiled at their choice of clothing because it made them look like a text-book lesbian couple: Carol, with red streaks in her black hair, unbuttoned black donkey jacket and black Dr. Martens boots, and Margie with her freshly blow-dried blonde hair, pink hoodie and green wellies. On another occasion she might have made a joke about it, but she had other things on her mind. She knew this was her moment and promptly phoned Jack. He picked up the phone after only a couple of rings.

'Hello Jack, it's Lotte. I hated how we left each other the day, and I wanted to say sorry for my part in that.'

'Lotte. I'm really glad you've phoned. I'm sorry, too. It's a horrible time for you, I know.'

They continued with their apologies, until Jack broke up the conversation by saying they shouldn't be talking on the phone, and suggested she come over in a couple of hours. Lotte promptly accepted, put the phone down, and returned to the kitchen. A few minutes later, Carol appeared at the back door holding up a long brown battered box. Before she could say anything, Lotte announced that she was going to see Jack.

'You be careful, Lotte', Carol said.

Lotte busied herself in her room. She applied a little makeup; just enough to cover up her exhausted face. No perfume because she knew Jack didn't like it. She pulled out her red jumper and green skirt from the wardrobe, because he'd previously said he liked both. She drove off, trying not to prepare any scripts. Had he suggested coming to his flat because he didn't want to be seen in public with her? Her mind wandered: to her husband's fist; to her smiling students; that abandoned conference paper. She pushed a CD into the slot on the dashboard. Chuck Berry's *No Particular Place to Go* started playing. She turned up the volume and smiled to herself as she tapped the steering wheel.

***

Jack wished he hadn't said 'in a couple of hours'. His mind had begun racing and he wished she was already in his flat. He wanted to see that mischievous smile on her face, but what if she was angry and looking for an argument? But why would she have phoned if she didn't want to see him? Or would she arrive and then say she didn't want to see him anymore? His mind switched to thinking about how well his recent conference paper had been received, but then quickly moved on to his contempt for Ralph Smythe, the Head of Research at the University. Finally, his buzzer rang and within minutes Lotte was in his flat.

Lotte joked about whether Jack had attempted any tidying up before she arrived, and whether any effort had gone into his clothing choice: an obviously un-ironed check-shirt and heavily worn Levi's.

'You know me Lotte. I like to keep a tidy flat and and you know it takes hours to prepare my unprepared look.'

'Yeah, right,' Lotte replied, with a wry smile. There it was. Just a hint of mischievousness, but enough to arouse him. He brought the two of them together in an embrace, and rubbed his nose against hers.

'Jack?' She hanged onto his name, then looked into his eyes. She wanted him to undress her.

Jack walked Lotte to the bedroom, where they proceeded to have the wildest sex in the all the time they had known each other. Jack could feel a slightly uncomfortable tingle from the scratch marks Lotte was making all over his back. In response, he started to bite her. She encouraged him. No matter how hard he bit, she wanted more, and he could see where his mouth had been from the bruising it was causing on her skin. Lotte didn't want any moments of relaxation, and whenever she felt him moving away from her, she encouraged him back. Eventually, they both fell on their backs, holding hands.

'Lotte, I feel like I've just come out of a war zone.'

'We're good together, Jack Lowell.'

They took it in terms to use the bathroom, and then lay back on the bed, dragging the duvet up from the floor and placing it over themselves.

'Do you think they will replace Richard McGiffen?' Lotte asked.

'They'll have to…What made you say that?'

'I was just thinking forward to next term.'

'It'll be very strange for a while; that's for sure.'

Jack's mind started to wander again, around the repercussions of the argument that had taken place in Richard's office: 'I guess no one will now want to say anymore about the Psychology review.'

'I don't understand why they did so badly, Jack.'

'Well, what I don't understand, Lotte Rudolph, is why your colleagues don't seem to give a monkeys about the quality agenda at all. That's ironic for a philosophy department, don't you think? Quality is a key philosophical concept, isn't it?'

'Oh, we care about quality, just not quality processes.'

'Well, it'll be interesting to see how you do in *your* review.'

The Philosophy Department was due for a visit from the Quality Assurance Agency in the following term.

'I'm not that involved,' Lotte said, 'but we do have a small team working on it.'

'So what will be your strategy, do you know?'

'Oh, we'll just lie our way through it.'

'And to think I gave you all that advice about teaching and learning strategies. What did you do with it...put it in the bin?' Jack beamed a big smile close to her face as he finished speaking.

'Oh, we'll be using all of it, I'm sure. We've also had someone in from another Philosophy Department that did well, to help us rehearse some scripts. And someone has been churning out some learning outcomes for all our teaching sessions. McFuckface would probably have got off on them. I doubt anyone will actually use them, except in the review, of course.'

'Lotte! Stop enjoying this!'

Jack pulled the duvet tightly over her head, as if to suffocate her: 'Have you no shame, Dr Charlotte Rudolph?'

'None whatsoever, and you love me for it.'

'Don't you feel any guilt about bullshitting?'

'No, of course not. We'll tell them what they want to hear. They'll go away happy and so will we. Anyway, you've been my mentor, don't forget.'

'How so?'

'Don't you remember when we first met, when I was worried about whether I'd survive my probation, you said to always have faith in the greater authority of your expert knowledge, so that's what I did.'

'Karl Marx...Max Weber...Emile Durkheim,' Jack said, in the manner of announcing their entrance at an exclusive party.

'Yep, so I turned to Nietzsche...Fredrick Nietzsche! Also sprach Zarathustra.'

'Lotte, I've got to hand it to you...you really are very talented...at mischief.'

As he said it, he felt himself being aroused by her playful subversion, but suggested instead that they have some lunch. She wanted more sex, but agreed to the lunch suggestion. While Jack was in the kitchen, Lotte picked up his tee-shirt and held it to her nose. She decided to wear it for another trip to the bathroom. Jack caught sight of her just before she disappeared into the bathroom and noticed she was wearing it. He thought about following her into the bathroom, but the toast popped up and he decided to pay attention to that.

They sat in bed with toast and espresso coffee, after which they fell asleep for a couple of hours. When they awoke, Jack complained that the scratch marks on his back were itching, which prompted Lotte to lick them, after which they pushed everything off the bed, and had wild sex again. They got dressed just before five o'clock. Jack said they should buy a takeaway and eat while watching the TV. Lotte agreed, wondering where the evening might now be heading. They had never spent the night together.

Around nine o'clock Lotte sat on the loo weighing up whether she should stay. She was determined not to spoil such a good day, and Jack did like his own space. She came back into the front room and announced that she really ought to go home. She could see that Jack was disappointed. She explained that Carol was very protective of her and she owed it to her to go home.

'Why not ring her?' Jack said.

'No. She was going out this evening with Margie and wouldn't be back until late, so I don't think it would be right.'

She had lied, but it was only a white one in her eyes, and Jack looked reconciled to the situation. She was sure that she had done enough for Jack to miss her, even if he spent the whole of the Christmas period at his parents.

***

Jack returned from his parents' house before the new year, but chose to spend New Year's Eve on his own, listening to music. He had been in a pensive mood for most of the week. The Eagles, *Greatest Hits*, hit the spot, and he laid back on the sofa. He toasted the New Year at the stroke of midnight, wondering when he might see Lotte again. It was pretty clear that Angela would not want to see him again.

***

Lotte spent New Year's Eve alone. She had been invited to a party being held by some of Carol's friends, but she didn't feel comfortable with the idea, in case she ended up speaking about her circumstances. She toasted in the New Year, pleased that she had heard nothing from her husband and wondering when Jack might be back from his parents. The coming year definitely now had some promise.

Chapter 10

The Spring term was still a week away, but all staff had been contacted to say that the Vice-Chancellor would be holding an all-staff meeting at eleven o'clock on Thursday 6th January, in the old gym. The University had opened a new sports complex just off campus a few years back, and the old gym space was now only used to hold large meetings. The Vice-Chancellor usually welcomed everyone back via email these days, so it was pretty clear that the meeting had been primarily called to provide an update on the death of Dr. Richard McGiffen.

The previous day Jack had cycled onto campus, to get some exercise and check his pigeon-hole to see if there were any incriminating messages there. He was looking for a letter from the police, but there was nothing, and there were no answering machine messages either. There must be some kind of resolution, he thought, unless the VC had some other grim news for everyone. He decided that he should phone Lotte because it wouldn't look good if the first time they spoke to each other was at the VC's meeting. He decided he would put the phone down if either of Lotte's housemates answered. He really didn't want to speak to them because of the guilt he felt about the whole situation with Lotte. Luckily, Lotte answered. She seemed pleased to hear his voice.

'Sorry for being slow to ring you, Lotte, but I was a bit nervous about your housemates answering and I stayed longer with my parents than I intended.'

'How *are* your parents, Jack?'

'Thanks for asking, they're both fine.'

'So, I'm honoured that you've rang, my Lord.'

'Hey, I was just a bit nervous, that's all. Look, are you going to the VC's talk tomorrow, because we could have lunch afterwards, if you like?'

'What meeting?'

'I think it's to give an update on Richard McGiffen.'

'That makes sense. I haven't been on campus, and nothing's been forwarded to me. What *is* the update?'

'Don't know; we'll have to wait. So, lunch?'

'Yes, that would be lovely.'

The following morning Jack parked in his usual place. There were a few cars already there, but none of the busyness you would normally expect to see had this been the first day of term. He walked to his office alongside Marion Barton, who provided him with the pre-meeting gossip, as she saw it. She had been speaking on the phone with Roger Fergusson, who had told her he was now eliminated from the police enquiries. She went on to say that it looked like it will be recorded as an accidental death, and that the case would be closed. Jack enquired as to how she knew that, but she just pushed her forefinger on the side of her nose. Jack was aware that Marion had friends in high places and took her gesture in the good spirit it was intended. They approached the old gym alongside the small groups of other colleagues. Jack noted that the end which housed Richard's old office was still closed off.

Jack scanned the old gym, looking for Lotte, but couldn't see her. In fact, he couldn't see anyone from the Philosophy Department. Surely they wouldn't boycott *this* meeting, he thought. But there were lots of empty chairs, so maybe several members of staff might not have got the message or were still away for the New Year break. At exactly eleven o'clock the VC delivered the news pretty much as Marion had predicted, but he added a few more details, including the police conclusion that he had most likely fallen while trying to carry six full box-files down the stairs. Just as the VC was stating that the police case was now closed, Jack saw Lotte out of the corner of his eye, standing to the edge of the room alongside the others who'd arrived late. Their eyes meet, but then Lotte raised her eyes briefly to the ceiling. Jack reacted by smiling, but then immediately looked forward and then down.

The meeting was only fifteen minutes long. The VC made it clear that he felt it inappropriate to entertain any questions. Everybody slowly filed out of the room, nobody speaking until they were away from the building. Jack made a beeline for Lotte but not so as to make it look obvious. He said he would meet her in one hour outside her department. As he was heading off to his office, Roger Fergusson tapped him on the shoulder and said that several colleagues were going to have a coffee in the staff common room. As they walked, the two of them confirmed with each other that the box-files Richard had been carrying must have been the teaching and learning documentation from the Psychology subject review.

'Do you think that Richard was taking it all home?' Jack asked.

'I'm sure he was,' Roger replied. 'After our bust up he said he would go over everything again. I took it as an acknowledgement that he accepted some of our criticisms.'

'Really sad that he felt he needed to do that over the weekend,' Jack replied.

At that point they were joined by Dr. Thomas Minot, from the Business School. Jack and Thomas had become friends after they realised their doctoral studies neatly overlapped. Thomas had written his thesis on the role of the workers' co-operative movement and its links with Marxist theory. He was the only person in the Business School with an interest in Marxist economics and felt somewhat ostracised because of it. He was also one of the few black academics on campus. He valued his friendship with Jack, which had spilled over into becoming friendly with other radical thinkers at the University. He didn't feel threatened by his Business School colleagues though, because he knew he taught one of the most popular undergraduate courses in the University, on developing entrepreneurship.

'Hi Thomas,' Jack said, 'we're off to the common room if you want to join us?'

'Thanks, I will. Horrible business...but I suppose at least we get a breather from all the quality mumbo-jumbo for a while?'

'There is that,' Roger replied.

Once in the staff common room, Jack went to get the coffees while his colleagues found a table. There were a few people milling around but it was nowhere near as busy as a term-time day. Jack could see that Roger and Thomas had joined Norman Thornhill, who was in conversation with two other colleagues, Dr. Brian Grealish, whose specialism was the politics of organisations, and Dr Janet Cripps, whose specialism was globalisation.

Before Jack even had a chance to sit down, Norman announced to the group:

'Ah, Jack, looks like you were implicated in Richard's death then?'

Roger and Jack exchanged glances.

'How so?' Jack asked.

'Well, the rumour is that McGiffen was carrying the teaching and learning box-files from the Psychology subject review. Didn't you provide a lot of that gumpf? I think some of it made it all the way to the ground floor after he fell. That's the real reason that part of the building is closed: the staff development team couldn't get in their offices because of the paper mountain.'

Jack laughed along with his colleagues, relieved that it was a joke, but noticed that Roger had remained stony-faced. Jack put his hand on Roger's shoulder, which Norman acknowledged: 'Sorry Roger; poor joke. You must have been the last person to see Richard alive.'

Roger accepted his apology with a nod before speaking: 'A weighty conclusion, Norman.' Because Roger laughed at his own comment, it prompted everyone else to laugh again.

Jack was beginning to feel uncomfortable, so made his excuses: 'Sorry guys, I need to get to some things from my office. See you all next week.'

Jack walked quickly towards his department, stopping at his pigeon-hole to pick up a couple of items, and then into his office, to check his emails. Still nothing incriminating. He put his feet up on his desk and stared across the campus.

***

Lotte Rudolph watched a conversation between three members of staff from her office window, thinking about how she might retrieve the rest of her things from the marital home. She looked at her desk top, happy that she had what she needed to begin her teaching the following week. Anything to avoid an ugly confrontation with her husband, she thought. She was happy at Carol's for the time being, and happy with the prospect of spending more time with Jack in his flat, if he was happy. Jack was very much work in progress, and she smiled at the prospect of teasing him on the subject. She looked at the clock on her wall and hoped that Jack hadn't changed his mind. She craned her neck to see if she could see him coming along the path to the Department. Sitting back in her chair she decided that a little bit of red lipstick was in order. At that moment there was a knock at the door: 'Come in, Jack.'

'Sorry, Lotte, just popped my head in to say Happy New Year. I saw you coming into the building.'

It was Professor Milton Townsend, the Department's senior member of staff and author of several books on Greek philosophy. The Department's successes in the previous two research assessment exercises were in no small measure down to his scholarly articles on ethics and wisdom. Lotte respected him enormously, and she was very grateful when he had agreed to be her probation mentor. She had also been proud to tell her father that news, knowing that the two of them were familiar with each other's work.

'And Happy New Year to you, Milton. What brings you in?'

'I felt obliged to attend the VC's meeting this morning. I'd never spoken to Richard McGiffen, but what an awful turn of events.'

'Yes, I was there, too. I was just turning my attention to the start of term before I meet someone for lunch.'

'It's at the beginning of term when I most miss teaching. I always liked that pregnant anticipation as the students file into the lecture hall.'

'I'm sure the first years would love to hear you speak, Milton.'

'Unfortunately, I know my place and that place seems to be research these days, and grinding out those papers. Avoid it for as long as you can, Lotte. I'll let you get on.'

Lotte looked at the clock again. The hour was up so she put on her coat and made her way outside. Jack was coming towards her. A good sign, she thought: he's on time.

'Fancy seeing you here,' Jack said, as he approached her.

They smiled and began their walk towards town.

'Maybe we could hold hands now, Jack?' Lotte asked the question knowing that it would make him feel uncomfortable.

'Maybe…maybe not.'

But as soon as they were close to the river, Jack picked up Lotte's hand and kissed it. Once in town Jack steered them towards a coffee shop: 'I came here once and thought it was nice,' he announced, as they approached the door.

Lotte thought about who had been here with and whether he would be happy being seen there. He motioned them towards a table at the rear.

They chatted about the classes they were due to teach the following week and how unprepared they were.

'Here's a plan,' Jack suddenly announced. 'Once term is underway why don't we go back to the Victorian and Albert Museum.'

'What made you say that?'

'I think we have unfinished business there, don't you? I think we should do a take-two. I want you to show me around the museum.'

'Okay,' she said, slowly.

'And, how about we extend that conversation about Nietzsche while we're there?'

'And then some sex in a forbidden place?'

'Why not,' he said. 'A little spice sounds good.'

Maybe he was coming round to her way of thinking, she thought.

Chapter 11

Lotte's bedroom window looked towards the street, enabling her to see her husband's car when it pulled up. He had agreed to drop off some boxes after Carol had put her foot down about Lotte returning to the marital home. Now that his arrival was imminent it didn't seem such a good idea. Carol told her to stay upstairs; that she would answer the door; and take possession of Lotte's things.

Nearly fifty minutes later than planned, Lotte watched her husband park his estate car in the street, and then take a large box from the back. He looked calm, but it didn't stop her thinking that he might storm about the house looking for her. She had prepared for this possibility by edging a chest of drawers closer to the door. She listened by the bedroom door as he explained to Carol that there was one more box in the car. On his return he asked if he might speak to Lotte. Carol calmly explained that this had not been agreed and she didn't want a scene.

Lotte watched as he walked away, thinking that his quick departure was probably aimed at impressing on Carol that he was a reasonable man. She continued to watch until his car turned the corner, after which she headed downstairs to inspect the boxes. All the things she had asked for were there, along with a few extra things and a note explaining the additions. On the back of the note was a short message asking her to ring him. She decided not to mention this to Carol, who had by then gone into the kitchen. The second box was full of books: Plato, Aristotle, Hume, Kant, Hegel… All there as requested, and still in the right order. All ready for the Introduction to Philosophy course she was teaching. That was kind, she thought.

***

Jack was not keen to attend Richard McGiffen's funeral. He agreed to go along because Richard's death was so untimely, and he couldn't face having to answer to his absence. He had a dark suit but no black tie, so he knew he would have to pop into town before heading off. At the last minute he decided to polish his shoes. After opening the shoe polish tin for the first time, he was pleased to see the unused brush in the same draw. As he brushed, his thoughts wandered: was a job at another university a possibility; was it worth giving up his flat? At least his relationship with Lotte seemed to be in a good place.

The funeral was the solemn affair that Jack had anticipated. Richard's extended family and other relatives were visibly distraught, and because none of them worked in higher education there was a polite mismatch between them and the small collection of academics who attended. Jack had little idea what to say to Richard's wife and tried to avoid speaking with her. He had already introduced himself to her and was reassured by the fact that she hadn't appeared to want a conversation.

Jack didn't want to be the first to leave and was relieved when some people started to make their way to their cars. Just as he was approaching his car, Roger Fergusson strode towards him: 'Didn't want to mention this earlier, Jack, but Marion told me yesterday that she thinks the advert for Richard's replacement will be going out next week.'

'Blimey, that seems a bit insensitive.'

'I guess the VC thinks he doesn't have a choice. He certainly won't want a repeat of our inspection fiasco, and it's Philosophy's turn soon. That should be interesting, to say the least.'

'Certainly should be,' Jack replied, his thoughts instantly turning to Lotte. 'That's almost making me hope they replace Richard quickly. The thought of Philosophy versus the new Quality Officer sounds like a good match.'

'Sounds like a grudge match,' Richard replied.

At which point both men placed their hands in their pockets, to retrieve their car keys.

'I assume you're not going to the wake,' Roger said.

'I made my excuses,' Jack replied.

As Jack drove towards the car parking spaces close to his flat, he passed an old, large, bright blue estate car parked by the side of the road. He had seen the same car a couple of days earlier and he looked back at it in his rear-view mirror. There was a guy with a beard sitting in the driver's seat. He wondered if it might be Lotte's husband, but dismissed the thought on the grounds of paranoia. But it didn't stop the thought returning to his mind throughout the rest of the day.

***

Lotte had made up her mind that it would be a good idea to phone her husband. She couldn't stand the thought of him making a scene at Carol's house, but she was also hopeful that he might be coming round to the fact that an amicable split was best for both of them. Carol and Marjorie were both out, but likely to be around the house the following day, so now would be a good time to make the call. If nothing else, at least it would get it out of the way. They spoke for around thirty minutes. Lotte was hoping he might say something which would spark a discussion about a more permanent split, but instead he kept steering the conversation towards the two of them meeting up, and how much he would like her to see his new art collection. Because the conversation was pleasant she decided not to risk introducing anything that might make him angry. It would also make it unlikely he would now show up unannounced and cause a scene. She agreed to think about them meeting up and that she would ring him again towards the end of the week. At least the next few days were now likely to be uneventful, she thought.

Lotte spent the rest of the evening preparing some notes on post-Aristotelian ancient Greek philosophy. Thinking about her students always put her in a good frame of mind, but the main reason for working on a Saturday evening was so she might then be able to spend some time with Jack the following day. The beginning of term had been hectic for both of them and they'd spent next to no time together. She wanted to ask his advice about her teaching, but she was also determined that the two of them should spend some of the time the following afternoon in his bed. She started fantasising about taking off her clothes in his front room while he made coffee in his kitchen. Those thoughts hastened the call to Jack.

***

After speaking with Lotte on the phone, Jack sat in his flat thinking about how the two of them would not even say hello to each other when he opened his door the following afternoon. Instead, she would just usher him to his bedroom. His revelry was interrupted by the thought that he would definitely need to tidy his flat before her arrival. He decided to put off the cleaning until the following morning and started working on his next teaching session: on the pros and cons of sociologists engaging in participant observation studies. He was keen to get his students discussing the ethics of a researcher becoming a gang member in order to understand gang culture. After a round of note-taking, he decided to leave it to his students to figure out the issues for themselves, after a few prompts.

Lotte arrived at Jack's flat just after 2pm, as they had agreed. She was carrying a large lever-arch folder. She explained that she would like his help on how to make her lectures more engaging for her students, and the folder contained her collection of lecture notes. He asked her to say more about what she thought the problem was while he made some coffee. As they sipped the coffee in his front room, he caught sight of her thigh as she moved to release some papers from her folder. Lotte saw Jack's eyes move between the papers and her thigh and she enquired if he was distracted.

'Show me more,' Jack said.

She smiled and proceeded to release more papers. Jack's mind wandered to the thought that a conversation about higher education pedagogy could become a prolonged form of foreplay. He looked at Lotte's notes for a minute and then said: 'I think you should consider your lectures less as a series of answers and more as a series of questions. In other words, rather than just giving your students the information they need, you should prompt them to think more.'

'But my students are dependent on me knowing more than them, surely, so why shouldn't I just tell them what they need to know?'

'Okay,' Jack said, 'then why not meet halfway and start introducing some key questions, say, every fifteen minutes or so, and see how it goes down?'

Jack was becoming aroused by Lotte's obvious leg movements and decided to stand up in the hope that she might do the same. Lotte followed Jack towards his large front room window, but just he was about to take hold of her, he saw her face visibly drop. He looked out to see what she might have seen. That bright blue estate car was there again. Lotte moved away from the window. Jack asked if she was okay. If it *was* her husband's car he didn't want her to know that he was affected by it, so said nothing.

After ten minutes of stilted conversation, about the role of lectures in higher education, Lotte apologised for her lack of engagement. She explained that she was feeling under the weather and really needed a good night's sleep before her first lecture of the week the following morning. She thanked him for his ideas and said she would let him know how she got on. They kissed at his front door.

'Are you sure you're okay, Lotte?'

'Yes, sorry, I didn't realise just how tired I was, and I really wanted to see you.'

***

Lotte drove home constantly checking her mirrors. She decided to make a detour to the marital home. His car was parked in the driveway. She had no intention of confronting him, and turned her car round so she didn't need to pass the house. She thumped hard on the steering wheel and shouted 'fucking arsehole!', but then realised that she might be holding a trump card because he was probably unaware that she knew what he was up to. He appeared to be reading something when she saw him through Jack's window. On the other hand, it may have been his intention that he was seen. After all, he wasn't exactly hiding. She could feel anger rising inside herself again, but took some comfort from the thought that at least she had not told Jack what she had seen from his front room window.

***

Jack spent the evening thinking about how he might get one up on the stalker. He could put a screwdriver into one of the car's tyres, or quietly smash a rear-light lens. Or would it be better to confront him: 'I know you're a wife beater.' In the end he decided that doing nothing would be best. He certainly didn't want the guy knowing he was in any way rattled by his behaviour, and he didn't want Lotte knowing that either. Lying in bed, he came to the uncomfortable conclusion that Lotte might not have said anything because she wanted to get back with her husband. Perhaps she was viewing his stalking as some kind of affectionate gesture? He stared up at the ceiling, with snippets of the tune *Lyin' Eyes* going round on a loop in his head.

Chapter 12

Lotte was pleased that the Spring term was now well under way because it meant she could invest her energies in her teaching, and in her students. On Wednesday morning she was having a coffee with a handful of them who were keen to learn more about her PhD. The subject had come up in the seminar she had just led and she said that she would be happy to say more in the Student Union building, but right in the middle of the conversation her mind jumped to thoughts about whether she should confront her husband about seeing his car outside Jack's flat.

Back in her office, she decided she would have to ring her husband and arrange that face-to face meeting. There were three birds to be killed with one stone here: a chance to get back into her home; a chance to broach the subject of a formal separation; and - if the moment was right - to ask what the hell he thought he was doing at Jack's flat. She knew he would be really angry about the last bird so she planned to mention Jack early on in the conversation, as someone who had been helping her with her teaching. That wasn't strictly untrue, and it would enable her to watch the look on his face when Jack's name was mentioned.

Lotte agreed to meet her husband at their home on Sunday afternoon. She would have to lie to Carol, but just another white lie, she thought. She would be missing the opportunity to spend valuable time with Jack, but their brief coffee break the previous day hadn't gone well. He said he would probably be visiting his parents at the weekend, which probably meant he wanted to be alone.

***

Jack never took time off work, and didn't consider that his mood could affect his teaching. But, as soon as each class finished, he rushed back to his office. If anyone said anything to him, he would just use the line that he needed to make some corrections to a pre-publication paper. Jack was now completely obsessed with the idea that Lotte wanted to get back with her husband, but also angry about the stalking situation. He needed to turn the tables. Some reconnaissance was in order, he thought. He knew Lotte's village because she had mentioned it, but he'd never been there and didn't know the address. His thoughts were interrupted by a knock on the door.

'Come in!'

It was Angela Salaman.

'I'm really sorry to bother you Jack, but something has come up and I feel I need to discuss it with you.'

'Of course. Come in, sit down.'

'Not now, I can't. It's my PhD viva on Friday and I'm having a run-through with my supervisor shortly, and then I need to spend tomorrow preparing.'

'Damn, sorry, Angela, I should have known about that.'

'How could you? The date has been changed several times.'

'Do you feel ready for it?' Jack was genuinely interested in Angela's answer, but desperate to know why she needed to see him.

'Ready as I'll ever be, I suppose. I like what I've written, but I've been warned to expect some harsh questioning from one of the examiners.'

'Don't be thrown. If you don't like a question, steer it towards what you think are the key issues.'

'Thanks Jack.'

'If it's not your PhD, what's on your mind?'

'I can't really talk about it now.'

'Well, can you tell me the subject at least?'

'I'd rather not. Can we speak after Friday?'

'Well, I can't wait the whole weekend to find out. How about we have a coffee in town on Saturday morning?'

'Okay. Send me an email to confirm the time and place and I'll be there. I'd better go.'

Jack stared out of his office window. Was she pregnant; does she have an STD; does she know something about Lotte? Maybe she's been offered that job in Scotland and just wanted to talk it through. It was a relief when he turned back to the stalker situation, which now seemed rather mundane. He concluded that he hadn't got anything to lose by taking a trip over to Lotte's village at the weekend. Perhaps it would be good idea to put the cycling gear on and go by bike; less conspicuous.

***

Lotte spent Friday evening wondering how best to make contact with Jack. Had her behaviour last Sunday pushed him back into the arms of Angela Salaman, assuming he had ever left them. After breakfast the following morning she decided there was nothing for it. At least by driving over to Jack's flat she could check if his car was there. If it was gone there would be a good chance that he *did* make the trip to his parents. If it was there, then who knows. As she approached his flat she decided that an absent car would definitely be the best outcome. But no, the car was there. She parked her car, but then decided against pushing his buzzer, and drove off in the direction of town.

***

Jack had left his flat just after 10.30, on his bike. He was due to meet Angela at eleven o'clock, but not in the coffee shop where they usually met. Angela had decided that they should meet in another one: the place where Jack had met up with Lotte the last time they were in town together. As he cycled, he went over the possibility again that Angela had seen him with Lotte in that place and this is why she was having them meet there. He locked his bike to a lamp post across the street from the cafe and then looked up to see Angela already sitting at a table by the window. She waved when she saw him. Well, she doesn't looked angry, he thought.

After Angela had got two coffees they sat facing each other.

'I feel like we're in a goldfish bowl here,' Jack said 'So, what's on your mind? Sorry, what am I thinking! How did the viva go?'

'Very well, actually. I just need to make some minor amendments and I'm done!'

'Well, good morning Dr Salaman.'

'Almost! Not sure I feel comfortable with that title, though, so none of that, please...Look, I'll cut to the chase. I overheard some of my colleagues talking last week. They were gossiping about whether Richard McGiffen's death was really an accident and that perhaps it was staged to look like it was.'

'Talk about gossip. Sounds like they all need to get a life.'

'Well yes, that's what I thought, but then one of them said that he had seen you coming out of Richard's building with Charlotte Rudolph about the same time that Richard had died. Was that malicious gossip or was that true?'

Knowing that the topic of Lotte could come up, he had prepared an answer on why he might have been seen with her around campus.

'Yes, it is true that I was in the building. I had been helping Lotte with her teaching. She had asked me for some advice so we were using one of the classrooms to go over some ideas.'

'That does sound a bit weird, don't you think, Jack? Friday evening on the last day of term?'

'I suppose it does, but we had been putting it off, and Lotte said that she didn't want to leave things until the new year because she had some preparation to do over the holiday period.'

'So there's no connection with Richard then?'

'No, of course not! We were at the other end of the building anyway. That's why I didn't go the police. I didn't want to waste their time.'

'But you can see why people might be a little suspicious. Certainly suspicious enough to start some juicy gossip. Anyway, I just thought you needed to know.'

'Well yes, thanks, I'm glad you've told me. This is why gossip is so dangerous. I hope you put them right?'

'Well no, I didn't. I was *overhearing* this conversation, and I didn't know what to say. We were supposed to be a couple then, remember? I felt embarrassed that I didn't know anything.'

Jack changed the subject back to Angela's viva and they spoke for a further twenty minutes about her interrogation. At which point Angela looked at her watch and announced that she had a lunch date and needed to get going. Jack said he would stay for another coffee. They stood up for an awkward embrace. He enjoyed feeling her back and began wondering if her lunch date was with another man.

'I still have feelings for you, Jack, even though I know I shouldn't.'

'Me too.'

At which point, Angela broke their embrace, and headed for the door without looking back.

***

Just as she was about to park in town, Lotte thought better of it and turned round to make her way home. She was not in the mood for shopping and was still winding herself up about Jack. She was sure that he was in his flat, either with Angela fucking Salaman, or with another woman. She thought about driving back to his flat, but decided against it because she knew he wouldn't answer, even if he was alone. She returned home to do some teaching preparation, but kept thinking about whether she should phone him. She also had to get her script ready for the visit to her husband the following afternoon.

***

Mid-Sunday morning, Jack decided to do some teaching preparation after lunch and then drive or cycle over to see if he could find the stalker's car. Unable to concentrate, he decided to flip the plan so he could get the stalker visit out of the way and then concentrate on his work. He decided to drive, to get the job done quickly, and set off just after one o'clock. He had already checked the map and could see that the village was very small, so a quick drive around should be enough. As he passed the village sign, it didn't look like there was anywhere obvious to park so he headed into the centre. It all looked very twee. The only thing missing was the cricket game on the large green, he thought. There it was: the bright blue estate car, sitting in a driveway. Well, that was easy. He was satisfied that he now had the upper hand, so he drove out of the village and began heading home. It crossed his mind to pay a visit to Lotte's new home, but dismissed the idea for fear of an odd scene in front of Lotte's housemates. Perhaps a phone call when he got home was the best idea.

'Hello Carol. This is Jack Lowell. Is Lotte there?'

'Hello Jack. I thought she was with you. Maybe she hasn't arrived yet.'

'Yes, that's why I was ringing. I've been expecting her. I'm sure she'll arrive soon.'

Was she on her way to see him, and why, or was she on her way to see her husband? He looked out of his front room window, then paced round the room, returning to the window. It seemed unlikely she wasn't going to show up. There's nothing for it, he thought, a trip back to the village was now inevitable, but after another round of pacing, he decided against it. If she was there and wanted to be with with her husband, what good would it do for him to turn up? And it would confirm *me* as a stalker, he thought.

***

Lotte left her marital home a little after 3.30. As she drove off, she thought about how different the house had smelt when she entered the hallway. The house didn't look any different, just that musty smell. The visit had been a disaster. Her husband didn't mention Jack, and she decided that for her to do so would make her look guilty. She said she was happy at Carol's place, and mentioned the subject of separating. He said that they were effectively having a trial separation. She mentioned making it more permanent, at which point she could see his body beginning to tense and, fearing an explosion, she didn't take it any further. The one positive result was his reassurance that he had no intention of making a scene at Carol's house. She decided that it was probably best to leave it at that. Determined to leave on a good note, she congratulated him on how his latest art work was coming along. At least the situation was no worse than before, she thought.

It was too early to return to Carol's house, so Lotte drove in the direction of Jack's flat. She had no intention of pushing his buzzer, certainly not after having just seen her husband. But she needed to drive somewhere, and should Carol ask her how her trip had gone, it might sound more convincing if she had at least been on the road to Jack's flat. After a couple of hours she arrived back at Carol's house.

'Ah, Lotte,' Carol said. 'We were concerned when Jack rang, asking after you.'

One disaster after another, she thought. 'I got stuck behind a tractor and couldn't get passed, so it took me forever to get there.'

Lotte told Carol and Marjorie that she needed to finish some lecture notes and disappeared upstairs. She lay on the bed, imagining what Jack might now be thinking.

Part Two

Anger

*"Yeh, that's right, report me to
the headmaster, you coward."*

(January 22nd 2001 – May 18th 2001)

Chapter 1

It was unusual for the Vice Chancellor to call a meeting to introduce a new member of staff; a new professor, perhaps, but not someone from the Quality team. The word in the staff common room was that he was worried about the potential damage to the University's reputation if there was a repeat of the recent Quality Assurance Agency report on the Psychology Department. Not that 20 out of 24 was an awful result; it was just the lowest to date.

In the common room a small group of staff were having their morning coffee break. Roger Fergusson was explaining the situation as he saw it. 'I think the VC is worried that the philosophers will not toe the line when they get their visit.'

'I get the impression he likes the philosophers,' Thomas Minot replied. 'I don't think he's got any time for this QAA malarkey. He's just going along with it.'

'And isn't that the real reason why VCs are now paid so much; to buy their silence?' Norman Thornhill asked the question, but it was delivered like a statement.

'Regardless,' Roger began, 'it'll be interesting to meet this mysterious new Quality Officer. How did they manage to recruit someone so soon? Do they build them somewhere and then post them out? I wonder if they come with the batteries already fitted,?' Roger got up and moved his arms like a robot, then spoke with a robotic voice: 'You must do things my way or be exterminated!'

Marion Barton explained to the group that there was nothing mysterious about the new Quality Officer: 'Her name is Lucy Martens. The VC wasn't expecting to appoint so quickly but she left her old post last October so she was free to start immediately.'

'*Left* her old post? Booted out more likely,' Thomas said. 'Strange time to leave.'

'Is she Dr Martens?' Roger asked. 'Maybe it's you she will be booting, Thomas, when she finds out what you think about the QAA.'

'I don't think she has a doctorate, only a master's in Educational Management,' Marion replied.

'Sorry Marion, I was referring to the boot company: Dr Martens; yes?'

'I hope she doesn't have a PhD,' Norman said, 'or we may have to take her seriously.'

Marion smiled, and Roger continued: 'Call yourself a sociologist, Marion. I thought it was compulsory in your department to have a pair of Dr Martens?'

At that point, those who were teaching at eleven o'clock rose and left.

The VC's meeting was again being held in the old gym. The last time most people would probably have been in there was when the Vice-Chancellor announced the police conclusion about Richard McGiffen's death. Jack Lowell had arrived early. Was the venue inappropriate or strangely fitting, he thought. As his colleagues filed in, he pondered each person's decision to attend, splitting them into two groups: do-gooders - those who dutifully turn up to anything associated with senior management - and intriguers - those who couldn't resist the spectacle of hearing about the next chapter in quality compliance. He wasn't expecting Lotte to show up, but he kept scanning for her. Nobody from the Philosophy Department had come through the door. Maybe the VC would be relieved about that; if they weren't there they wouldn't be able to ask any awkward questions.

The Vice-Chancellor began by talking about the importance of the University's mission to secure a joint reputation for high quality teaching and learning alongside a strong research ethos. The words sounded vacuous, but Jack admired the ability of the VC to sound as if he was committing the University to something deep and meaningful. The new Quality Officer, Lucy Martens, was sitting upright a few feet from the Vice-Chancellor, nodding enthusiastically. Jack stared at her, thinking that her short hair and grey trouser suit made her look a bit like Richard McGiffen. It sounded sexist, so he dismissed the thought immediately. The VC continued: 'As you will all be aware, the Quality Assurance Agency is in the process of amending its review process which will usher in new demands on universities with the aim of further enhancing the quality of the learning and teaching experience for students. Because of this I am extremely pleased that we have been able to appoint someone with such a thorough knowledge of quality matters in higher education and I look forward to the University enhancing its reputation under her guidance.'

Lucy Martens took her cue and walked towards the lectern: 'Thank you, Vice Chancellor, for such a warm welcome and I look forward to working with everyone, as we embrace the new change agenda for higher education in the UK.'

Jack glanced quickly left and right to see if he could gauge how many others were choking on the banality of the words. He saw some colleagues from the Education Faculty, who appeared enthusiastic, or were they just feigning interest in the hope that teacher wouldn't pick on them?

Jack sensed that the next few months would to be difficult for him. He believed in raising the profile of teaching and learning, and felt that academics should spend more of their time on preparing their lectures and seminars and engaging with their students. But the phrase 'change agenda' sounded way too much like management-speak, and a mechanism for controlling recalcitrant workers. His mind wandered back to when he was a Sociology student, being introduced to the work of Fredrick Taylor, and the ways in which managers wrestled control of the production process from skilled workers, in order to increase profitability, but in the name of efficiency. Surely, this couldn't now be happening to professional workers? His mind began to race, but he was brought back to the old gym when he heard the VC announce that the floor was now open for questions.

The first question came from the back of the room. Jack looked round and saw that Milton Townsend was speaking: 'Thank you, Vice Chancellor. As I was listening I couldn't help but think about whether the quality of an object is inherent - is located within it, so to speak - or whether it is an external judgement placed on it, and how much faith should we have in those who are testifying to this quality?'

Thank you, thank you, Jack thought.

Just as the Vice Chancellor was about to speak, Lucy Martens asked if she might take the question. He nodded in a deferential manner.

'Thank you for your question. I take it that you are a philosopher?'

Lucy Martens smiled as she asked her question and then proceeded to address Milton's question: 'I think it's incumbent on all of us to understand what is required to ensure that any judgements made on us will demonstrate not only that we are maintaining standards but also that we are constantly seeking excellence and always looking to go beyond.'

Out of the corner of his eye Jack could see that Norman Thornhill had his hand fully raised, which the Vice-Chancellor acknowledged.

'If that is the case, Lucy, I'm wondering what a university which has moved beyond excellence might look like?'

Another beautiful and subversive question, Jack thought. The idea of something being more excellent than excellent reminded him of the infinite regress problem, and the earth being held up by a series of turtles, each one below the previous one.

'Thank you for your question,' Lucy Martens began. 'It's important not to run before we are walking. We need to ensure that we are competent walkers before we can become excellent runners. We need to cross each bridge as we come upon it.'

Jack smiled to himself about the mixed metaphors, and hoped for more to come. Unfortunately the third question came from someone in the Nursing Faculty, about how well the proposed new QAA infrastructure would dovetail with the standards set by the Nursing and Midwifery Council. Damn, Jack thought; that'll be an easy one for a Quality Officer, and might well take the meeting into a much more mundane place. Fortunately, Lucy Martens finished her answer by suggesting that we won't go far wrong if we keep delivering what the system requires of us. Jack smiled to himself again, satisfied that this comment would give more than enough subversive food-for-thought for his colleagues over the next few days.

Shortly after that question the meeting was called to a close, but not before the Vice-Chancellor announced that Lucy Martens would officially start work at the beginning of February and would be visiting each department over the next couple of months, starting with the Philosophy Department. That was no surprise given their impending visit by the Quality Assurance Agency. As Jack got up he glanced up at the ceiling and thought of Lotte. The rock band Rage Against the Machine popped into his head as he was leaving.

Chapter 2

Lotte Rudolph was sitting in the cafe of the garden centre where Operation Remove Lotte had begun. Was it really nearly two months since that meeting with Carol, she thought. She looked up at the neon sign, which read 'White's Coffee Shop', on the wall behind the large retro Italian coffee maker. As she moved her coffee cup towards her lips, she took in the aroma and began wondering what might have happened had that meeting with Carol not taken place. It was just possible that she might have been able to strike a deal with her husband, one where he promised to work on his drinking and anger management. But then she thought about all the investment she had made in Jack, not knowing that it would amount to nothing. She thought about what Jack might be doing at this time on a Saturday morning, but after looking at her watch her thoughts returned to the reason why she was in the cafe. Carol had asked Lotte to go out for the morning while she took possession of the final boxes of Lotte's things from the marital home.

It was now 11.50am and there was a good chance that the delivery would have been made. She had promised Carol she wouldn't return until one o'clock, just to be on the safe side. In her head she saw her husband's suede shoe attempting to block the closing of the front door. But Carol would have known exactly what to say to him, had he made a scene. It was time to move on - without her husband, and without Jack. She thought about her students, which then turned to thoughts about the meeting she'd had with her Head of Department the previous day. He'd asked if she would be interested in joining the small team who would be coordinating the preparation for the forthcoming visit by the Quality Assurance Agency.

Lotte had told her Head of Department that she needed to think about his kind offer. 'Engage with inspection morons', she had said to herself when the offer was made, but a few hours later she phoned him to agree to the offer. Now that she didn't have to concern herself with her husband's jealousy, she thought it would be a good way to get more involved with the work of the Department. And it would mean she would be less likely to be asked about her research. She also felt confident that she could contribute something positive to a departmental narrative about teaching and learning, based on her previous conversations with Jack, and the articles he had given her. Nothing to lose, really, she thought. Her thoughts then turned back to Jack, at which point she rose from the table in order to look round the garden centre. Knowing that she was likely to be staying in Carol's house for the foreseeable future she wanted to buy some ceramic pots and plants for her windowsill, and something to thank Carol for her kindness.

When Lotte returned to Carol's house she could see that her husband's car wasn't in the street. Perhaps he hadn't even been? But as she pushed open the front door she saw a stack of brown boxes in the corridor leading to the kitchen. The smells and sounds coming down the corridor meant that someone was cooking. As she entered the kitchen Lotte saw that Carol was alone.

'Hi Lotte. All good. He's gone. No trouble. I'm rustling up a late fried brunch, in the hope you might join me. Margie has gone to London to meet up with some friends.'

Lotte offered up a pot plant in Carol's direction: 'A small gift to say thank you, and yes, brunch would be lovely, Carol.'

'I thought you were going to buy *yourself* some plants?'

'I did; they're still in the car. I couldn't carry them all.'

'Can you leave them for now? The food is almost ready.'

As Lotte sat down she asked after her husband's mood. Carol stopped the conversation dead by proclaiming that it was time to move on: 'Let's see that row of boxes out there as a line in the sand,' Carol said.

'Okay, but he wasn't rude, was he?'

'He wasn't anything, Lotte. Tell me about Jack. You haven't mentioned him for a while.'

'To be honest, we've fallen out. I don't think we will seeing each other again.'

'Oh, I'm sorry, I didn't mean to intrude. How do you feel about that?'

'It is what it is. I just feel very disoriented at the moment.'

'Well, you can probably guess what I'm about to say: Don't let your life be determined by your relationship with men. It took me far too long to learn that lesson.'

'I think I was unlucky with my husband and it could have worked out differently with Jack.'

'Don't go blaming yourself; it just lets them off the hook. It's not your fault when men let you down. Remember that.'

'But Carol…you don't like men. I don't see the world like that. I *do* like men. Do you have *no* feelings for men anymore?'

'I've had my moments, you know that, but just like when I gave up eating meat, I craved it for a while and had to wean myself off it. I can't go back now.'

Lotte smirked, and Carol saw the joke.

'Okay, bad comparison,' Carol said, 'but you know what I mean. I'm sure Margie won't mind me saying this, but she knows she's always been a lesbian. It's genetic. For me, it's always felt more like a conscious decision. I don't like saying I'm a political lesbian…we don't need to rehearse that…but I am still something of a separatist.'

'You were the first woman I interviewed for my PhD, don't forget.'

'And I still think that men have a fundamental design flaw and that *is* genetic. They're hardwired. You can't retrain them. You really would have more luck teaching an old dog new tricks.'

'Thanks for making this food, Carol. We haven't chatted like this for ages.'

'To be honest, that's why I did it. I thought this might be the right moment. And just nice to talk again, like we used to.'

'Do you remember that essay I wrote on the MA, when I got told off by that tutor, for making a comparison between Malcolm X and political lesbianism: 'Combining liberation politics in unhelpful ways; that's what she wrote on my essay. I still remember it, because it's what decided my PhD topic for me.'

'I never liked that tutor; too much theory and not enough lived experience. But that's the thing, isn't it? *You* know the theory...better than most...and, yes, it's important it gets documented. But I'm living it. It's always been more of an emotional thing for me and sometimes that means *battling* with emotions and not giving into them.'

'I don't think I ever told you, but that's the reason I didn't do much with my PhD. I couldn't handle those feminists at the conferences. You're excluded, of course. Those who kept shutting down comments by people who wanted an academic debate. I felt sorry for some of those men who wanted to engage with the issues. The final straw was that woman who got up and said I had no right to be speaking about Feminism if I was happy for men to be in the room.'

'No, you didn't tell me that...but...here we are...*we* disagree, but we understand each other's positions...it's not strident and dogmatic...But, Lotte, what about the next couple of months? You know I'm very happy for you to stay here as long as you want. I think it'll give you the space you need to properly think things through.'

'I can't see myself becoming anti-men though.' Lotte smiled, which Carol acknowledged by smiling back.

'Just be careful, that's all I ask, Lotte.'

After clearing away the lunch things, Carol said she would find some space in the cellar, leaving Lotte to decide what to take upstairs from her boxes first.

Chapter 3

Jack Lowell was sitting at his office desk looking out across the campus. In a hour's time he had a meeting with Lucy Martens. She had asked to meet with everyone from the Quality Office, the Staff Development team, and anyone else who had worked on learning and teaching enhancement. He had half a mind to make his excuses, but intrigue had got the better of him, and there was always the possibility that she might actually be interested in what he had to say. He looked at his phone, hoping that Lotte might ring. He was far too proud to ring her. He turned to the article on his desk and began reading about Durkheim's notion of sacred objects and whether it was still possible for something to become a sacred object in modern societies.

Jack decided to join the meeting with Lucy Martens a few minutes late in order to avoid any small talk with colleagues he didn't know very well. The meeting had begun when he entered the room and Lucy Martens beckoned him to take an empty seat near the front. The room had a sweet perfume smell, and he was instantly intrigued by the projected image behind Lucy Marten's head. It was entitled 'The Place of Quality in the New University' and featured a spider diagram with the word 'Quality' in the middle and branches leading off to an array of words commonly associated with university functions: 'student recruitment', 'library and resources', and so on. The diagram was vacuousness personified, he thought, and he was eager to see how it was going to be addressed.

Lucy Martens did not disappoint. She proceeded to explain that quality needed to be at the heart of everything that the University does. But she didn't provide any definition of what quality actually was. No surprise there, Jack thought. He was disappointed that there weren't any slides with slogans like 'the one constant is change', but she came close with a sentence which ended with 'to improve is to do'. In his head, he rehearsed the old joke about Descartes, Sartre and Frank Sinatra: 'to be is to do' - Descartes; 'to do is to be' - Sartre; and 'do be do be do' - Sinatra, and he hummed the Sinatra tune in his head for the rest of the meeting.

Jack took some notes on whether a concept like quality could ever achieve totemic sacred status in society. He concluded that it was far too amorphous an idea to coalesce around, and, regardless, totemic symbols only truly work when they organically grow within a community, not when they are imposed on people. Jack was satisfied that the meeting had, ironically, been very useful and that he now had some ideas to work on. The meeting ended with some questions, but they were all administrative in nature; about the timetable of events, with people chipping in about how busy they were. He couldn't see any point trying to shoe-in a more issue-oriented question.

The meeting lasted one hour. Just as he reached the door to leave he saw that he was being ushered back by Stephanie Leyland-Ball, the Head of Staff Development, who was huddled with Lucy Martens against the backdrop of her final slide which featured an image of a steaming cup of tea with 'any questions' underneath it.

'Jack, have you met Lucy yet?'

'No, not formally.'

'We've just been talking,' Stephanie continued, 'about the importance of having an academic voice in the room when Lucy meets with the Philosophy Department shortly. You know what they're like, with their long words and concepts.'

Jack instantly translated the coded message to read: '..with their distrust of idiots and idiotic ideas.'

'We thought that you could be just the person.' Stephanie looked at Lucy Martens as she completed her sentence.

Lucy Martens then looked straight at Jack: 'How about we have a meeting in my office sometime in the next week? I'll have to look in my diary and let you know a time.'

Jack nodded in agreement, while thinking about that Woody Allen film, where the subtitles explain what people are really thinking.

As he walked back to his office, his head started to spin. Should he just say no to the meeting with the philosophers; should he attend and be subversive in the knowledge that the philosophers would know what he was doing but Lucy Martens would be oblivious; but what if the philosophers assumed that he'd gone native with the philistines; and what about Lotte? Perhaps he could make a link with Durkheim's elementary forms of religious life and talk about the need for universities to produce forms of social solidarity around concepts like quality; that quality was not actually a philosophical idea but a social construction designed to help cement social order. Satisfied that he was on to something he strolled purposively up to his office door, ready to take some notes.

At his desk, his thoughts kept returning to Lucy Martens and Stephanie Leyland-Ball. How had he managed to get into bed with these two? He thought of Lotte, and started imagining the two of them leaving the upcoming meeting with the philosophers, and heading for the old gym. He went back to the article he was reading earlier, after which he began pondering how many of Lucy Martens' university functions - the ones on her slide - might be considered profane examples of everyday activities, with no real cultural significance or true meaning.

Jack had cycled to work that day and after looking out of the window to see how dark it was getting, he decided it was time to head home. He packed up some notes for his teaching the following day. Tomorrow was Friday and the thought of not having to think about quality matters over the weekend came as a relief. But I do want to think about quality, he thought, just not quality *processes* and *systems*. As he said it, he could see Lotte's face, and the time he had pulled his duvet over her head in his bedroom.

As he cycled, he thought about what happens when you turn an activity into a system. He thought about how much he used to enjoy having tutorials with his students, but how he had come to dislike them when they became part of a tutorial *system*, requiring documentation. He then thought about the old Harold Garfinkel article on 'good organisational reasons for bad clinical records'; about how doctors produce official records for bureaucratic reasons, not clinical reasons, and how this neatly connected with Lucy Martens' comment about providing the system with want the system requires. There was the light bulb, he thought: two ideas of efficiency - the bureaucratic one and the professional one. No, we shouldn't always do what the system requires of us, particularly if it clashes with what we think we *really* should be doing, or perhaps, as Garfinkel concluded, we should keep the front desk appropriately misinformed, only so we can then be left alone to get on with the job. Perhaps there were two realities: the bureaucrats in one, and the academics in another; or, perhaps better, the academics have learnt how to switch between the two.

'Nobody expects the Spanish Inquisition!' He said out loud as he approached his front door. Perhaps the true job of a Quality Officer is to be Michael Palin, interrogating people on whether they are just mouthing what they think they should say, or whether they are true believers. That's it, he thought: academics will never be true believers in the quality agenda, but they could learn to mouth what the system requires of them. Maybe that's enough. Maybe, if they say the right thing when required, they might then be let off for good behaviour, and be allowed to get back to being the academics they really want to be.

Once inside his flat, his thoughts continued. Maybe there are two types of Quality Officer: ones who really believe in what they are doing, and those who know it's a game and do whatever it takes to win it. Perhaps we should feel sorry for the former, because surely it would be easier to game-play; it must be easier to enhance a university's reputation that way? Satisfied that he had now earned his dinner, he quickly jotted down some notes, realising in the process that he could use a lot of this with his master's students the following day.

After dinner and more note taking, Jack started to become despondent. He would be on his own all weekend, with no prospect of any contact with Lotte. No doubt, she would be with her husband, probably at some exhibition or arty event. Was his violent past now behind him? He thumbed through his address book and decided to ring Angela Salaman. Maybe she might enjoy a coffee on Saturday morning; he had nothing to lose. He picked up the phone: 'Hello Angela, it's Jack Lowell. Do you have a few minutes?'

'Hello stranger. Well, this is a surprise.'

'I was just thinking about you, and thought I would ring you.'

'That's nice. I was thinking about you the other day, after that meeting with the new quality person.'

'Oh, I didn't see you there.'

'No, I arrived late and had to leave early, so I just snuck in at the back. I thought I should learn a bit more about what is going on. What did you make of it all? My colleagues are dreading her coming to the Department armed with a load of nonsense which has nothing to do with our work.'

'I don't think it will come to that. Bizarrely, I have a meeting with her next week, so I'll let you know what she's planning.'

'I'm hoping I can avoid it all. They've given me another course to teach, but I'll still be part-time.'

'Look, do you fancy a coffee in town on Saturday morning. It would be great to catch up on everything.'

'Yes, that would be nice. Our old place at 10.30?'

Chapter 4

Jack cycled into town on Saturday morning and arrived at the old coffee shop where he used to meet with Angela. She was coming towards him as he locked his bike. He instantly liked the way she looked, with her blond hair tied back behind her ears and wearing a tweed jacket and short skirt. They embraced and entered the coffee shop. The place was busy, but they found a table for two towards the back.

'So, tell me about the new course you'll be teaching,' Jack said, as they sat down.

'Well, I'm sharing a course on 20th century American Literature, and we've had great fun deciding who would teach what.'

'Bit of Kerouac in there?' Jack thought he'd get in quick, not knowing much about American literature.

'Yep, he's there, but Karen is doing the Beat writers. I follow up with the post-modern turn.'

'That's great. Right up your street; yep?'

They continued talking for an hour, after which Jack suggested that they spend the afternoon together. Angela apologised and said that she had some errands to do, but asked whether Jack would like to come round for dinner later. Jack cycled back to his flat, pleased that he had the afternoon to listen to some music, and knowing that he had the prospect of an interesting evening with Angela to come. Just a niggling thought about the person she shared the house with.

Jack drove to Angela's house and knocked on the door just after eight. He handed her the bottle of red wine he had bought on the way over. In the dining room the table was set and adorned with flowers and candles.

'Well, this looks lovely,' he said, as Angela disappeared into the kitchen.

'Yeah, I thought it would be nice!', she shouted from the kitchen. 'I don't get many opportunities to do this. Sit yourself down. Do you want a beer? And no, I don't need any help. It's just some pasta.'

'Well, whatever it is, it smells great!' Jack shouted. 'And yes, I'll have that beer.'

Jack sat in the middle of the sofa in the L-shaped dining room, looking up at the book shelves; mainly literary criticism. A few chunky hardbacks stood out: *Moby Dick, War and Peace, The Master and Margarita.*

'Where's the person you share the house with? I've forgotten her name.'

'It's Julie, and she's away for the weekend.'

Angela then strode into the room holding a bottle of beer, a small bowl of pistachio nuts, and salt and pepper grinders for the table. Jack enjoyed her walk, the way she leaned across the table to place the grinders, and her turn which revealed a big smile on her face. The next time she appeared she had a big bowl of pasta in one hand and a smaller bowl of bread in the other. She ushered Jack to the table.

'Do *you* think the quality agenda in higher education is troubling, Jack?'

'What made you say that?'

'Well, while I was preparing the things for dinner, I started thinking about our conversation earlier, and whether a lot of what is now happening in universities is actually no bad thing. I was thinking back to when I was an undergraduate; sometimes lecturers didn't turn up for lectures; sometimes I wasn't even sure what the course was about.'

'I agree. That's one of the reasons I got involved in running teaching and learning workshops. But the problem is this tendency to think that there's just one way to do it; that teaching means this, and learning means that. And worse, that because you have some learning outcomes for your teaching sessions, then you can just turn learning on and off like it was a tap.'

'Okay; I get that. I'm not clear what a learning outcome is, but everyone does know a bad teacher, don't they?'

'I think it's complicated. But the idea of a learning outcome is actually quite simple, if you think about it as question of transparency…making it clear to students what they need to learn. Learning outcomes, as a concept, have a bad reputation for many academics, because it feels like they're being imposed, and they sound school-like. But the danger for me is that they could make learning robotic. I remember some really odd teachers, but looking back I rather enjoyed their eccentricities. I think it would be a tragedy if we made every teacher the same. I think that's the dilemma. There's a sociologist in the States, George Ritzer, who talks about McJobs; McDonald's type jobs, where everything is so controlled; that the worker doesn't have to think about anything; and they can be replaced by anyone else. McTeaching jobs would be terrible, wouldn't they?'

'Yes, I can see that. But it should be clear what a course is about. I remember talking to my friends from school…we were doing English at different universities and it was like we were doing completely different courses. The teachers seemed to teach whatever they wanted.'

'Yeah; okay…but we do need to be careful. Another way to look at it might be to say that the students are getting privileged access to the specialist knowledge of those teachers. They could well be speaking about the research they've done, over a number of years. If it was just generic knowledge, then, yes, pretty much anybody could teach *that*.'

'It's tricky though, isn't it? Although I've longed to teach my specialism, I can see that undergraduates, especially first years, do need a good grounding in the basics of the subject. That's important, surely?'

'I suppose one way to look at is to say that there's nothing wrong with standardisation of the curriculum. That's what these new subject benchmark statements and programmes specifications are all about. Making it clear to students what they might expect from a course. That would address your question of what exactly *is* a degree in English. But if you then stretch that to include how you should teach a particular subject, and then rank the institutions according to who is doing it best. That's when it goes wrong, I think.'

'That makes sense. A bit like taking a large hammer to crack a small nut.'

'For a start you've got to trust that the people making the judgements are up to the job. Let's be honest, if you enjoyed teaching and researching, why would you want to waste your time inspecting other people doing that? What's that old saying: only people who can't do something teach it. And only those who can't teach it then inspect others.'

'Very good, Jack, I like it.'

At that point, Angela stood up in a theatrical style, with arms aloft, and apologised that she'd forgotten the wine: 'Forgive me, Jack. Red or white?'

'Well, I'd like a red. But I've had that beer, and I've got the car with me.'

'It's up to you. If you'd like one we could always get you a taxi.'

'Okay, I'm persuaded.' As Angela disappeared once more into the kitchen, Jack thought to himself, if Angela drinks, then so be it.

Angela returned with a bottle of red and two glasses, and announced that the washing up was for tomorrow. She motioned to Jack that they should sit in the front room and then closed off the dining room from the front room with the two dividing doors. They sat at either end of the three-seater sofa, but after a second glass of wine, Jack edged closer when Angela moved her arm towards him. They kissed.

***

Jack awoke and looked at his watch: 7.12am. He looked across to see Angela facing him but fast asleep. He looked up at the ceiling. He was glad not to be back at his flat, but concerned that some of Angela's talk the previous night was very focused on establishing a firm relationship between them again. He satisfied himself that there was no need to think that one through; for a while, at least.

Chapter 5

Lotte walked briskly across the campus to the seminar room where her first meeting with the Department's subject review team was being held. As she walked up the stairs in the old gym building she had a mental image of herself in the storeroom with Jack. On the second floor, she paused to look up at the final set of stairs before turning towards the seminar room. Through the glass window in the door she could see her Head of Department, Dr Steve Jackman, who was standing by a coffee maker with two of her colleagues: Dr Josephine Conway and Dr Julian Ashwood. She paused to asked herself again whether she should be getting involved with inspection matters; her mother came into her head. She then held down the door handle to enter the room.

'Hello Lotte,' Steve Jackman said. 'Really glad you could join us. Sorry, we were just enjoying the coffee and biscuits I ordered. Can I pour you a coffee?'

Lotte was glad that Julian was in the room. He had only been with the Department for three years, after completing a PhD on the differences between the writings of Simone de Beauvoir and Jean-Paul Sartre, specifically on the question of bad faith. He was just a couple of years older than Lotte, and like her, took his teaching very seriously. The other two were specialists in the philosophy of religion. Josephine Conway's PhD was on liberation theology and the Sandinista movement in Nicaragua and she had recently published a book on Catholic schooling. Steve Jackman was a respected expert on world religions. Lotte didn't know Josephine very well, but, being the only two women in the Department, they had spent some time together, and joked about being imposters in a male temple.

'Okay,' Steve Jackman announced, 'shall we get started? Lotte, if I address you for a few minutes, that might be a good way of summarising where we are at the moment. As you all know the visit by the review team is imminent, and we need to be firming up the key points for our narrative. I think we have a good story, and, as you also know, I've received some great intelligence from colleagues elsewhere. And thanks again, Jos, for checking up on some of the likely inspectors…sorry, reviewers. Our next stumbling block would appear to be the new bureaucrat on the block, the Head of Quality, who has confirmed that she will be visiting the Department next Wednesday.'

'Could we tell her that we already have everything sorted?' Josephine asked.

'I had thought of that but given that she will be visiting all the departments I don't think we have a choice. But we could try to sidestep the question of the QAA visit by bombarding her with general questions.'

'I suppose,' Josephine continued, 'we could ask her some questions about the relationship between teaching and research. She's probably never done any research in her life. That should keep her quiet.'

Until that point Lotte had been enjoying the conversation. There was more than a healthy disrespect for the inspectors, but the R-word - the word that should not be uttered - had now made an entrance and it made her uneasy.

Steve Jackman kept the meeting on track: 'Quite...But let's focus on our preparation. I will continue to work on all aspects of the general management of our programmes. Jos, if you could keep working on our student progression work, that would be great. And Lotte, if it's okay with you, I'd like you to work with Julian on strengthening our narrative on student learning. As you know, we've got a bit of a battle here. We've got to make sure that we don't alienate our colleagues by forcing them to use fake learning outcomes, but we've also got to convince the QAA team that we are making the learning explicit. We are philosophers, so we should be able to pull this off, or at least pull the wool, blah, blah, blah.'

'Well, Steve,' Josephine said, 'as I see it, if I do a cut and paste job, where I change all our references to "student progression" and put "personal development" instead, and we re-badge our end of term "student tutorials" as "learner profiles", I think we should be in a good position. I've gone back through the Dearing Report on higher education and this seems to be the new language. Intelligence from colleagues elsewhere shows that the QAA seem to like this talk. What I'll need to convince everyone is that we won't be doing anything any differently, just changing its name - simple nominalism.'

'That's neat, Jos. Thanks.'

As soon as Steve Jackman finished his sentence, Julian Ashwood became animated: 'Personally, I don't like this subtle change from student to learner. What work does the word learner do that the word student doesn't? We are students of philosophy, aren't we, not learners of philosophy?'

'I agree,' Steve Jackman said, 'but I think it helps if we take a broad look at what is going on. As I see it, all the years of developing our disciplines have given academics a lot of professional power. Changing the language is an important step in trying to create a new form of professionalism, where the power is concentrated in the management of a university, not in the disciplines. So, the more we learn to speak a generic language of learning, the easier it will be to control us. And how could universities be ranked if there isn't some common standard to rank them against? Don't get me wrong, I'm not advocating this, just recognising the new reality.'

'Okay,' Julian replied, 'I don't want to hijack the meeting with this.'

Josephine then moved forward on her chair and raised her voice slightly: 'Let's just do what we have to do in order to get these people off our backs; yes?'

'Yes,' Steve Jackman agreed. 'So, your task, as I see it, Julian, is to try to get a compelling narrative together to link Jos' work on student...sorry...learner development. Perhaps we have another cut and paste job there? We need to combine Jos' work with some learning outcomes for our students...sorry...learners...Ah, wait a minute...I have a new idea. Perhaps we need to wire ourselves up for a few weeks... our own Milgram experiment...where every time we use the wrong word, we get a small correctional electric shock?'

While everyone was still enjoying Steve Jackman's joke, it gave Lotte the breathing space to compose her contribution: 'I've been reading some articles by Carl Rogers, where he says it's ridiculous to decide the learning outcomes in advance of meeting your students. I'm not sure he actually uses the term "learning outcome" and I suspect he probably meant something a bit different from how it's now being used, but what I got from his discussion is that we should be *negotiating* learning outcomes with our students. Perhaps at the beginning of the course, or even every seminar?'

'Or,' Josephine said, '...why not negotiate the learning outcomes at the end, so, rather than announcing at the beginning that this is what everyone *will* learn, we encourage students to say something about what they have *actually* learnt. I can see a neat link there with our student progression work. It's effectively what we are doing in the end of term student tutorials, so why don't we extend it to include mini versions at the end of each session?'

'I do that already,' Lotte said, 'or something like it.'

'It's a good idea, yes, but speaking as Head of Department, I think I would have trouble selling that idea to every colleague. It does sound a bit burdensome and would possibly eat into course content.'

Steve Jackman then looked everyone in the eye. After a long pause, Josephine continued the conversation: 'Well, if we are to maintain our integrity through this attempt turn the University into a prison panopticon, we should at least be able to keep the barbarians from the *seminar* door. Of all seminars, surely a philosophy seminar is not something you should be able to predict. It could go anywhere; indeed, it should. How could you possibly know beforehand where it will go? As Wilheim von Humboldt argued, 200 years ago, a university is defined, not by what we know - that's for schools - but by what we don't know - *wissenshaft*...scholarship...leaps into the dark with our students. At least, it should be.'

'Lotte, Julian, what do you think?' Steve Jackman asked.

'Well,' Julian began, 'I suppose one compromise...middle ground, if you will... is to write some clever non-behavioural learning outcomes. I know the pressure is on to produce some kind of Skinner utopia - a *Walden II* - where we only measure the outward manifestation of a change in a person's behaviour brought about by an engineered external stimulus; a pure form of behaviourism...*But,* we should be challenging this, and I think that clever non-behavioural learning outcomes could be the way forward for us.'

Josephine looked forward again and said: 'At the end of the session the student will be able to challenge the need for there to be a discreet learning outcome for the end of the session.'

'Very good, Jos,' Steve Jackman said. 'I'm not averse to this. But I think we have to be a bit more conservative for the moment. Once the barbarians have gone back to Ba-Ba-Land perhaps we could think this one through a bit more. Lotte and Julian, could I ask you to spend some time together working on this middle ground, as you put it, Julian?'

Lotte and Julian looked at each other and nodded.

'It would be good,' Steve Jackman continued, 'if the two of you had something for us ahead of the meeting with that quality person next week. Would that be okay?'

Lotte and Julian looked at each other again and agreed.

'Maybe we could meet late tomorrow, Lotte? Strike while the iron's hot?' Julian asked.

'Yes, that would fine,' Lotte said. 'I'm teaching until four; what about 4.30? Shall I come to your room?'

The rest of the meeting was taken up by the Head of Department ticking off everything that needed to be boxed off, including a double tick for those things which had already been done. He then rounded off the meeting by explaining that a room had now been allocated where everything would be stored, under lock and key, and that the key would be kept with the Department's administrator, Beverley Sykes.

'I like the key as a symbol,' Josephine said, 'a key to unlock an alternative universe, one where everything makes sense in its own terms, unlike the messy, unpredictable universe outside, and long may the latter reign.'

At which point Steve Jackman smiled, shuffled his papers, and agreed that this was a good note to finish on.

Chapter 6

Lotte arrived at Julian's office just after 4.30pm. He offered her a chair at the end of his desk and explained that he had spent the afternoon working on some non-behavioural learning outcomes. He suggested they go through them, adding and taking away, as they saw fit. Julian read aloud: 'By the end of the session students will be able to reflect on the value of a deontological approach to ethics.'

'Julian, can I stop you there for a minute. What exactly is a learning outcome? Is there a definition?'

'There certainly is.' Julian stretched across his desk for a note book and after turning a couple of pages, he read out loud: 'A learning outcome is a statement of what a learner will either know or be to do after a set period of learning.'

'Is that an official statement from the QAA?' Lotte asked.

'No, it's my statement based on what I've been reading.'

'Okay; so, do you know that this is what the QAA want, or could we do it differently?'

'I see where you're coming from Lotte, but I think it would be very risky. You seemed comfortable in the meeting yesterday.'

'No, not really. I've been thinking about what Jos said; about how all this is bit un-HE, if you like. Isn't it all a bit childish, with the QAA acting as angry patriarchal Dad? Why can't we just be trusted to get on with our jobs?'

'Well, you know I don't disagree on that front, but we do owe it to our students to make it clear what they should be learning; don't we?'

'Yes; of course. But can't we show that by preparing interesting sessions, and caring about what we do? When I asked my students about this over coffee this morning they said what they liked in a lecturer was…knowledge…passion…enthusiasm. Surely, that's it; isn't it?'

Lotte could see that Julian looked a bit concerned. She liked him and didn't want to hurt his feelings.

'Sorry, Julian, I'm drifting away from the plan, aren't I? Let's continue and see where it takes us? Let's take a look at that non-behavioural outcome again.'

'Okay; so…by the end of the session students will be able to reflect on the value of a deontological approach to ethics.'

'I can see,' began Lotte, 'that this doesn't result in an actual change of behaviour, making it non-behavioural, but it does imply that there would an action…of mind…so does that make it behavioural again?'

'But, understanding the basis for acting in a particular way, doesn't imply that you will actually act on, does it?'

'Unless you're a Greek philosopher, of course. If you know it, you'll do it.'

'Very good, Lotte. Perhaps we should ask the students to imagine that they are Greek philosophers?'

'But we do now have another problem. What would a student look like who was imagining or reflecting? Do we concede to the barbarians that if we can't actually measure the change, then it might as well not have happened?'

'Quite,' said Julian. 'But the key for us, as academics, is surely not to ask our students to act or be particular types of people, but to understand the foundation for thinking in particular ways. I can see a slippery slope here. We start by measuring only those things that are easy to measure, and then we start believing that education should be about producing a particular type of person...a skilled worker rather than an educated mind; perhaps? The barbarians *are* at the gate. Sorry; I'm undermining my own argument for learning outcomes here, aren't I?'

'This is now beginning to make me annoyed, Julian.'

'Okay; let's be more strategic about this. The QAA are definitely coming. We can't change that. Our colleagues don't like it. But we should do what we can to minimise the potential harm; yes? Isn't that the job we've been given?'

They agreed they might be able to persuade their colleagues that non-behavioural learning outcomes were just another way of expressing what the Department was already doing. They also agreed that their colleagues might appreciate that, by being handed some learning outcomes, they were, in effect, being shielded from the inspectors. And should any of the review team wish to visit them to discuss a teaching session, that the two of them would be willing to prepare a good script for them to rehearse from.

After two hours of discussion, Julian suggested that they should stop and take stock. He then asked if she would like to join him for a drink in town. She was pleased he had asked. This would be her first true off-campus social meeting with one of her immediate colleagues and she liked the intrigue.

Lotte told Julian that she needed to return to her office to do a few things and that she would meet him downstairs in ten minutes. She phoned Carol to say that she would be late home, then checked her hair in the mirror and applied a little lipstick. She put some notes and books in her bag, to take to her car, so she wouldn't need to come back to the office. She then phoned Julian to tell him that she would meet him in the car park in five minutes. As she walked to her car she wondered if she might see Jack, and whether her behaviour would indicate that she was on a date. She stopped her train of thought when she realised that she actually knew very little about Julian. Was he married; in a relationship; gay, maybe?

As they walked, Julian and Lotte agreed they would rather not be in the position they now found themselves.

'I think we got lumbered with inspection,' Julian said, 'because we are the new kids on the block.'

Lotte agreed, but her mind had started to wander, to whether she might see people she knew in town. A few people from her husband's art college lived in town, but it was unlikely that any of them would be in a pub this early on a Tuesday evening. Julian gestured to Lotte that she should enter the pub first. Lotte relaxed after seeing that the place was pretty much empty. She surveyed the room one more time while Julian was at the bar, ordering the drinks. He returned and placed two glasses of red wine on their table: 'Do you have any plans to move on, Lotte, or are you happy with the place?'

'I like my teaching and I love my students. I'm just a little concerned that I don't have a research profile. Why do you ask?'

'Oh, I was just wondering earlier what would happen if we don't do well in the subject review. Most philosophy departments have done really well so far.'

'What? You think we might get disciplined or something?'

'No, not at all! If it did come to that, the question would most likely be put to Steve. That is, why did you have those two youngsters do so much of the preparation?'

They agreed that they should change the subject, which prompted Julian to say that he had been watching some Jean Genet films over the weekend, which then made him turn to his bookshelves to pull out *The Outsider* by Albert Camus.

'I never did ask you about Simone de Beauvoir,' Lotte said.

'I've got a lot to say about her. Perhaps we could meet up again? I really need to get going shortly. I'll walk you back to your car first though.'

He looked at his watch, then lifted his glass to drink the last of his wine.

'No, there's no need to do that. You get going.'

Lotte drank the last of her wine, smiling to herself that her date hardly deserved the name.

Walking back to her car alone, she reconciled herself to the situation. It was only a first outing and there could be more. She was satisfied that she had made a good impression; that she had made herself clear about the QAA visit; and that she was comfortable about her attraction to him. She smiled as she thought about his boyish-philosopher look, with his horn-rimmed glasses and corduroy jacket. All in all, a good day's work. But the thought of the QAA visit came back into her head, which began festering by the time she got into her car. She started to sing *I Fought the Law*, then shuffled around the small collection of CDs in her glove compartment, settling for Bo Diddley.

As she walked up to Carol's front door, Bo Diddley had morphed in her head into lines from David Bowie's tune *The Jean Genie*.

Chapter 7

Jack opened Lucy Martens' office door, and was surprised to see Stephanie Leyland-Ball.

'Hello Jack, come in. Stephanie and I were just discussing the best way to approach our meeting with the Philosophy Department. I've been learning a bit more about why we might get a bit of a hard time.'

Well *you* certainly will, Jack thought. And who were the 'we' in that sentence? Did that mean that Stephanie would be coming as well? Fight or flight, he thought.

'We were thinking,' Stephanie began, 'that perhaps we might put on some learning and teaching workshops for them. Jack, do you think you could do something on delivering excellent teaching?'

Jack winced inwardly at the very thought.

'Well, it's a thought,' Jack said, 'but I don't think we could do that in a few workshops.' That came out well, he thought: it sounded like he was saying the philosophers would need a lot of help, but what he really meant was that the words 'delivery', 'excellent' and 'teaching' all needed deconstructing. The idea of 'delivering' teaching made it sound like students were being handed a parcel, which they just had to unwrap. He was tempted to recommend that they both read Bill Reading's book *The University in Ruins*, but he was sure they wouldn't recognise themselves as agents of the ruin.

Lucy Martens jumped into the conversation: 'But you could do some tips for teachers; yes?'

The worst comment, Jack thought; to reduce learning and teaching to a series of mechanical techniques. McJobs were on their way and the lunatics *were* taking over the asylum.

'I think it would work better,' he said, 'to talk more generally about pedagogical principles and the role of autonomous learning in higher education.'

'Excellent Jack,' Lucy Martens announced. 'I could link that with the QAA precepts and the importance of independent learning. We're on the same page here. Good.'

What was worse, he thought, Lucy Martens completely disagreeing with him, or agreeing to work as a double-act? A disaster, and in front of Lotte.

'How about..,' Stephanie began again, '...I open the meeting by saying a few words about the importance of investing in continuing professional development, then you come in, Lucy, on outlining the QAA agenda for improving teaching in higher education, and then you finish, Jack, by talking about how to produce an independent learner?'

You wouldn't know an independent learner if she slapped you in the face, he thought, but then said: 'I could work with that.'

Lucy Martens announced that the meeting with the philosophers would be one hour long and that the three of them should produce some slides and each speak for twenty minutes.

'Could we reduce the time to fifteen minutes each, so we could have some questions and discussion?' Jack asked.

'I don't think we can afford any debate about such important matters for the University's reputation,' Stephanie replied.

'But people do need space to assimilate change,' Jack said.

Lucy Martens agreed, so the timings were adjusted.

By the time he got back to his office, Jack had three slides pretty well composed in his head. Three would be enough, he thought; enabling some space to talk around the ideas. He needed a slide on the concept of constructive alignment - that learning outcomes need to be tied explicitly to the learning strategies and to assessment strategies. That shouldn't be too controversial, he thought, particularly if he could relate that to issues of transparency and clarity of intentions. He needed something on the uniqueness of university education; that higher education was about criticality and challenging accepted knowledge, and the importance of students becoming part of that process. And then something on the process of taking students from dependency in year-one to independence by year-three. That last slide would enable him to introduce the work of Carl Rogers, the psychologist that Roger Fergusson was always talking about. Enough for now, he thought. Keep it simple. No need to be deliberately provocative.

***

An hour before the meeting with the philosophers, Jack thought about phoning or emailing Lotte. He hadn't heard from her. She *must* be back with her husband. There had been no recent sightings of the stalker or his car. Maybe she wouldn't come to the meeting.

The meeting was being held in a seminar room on the third floor above Lotte's office. On his way to the room, Jack stopped off on the second floor in the hope that he might bump into her and at least get the chance to say something. He wandered down her corridor, thinking that he could use the excuse that he'd forgotten the room number for the meeting. 'Dr Charlotte Rudolph' said the plaque on her door. He felt like the naughty school kid on his way to see the headmaster, so he turned round and headed straight for the seminar room. He was ten minutes early, but took it as an opportunity to get into conversation with some of the philosophers ahead of the meeting. There was a paper note on the door confirming the meeting, but no one inside. Lucy Martens had asked for all the slides ahead of the meeting so there was no need to prepare anything, so he walked into the room and over to the window. Looking out, he started thinking about how easy it would be to concentrate on his sociology work and just forget about quality in teaching and learning.

'Hello, you must be Jack Lowell,' Steve Jackson said, as he let the door close itself behind him. 'I'm Steve. I don't think we've met.'

'I'm Jack. I was asked to tag along to say something about HE pedagogy. I hope it will tally with how you see things.'

'Indeed. I'm not sure who's coming. I didn't impose a three-line whip. My QAA preparation group will be here, I'm sure. You're a sociologist, I believe.'

'Yes, my main research interest is the work of Emile Durkheim.'

'Interesting. I read Durkheim some time ago now; on the elementary forms of religious life, when I was doing my PhD.'

At that point, Lucy Martens and Stephanie Leyland-Ball came into the room, followed by Josephine Conway.

'Excellent,' Steve Jackson announced. 'We're filling up. I'll leave you to set things up, while I check if the tea and coffee I ordered is on its way.'

As he opened the door to leave, Julian Ashwood appeared.

'Have you seen Lotte?' Steve asked Julian.

'No. I expect she's on her way,' Julian replied.

At five past the hour, Steve Jackson suggested that the meeting should begin: 'I think we should have a few more people coming along; certainly one more, but let's get started, shall we?'

Only three versus three, Jack thought; the philosophers never disappoint in their non-appearance.

Lucy Martens introduced herself as the new Head of Quality, and that she would be steering the Department through the impending QAA review visit, as the institutional facilitator.

'Could I stop you there,' Steve Jackson said. 'I understand that role, but isn't it the Head of Department's job to do the steering? Aren't you there to support us? Just trying to be clear.'

'Quite,' Lucy Martens said. 'We're looking for a strong outcome this time. As you know, we had some problems last time round with the Psychology review. Let's say that we will be working closely as a team. I'm sure we'll have plenty of meetings in the coming weeks. Shall we proceed with the slides?'

'Please do.'

Jack turned his neck to read the first slide, which announced that continuing professional development was a total quality commitment on behalf of an institution; an investment in improvement; in value for money; and customer satisfaction. Stephanie Leyland-Ball went on to explain that universities are businesses and their future survival required a change of mindset. Jack wanted eye contact with the philosophers, but his neck felt stuck in its position, and he continued looking up at the screen. Thoughts started to whirl around in his head: was she trying to start an insurrection? She finished her little speech with the phrase 'going forward.' Perfect, Jack thought, vacuousness personified, and topped off with a meaningless phrase. At least Lotte wasn't in the room. But, exactly at that moment, the door opened and there she was. This time, Jack's neck loosened and he watched her tip-toe to the nearest seat. Her dark hair looked longer and her eyes looked bigger.

Lucy Martens' first slide was the quality spider diagram - the one he had seen before. She then went on to outline the new QAA infrastructure for higher education, including a list of precepts, stating that this is what universities will now be expected to comply, with, 'going forward'; that phrase again. She then went on to state that the student learning experience was everything, and that the reviewers in the forthcoming visit will be looking for transparency in the student offer. Josephine Conway raised her hand: 'Surely, we don't want *absolute* transparency, otherwise where will the scholarship come from...the leap in dark, so to speak?'

'Thank you for the question,' Lucy said. 'Could we come back to that at the end? I'd like to hand over to Jack Lowell at this point.'

There were only ten minutes left to speak if they were going to stick to the timings, so Jack quickly explained the concept of constructive alignment, and the importance of students seeing the connection between what they were being taught, how they would be assessed, and how both would enable them to meet the relevant learning outcomes for the session. He said that this was a good way to conceive of transparency. He then went on to explain the path from student dependency to student autonomy, using the word 'scholarship' - mirroring Josephine Conway - to explain how students, with the right research tools, could be pushed to the edge of a discipline's knowledge. He finished with the phrase he had learnt from Carl Rogers: 'freedom to learn'; that once students were in charge of their learning they would be empowered to learn without guidance from teachers.

'Jack, could I pick you up on that last point, about autonomy,' Steve Jackman said. 'Surely, students will continue to need guidance from their teachers, otherwise there would be no point in having master's qualifications or a PhD supervisor.'

'I take your point Steve, but I would still insist that there should be a distinct path towards autonomy. And, naturally, some students will be further down the road than others.'

'Jack, Jos Conway. Hello. I liked your use of the word scholarship there, implying that universities are very different from schools; that both students and their teachers should view themselves as being in the service of scholarship; not more rote learning; that students should be discovering things for themselves; that what is in the textbook today is likely to be proved wrong tomorrow. Straight from the famous Wilheim von Humboldt 1810 memorandum.'

'Yes, absolutely,' Jack said, making a mental note to go and find that memorandum. 'I suppose we might say that in higher education we need to be a bit more discursive, and a bit less didactic.'

'Precisely', said Josephine, 'so would you say that this QAA infrastructure - did I say that correctly? - is rather a little too prescriptive and not in the spirit of Humboldt?'

Just as Jack was about to reply, Lucy Martens' jumped in: 'Yes, but it's imperative at the moment that we stick to what the QAA reviewers will be looking for when they arrive.'

'Well', said Josephine, 'if they're not looking for what we are talking about, should they even be employed as reviewers?'

'Okay, let's hold that thought,' Steve Jackman said. 'I think we'll need a whole day for that debate to run its course. We have a couple of minutes left, so are there any more questions from the floor, specifically on the review process?'

'Yes,' Julian Ashwood said. 'On the subject of learning outcomes; what would happen if we chose not to use them and went another way? What I mean is: have learning outcomes been imposed on us by the QAA?'

'They are considered good practice,' Lucy Martens said, 'in which case I think it would be very foolish to ignore them, assuming you want to do well in the review?'

'But where did they come from?' Julian asked.

'Could I take that Lucy?' Jack asked. 'Well, it's not from the QAA. They come from educational theory and practice. Yes, a lot of the original work came from schools, but we could be much more imaginative with them in higher education. I think that's the challenge. Remember, the reviewers are only looking to see whether you do what you say you do. They are not Ofsted school inspectors.'

'Thanks Jack,' Steve Jackman said. 'Much to mull over. I think we need to stop there. Lucy, I guess we will be in touch in the coming weeks?'

'Yes, yes,' Lucy Martens said. 'I'll check my diary when I get back to my office and send you an email.'

Jack walked back to his office alongside Stephanie Leyland-Ball and Lucy Martens. Why had Lotte not said anything? At least he now had a reason to email her, he thought.

'I see what you mean,' Lucy Martens said. 'They certainly are a difficult crowd, and why only four people? We've got our work cut out here. I don't think the VC will be very happy. Jack, how do you see it?'

'I think they've got a good story to tell. I've never heard a bad word about them. They do have a lot going for them.'

'But,' Stephanie Leyland-Ball began, 'we've got to get them using the right terms; it's not the 19th century anymore, it's the 21st century.'

'Quite,' Lucy Martens said. 'I'll make that clear at my first meeting with the Head of Department. They seemed very enamoured by you, Jack. Perhaps, you could support me?'

'Okay,' Jack said, before peeling off to his office. Hopefully, she'll forget, he thought. Or he could say that it might be better to hold his own workshops with them, leaving the management of the QAA visit to her.

Chapter 8

The Philosophy Department subject review preparation team were gathering in the new box room.

'Come in Julian,' Steve Jackman said. 'Okay, that's all of us. So, here is our room, in all it's glory, or should I say, gory? Each shelf is labelled according to the six areas we will be inspected on. As soon as you have something for one of the box-files, could you hand that to Bev first, who will check it with me, and then it will go into the relevant box. Is that okay, Bev? I will need to check that any new text doesn't contradict our SAD.'

Everyone nodded in agreement. Steve Jackman continued: 'If any of you need to get into the room to check anything, please ask Bev, who will make sure the room is locked at all times. Please support Bev. Naturally, this will be a major operation. Unless anyone needs to check a box now, I suggest we depart. Bev, could you do the honours?'

'Can I buy you a coffee, Lotte?' Jos asked, as they walked together down the corridor.

'That would be nice.'

'Have you noticed the gendered nature of all this inspection work?' Jos asked.

'How do you mean?'

'Well, it's the women who are busying themselves with all the preparation work. I'm not just talking about our department, but ours is a good example, don't you think?'

'Yeah. It does look like the men feel that they have more important things to be getting on with. But I think that myself, of course'

'So how is it that we feel we have to get so involved? Why don't we just say no? I'll answer my own question: it's because the men, unconsciously perhaps, think that we are the ones who will be good at organising all the paperwork, and demonstrating that we care about our students; difficult to say no to that.'

'Between you and me, Jos, I feel really angry about the whole thing. What is this all for? And what was that fridge doing in that room? I didn't want to ask Steve.'

'Ah, the sacrificial fridge. That's an attempt to put the inspectors in a good mood. It will be stocked with exotic fruit and drinks, while they are looking at all the paperwork we've collated.'

'Really? That's ridiculous. I thought we were being asked to *save* money, not throw it away.'

'Quite; but don't get angry. See it as an exercise in getting one over on them. And don't forget, the people coming are...or were...philosophers, of sorts. I've checked them out. I think we will be okay. Just one guy who might prove problematic. I'm very philosophical about it; excuse the pun.'

'That makes me more angry, Jos. Why would people play Judas? Can't they see they're undermining their own profession? And what was that SAD thing that Steve mentioned.'

'The Self-Assessment Document. Very appropriate acronym, don't you think? It's the document we send to the QAA, which has the gist of our story.'

'I remember now. Just hadn't heard it called a SAD. Yes, great acronym; you couldn't make this up, could you?'

They walked back to the Philosophy Department. Lotte wanted to speak with Jack. 'Undermining their own profession' was a phrase she'd heard him use. As she stared out of her office window, she began composing an email in her head. Unable to decide whether it was a good idea, she turned to thinking about the whole concept of quality. How did we get to a situation where we would be searching for quality in a room full of box-files? And then you had to wait to be told by a sad bunch of little Hitlers if any quality had been found. 'This is a bloody nightmare', she said out loud to herself. She looked across at Aristotle's *Nicomachean Ethics*, which was open and face down on her desk. He would turn in his grave, she thought, except he would have been reincarnated, of course. But certainly not hanging around a UK university in the 21st century. A chat with Milton was in order.

'Come in Lotte. Good to see you. You sounded a bit agitated on the phone.'

'Sorry Milton, I'm not disturbing you too much, am I?'

'Not at all. I've done my bit for the day. I've been reviewing an article on whether Socrates was a real person.'

'You mean he was mythological?'

'Sort of; a postmodern take, based on the idea that we only know him through the interpretations of others.'

'Ah, very good. That's not a million miles away from what I wanted to ask you about…You know I've got involved in the QAA subject review. It seemed like a good idea, but now I just want rid of the whole thing. I don't think these people know anything about quality, but aren't we all to blame for letting this happen?'

'Well, I suppose we are, but that's because concepts like quality are rather slippery, aren't they? It's not a straightforward concept, which I think has made it easier for these cruder notions…mainly taken from the world of business…to take hold.'

'So, what do we do? Just live with it?'

'Well, thinking about it logically, we have two choices - or is it one choice, with two options?…we can either beat them at their own game, or fight them in order to play another game.'

'Jos Conway seems to think that we might be able to pull the wool over their eyes. Is that a third option?'

'I suppose it is. I see it more in terms of integrity. I have a duty with regard to truth, if you like. In which case, so long as that is not undermined, I can live with these…what shall I call them?'

'…Barbarians?'

'Yes, very good word. They speak gobbledygook, or that's how it sounds to us. It makes sense to them, because they've been trained to speak and think in a certain way, and they've been allowed to infiltrate the Academy. But, we continue to conceive of things very differently. Take the Research Assessment Exercise. It's a very crude mechanism for judging the quality of research. Indeed, it's not really a judgement on quality at all. It just fulfils a political role...as a means to allocate limited public funds. But...I know the game they are playing, and I know how to play it: I churn out peer reviewed articles; single-authored; in well-known journals; and I do my best to make sure I'm read and cited when I attend conferences. All of these things can be managed and manipulated. But what I have to ask myself is whether my integrity has been compromised in the process. Yes, without the RAE I might well have published fewer articles of a higher quality, and I may have published them in other ways or in other places, but the ideas wouldn't have been that different. So, I can live with the barbarians...and their strange ways...to *some* extent.'

'That's helpful. But what happens when your line is crossed? You know my father has just retired because of this nonsense. He couldn't handle it. Perhaps he let his anger get the better of him...but now we have this teaching assessment as well, which seems even more crude and it surely *does* undermine *everyone's* integrity.'

'How *is* your father?'

'Glad to be out of it, I think. He's now writing the books he always wanted to write.'

'Well, don't get me wrong. The line could easily be crossed for me, as well. And don't forget, they have to change the criteria for all these daft exercises because of the game playing, which just confirms that it is, indeed, a game. You just have to hope it it will all unravel at some point. I enjoy thinking of examples from the past: Einstein probably would have been sacked from his post, because his rate of publication would have made him ineligible for the RAE. Some people defend the RAE because of the prolific rate of publication for UK-based academics these days, but if you take a wider view you can see that a lot of it is the recycling of old ideas in new journals. And some journals only seem to have been created so that people will have somewhere to put their newly assessable work.'

'Milton! You're depressing me. Are we stuck with all this nonsense? Were we just born in the wrong age?'

'Yes, but don't forget that phrases like "publish or perish" came from the United States, and that wasn't because of the QAA. And the Athenian State put Socrates to death. I don't think Blair or Thatcher ever had *that* in mind.'

'Good point. That's sort of comforting. But one thing I really envied in the States was the freedom and respect that academics seemed to have. They seem to do all right without an RAE and a QAA.'

'I can't see any of what we've been subject to happening there, but there are always prices to be paid. You could say that we have only been playing around with the idea of bringing the market place to universities. Over there, they only really have the market place. Elite universities thrive because they are largely unshackled from the State, but in following private money some of them could be accused of engaging in some very unsavoury research - often funded by large corporations - and some of their students are paying extortionate fees for the privilege of attendance. They are free in one sense, but they are not unencumbered.'

'Yes, I can see that. I suppose we're all encumbered by something. Perhaps the line gets crossed when the means start determining the ends.'

'Yes, that's a good way to put it. My big fear is that philosophy, as a subject, far from being viewed as the foundation for all thinking, is increasingly being viewed as a luxury the country can't afford, or even worse, as a subject that must be re-couched in the language of increasing the country's productivity. If I thought for one minute that I was being pushed to do research that wasn't strictly in the pursuit of the truth, however defined, or to work on a project just because it brought in a lot of money, that would be the day *I* retire.'

'And then where would we be if everyone like you left?'

'Well, I know where I'd be; like your father I'd be writing that book I've always wanted to write, on the pursuit of the good life. It's a shame that I have to retire to write something that I think just might do some good. Sorry that was an unintentional pun.'

'That book would be popular with our students, I'm sure. I'd certainly use it on the Introduction to Philosophy course. But it could also go into the Research Assessment Exercise; couldn't it?'

'Yes; but if only this audit life was that simple. For a start, a popular book would not be rated as highly as a cited journal article, and the whiff of a textbook often doesn't go down very well either. Which itself points to a new problem we've created: the pulling apart of teaching and research. I think this is the most destructive part of what these barbarians have been doing, but, because they *are* barbarians, they don't even know they're doing it. The people behind the RAE and the QAA don't speak to each other and they can't see that one half-decent measure of how well a university was doing would be to look, precisely, at the *unity* of teaching with research; that's pretty much a definition of what a university is. But how can they be united if one group of academics are being told to concentrate on research and another group are being told to concentrate on teaching? We're actually tearing universities apart if you think about it. But that's what happens when you let the barbarians infiltrate… particularly those brandishing business manuals.'

'It's more serious than I thought.'

'I need to get going shortly, but let me finish with something practical. After you phoned earlier I started thinking about two ancient Greek words that relate to quality: *arete*; viewing excellence as a form of virtue, and the word *kalon*; the beauty that comes from someone feeling that what he or she has produced has a perfect harmony to it.'

'Brilliant; thanks Milton. I suppose I came to see you because I needed cheering up. At one point there I wanted to hang myself, but you've given me food-for-thought, as ever. Thanks for your time. You know I really appreciate it.'

'I'd stay longer but I need to get to the supermarket and I'm expecting a phone call later from a colleague in New York. Last time we spoke, he told me about a new

TV series, *The Sopranos;* about The Mob in New Jersey; now there's a group of people who know how to deal with trouble makers, it seems.'

'Thanks; some tips there, maybe?'

'Oh, and one more thing I often find myself repeating to myself: universities may be businesses, but higher education is not. The two need to be kept apart.'

'Thanks again, Milton. Perhaps that should be our departmental mantra?'

Lotte walked from her office to the car park, taken by the idea of viewing quality as a virtue; an Aristotelian disposition. Perhaps quality and excellence were interchangeable words? That would need checking. She glanced across at the English Department and saw Jack leaving the building. Angela fucking Salmon-Face; for what other reason would he be in that building? She darted into the Nursing Faculty building to avoid being seen. Coast clear, she then headed for the car park. As she pulled away, she pushed Lightening Jay Hawkins into the CD slot. She thought about whether it wasn't too late to duck out of the quality agenda and just immerse herself in philosophy and her students. But maybe Lucy Martens' needed a piece of her mind first? Angela Fucking Salmon-Face certainly did.

Lotte's thoughts turned to her father; at home in his study, standing by the window.

'Just think, Charlotte, about the full implications of God being dead. Will to power would then be the life force'. Her thoughts went back to the QAA. Will to power. Inspections of research and teaching are control mechanisms, political acts, masquerading as objective assessments. But why do we submit to them? Jos Conway was right: they're trying to pull the wool over our eyes, so why shouldn't we do the same back. Particularly if our resistance sits on a stronger moral foundation, or it would do if we could articulate it better. *Arete*? Quality, not residing in the outcomes of actions, but in the motivations of the actors. That just sounds right, she thought. It would also mean that Nietzsche and Aristotle could be connected; not something she had contemplated before now.

As she turned into Carol's road, she patted the steering wheel. A glass of red wine after dinner, and a re-reading of Nietzsche sounded like an attractive proposition. And perhaps even a phone call to her parents.

The sodium street light was casting a pleasant orange glow in her bedroom as she settled down. She opened her notebook: "The Roman Caesar with Christ's soul." The phrase came from Nietzsche and it had always fascinated her. Here was Nietzsche's superman, the misunderstood over-man, the person whose soul is chiseled from his own strong will. The master of his destiny, not the slave to a dead weight bearing down on him. The quality agenda is a form of will to power, but also a dead weight: when it makes slaves of everyone who subject themselves to it. Lucy Martens, the archetypal *under*-woman, she thought.

But, Jack? She hated not been able to make eye-contact with him during the meeting with her colleagues. But his idea of being imaginative with learning outcomes had stuck with her. If it was true that the QAA only want check you were doing what you said you were doing, then the Department should certainly stick to its guns. 'The Quality Assurance Agency', she said out loud. Even the name sounded wrong: 'assurance' sounded like a dead weight, and 'agency'? That was ironic, for a body actively curbing the free spirit. Nietzsche would have enjoyed messing with state quangos, she thought. She looked at her watch. It was now too late to ring her parents. She checked that she had her notes ready for the seminar in the morning, on Stoicism. She had another meeting with Julian in the afternoon. Perhaps it was time to put her foot down with him. But there was also the prospect that he might ask her out again. As she drifted off to sleep, she wished she could put a bloody spell on bloody Jack Lowell.

Chapter 9

Lotte's meeting with Julian Ashwood was set for 4.30pm. She was now determined that the Department should not kowtow to the QAA inspectors. She had raised the issue of quality in teaching with some of her students over lunch. They had reached an agreement: that a good taught session was one where the teacher had been able to sustain student interest, particularly in something which didn't seem very interesting, and where a teacher demonstrated that they cared. One student had been vehement, that what she hated most was when a lecturer seemed disinterested, as if they would rather be somewhere else. Lotte raised the question of learning outcomes, and whether they thought they would help to make sessions clearer. Not if a lecturer was boring, they agreed.

Fifteen minutes before the meeting with Julian the phone rang: 'Lotte Rudolph, how can I help?'

'Ah, Lotte. It's Nigel, Nigel Eames. I wasn't sure whether it would be a good idea to ring, but then I thought, why not?'

Nigel Eames worked at her husband's art college. Both men were good friends.

'Nigel. Well, well. How are you?'

'Good, thanks. I'm really sorry I haven't been in touch. Stuart told me what happened, of course. I wanted to reach out, but...taking sides, and all that. And an email felt very cold, if you know what I mean.'

'You don't need to apologise, I understand. So, what changed your mind?'

'Oh, Stuart and I had an argument last week, so it started me thinking.'

'What were you arguing about?'

'Silly, really...Rachel, the postgraduate student. You remember her?'

'Yes. You mean the one you had a thing for?'

'I got pissed off with Stuart, because he didn't tell me he'd been seeing her. You know she got that teaching post in London. He's being staying at her flat. I guess you weren't too pleased about that yourself.'

'Sorry, Nigel. I've just realised I need to be at a meeting. Could we continue this conversation tomorrow.'

'Sure.'

'Fine. I'll ring you. Need to go; sorry.'

She looked down at her hand on the phone. Well, that explains a lot, she thought. No wonder she hadn't heard from her husband. And Rachel, the postgraduate student. How long had that been going on for? There hadn't been any evidence at their house. Maybe it was recent or only in London? Should I warn her? She must be at least thirty years old; she can fend for herself; she'll think I want him back if I say something. What's Carol going to say about this? Do I admit to Nigel that I didn't know anything?

***

'Hello Julian, sorry I'm late, something came up.'

'Hello Lotte. Come in. Let's try and crack this today, shall we? I'll feel a lot better when we've got that box-file full up. I went to the box room earlier. Steve has been adding boxes and paper like crazy. The teaching and learning ones are still pretty empty and looking a bit forlorn.'

'Yes, agreed. I've been thinking about this. I'd like us to go for non-behavioural learning outcomes for the lectures, but negotiated learning outcomes, with students, at the beginning of the seminars. I think that's a good compromise.'

'Are you sure? That sounds a bit radical. I got the impression that the quality person, Lucy, doesn't want any risk-taking.'

'I know. But seriously, Julian, what the hell does she know about teaching, let alone teaching philosophy.'

'But she does seem to know a lot about what the QAA want to see. Why don't we go along and see Jack Lowell. You know him, don't you?'

'How about this compromise: You finish off the learning outcomes for the lectures and I do something for the seminars? They may never see the light of day if the inspectors only look at the learning outcomes for the whole course.'

'Okay. I've got the course learning outcomes pretty well covered already. Steve will definitely want to see some session learning outcomes though…both for lectures and seminars…I'm sure. Especially for the sessions they intend to visit.'

'But aren't we wasting too much of our time on this? Don't you get the distinct impression that we are doing all this only to impress some idiot inspectors? We should be impressing our students. Why don't we just ask our students what *they* think and cut out out this bogus middle man?'

'The reviewers *will* speak with the students, of course. I'm sure the students will speak highly of us…especially you.'

'Are you trying to flatter me? But that's not what I meant though, is it? I don't think students are that bothered about the things inspectors are interested in. Students know what they like.'

'Like art? I know what I like even if I don't know why?'

'I think students are more like art *critics* than layman.'

'Possibly, but they are surely lacking in the language of pedagogy.'

'But do you think that inspection is really about pedagogy? Isn't it really about attacking the professionalism of academics in order to control them? Like Steve has been implying…without directly coming out with out?'

'I do see that, of course, but Steve does clearly want us to do well out of this review. He's caught in the middle, I suppose…So, we do still have a job of work here. I don't think we can avoid it. They'll be here in a couple weeks. I think we just need to crack on.'

***

Who Stole Quality?

Lotte was relieved to hear her office door close behind her. She had spent two hours with Julian, at the end of which he had asked her out for another drink. Turning him down had been the right move; best that liaison finished now. He was starting to sound a bit creepy and cowardly. But what was Nigel Eames up to? Did he contact her because he felt the coast was now clear? She remembered a party a while back, where he had run his fingers up her arm. Perhaps he just wanted to share some gossip? He must have known I wouldn't know anything about Rachel?

She packed up her things, decided she didn't want to speak to anyone, and started looking forward to another evening with Nietzsche. Tomorrow was Friday; just one seminar in the afternoon. The walk to the car park raised her spirits: the light on the path was coming from the setting sun rather than the campus lights. Spring was on its way. This quality agenda is a straitjacket, she thought. We need acts of over-becoming: *Also Sprack Zarathustra*.

Chapter 10

The senior common room was empty when Jack Lowell and Roger Fergusson walked across it to greet Norman Thornhill. It was late Friday afternoon and most people were either on their way home or thinking about it. The three of them had agreed to meet up to take stock of developments on the quality front.

'So, Norman, come on, spill the beans, how did the History Department meeting with Lucy Martens go?' Roger asked.

'Give me a moment, please. I need to compose myself.' Norman smiled broadly before continuing: 'Well, for a start most of us were there, unlike the meeting with the philosophers, Jack. I had put the word round that we needed to stand up to her.'

'Good,' Jack said.

'The fact that we got 23 out of 24 for our subject review certainly helped us, which she acknowledged. But she then started talking about the *new* quality agenda, as if what happened in the past was now irrelevant. She kept banging on about student records of achievement, graduate skills, and graduate jobs, and the best one of all, performance indicators. You can imagine how that went down.'

'Performance related pay, that'll be the next thing,' Roger said.

'I'm pretty sure the Union will resist that,' Jack added.

'I get the distinct impression,' Norman continued, 'that her aim is to impose some kind of monolithic structure across the University, where every course fits within the same template.'

'That's patently ridiculous, Norman, I hope you told her,' Roger said.

'Indeed we did, but I can see a huge divide emerging, between the humanities subjects and the Education Faculty and the Nursing Faculty. Those two are huge, and their courses are largely vocational. I can't see them having much trouble with all this change.'

'The old education versus training debate,' Jack said 'Yep, I think we might well be up against a juggernaut here. What we need are some people in those faculties to stand up and defend education for its own sake, and the importance of criticality; that's *the* key skill, surely?'

'Quite,' Norman said. 'But I think it's even worse. When we challenged her on whether these graduate skills…I think that's what she called them…were generic across disciplines she said that they were, but she also agreed that the key skill was, indeed, criticality.'

'But,' Roger began, 'criticality just isn't a generic skill; it varies from discipline to discipline.'

'But with respect Roger,' Norman began, 'I don't think we should call criticality a skill at all. I think it belittles it. It's really more like a disposition; not how we normally conceive a skill. But, besides that, I think the more important point is that we are surely now experiencing a concerted attempt to undermine disciplined-based knowledge.'

'This fits neatly with Basil Bernstein's latest work,' Jack said.

'You mean the children's speech-code guy,' Roger interjected.

'Yep, same guy, but recently he's been writing about how knowledge in universities has changed. Traditionally, knowledge was developed within the cloistered confines of a university discipline. In the language of Durkheim, this would be considered sacred knowledge, uncontaminated by the outside world; pure knowledge. But we now live in a world where the World, literally, is imposing itself on the Word - the word as constructed by the discipline.'

'I like that Jack,' Norman said, 'I can see how that fits with the ancient university curriculum where the trivium subjects, like Logic and Rhetoric, are considered primary: in the beginning was the Word.'

'Precisely,' Jack said. 'That's where he gets the idea, I think. He has a chapter on that distinction.'

'But there's a problem here surely,' Roger said, 'because it makes it sound like rhetoric and logic *are* actually key skills,...sorry Norman...key dispositions.'

'Yes,' replied Jack, 'but I think Bernstein is trying to emphasise that the building blocks of a discipline's knowledge are insular...singular, uncontaminated by the World and its politics. That doesn't make them detached and merely academic; actually the opposite...it would make any skill an embodied one; embodied by its discipline context. In which case, I think Bernstein would be agreeing with you, Roger.'

'I think that's right Jack,' Norman said, 'but we shouldn't forget that for centuries the Oxford and Cambridge colleges were more like professional formation centres. They prepared young men for their calling; their vocations. It was much later, probably not until the 19th century, that they became breeding grounds for the disciplines as we now know them.'

'Well,' Jack said, 'they certainly weren't like the training centres we now have today; where the knowledge being taught is *brought to* a university - what Bernstein calls generic knowledge...there's your key skills, Roger, but disembodied ones. To be fair to Bernstein though, he does talk about...what he calls...the regions...those disciplines that have always had a foot in both camps, so to speak; they develop knowledge within the confines of the discipline, but the knowledge looks outward to the places it will be applied...like Medicine, Architecture, and Law.'

'Good,' Roger said, 'I can see how this fits with audit culture, and why it is so objectionable. What the QAA is really reviewing is not discipline knowledge, but how well a university has adapted to the new demands being put on it. Just look at how many comments in the subject reviews are about student preparedness for the world of work; how a university needs to be preparing students for future employment; not the love of subject, or of knowledge.'

'Yes, they are increasingly inspecting the generic knowledge,' Jack interjected.

'But,' Roger said, 'I think it's complicated in a subject like Psychology, because it's a relatively young subject compared with, say, Theology or Law, and because of that it has come under the influence of the World much more than they would have. It annoys me that some of my clinical psychology friends seem much more comfortable with what is going on, because they can see the jobs that the students will go into. I just don't consider myself preparing my students for any particular job, otherwise my "Introduction to Freud" course would have to renamed, "Introduction to becoming a therapist".'

'I suppose one way to look at it,' Norman began, 'would be to say that the more ancient the subject is, the more insular it probably will be. These are the subjects and people who will suffer most from what is currently going on, because it's much clearer to them that their work is being undermined; that the World *is* encroaching on the Word. Those subjects which are more outward looking...the ancient professions...might also feel aggrieved, but the younger, newer, professions might not feel aggrieved at all, because the curriculum always felt like it was being delivered to a university rather than being constructed within it. On that, I think you're right Jack. Disciplines like Education and Nursing might not even see the problem. It would be good if we had a traditional Medicine Department working alongside Nursing. That might put the cat amongst the pigeons. But therein lies a problem with a university like ours: we tend to specialise in the more applied subjects, anyway. Ancient universities teach ancient subjects. We shouldn't forget that we were a polytechnic less than ten years ago. Perhaps it's people like *us* who are actually the problem, because we teach ancient subjects within a very modern, generic knowledge context. Does Bernstein talk about that, Jack?'

'I need to check; not sure. I think it would be safe to say that further education colleges have now become generic training centres, so perhaps it's a question of how far we are willing to let the encroachment go.'

'On that note, Jack, I need to get going,' Norman said.

On the walk back to his office, Jack could see the clouds gathering in the sky. If he was going to make it home before the rain, he would need to be on his bike before long. While he was tidying up the papers on his desk he saw the post-it note with 'Wilheim von Humboldt' written on it. He calculated that there was time before the rain to walk across to the University's library to order a copy of Humboldt's 1810 memorandum from the British Library. He looked up again at the clouds as he left the library. Luckily, he found himself cycling towards blue sky rather than grey, which provided some space for his mind to wander. Although Sociology was a relatively recent subject - Auguste Comte, 1840, he reminded himself - it did have a strong case for being considered an insular or singular subject. Nice irony there: that Durkheim's distinction between sacred and profane knowledge was itself part of the sacred knowledge of Sociology.

Perhaps this is the real reason why the QAA was so problematic, he thought. Rather than the discipline interrogating its own knowledge practices, it was being undertaken from the outside. What profession, or professional wants to be held to account in this way? What's the point of becoming a professional; being ask to guard professional knowledge; being granted professional autonomy, only to surrender it to a government agency? But generating sociological knowledge was not the same as teaching it. Perhaps this is where the real problem lay: that pedagogical considerations have become divorced from subject knowledge.

Who Stole Quality?

The absent-minded professor. Perhaps he's been the problem all along? The person who is so engrossed, so in love with his subject knowledge, that he has become other-worldly, with no ability to communicate his knowledge to his students. Teaching is the World, not the Word; that needs exploring, he thought. But wouldn't it be better if Sociology teachers got their own house in order? Does it need somebody to come in from the outside and tell them how to do it? Unless you wanted to steer the curriculum in a particular way, perhaps? Or you wanted to standardise the curriculum so that a league table could be created. It was back to the same old problem; the Thatcherite problem: that public sector professionals couldn't be trusted; they were just as bad as mine workers. Could it be that simple?

Jack wheeled his bike down the corridor towards his flat, satisfied that he had earned his dinner. Some unfinished questions for Norman, he thought. Perhaps a phone call in the morning was in order. It would have to be in the morning, because he was due at Angela's house the following afternoon. He had promised Angela that he would help with the preparations for a dinner party later in the evening. The dinner party. Not something to look forward to, he thought. But at least there was *this* evening; a chance to listen to some music: Neil Young, or perhaps Joni Mitchell.

Less than ten minutes into *Ladies of the Canyon,* his mind wandered away from the music, back to the question of professional integrity. He thumbed through his phone book, looking for Norman's number. Eight o'clock; not too late to ring. He let Joni Mitchell run to the end, then made the call.

Chapter 11

The sun was streaming into Jack's bedroom as he drank his morning espresso. Norman and Roger had agreed to meet him for a coffee at 10.30 in town. Jack hadn't been comfortable leaving Roger out of the conversation and was pleased when he said he would be able to join them. Saturday morning was football practice for Roger's identical twin boys, giving him a two hour window between drop off and pick up. Jack smiled at the thought that Roger and his wife had produced their own psychology experiment.

The three of them had agreed to meet in the coffee shop where Jack normally met with Angela. Jack locked his bike against his usual lamp post, and as he rose he saw Norman waving at him from inside. Jack smiled to himself: Norman was looking more like Oscar Wilde every time he saw him; possibly Stephen Fry playing Oscar Wilde.

'Hello Norman. Thanks for agreeing to this.'

'How could I not agree. You sounded like you were plotting last night.'

'Yes, sorry about that. I think I was. Shall we wait for Roger?'

'Okay. Coffee?'

'Yes, thanks Norman. Americano, black, no sugar.'

At that point Roger came in, sounding breathless: 'Sorry guys. Crisis on the domestic front. Missing football boot.'

Roger was wearing track suit bottoms and running shoes, even though it was his children who would be undertaking the real exercise. Not that he didn't look fit. He was over six feet tall, slender, and his beard gave him a rugged mountaineer's look, which somehow seemed more apparent off-campus.

'Coffee, Roger?' Norman asked.

'Yes please. I need it. Americano, thanks.' Roger then turned to Jack: 'So, what's this all about then?'

'My mind started wandering yesterday evening and I wanted to get your reaction.'

Jack resumed when Norman returned with the coffees: 'We agree that our professionalism is under attack?'

Norman and Roger looked at each other, then nodded.

'So, how about we fight back, by creating our own teaching and learning course, for all new academics, run by us? No outside imposition.'

'You mean like a school teacher post-graduate course,' Roger began. 'I know that some universities now have these, but aren't they run by the quality people? We'll be ostracised by our colleagues, surely?'

'I suppose what I'm thinking is, why not get in before them? Go straight to the VC and say that we want to extend the workshops that Richard McGiffen started, and turn them into a course. We would then have control.'

'The problem, as I see it,' Norman said, 'is that we wouldn't be imposing something from the outside, but we would still be imposing...from the inside. Wouldn't it better if each discipline, or subject area, was responsible for their own course? If we just have one course, I think it would still be perceived as the Devil's work. Correct me if I'm wrong, Jack, but wasn't Bernstein's point that we shouldn't allow discipline knowledge to be undermined by generic knowledge - brought in from outside?'

'On my PGCE course,' Roger said, 'we had some generic content and some subject specific stuff.'

'I didn't know you had a PGCE, Roger,' Jack said.

'I wasn't hiding the fact. Actually, I taught in a school for ten years; Maths. I took my master's in Psychology and then my PhD while I was still teaching. That's how I got interested in the question of HE pedagogy, especially when I realised just how many people in the University didn't seem to know the first thing about basic teaching concepts. It's completely different though, because in schools you get qualified before you teach. Presumably here, we are talking about academics taking a qualification after they've already got a job. The interview I underwent here was all about my PhD research, not about my ability to teach, or my PGCE. That didn't even come up.'

'Does that mean,' Norman said, 'that you have two master's qualifications? One in Psychology and one in Teaching?'

'No. My Post-Graduate Certificate in Education was not at master's level. The post-grad bit just meant you had to have a degree first. It was a time-served definition, not an academic level one.'

'Ah, I see,' Norman said. 'That's interesting if we look at this historically. I think the VC's view is that people are qualified to work here because they have PhDs. For a new university we certainly do have a lot of PhDs. I don't know whether it's a policy decision, but haven't you noticed how it's always the people with the PhD who get the job? Then we find out later that they either can't teach, or don't want to teach. Certainly the case in the History Department.'

'And your historical point, Norman?' Roger asked.

'My point is that a PhD...if it qualifies you for doing anything...is a qualification in research. It validates your ability to do research, not to teach. The problem is deep rooted. The original master's qualifications *were* teaching qualifications. Now they're just academic stepping stones to PhDs. They've lost their pedagogic basis. And don't forget they weren't really courses. You proved you had the knowledge with your bachelor's degree, then you came down from Oxford or Cambridge to London and spent a couple of years as a journeyman, disseminating that knowledge...engaging in professional formation, if you will. Then you returned to your Oxbridge college to be granted your master's.'

'So,' Jack said, 'what we should be doing is granting everyone a master's in Pedagogy once they have proven that they can do some decent teaching?'

'Well, yes,' Norman said, 'in a way I *am* saying that. There's no need for a course, but there could be some kind of professional formation process, particularly if it was linked to a professional or discipline association."

'Like the British Psychological Association, or The Law Society?' Roger asked. 'Of course, there is already something like this. I was looking at the materials on the Psychology LTSN the other day. It was actually pretty good.'

'LTSN?', Norman asked.

'I think it stands for "learning and teaching subject network". Is that right, Jack?'

'Yes. I've heard of these networks. I looked at the Sociology one a while back. I suppose each one could become its own professional teaching association, which could then validate teaching competence. Ouch! I just said "competence"; I don't mean that, do I?'

'There's the problem again, Jack,' Norman said. 'If Teaching, or Pedagogy, really is a discipline in its own right, then do we induct *everyone* in to *that*, or do we recognise that each discipline does have its own approach to teaching? If it's the latter, then each subject area would have to have its own master's route. In the language of Bernstein, it would be "regional knowledge"...knowledge looking out towards the world...in this case the classroom...but its root would still lie in the discipline. '

'I think what we might have here,' Jack said, 'is a political problem masquerading as an epistemological problem...the profane overrunning the sacred, in the language of Durkheim.'

'Explain,' Norman said.

'I think the differences between all university disciplines...in terms of pedagogy... are actually quite small...there really isn't *that* much difference between teaching Maths and Sociology, surely, but it pays for the disciplines to claim that there is, because it's a way of keeping out the quality bureaucrats. It's a political bulwark; deliberately set up to stop incursions. Sorry for the sociology lesson, but it's a Weberian mode of social closure; a deliberate attempt to put your arms around your secret society in order to help make it special, or sacred. Clearly, it pays to do this. But you've now got me thinking, Norman: maybe *all* disciplines have "regional" dimensions...in terms of pedagogy at least. It's rarely a matter of "singular" knowledge only. We just have to be on guard when it comes to the "generic" incursions. Maybe this is what Bernstein means by the recontextualisation of knowledge. Need to get back to you on that! '

'The way I see it,' Roger began, 'is that a post-graduate course in HE Pedagogy would provide the space to discuss *all* these things. How often do any of us actually talk about these things?'

'Well, *we* do,' Norman said. 'But I take your point. It's not normally a topic of conversation in the senior common room, and perhaps it should be. Personally speaking, I'd love to have a little module on a pedagogy course where I could talk about the first priority of a university being to teach and disseminate. If it was just to do research...which I think some of our colleagues believe...then why bother with having any students around. They'll only get in the way. Sorry, that's *my* history lesson. I was paraphrasing Cardinal Newman there.'

'Well, quite, Norman,' Jack said. 'which also raises the question of whether the primary focus in teaching should be on knowledge transmission and generation; or on moral formation; or even plain old self-development.'

'That suits me,' Roger said, '...that would provide me with the space to discuss exactly what self-development really means, from a psychological perspective.'

'This is good,' Norman said. 'But can we continue on another day because I need to get to the station soon to meet my partner. Sorry, I should have said earlier. He'll be annoyed if we miss our train. We're off to London for the rest of the day.'

After Norman's departure, Jack and Roger stayed on.

'It's funny, how we...sort of...know each other, but not really,' Roger said, as he sat down with two fresh coffees.

'How do you mean?'

'I love old Norman, but I don't really know much about him. Have you ever met his partner? We talk about ideas, but not really about each other. What does that say about us?'

'That we're academics, I suppose...I didn't know you had a PGCE and taught for *ten years* in a school.'

'Just never came up, I suppose. But this hits the nail on the head, doesn't it? We *do* mainly only talk about academic things. We *are* somewhat cloistered. The emphasis on knowledge production and PhDs *has* turned us inwards, and not in a good way. I take Bernstein's point about insularity, but surely we do need to get out more?'

'You've just reminded me of a book by Russell Jacoby, *The Last Intellectuals*, where he speaks precisely to that question. We *don't* need more academics, we need more public intellectuals. People who contribute to public debate, not just write academic articles that very few people actually read. It really would be great to have a space where we talk about the type of knowledge that we trade in. I think our course in HE pedagogy could be that space.'

'I agree,' Roger said. 'but we're up against. We haven't even got Norman on our side, have we?'

'But I think he would agree on the academics versus intellectuals issue. And surely there's a middle ground here: if academics from each discipline all came together on a course, wouldn't we all be learning from each other? And it would certainly be collegiate in nature, not managerial.'

'But what happens, Jack, when the course clashes with what Lucy Martens and her crew want to impose? Won't they just win out? It's possible that we might be able to enhance learning and teaching significantly, but we might still do badly in a QAA visit, because we didn't do things as *they* wanted. I think that's the big issue.'

'Well, I certainly think we should discuss this more. I think Marion Barton and Thomas Minot would agree with us, for a start.'

At that point Roger looked around the room and then edged his seat nearer to the table: 'I've been meaning to ask you about Richard McGiffen.'

'What do you mean?' Jack asked.

'I still keep thinking that the police are going to get in contact again and ask me more questions. I know that's paranoia.'

'Well, it may well be, but I do the same, if it's any comfort. I sometimes wake up in the early hours thinking that someone has gone to the police and they want to speak to *me*.'

'Why *were* you in the building that evening, Jack?'

'Oh, you heard about that then? I was with Charlotte Rudolph.'

'When you say *with*, what do you mean?'

'Hey, Roger, now you're making *me* paranoid, again.'

'Sorry Jack. No more questions on that.'

'One thing I do keep thinking about though is how good old Dickie Mac was, especially compared with Lucy Martens. Sometimes you really don't know what you've got until it's actually gone.'

'A horrible thing to say I know, but we'd probably be better off if *she'd* died and got replaced by Richard. At least that way I would have had a blazing row with her and not Richard. You're right; he was a good egg. It's horrible how we got pitted against each other.'

'I think…in Richard…we might have seen the last real quality officer; misguided, perhaps, but he did care.'

At that point, Roger looked at his watch and announced that he needed to be on his way, to pick up his boys.

'Don't forget, it's the last QAA visit next week. The philosophers.'

'I know,' Jack said. 'How *could* I forget.'

Chapter 12

Jack heard his mother's voice in his head as he rode away from the cafe: 'You might have a degree, but it's certainly not in common sense.' There is a real issue here, he thought; another quality issue, perhaps; is academic knowledge all its cracked up to be? That would make a good article, he thought, but then realised the irony of writing an academic article about why we shouldn't always write academic articles. Even more so if nobody read it. Could still be fun, though. Except Ralph Smythe, that miserable little Director of Research, would probably put his fountain pen right through it.

He arrived back at his flat, just after one o'clock. Plenty of time for lunch and a sit down. He was not expected at Angela's until three o'clock. Her dinner party was set for eight o'clock. Perhaps the conversation there might move away from the subject of literature and onto politics? Or perhaps he could steer it that way: is Tony Blair's Third Way just Thatcherism in disguise? 'Mrs Thatcher without a handbag' - a comment he remembered the sociologist, Anthony Giddens, once using when addressing his critics. Or maybe a discussion about whether writing in the third person is just first person writing in disguise. But could get hopelessly out of my depth there, he thought.

***

'Hi Jack, come in.' Angela kissed him on the cheek being careful not to touch him. Jack looked at the cement-like substance on her hands and up her arms.

'Don't mind me. As you can see I've started already.'

Jack followed her into the kitchen.

'Do you think you could make some guacamole, Jack?'

'If you tell me what it is and how to do it.'

'See that chopping board, all the ingredients are next to it. Start chopping and mashing.'

'So, who's coming tonight?'

'We've got Keith, Graham, and Gemma from the English Department. And Alex and Brian coming from London. And Julie, my housemate, of course. She'll be back shortly. She's gone to the supermarket.'

'Wow, full house. You don't think I will stand out a bit? Everyone poking fun at the sociologist.'

'Don't be silly. Just enjoy yourself. There'll be plenty to drink. You'll be staying over?'

Jack smiled, but in his head he wished he had previously said that he was going to his parents early next morning. Perhaps he could still say that.

'Hey, Angela, I've been thinking about subject knowledge lately. Would you say that English has to be taught in a particular way, and how would you describe literary knowledge?'

'Nice, Jack, start with the easy ones, why don't you.'

'Sorry, I sound like a madman. The nature of subject knowledge has been on my mind, that's all.'

'I think you'll enjoy talking to Brian. He's really angry about what's been going on at his place.'

'How so?'

'I think they're making all their courses follow a set pattern and all the students have to fill in a form about their employment aspirations. Something like that; I wasn't really listening, to be honest. He thinks it's because they haven't done very well in the subject reviews.'

'Yeah. I can see that sort of thing happening more and more.'

'Time for me to move on if that happens. I just don't see English as a vocational subject.'

'But how about if we distinguish vocationalism from employability; the new term on the block. That the subject of English doesn't prepare you for a particular job, but English graduates *are* employable.'

'Well yes, they are employable; very employable, so what's the problem? They get jobs; all sorts of jobs.'

'I agree. It's the same for Sociology students. I think the problem stems partly from those in government who want undergraduate students to be more focused on work, and to blame themselves if they don't find it, but also those old reactionary types who hate students doing Mickey Mouse degrees, as they like to call them.'

'Well that's rich; isn't it? How many prime ministers and civil servants have studied Classics at Oxford. How did that prepare them for *their* jobs? Surely, it's having a degree…in anything…that's important. It's the critical skills and self-confidence, that's the important thing…yes?'

'But what was it about your degree that gave you that criticality and self-confidence?'

'In my case it was when I was introduced to postmodern ideas. It was then that I realised that my faith in knowledge was just that…a faith. You had to believe in it; it wasn't self-evident. It was like a bedtime story you told yourself in order to feel safe and secure. Breaking away from that was very liberating for me.'

'But does that mean you now have no faith? That sounds a bit depressing.'

'But surely it's more depressing to believe in a reality that isn't really there? Coming to that realisation late could be crushing. Hey, that lemon hasn't been cut open yet.'

'Sorry, I didn't realise that needed to go in…I want to say that there is a reality out there; it's just that we can't be sure that we understand it properly. I think it was Einstein who said that studying the world was like trying to understand an unopened watch. We think about it; we imagine; we theorise; but what we can't do is pop round the back to check that we have got it right.'

'I suppose I would just go one step further and say that the reality - if we must use that word - is a reflection of how we see it, not the other way round. Don't forget, we bring language *to* our reality.'

'Good; that fits neatly with what I've been thinking about. But that's not how all your colleagues see it?'

'Good God, no! There's plenty of them who have an aesthetic sensibility.'

'Is that what gives literature its quality? Can that be taught?'

'Sure. Sign up for a degree in English and American Literature.'

'But, seriously, do you have to teach English in a particular way?' Before Jack could get an answer, Julie came through the front door with the shopping.

'Hi Jack, nice to see you. Do you think you could help me get the rest of the bags out of the car? Better still, could you bring the wine in?'

'Okay. I think this guacamole is ready. Do you want to taste it?'

***

Just before nine o'clock Angela called everyone to take their places at the table. Above the sound of chair legs being scrapped on floor boards, she began explaining all the food items, and encouraged everyone to help themselves. She picked up one of the large spoons by way of demonstration. The small talk introductions had already taken place. Jack knew Graham, Gemma and Keith, but had never gone beyond the odd 'hello, how are you?' Julie had recently got a job at the British Library. Because of the journey into London she often stayed over in a friend's flat, so he hadn't got to know her very well either. Alex and Brian were partners, working at different London universities. Alex and Angela had been friends from their undergraduate days. It was already clear that Brian was the most outspoken of the group.

'So, Jack,' Brian began, 'tell me more about this staff development role you play. It looks like you've picked up a poisoned chalice there.'

'Yep,' Jack replied. 'It does feel like that sometimes. I still consider myself a sociologist, so this is something I do on the side, so to speak.'

'At my place, staff development used to be people you could ignore. But their power has grown. No department has got 24 from the QAA, so I suppose that was inevitable.'

'How did that pan out?' Jack asked. 'What I mean is, was it teaching and learning issues or management issues that brought the scores down?'

'I think it was both. I didn't take much notice, to be honest. I was working to get my final article published for the upcoming RAE.'

'So, perhaps there was a *real* problem with the teaching and learning environment?'

'Are you sure you're not a staff development person? That's how they talk. Most of us have dedicated years to our subjects. Who the hell do they think they are?'

'Brian! Really!' Alex interjected. 'We don't need your lecture on this again, not here. Jack is only doing his job.'

'That's okay Alex,' Jack said, 'I enjoy talking about this.'

'I think there is a problem,' Alex said, 'but I'm not sure the subject reviews are the solution. Do you remember, Angela, when we were talking about that awful lecturer we had as students? The one who didn't show up and when he did nobody knew what he was talking about.'

Before Angela could speak, Brian interrupted: 'Well, yes, we can all think of those cases, but they are exceptional and largely anecdotal.'

'Look, there's red and white on the table. Do please help yourselves. And there's a lot of salad untouched, so please go ahead.'

'I agree,' began Gemma. 'Look at the way the evidence for *our* QAA visit was compiled. It was easy to hide the skeletons in the cupboard.'

'Gemma's right,' Angela said. 'That guy shouldn't really have been teaching us, but would any kind of formal review have actually dealt with it.'

'But I bet he had a good research record,' Brian added, 'that's the main reason for working at a university, surely?'

'But there's the problem, Brian,' Jack said. 'The way that researchers have come to dominate over teachers. They should at least be better balanced, surely?'

'I want to take a different line on this.' Graham said. 'If you look at the Dearing Report, where a lot of current government ideas can be found, it says there that one of the issues is the current influx of students who have no background in higher education. Their parents won't have degrees, meaning they will need more support. It's hard to disagree with that, particularly for a post-92 university like ours.'

'Well,' Brian said, 'I *do* disagree with that. Why the hell has Blair, and his cronies, committed us to having 50% of the population with degrees? That's just barmy. We don't need that number of graduates. Next thing you know your plumber will have a degree in Media Studies.'

'I suppose he could recommend films while he was fixing the sink?' Keith chipped in.

'But this is serious,' Brian continued. 'The real point is that we're now expected to deal with remedial students, who shouldn't be at university.'

'Hey, come on Brian,' Jack said, 'that's not fair. Higher education has been the privilege of the middle-classes for far too long. Widening participation is long overdue. Just because some people happen to have the right parents, and went to posh schools, why should they then get given privileged access to university?'

'Are you sure you're not one of those staff development types, Jack?' Brian replied.

'Brian, the sociological evidence about privilege in this country is overwhelming. Why would you want to defend that?'

'What I want to defend are standards. Standards in higher education are slipping each year, and they will continue to drop all the while Blair is in office.'

'So you're a Tory, Brian. Is that what you're telling us?' Jack said.

'Hey guys,' Angela interrupted, 'perhaps we could change the subject now?'

For the next ten minutes the sound of cutlery on plates and bowls resonated around the room, and the group settled into the odd comment about the quality of the food.

'Jack, could you help me in the kitchen?' Angela asked.

He scrapped his chair back and dutifully followed her into the kitchen.

'What the hell, Jack. What was that all about?' Angela whispered.

'He's getting on my fucking nerves. Arrogant prick.'

'Jack, please. Lower your voice; he'll hear you.'

'Well good. I want him to. Don't tell me you agree with him?'

'No, but he's entitled to his opinion.'

'I don't care about his opinion. I want him to produce some fucking evidence.'

'Jack, can you stop swearing. You need to apologise to him, so we can move on.'

Angela returned to the dinning table with the main course, Jack in tow.

'Here we are everyone, tuck in. This one is meat based, and the one Jack has is the veggie option. I'll just get some more bread.'

'So,' Keith began, 'anyone got plans for the summer yet?'

'I've signed up for a writing retreat in New England,' Gemma said.

'Not run by Stephen King, is it?' Keith replied.

'Don't think so, but I do think he's a better writer than some of us would give him credit for.'

'Standards again,' Brian said.

Alex jumped in quickly: 'We're going to stay in my parents' summer house in Tuscany.'

'Nice,' Julie said. 'My parents have a house in Provence. Perhaps we could swap for a week?'

'That would be fun,' Gemma said.

'Angela, weren't you talking about Portugal?' Keith asked.

Jack reached for a top-up on the red wine, noticing that the bottle still had a fair amount in it.

'Just a thought,' Angela said.

'A nice one,' Keith replied.

Jack glanced at his watch without being obvious: 10.30pm. How much longer, he thought. It was too late to say he would be driving home. He was now on his fourth glass of red wine. Brian was sitting directly opposite him, making it hard to avoid eye contact. He turned to Julie, who was sitting next to him, and asked some questions about The British Library. He managed to stretch out a conversation about Karl Marx and his favourite seat in the old reading room.

Just before midnight, Graham asked if he could use the phone to book a taxi. Jack was tempted to ask if he could share the ride, but he knew this wouldn't go down well with Angela. It had been obvious for the last couple of hours that Brian and Alex were staying overnight. But what was worse: attempting escape, or laying low? He decided to stay quiet, while using his body language to make it as clear as possible to Brian that he thought he was a prick.

Just after midnight, Angela's clean-up operation was in full swing. Jack was given front room clean up, along with Julie and Alex. The rest were put to work in the kitchen. At 12.40am the taxi arrived, which formally closed the evening. Keith, Graham, and Gemma departed together, sharing the taxi, and by 1.15am everyone left in the house had gone to bed.

Angela walked into her bedroom after brushing her teeth and looked at Jack who was sitting by the side of the bed: 'Did you apologise to Brian, Jack?' she whispered.

'He should have apologised to *me*.'

'Jack, for goodness sake. What is wrong with you.'

'What's wrong with *me*?'

'Just go to sleep, will you.'

Angela turned her back on him and pulled the quilt towards her. This left Jack partly exposed, but he didn't fight back. He stared up at the ceiling, wishing he was back at his flat. I could feign a bit of illness in the morning, he thought, as he drifted off.

***

Jack heard Angela leave the bedroom just after eight in the morning. The next time he awoke he could hear Angela saying her goodbyes to Brian and Alex. He looked across at the clock on the bedside table: 9.35am. The bedroom door then opened.

'How embarrassing, Jack. I had to pretend you had too much to drink last night.'

'Sorry. I did have a lot to drink, so you weren't lying.'

'But I *was* lying. The drink had nothing to do with it, did it?'

'Sorry, but I couldn't let him get away with his comments.'

'But didn't you think about everyone else? It was supposed to be a nice get together. You could at least apologise to me?'

'Okay. I'm sorry.'

'Well, say it like you mean it. You've been so moody lately, Jack. Don't you want us anymore?'

'Look, I'm sorry, I really am. What do you want me to say. I tell it like it is. Why should I have to change?'

'Your call, Jack. I'm not happy, let's just leave it at that.'

Chapter 13

Lotte had spent a good deal of the weekend on the phone with Steve Jackman and Julian Ashwood. The box files for the QAA subject review were pretty much complete except for some gaps in the teaching and learning ones. Julian had been in his office at the University for most of Saturday, busy typing up what was being agreed and then transporting it to the box room. Lotte's frustration with both of them had been growing. It was clear to Lotte that Steve had got cold feet and that Julian had been enthusiastically agreeing with everything he said, then running away to adjust the Department's story accordingly.

Late Sunday afternoon Steve phoned Lotte to confirm that he would be trying to engineer proceedings to ensure that Lotte's teaching was observed by one of the QAA review team. Steve was also keen that the reviewer who looked the most troublesome should be the one who observed Lotte, if at all possible. He saw her as the departmental trump card when it came to enthusiastic teaching. He asked her to be prepared to be observed on another occasion if he was having trouble orchestrating everything. He also confirmed that the hand-picked students would be interviewed late Wednesday afternoon. Steve had deferred to Lotte and Jos on who these students should be. That was the only thing that Lotte was comfortable with. Everything else seemed to have moved some distance from what they had originally agreed on.

'Lotte! Dinner's ready!' Carol shouted up the stairs. Carol and Marjorie had seen Lotte's stress growing over the weekend and had agreed to cook a Sunday roast for the evening.

'Thanks you two,' Lotte said as she entered the kitchen. 'It smells great.'

'I hope you're all done up there,' Carol said.

'Yeh. Not much I can do now. They arrive tomorrow. I'm thoroughly pissed off with the whole thing.'

'I've seen people brought to tears at my place,' Marjorie said. 'I thought the universities were much more powerful than further education colleges when it came to inspection.'

Lotte thought of her mother, then said: 'I would have agreed with you, until a couple of months ago, but I now think the universities are rolling over as well.'

'I appreciate that I'm only sitting on the edge, in student support,' Marjorie said, 'but I do hear all the gossip at my place. There are a lot people who want out. It's about to be made compulsory to hold a teaching qualification, and a lot of the teachers are really angry about it. One of them told me that they've all got to tick off this huge long list of teaching competencies. He wasn't convinced that any of it would make him a better teacher, just a paper-qualified one. I think that was the term he used. Some of them are thinking about going back into the industries they came from.'

'I can see why,' Lotte said. 'At least they've got somewhere to go. The problem in universities is that the profession is not the one you came from, it's academia itself, and it's being torn apart by all of this.'

'I can see you are hurting, Lotte,' Carol said. 'It must be worse for somebody like you, who believes in academia, but there must be some of your colleagues who wish that the links with the real world and the professions were stronger.'

'Yeah, but don't forget, Carol, academia is the real world. It's just as real as any other real. I'm caught, though, you know that, because I want to defend knowledge for its own sake, but my own research profile is non-existent. And I can only see that getting worse, if I am pushed more and more into a teaching role. I got *really* pissed off this afternoon because my Head of Department was talking as if I was some kind of teaching saviour for the Department.'

'There are more roast potatoes in the pan on the draining board, so don't hesitate,' Carol said.

'One thing I know pisses people off at my place,' Marjorie began, 'is that more and more money is being spent on marketing and making the place look pretty, but it's just a facade because a lot of the classrooms haven't changed in years, and the biggest complaint from the students is the lack of books in the library. I overheard one lecturer saying that an inspection must be coming up because the corridor smelt of fresh paint. Kinda sums it up.'

'I think this is pretty universal in the public sector professions,' Carol said. 'At the same time that the government has become obsessed with improvement and value for money, it has been reducing the unit cost, so quality will decrease, unless creative ways to stage-manage things are found. Which, of course, increases costs because managers have to be found to do the stage-management. It's a pretty sad state of affairs really. Blair has turned out to be Thatcher Mark Two.'

'We've certainly got a bloody annoying quality manager at my place.' Lotte said. 'She's been pissing me off for weeks.'

'Here's an odd thing,' Marjorie said. 'I came into work last Monday, to find a guy putting up new signs. I knew our department name was changing from "Student Support" to "Learner Support", but he was also taking down the library sign and replacing it with "Learning Resource Centre", and next to his ladder he had a sign with "Accessible" on it. I asked him about it and he said his next job was to take down the "Disabled" toilet sign and replace it with the accessible one. It got me thinking that the college hadn't changed at all, but the way we were supposed to speak about it had.'

'I think they call it verbal hygiene,' Carol said.

'Well, as long as the toilet stays hygienic,' Marjorie said. 'The next thing will be students coming up to me asking whether they are allowed to use that toilet.'

'There is a genuine issue here, though,' Carol said. 'Referring to women as bitches or black people as the n-word *is* wrong; we shouldn't tolerate that. Some name changing *is* just political correctness, but some clearly isn't.'

'But what about a bit of postmodern irony?' Lotte said. 'What if women or black people start calling themselves those things. Just like the gay community appropriated the word "queer". Yeh, I'm queer, what are you going to do about it?'

'Glad to have you on board, Lotte,' Carol joked.

'But seriously, something does need to change,' Lotte said. 'I feel I could explode at the moment.'

Chapter 14

Lotte walked to her car just before 8.30 on Monday morning. It was warm and she removed her black wool jacket before getting in the car. The Bo Diddley CD was on the top of the pile in the glove compartment. She pushed it into the CD slot, opened the window., and checked the time. She wasn't teaching until the afternoon, but she felt obliged to be around all morning in case any more boxes needed some last minute attention. The QAA review team were due to arrive at midday. Steve Jackman had told her that she would only be needed for two meetings: the teaching and learning meeting the following morning, and the student welfare meeting set for Thursday morning. Everything was in place. By Friday they would be gone and things could return to normal.

She walked into her corridor, to discover Beverley, the Department's administrator, frantically running back to her office, with an armful of paper.

'Morning Lotte. I feel like I've done a week's work already. I've been here since 6.30, can you believe?'

'Let me help,' Lotte said, as she placed her bag down on Bev's desk.

'Thanks, but I think I'm okay. Steve and Julian have just given me this lot. I've put different coloured stickies on each wodge of paper. I just need to slot them into the relevant boxes. I'm going straight over there now. Jos is already there, taking out the old paper, so, we should be fine. Steve is in his office if you want to see him.'

'Morning Lotte,' Steve said, as he looked up from behind his desk. Julian was leaning across him, shuffling paper: 'After my phone call with you, I started to panic again. Nothing to do with you. I just felt that some of the learning outcomes needed to be more transparent. Julian's been up all night making the adjustments.'

'Nearly there,' Julian said.

'I also started panicking about student welfare,' Steve said. 'I do think we've got a great story, but Lucy Martens wants it to dovetail better with the central system. She thinks we will be pulled up on it. I wasn't worried before, but now I am.'

'What can I do?' Lotte asked.

'Thanks Lotte, but I think we're there. I just need to get the message out to everyone that we must say that we use the central recording system for student progression. And that Julian has the session plans for anyone who may be observed teaching.'

Julian dutifully waved another load of paper in the air.

Lotte retrieved her bag from Bev's office, then sat in her own office, with the door closed. 'Fuck,' she said out loud. 'What a bunch of cowards.' She then thought of Jos and Bev in the box room and decided to head over there.

'Hello Lotte,' Jos said. 'Welcome to the madhouse. I think we should put a sticker on the door: The Kafka Room. We have no idea what we've done wrong, but we're going to be convicted anyway.'

'Sorry Jos,' Bev said, 'can I leave this with you? I need to go and buy the stuff to put in the fridge.'

'I'll help Jos,' Lotte said.

'Thanks,' Jos said. 'The pile on the left is the old stuff we need to get rid of, and the pile on the right is the new stuff, which needs to go in the boxes, according to what it says on the stickie. Can you make sure the stickies come off. There are some incriminating comments on them.'

'Like what?' Lotte smiled as she asked the question.

'There's one there, I just pulled it off.'

Lotte read out loud: 'Put at bottom of box. Should be bored before they get to it.'

Lotte recognised Steve Jackman's handwriting.

'The big question though is which pile tells the real story?'

'I would say it's a trick question. Neither does.'

'Correct,' Jos said. 'Or perhaps we might say that what is now in the boxes is more real, because it reflects QAA reality better. I read something the other day about *Qaa-heli*. The language of the QAA. I think I've done a crash course in it over the last two weeks.'

'Not a language I have any desire to master, I'm afraid,' Lotte said. 'Do you think there's a chance that we won't do very well out of this?'

'Yes, I think there is. That's why Steve is panicking.'

'He seemed quite relaxed about it all in that first meeting I went to.'

'I think he was, until Lucy Martens got in on the act. I think she's got to him. Poor sod.'

'I'll be glad when it's Friday.'

'Don't panic. I'll be working on some crib sheets this afternoon. Just cast your eye over them before you go into any meetings with the review team. As I said before, I'm not impressed with them as philosophers. What they're like when they've got an inspector's uniform on is another matter. We certainly have that one guy to worry about. His department got 21 out of 24, and he was very aggrieved, apparently. He might be out for some revenge, or just be very nit-picky. Either way, we have to watch him. The rest should be okay. Unless the whole review team have already decided they want to pull us up.'

'How do you mean? Why?'

'It looks like Philosophy up and down the country is doing rather well, so we could become a scapegoat, to create a better spread of marks.'

'Ah, the old norm referencing problem.'

'Indeed. Let's get this box-filling finished as quick as we can. This room will be out of bounds once Bev gets back.'

A little after one o'clock, Lotte sat in her office with a sandwich and a coffee. She looked across her desk and saw the post-it note with Nigel Eames' telephone number on it. She hadn't rung him. He might cheer her up, she thought. He was a radical non-conformist, just what she needed right now. Given it was lunchtime, he might be in his office.

'Hello Nigel, it's Lotte Rudolph. Do you have a minute to talk?'

'Of course. I thought I'd offended you.'

'No, sorry. I've been preparing for a QAA inspection visit. It's taken up all of my time.'

'Not those clowns. You too?'

'Yes, they're here now, or at least I think they are.'

'Why not let their tyres down.'

'Don't tempt me.'

'They've been here already. Luckily all our higher education work is validated by two universities and it was them who had to deal with it all. They did come to the college one day, but I made sure I wasn't around. I don't know what happened, but we're still here.'

'I wish I wasn't here right now. It's made me so angry.'

'Sounds like you need a drink. Why don't you come over later and we can talk about it?'

'Okay. I'm teaching until three, then I'm free, unless I get summoned, of course.'

'I'll email you directions to my place. I'll be there from four onwards.'

Although she knew Nigel reasonably well, she'd never been in his house. If it was anything like him, the visit should be interesting, she thought. And something to look forward to. The last time she saw him he looked like a cross between Sid Vicious and Johnny Cash: his hair was always a bit spiky and he always wore black clothes. She turned to her lecture notes; she was due to give a lecture on David Hume to the first years at two o'clock.

Lotte arrived in Nigel's street just after four o'clock. The Victorian house had been turned into three flats. She rang the top bell, marked 'Eames'.

'Come up, Lotte. I'm on the top floor.'

The flat did not disappoint. The front room was an artist's studio, with a mix of materials and easels. On the large wall in front of her was a neon sign, announcing 'Burlesque.' The large bay window was bathing the room in sunlight and the place felt warm and inviting.

'Home sweet home,' he announced.'So, drink? I've got vodka, wine, tea, coffee.' As he spoke, he waved the vodka bottle in the air.

'Why not, she said. 'Fuck it.'

'Hey. You've cheered up. Anything in it?'

'Orange juice?'

'Sure. I've got some in the fridge.'

'She followed him to the kitchen. It was messy, but homely again.

'So, how's life? Stuart told me you were living with a couple of lesbians. Sounds like fun.'

'It is, but not in the way you're thinking. They've been very kind. Carol and I did a master's together. What about you?'

'You know me. I flit around.'

'Anything being exhibited?'

'Couple of things, nothing major. You know how it is. What I think is my best work doesn't get a look in. And then suddenly, something second rate gets taken up.'

'Knowing you, Nigel, that doesn't surprise me. I don't think you do yourself any favours.'

'Yeah, but what's in a gallery is only there because the gate keepers of the gallery like it. It's all arbitrary.'

'Yep, I can see that.'

'There's no objective standard for judging pieces of art. People think there is, because they've bought into the rules of the game. New rules, new game...I'd rather produce a piece of art that shocks, than one that follows some arbitrarily rules.'

'But does that go for everything else? Do you think there's such a thing as good teaching?'

'Ah, so you're not that relaxed. You're still thinking about those QAA clowns. They're just following the rules *they've* been given. Good teaching is what follows their rules. Brilliant teaching could be something entirely different.'

'So there's brilliant teaching is there?' Lotte smiled as she said it.

'Caught me there. You know what I mean. It's all rule-governed, but the rules are made up. There's no real meaning behind any of it. Rather than getting depressed about, I just try to mess with it; play with it, subvert it...Another drink?'

'Better not. I've got the car with me. Not to say I wouldn't like another one.'

'Okay, here's the deal. You have another one and I'll book a taxi to get you home.'

'That'll cost a fortune.'

'On me. You look like you could do with another one. I've got something nice to smoke as well, if you'd like some?'

'Let's start with that drink. Are you sure about that taxi?'

'Yes, I'm sure. Why don't I order a takeaway and we make an evening of it?'

'It's QAA tomorrow. I can't be late getting home.'

'It's a shame we can't get something for *them* to smoke. That might create a whole different ball game. Look, it's only five o'clock. You could be home by nine o'clock.'

'But how will I get to work tomorrow? My car will be here.'

'I'll drive over and pick you up. Where's your house?'

'About an hour away.'

'Fine. It's done.'

With that, the vodka and orange was poured and thirty minutes later Nigel was waving a small bag of cannabis in the air. At around seven o'clock the Chinese meal arrived on the doorstep.

***

Lotte looked at her watch while she sat on the loo; 9.10pm. No taxi had been ordered and she felt drunk and tired. Just as she re-entered the front room, Nigel span her round and escorted her into his bedroom. The room was dark, incredibly dark, until she realised that the walls and the ceiling were all painted black. She smiled to herself: Nigel the nihilistic cliche, she thought. He began undressing himself but got his jeans caught on his legs and fell forwards onto the bed. He motioned for her to lie down and placed his arm across her stomach. He had drunk far more than she had, and smoked more cannabis. She reconciled herself to the fact that she was staying overnight. It would be better because she could just drive her own car in the morning. There would be time to get home and change. But she needed to phone Carol. She took Nigel's arm off her stomach and tip-toed back into the front room. She would have to say that she had made things up with Jack and she was staying over at his place.

Back in the bedroom, Nigel had manoeuvred himself further up the bed and disentangled his jeans from his legs. She lay next him, while he snuggled into her. She was still fully clothed and Nigel didn't look in much of a state to do anything. It was gone one o'clock when she made another trip to the bathroom. She glanced at her jacket hanging in the landing; she would need that in the morning. The rest of her clothes she could change when she got home. There wasn't an alarm clock in the bedroom, just a copy of the novel *Fight Club* laying open and face down on the bedside table. She turned off the bedside lamp and thought about whether she would wake up early enough. There were no curtains so she hoped the morning light would be enough to wake her.

Lotte glanced again at her watch, which was now on the floor: 'Fuck', she said; 8.24am. She looked across at Nigel who was still fast asleep, then down at her clothes. She still had her bra and knickers on, confirming that nothing much had happened in the night. She jumped up and went into the bathroom. There wasn't a shower, only a bath, so she started to run the hot water. The meeting with the QAA was set for ten o'clock. She could still make that meeting, but there wouldn't be time to get home first. She smelt her blouse; not good. She waved it around a bit, but still didn't feel comfortable putting it on. She lay in the bath, thinking that if she left the house by 9.00am she should be able to make the meeting. She looked down at her bra and knickers. She didn't feel comfortable putting them on again, either. She thought about the sports bag in the boot of her car, sitting there in case she ever decided to make a trip to the campus gym. That meant there would be some deodorant and perfume. And if she sped things up, there might be time to get a coffee somewhere. She dried off, used some mouthwash she found in the bathroom cabinet, slipped the blouse back on, but decided against the bra and knickers. If she buttoned up her jacket she should be fine. She pushed the bra and knickers into the pockets of her jacket as she past it on the landing. Her skirt was fine. She looked out of the window to see a blue sky, and it felt warm.

8.57am: time to go. There was a notepad and pen on the table by the front door, so she quickly scribbled: 'It was fun. Lotte.' Back at the car, she was pleased to see her toiletries in the sports bags and also a clean tee-shirt. Her bra strap was hanging out of her jacket pocket, so she pushed it further down, and jumped into the car. She checked her hair, and drove off. Bo Biddley was still in the CD player, so she jumped it forward to *Road Runner*. She opened the window to let the warm breeze in. On the ring road, she saw the familiar bright yellow arches just off a roundabout; time to get a takeaway coffee and a quick trip to the loo. She emerged with the clean tee-shirt on and her jacket tightly buttoned. Black jacket, white tee-shirt, black and white small checked skirt, black high heals; all fine. No underwear, but a hot cup of coffee. Thank you Ronald, she said to herself. 9.43am.

She turned into the campus carpark; 9.54. She was going to be late, but only by a few minutes. The traffic on the ring road had been kind and at least she was now on campus. Just need the office number for the meeting, she thought, as she turned the key to stop the engine. She pulled open her handbag, hoping that her desk diary was in there, otherwise she'd have to go to her office. Good, good: the diary was there and the room was close-by. She walked briskly but without running, to avoid looking dishevelled when she arrived. She could feel her breasts enjoying a freedom they'd never had on campus; apart from in the old gym storeroom. She was totally unprepared for the meeting, but she felt good.

The room smelt of men in suits. There was only one seat unoccupied so she started walking towards it. 'I'm so sorry I'm late. I got caught in traffic on the ring road.'

'That's okay. Take a seat and compose yourself for a minute. We've only just started. I was introducing myself, so I'll start again.'

Clearly, the Lead Reviewer, she thought. He was flanked by four people, two on either side: three men and one woman. The woman smiled as Lotte sat down. At that point she noticed Lucy Martens sitting at the right-angle of the pushed-together tables. Her short hair and grey jacket had made her merge with the male suits; appropriate, she thought. Jos Conway smiled when the two of them made eye contact with each other. Jos looked great, as always: black spiky hair, large ear-rings, dark mustard-coloured jacket and red blouse. Lotte checked that all the buttons of her jacket were still done up. Julian looked like Julian, in his corduroy jacket, but he had put a tie on. It looked like it was his old school tie. Steve Jackman had a dark suit on. She'd never seen it before; perhaps he'd bought it for the occasion. She was surprised to see that Stephen Jenkins was also there. He taught Political Philosophy in the Department. And one other person she didn't recognise.

Introductions over, from which it was clear that the unknown person worked in the Study Support team. Lotte thought back to the dinner conversation with Carol and Margie, then suddenly became startled: 'Fuck', she said to herself, 'please don't tell me my bra was hanging out my pocket as I walked to my seat.' She slipped her hand into the pocket, relieved to find that all of it was firmly tucked in. She then checked the other pocket and felt her knickers perfectly positioned at the bottom of the other pocket.

'I wonder if we might open some windows,' Steve Jackman said.

'By all means,' the Lead Reviewer replied. 'It is unseasonably hot today, but we shouldn't complain about that, should we? So, could I kick off, with a starter for ten, so to speak, and ask you to outline the essence of your learning and teaching regime. Who would like to take that? Steve, perhaps you to begin, as Head of Department?'

The meeting plodded on, with Steve Jackman and the lead reviewer exchanging witty philosophical comments. It got interesting when one of the sidekicks questioned how explicitly the Department explained to students their progression options, and how prepared they were for the world of work. Lotte was pleased with how provocative Stephen Jenkins was: 'Well, John Stuart Mill is a good guide, I feel. The priority is to educate, because the best preparation for employment is that education. We do make that very explicit to students in our personal development work.'

Need to remember these words, she thought. A few more questions were asked, which prompted Stephen to suggest that the review team might like to seek some clarification from the students themselves.

Jos then went into great detail about how everything was fully integrated, and how this was, indeed, transparent to students. Good word, she thought, "transparent". Julian then talked excessively about learning outcomes, as if he was trying to impress his primary school teacher. The person from student support piped up from time to time about the how the University was working hard to ensure that each department had access to robust data from central services. Another good word, she thought, "robust". It sounded right for the occasion, but strangely masculine, particularly when spoken by a female colleague. Would that person use that word outside of this meeting, I wonder?

Finally, Lotte got her chance to speak, in response to a question about developing critical skills: 'Well, of course criticality is the central core skill. We introduce students to the questioning of knowledge in the first year, and then start to build on that for the second years, by getting them to critique the foundation for philosophical argument. In the third year we try to get them thinking autonomously and exchanging ideas with us, more as our equals.'

Fuck, she thought, did I mean 'core' skill; should I have said another word? She thought of Jack. Without him she wouldn't have talked about student autonomy, and surely that was her key point. She hadn't listened to what the sidekick had said in reply, but Jos then came in and talked about the importance of seeing knowledge as contingent and the importance of students seeing the limits of the discipline's knowledge. Good old Jos, she thought. She recognised Jos' terminology from one of the meetings they'd had. Everybody seemed to be nodding away in agreement and Steve and the Lead Reviewer continued with their light-hearted banter. All except one of the sidekicks. It was clear he was the troublesome reviewer. He didn't smile once, and didn't seem that impressed with any of the answers.

And then it was over. The Lead Reviewer thanked everyone for a productive meeting, and said he would see everyone throughout the week. As Lotte rose, she checked that her bra was still firmly in her pocket, then checked her knickers again. The troublesome sidekick smiled at her as she approached the door, and motioned for her to leave before him. Creep, she thought. Outside, in the corridor, Steve Jackman flashed a quick smile in her direction, and winked with his right eye. Strange gesture, she thought, but he was obviously nervous and she understood the message. She gave a quick smile back. Now, onto the teaching observation. She was alone as she walked back to her office. Everyone else had peeled off in different directions. The word 'triangulation' came into her head. It had been used twice in the meeting, to indicate how important it was that everything should be explicitly tied together. It sounded slightly threatening; like a TV cop show when the villains realise they need to get their story straight. The maverick cop was bound to spot a crack somewhere; probably Troublesome Sidekick.

It was a relief for Lotte to get back to Carol's house, late in the afternoon, and have a shower. She spent the evening going over her seminar notes in preparation for her teaching observation. She stopped when she thought of what her students would make of her if she was not her natural self. I'm not an actor, I'm a teacher, she thought, but then proceeded to think about how teaching *was* a form of performance, but not a false one, surely? She satisfied herself that her students were smart enough to know what was going on and would support her. Particularly when they caught a glimpse of po-faced Troublesome Sidekick.

She looked over the pre-read sheet she had given the students at the last seminar. She always gave them some questions to think about. The seminar was on the work of Bishop Berkeley. '*Esse est percipi,*' she read out loud to herself. The first question: Are you convinced by the argument that 'to be is to be perceived'? Question Two: What arguments would you put forward against Berkeley's major proposition? Question three: Would Berkeley have faced stronger criticism in today's more materialistic world? It was too late to change the questions, but she was happy that the students would have some things to say; they were a good bunch. She just had to hope they would have read the extracts from Berkeley himself. She satisfied herself that she had been clear about Berkeley's world in the previous lecture. Shame that Troublesome Sidekick hadn't come to that lecture.

Lotte picked up the session plan that Julian Ashwood had prepared for her. The learning outcomes were different from the ones they had worked on, but, other than that, it was just a formal written version of what she intended to do anyway. She thought about whether she should write the learning outcomes on the board, as Julian had suggested, but then thought how false this would look to the students, and it might well confuse them. She remembered Jos saying that it shouldn't be necessary to actually write out the learning outcomes. She checked them again: they didn't really say anything different from what was implied in her pre-read questions, so she decided just to read them out at the beginning. Stick to your guns, she thought, and check with the students what they had learnt at the end; as she'd always done.

***

The teaching observation was set for three o'clock, but Lotte had been warned to make herself available ten minutes before to have a preliminary discussion with the reviewer. Troublesome Sidekick knocked, entered the room, and Lotte wondered if he would be able to crack a smile from his po-face. She rose from the desk at the front end of the seminar room and handed him a copy of the session plan that Julian had prepared.

'Just be yourself,' he said.

'Oh, I intend to be,' she said to herself.

'Thank you for this,' he continued. 'I'll review it as we go. I don't know much about Bishop Berkeley; I'm more political philosophy. It should be interesting.

Perhaps we could have a quick chat at the end? Only briefly, because I need to get to the meeting with the students straight after.'

'That's fine,' Lotte said.

Before anymore could be said the first small group of students came through the door. 'Is it okay if we come in?' one of them said.

'Of course, come in,' Lotte said. She then turned to Troublesome Sidekick and asked if she should introduce him.

'Not necessary,' he said, as he was positioning himself by the row of windows opposite the door.

At exactly three o'clock Lotte referred everyone to the questions on the pre-read sheet, read them out loud, then asked if everyone had done the reading. The group enthusiastically nodded. Lotte felt like saying, 'could you do that again, this time with meaning', but she knew they were all trying to be helpful, and she loved them for it. Everything had settled down by the time they got to the question about modern materialism. It finally felt like the students had forgotten the cameras were on.

One student asked a question about what Berkeley would have made of the film *The Matrix*, which started an animated discussion about the nature of reality. Someone then made reference to the film *The Truman Show*, and asked how we would know if we'd all got locked into a false university reality. This gave Lotte the perfect opportunity to claim that Berkeley's principle was very resilient to criticism because how would we know of the existence of an external world if our only access to it was through our minds. She then gave a summary of where she thought they had got to. The students saw the cue and discussed what new things they had learnt. Perfect, she thought. She finished by reminding them to use the discussion in the upcoming problem-based learning task, which was going to be formally assessed. Great, she thought: without Julian's session plan she might not have remembered to say that. The students already knew, of course, but Troublesome Sidekick needed to hear it. As the students filed out of the room a couple of them gave knowing smiles and nods in Lotte's direction, away from the gaze of Troublesome Sidekick.

'Well, I enjoyed that,' Troublesome Sidekick said.

'Thank you.'

'You obviously get on very well with your students. Some of them seemed a bit disconcerted at the end. Do you think they all understood the purpose of the session?'

'What makes you say that? I know these students very well. I could see from their faces that they were happy. And anyway, we always review things as we go, so if there *were* any issues they would certainly surface in the next week or so, and we would deal with them then. And also, of course, in our student progression work.'

Fuck, she thought, did I use the right phrase? Am I just babbling?

'Okay. Well, look, I need to get going. The team have the meeting with the students shortly.'

With that, he was gone. What a tosser, she thought. How dare he say that: he doesn't even know any of the students. She sat back at the desk, aware that no other groups used the room after her session. Not wishing to let down Steve Jackman, she decided to go back to her office and look over what she knew about student welfare, in preparation for the final meeting the following morning.

Just as she was packing up her things to go home there was a knock on Lotte's office door. It was three of her students, two from the earlier seminar. They had all been at the meeting with the review team.

'Lotte, sorry to bother you,' one of them said.

'Not at all, come in.'

Rachel, one of her students from the earlier seminar, spoke first: 'We just wanted to let you know what happened at the meeting. That person who was at our session, we felt he kept fishing. It was like he was looking for negative comments.'

'Like what?' Lotte asked.

Ella continued: 'He kept asking about whether everything was clear to us. We all said, absolutely, yes. But he didn't seem convinced. The other people were all very nice, and asked us about what we enjoy about philosophy, why we chose it, and what we wanted to do in the future.'

'Yes,' Lotte said, 'he's a bit of a po-face, that one.' They all laughed.

'We didn't let you down, did we?' Lisa asked.

'No, absolutely, not,' Lotte replied. 'They'll be gone next week, and we can get back to normal. Sorry if I wasn't quite myself. It was a bit intimidating having him in the room, if I'm honest.'

'We were talking about that,' Ella said. 'It seems unfair to do that to people. I told him we really enjoy your seminars and lectures.'

'Thank you; that was kind of you.' Lotte said. 'Thanks for popping in. I appreciate you coming.'

With that, they shuffled out of the office. Lotte sat back. Please let this nonsense be over, she thought. Picking up her bag to leave, she uttered 'My girls' in a Scottish accent. She kept singing the word 'please' over and other again as she drove home. She remembered hearing a song with this refrain at Jack's flat, but couldn't remember any of the other words.

Chapter 15

The student welfare meeting with the review team was set for ten o'clock on Thursday morning. It was in the same room as the teaching and learning meeting from Tuesday. Walking towards the room Lotte smiled to herself about not needing to check whether her underwear was going to make an appearance. That meeting seemed an eternity ago. The review team all sat in the same order. She imagined them all with bright snazzy suits and afro hair; like The Jackson 5. She glanced around the room as everyone else took their seats. No Stephen this time; perhaps he was on the naughty step. The person from the Study Support team was there again, this time with two other female colleagues she didn't know. Must be from Careers or Counselling, she thought. Everything then went quiet. Hands on buzzers, she thought, but the Lead Reviewer didn't look like he was in the mood for jokes this morning. Perhaps he'd been ground down by the whole thing and was looking forward to going home. With any luck he would have fallen out with Troublesome Sidekick by now. She flashed a quick look at Troublesome Sidekick. No sex life, she thought. She then focused on the female reviewer's outfit. She looked transformed from the other morning: long silver earrings and burgundy jacket. Perhaps she's going somewhere nice afterwards?

The meeting was dominated by discussions about data. Troublesome Sidekick seemed to have uncovered some mismatch between the Department's student progression files and what was held centrally. It became clear that there was left over business from the student progression meeting. There was talk about the need to drill down a bit. Another very masculine sounding phrase, she thought. Do women drill down? Her mind wandered around the idea of genderlects, and she thought back to her happy days on the Women's Studies master's course. She was brought back to the room when she was asked if she would like to comment on the measures being taken to retain first year students: 'We have an advantage, because most students opt for single honours Philosophy. It's naturally more problematic…I mean requires more active monitoring…when students are taking combined honours courses. But our personal development system kicks in very early, and we find that we can pick up on any issues, almost as soon as they happen. We make personal development part of the curriculum offer and the students see it as part of the course, not something extraneous.' Good answer, she thought, even if it sounded like someone else saying it. Reading Jos' notes the previous evening seemed to have done the trick.

Several other questions were asked about central service data. Lotte was saved from having to say anymore, because one of the woman from Student Services became very animated and spoke for a long time about how the University was working on streamlining the system to create a cradle-to-grave operation. Strange turn of phrase, Lotte thought, but it lightened the mood, particularly when Steve

Jackman talked about how it might be difficult for students to leave the place with this policy in place.

The meeting continued with its theme of data collection and its use, and finally came to an end when the Lead Reviewer announced that his team now had everything they needed to come to their judgements. He then stated that he would see everyone at the final assessment meeting later in the afternoon.

***

After lunch, Lotte walked to the library to return some books. She decided to head into the library itself. She took comfort in the smell of the shelves as she made her way towards the back of the building. She ran an index finger along a row of old hardback books. It felt like an oasis, or a walk in an academic forest. Here is the heart of the University, she thought. Not that bloody box room. Around twenty minutes later, she walked down the steps outside the library, only to find herself being wound up by the review process again. What a waste of a week. I could have been doing my job instead of talking to people about it. She looked up and saw Lucy Martens striding towards the old gym building. Too late, there was no where to hide.

'Hello Charlotte.'

'Everything going okay?' Lotte said.

'Yes, but some issues have come up.'

'Issues; how do you mean? The meeting with the students went very well, didn't it?'

'Yes, but it's not just about the students. We seem to have an issue with transparency of the learning outcomes. I have been telling your Head of Department for some weeks now about this issue. Some of your learning outcomes are very complicated.'

'But we're talking about a degree in Philosophy. It's supposed to be complicated.'

Lotte could feel her hackles rising as she spoke.

'Look, we shouldn't be talking about this here, not in the open. Come to my office for a minute, will you.'

They walked silently up the steps into the old gym building. On the third floor, Lucy Martens motioned to Lotte to enter her office. Lotte looked to the left before proceeding. The other door to the storeroom, she thought. But no shelf above the door.

'What's in there?' she asked.

'Just a store cupboard, I think. I've never been in there.'

Once inside her office, Lucy Martens stood in front of Lotte.

'Look, I think I've managed to limit the damage.'

'The damage?' Lotte's question came out like an exclamation.

'In my role I have to make important judgement calls. I'm afraid I agree, that everything is not as transparent as it might be.'

'Who's side are you on?'

'I'm on the side of quality.'

'I'm beginning to think you don't know what the word means.'

'I've been working with the quality agenda for the last ten years.'

'And I've been working on learning and teaching. I'm in the classroom, with students. Where are you?'

'I support people with their teaching.'

'Well, you're not supporting me right now. You're in danger of losing us marks. What's wrong with you?'

'It's a question of standards, Charlotte.'

'You're not wrong there. You don't seem to have any.'

'Charlotte, you can't talk to me like that.'

'I'll talk to you how I fucking like.'

'That's offensive. You need to stop immediately.'

'Me, offensive? You're the one who's being offensive.'

'I will have to speak to the VC about this. You do understand that?'

'Yeh, that's right, report me to the headmaster, you coward.'

'Do you want to apologise and we start again?'

'No! Fuck off!'

Lotte turned, slammed the office door behind her, looked again at the storeroom door, then strode back to her office. No sooner had she sat at her desk, when there was a knock at the door. It was Steve Jackman: 'Could I have a word, Lotte, in my office?'

Fuck, she thought, Lucy Fucking Martens had been on the phone already.

'Could you give me a minute, Steve?'

She liked Steve but was in no mood to back down.

'Come in, Lotte. Sorry for sounding a bit dramatic but something has come up.'

Here we go, she thought.

'We're in a tricky situation. Can you tell me what happened after your teaching observation? What specifically was said, can you remember?'

'Why? What's the problem.'

'This is highly confidential. I'm not sure we should know this, but that reviewer…I knew he would be trouble…it appears he wants us to lose a mark on our teaching and learning score.'

'How do you know that? I thought it was all supposed to be secretive.'

'So did I, but he was overhead talking to one of the other reviewers, about his concerns over transparency…something about clarity of learning outcomes.'

'Wow! Who overheard him?'

'Brian Grealish from Politics. He was outside on one of the picnic benches drinking coffee; their voices travelled. Brian was adamant about what he heard, although somebody did tell me he enjoys being scurrilous.'

'Well, I remember the reviewer was in a hurry to get to the student meeting, so we only spoke briefly. I *was* a little disappointed. I thought it was a good session. The students were great. He said he enjoyed the session, but then said something about the students possibly being a bit disconcerted. Disconcerted? What does that even mean?'

'Well, quite. I went to Lucy Martens, and she agreed that we needed to raise the issue with the chair.' Steve Jackman then lowered his voice. 'This is strictly between us, you understand. I was completely taken aback because Lucy Martens kept bringing the conversation back to accepting that we probably did need to lose a mark for teaching and learning. Can you believe that? The long and short of it is that she is going to speak with the review team and then they will come to a decision. I can't see us getting 24, but hopefully, it won't be another 20. We'd already had what they called a clarification meeting and it looked like student data was going to be our downfall. I had rather hoped that we'd managed to sort that in the student guidance meeting. That's why that meeting got somewhat hijacked by discussions around data. The whole thing is really annoying because our biggest problem now seems to our own Quality Officer.'

'I see. I have to tell you, Steve, that I've just had an argument with Lucy Martens. She stopped me on my way back from the library and said that there had been an issue with our teaching, so I had it out with her.'

'Don't worry. *Hopefully*, what you said will have strengthened her resolve to go back to the chair and argue our case. I think the Lead Reviewer understands the issues.' Steve looked at his watch: 3.45pm: 'The meeting to give us our final score was supposed to be at four o'clock. I can't see that happening now. Fingers crossed. If it doesn't go well, I will have to go to the VC, to see whether anything can be done.'

Lotte walked back to her office, closed the door and sat at her desk. She looked at Julian's scribbled notes on the learning outcomes document they had worked on. Get me out of this place, she thought. She saw the post-it note with Nigel Eames' name and telephone number. She was about to scrunch it up and put it in the bin, but then thought better of it. It could be useful if there was any more trouble with her husband, so she stuck it on the outside cover of her desk diary. She began composing an email to Jack in her head, but then picked up the phone. What the heck, she thought.

'Jack, is that you? It's Lotte'

'Lotte? How's the review going?'

'Terrible. I've just had an argument with Lucy Martens.'

'What's she done now?'

'Jack. Can I see you?'

'Of course. I'll come over. Are you in the office?'

'Yes, but I need to get off campus. Can I meet you in the car park.'

'I'm coming over now.'

Lotte watched Jack walk across the car park through the windscreen of her car. His light brown hair was getting longer and curlier. He opened the passenger door as soon as he could see how distraught she was.

'Jack. I've got to get out of this place.'

'Okay, just drive.'

'No, I mean this bloody job.'

'What's happened?'

'I think I'm going to be sacked.'

'They won't be able to do that. The Union will protect you.'

'I need to go somewhere where I can just get on with my job.'

'Let me know when you find that place. I'll be right behind you.'

He lifted his right arm towards her. She reciprocated by lifting her left arm to meet it. Their fingers touched. She had the feeling of electricity running up her arm. Jack's eyes felt piercing and she wanted to be lost in his embrace. He snuggled into her neck and kissed her ear lobe.

'I want you, Jack,' she whispered.

'I want you too, Lotte. Shall we drive?'

'Can we just stay here a while?'

'But we're in full view.'

'I don't care, Jack. Hold me.'

He licked her earlobe, then ran his fingers up her lower arm, under her blouse. After a couple of minutes he whispered: 'Workout?'

They closed the car doors behind them and walked across campus. Lotte noticed that Jack didn't look at the English Department as they passed. When the old gym building was in site, Jack spoke: 'So long as no one's in the seminar room on the third floor we should be fine. There won't be any more seminars starting at this time, I'm sure.'

'Ever Cautious Jack,' Lotte said, and then smiled at him.

'Ever Mischievous Lotte,' he replied.

They walked up the few steps into the building. Jack turned to look into the old gym through the small square windows at the top of the entrance doors: 'Bloody Hell,' he whispered. 'That's your QAA review team. Aren't you supposed to be in there? Quick, move away from sight.'

'There's no way I was going to that.'

'Did you know the final assessment meeting was in there? They're late. What's going on, do you think?'

'Probably Devil Dog Martens telling tales.'

'Well, this is risky, to say the least.'

'Well, risks are surely what makes the whole thing fun, Jack.'

She stared into his eyes. She could see he was ready to take the risk. As they made their way up the stairs they passed a seminar taking place on the first floor, but nothing beyond that. Standing outside the door to the storeroom, Lotte reached up and then waggled the key back and forth in front of her face.

Once inside, they stood opposite each other, pausing for a moment before locking their fingers together again. Jack rubbed his nose against her's, then started urgently pulling her top up over her head, forcing her arms into the air. He plunged his nose under one of her arm pits: 'You smell gorgeous.'

She pushed him backwards, then downwards, holding his head against her stomach. He slid his arms behind her and then growled as he began biting her.

'Hey, that's loud,' she whispered.

'Sorry,' he whispered back, but then added, 'no…I'm not.'

Their sex was as explosive as ever.

As they lay on the yoga mats, she smiled to herself: it felt like Jack had finally let himself go. She turned towards him to rest her head on his chest. His heart was racing, but just as she began moving her fingers towards one of his nipples, she stopped and let out a deep breath. They lay motionless and silent for around ten minutes. Lotte was the first to speak: 'Come on, we'd better get going. You know how nervous you are about everything.'   Jack laughed: 'We've just had sex above your QAA review team, and the VC.'

'I can't think of a better way to conclude the review,' she replied.

'Stay still. We're safe here for a while.'

'Unless the porters have changed their routine, Jack?'

'Not that much, surely? And your lot might still be down there.'

'You know this could be my last day working here.'

'That's not going to happen. If they did sack you, I'd leave as well.'

'So you do love me, Jack Lowell,' she said with a big smile.

'But…just as the man said, we really do need to get out of this place.'

'But is there really a better place for me and you?'

With that, they rose and tidied themselves up. Outside the room, Jack glanced down the stairwell to check that the coast was clear, while Lotte locked up. She was comforted by the musty smell which hung in the slight draft as the door closed. They walked in silence down the stairs. The seminar room on the first floor was now empty. Once on the ground floor, Jack motioned for Lotte to hang back while he took a peek through the windows on the gym doors. The coast was clear again. He waved his arm forward, to suggest they should go in. The large rectangle of tables and chairs were still there, but there was no other evidence that a meeting had just taken place. The room was large and the row of small windows towards the ceiling were still open. It had been another warm day.

'You can't even smell any evidence of a meeting,' Jack said.

'The desert of the real,' Lotte said.

'Jean Baudrillard?'

'Yes, but to be honest, I was quoting from *The Matrix*.'

'You're right though. The reality that the review statements refer to is its own reality. Now they're gone, the old reality is back, leaving no trace of this alternative universe.'

'Except, what's to say that our reality is real?'

'Hey, don't go all postmodern on me. I've had enough of that lately.'

'So have I, actually.'

'Okay, let's get out of this *particular* place, shall we? Fancy a drink and some dinner. And another workout?'

'Don't mind if we do.'

In Jack's flat they sat drinking red wine and eating a takeaway pizza.

'I'm thinking about that reality issue again,' Lotte said. 'The QAA's world is definitely illusory, but academic worlds are full of illusions, too.'

'How dare you bring the postmodernists into my flat?' Jack said.

'It's Nietzsche, actually. People choose to have faith in their illusions. That box room was a reality which you could put your faith in, if you chose to: here resides quality. That's what Lucy Fucking Martens has done. She's put all her faith in those bloody boxes. We just choose to put our faith elsewhere.'

'But didn't Hitler put his faith in Nietzsche?'

'Yes, but only through ignorance of what Nietzsche was actually saying. And before you say it, I think Nietzsche's views on women were also misunderstood.'

'Out of my depth, so I'm happy to let that go.'

'Have you read that *new* book by Baudrillard, *The Perfect Crime?*'

'No.'

'I started it but didn't get past the references to Nietzsche. The central idea did make sense, though. That a crime has been committed; somebody has killed reality. It's a perfect crime because we don't know the perpetrator and we don't know that we are the victims.'

'Or was it Lucy Martens, perhaps? Is she the perpetrator?'

'Or the victim?'

Lotte paused and looked at Jack. 'Sorry, shouldn't have said that; what with Richard McGiffen; figure of speech.'

'That's okay. I know what you meant. I think there's a big difference between Richard and Lucy Martens. I think Richard really cared. He actually wanted to enhance the quality of teaching and learning. I think Lucy Martens doesn't really care about teaching or learning, only that we do what we have to do in order to look good…But you could say that makes her a better quality officer…for the present situation…because if you know the rules of the game, and treat it like a game, you'll find it easier to win the game. I don't think Richard thought it was a game.'

'So are we talking about a Wittgenstein language game, where the reality beyond the game is not important, so long as all the players are happy within the game?'

'I've never read any Wittgenstein, but that does make sense. For me, that kind of rescues reality as well, because beyond the games we could still be talking about a reality.'

'Well, if reality isn't dead, it's certainly been wounded.'

'I think the problem is that the way the world *appears* has come to dominate. But you know Marx wrote about this in his theory of commodity fetishism…that we don't see the reality behind the appearance. That was before Nietzsche. At least I think it was.'

'In that case you could argue that Nietzsche is just taking it one step further and asking what is it about humans that makes them want to turn their allusions… appearances…into their reality?'

'But what we're left with…then…is all of us running around the University in worlds of our own making. The University is a fiction in that case, or a series of fictions.'

'Truth is an army of metaphors.'

'Don't tell me, Nietzsche again?'

'Correct. But don't forget it was you that told me to have faith in my subject knowledge.'

'I didn't say faith.'

'Oh yes you did!'

'That's me hoisted by own petard, then. Figure of speech again, though; surely?… Does that get me out of jail?'

'Maybe, or perhaps you are slowly groping towards Nietzsche.'

'But we do agree that there *is* a reality somewhere? We use words…our imagination…to help explain things. We all grope…towards reality, but we'll never really know it. Doesn't mean it isn't there. That's Einstein, I believe.'

'Does that mean we are together on this?'

'I think so. I like that fact that *we* are together. And I like the fact that we have created our own little world.'

'You really are an idiot sometimes, Jack. Perhaps inside your materialism is a romantic desperately trying to get out?'

***

Just before eight o'clock the phone rang in Jack's flat.

'Are you going to get that, Jack?'

'No. Who would be ringing me at this time?'

'It might be Carol. I gave her your number. I forgot to ring her. She was expecting me a couple of hours ago.'

Jack picked up the phone. It was Marion Barton.

'So sorry for ringing you so late, Jack. Good result for the philosophers.'

'What did they get?'

'23. But that's not the reason I'm ringing. Have you seen Charlotte Rudolph? Sorry to ask but I know you are good friends. Steve Jackman has been trying to get hold of her. He came over to the Department earlier to see if she was with you.'

'Why, what's the problem?'

'He rang her at home, but she's not there.'

'I saw her earlier on. She said she would be out all evening.'

'Okay. If you do manage to speak with her, could you ask her to contact Steve first thing in the morning.'

'Sounds a bit melodramatic, if you don't mind me saying.'

'Okay, Jack, in confidence. In the morning everyone will know anyway. Lucy Martens is in hospital.'

'Why? Has she choked on her own words?'

'It's serious, Jack, I'm afraid. It could be touch and go. She crashed on her way home.'

'Blimey.'

'I only know all this because I had a phone call from the VC. He asked me to be available in case he needs help, to make a formal statement. I've said too much. You know the score. Steve was worried about Lotte because he knew she had argued with Lucy and he wanted to reassure her.'

'Thanks, Marion.'

Jack put down the phone and looked at Lotte.

'Why didn't you say I was here?'

'I don't know, I panicked, I suppose. Did you hear everything?'

'Think so...Lucy Martens. She's in hospital. Car crash? Anyone else involved?'

'Don't know. Wow, what a phone call. But hey, you got 23 out of 24. That's good news.'

'I suppose so. I'm just so sick of it all; I couldn't care less what the number is. It's just a bloody number anyway. But hey, if I heard correctly, it looks like everyone thinks we are a couple. No need to tip-toe around anymore, Jack Lowell.'

'I wonder where you lost the mark?'

'Well, that was me, obviously.'

'You don't know that.'

'That's the real reason Steve Jackman wants to speak to me so urgently. Unless he wants to tell me off for not going to the review meeting. Who *was* that on the phone?'

'Marion. Marion Barton. Her office is next door to mine. I'm sure you've met her. She knows everything. She's lovely. Hey, come on, let's forget it all, for now, at least. There's nothing we can do. Top up?'

'Yep, go for it.'

'I want you to stay over.'

'Are you sure, Jack? Somebody might find out and spread it around the University, you know.'

'Don't care; I want you close to me.'

'Good. I want to be close to you. But I haven't got any clean clothes for the morning.'

'Good. I love the smell of your clothes when you've been wearing them.'

'I'm being serious.'

'So am I. What do you need? Why don't you wear one of my shirts?'

'I could do that. I've got some toiletries in the car.'

'Go get them now. I want you in my bed.'

'I need to phone Carol. Is that okay?'

While Lotte was collecting her things from her car, Jack went to his desk in the spare room and wrote on a post-it note: 'Who stole reality?' He had forgotten the actual title of the book, but the prompt was enough. The question also had a nice ring about it, even if it was postmodern. Back in the front room, he could see Lotte's opened handbag on the coffee table. Her desk diary was visible, along with some of her make up items. In her rush to pull out her car keys, some of the things had spilled out. He stared at them, loving that her little artefacts were back in his life. Except the post-it note with 'Nigel Eames' written on it and a telephone number. Who was he?

Chapter 16

Jack's alarm went off at 7.30am. Lotte looked across at Jack. He was sleeping, which made her smile. Perhaps they had finally turned a corner, she thought. She lay back and looked up at the ceiling. Did Lucy Martens crash because of their argument? She couldn't shake the thought from her head. Perhaps *that* was what Steve Jackman wanted to talk about. She looked again at Jack. Why the hell hadn't they been speaking for the last three months? She made her way to the bathroom with her clothes in her hands. Looking in the mirror, she smiled. She picked up her bra and knickers from the floor. Perhaps another day without them would be nice. She would need a top, though. She went back into Jack's bedroom. He looked up at her and said: 'Hello Gorgeous. You haven't been in the shower, have you?'

'No, not yet.'

'Then get back in bed.'

'Jack. I've got to get to work.'

'That can wait ten minutes, surely?'

'Okay, if you find me a top, please.'

'Deal.'

Lotte left Jack's flat just before 9am. It was cloudy and a bit chilly. She was glad she had decided to wear her bra. She looked down at Jack's check shirt under her unbuttoned jacket. She had deliberately left her knickers on the floor of Jack's bathroom, and she smiled to herself at the thought of him finding them. He must have seen them, but hadn't said anything. In the car, she shuffled around in the glove compartment and found *Led Zeppelin IV*; why not, she thought. She wasn't sure of the route to campus through the town so went out onto the ring road. She entered from the roundabout and looked across at the yellow arches. Her brief visit there seemed like ages ago. She'd had a strong espresso at Jack's flat and was grateful for that boost, but her nerves were now beginning to get the better of her. She hoped she might be able to get back to Jack's flat later, but that hadn't been raised during their brief breakfast.

***

'Ah, Lotte,' Steve Jackman said. 'Come in, come in. You got my message. Sorry for the intrigue. You might have heard what's happened to Lucy Martens.'

'She's in hospital?'

'Certainly is. She's in intensive care, I understand. It sounds nasty. I think she left the road on a bend.'

Lotte sat rigid, waiting to hear her fate.

'I let slip with Marion Barton that you had argued with Lucy and I wanted to say sorry and to reassure you that we both agreed it should go no further. I can't see that it has any connection with Lucy's accident. But there is something else. I wanted you to hear this from me first, in case you hear anything else.'

'Hear what?'

'You know we got 23 out of 24. I'm so relieved. I went to bed on Wednesday evening thinking about a *Times Higher* headline: "Philosophy department fails to define quality, with lowest recorded score". But, here we are. We lost a mark, not for management, which I feared and not for teaching and learning, which, if I'm honest, I also feared, but because of student welfare. I know you care very much about our students and I'm very grateful for that, but the issue was about the mismatch between what we do and what central services do. It was nothing to do with you or your teaching observation, or your argument with Lucy Martens.'

'I see. I'm sorry I didn't make the meeting.'

'Yes. I wanted to ask about that. Are you okay?'

'Yes; I am now. The confrontation I had with Lucy Martens shook me up, and just couldn't face that meeting.'

'Well, that's understandable in the circumstances. To be honest, I didn't feel like going myself. But here's the rub: I really wanted to get hold of you before any Chinese whispers start going round. We *were* faced with a score of 22. It looked like that reviewer wanted to take away a mark for teaching and learning. But…long and short of it, we managed to get it restored. Unbelievably, Lucy Martens seemed happy for us to lose it. I assume that's what you were arguing about with her?'

'Yes. It was.'

'Well, to reassure you again…and you need to keep quiet about this…I had a word with the VC, and he said he would speak to Lucy Martens after the reviewers had left. He didn't seem best pleased, but he's difficult to read, of course. So, there we are, 23 out of 24. Given that nobody here has got 24, that makes us top of the pile. And most of the 24s in the country seem to have gone to the ancient universities. I think we can be very satisfied. I'm going home at lunchtime; it's been a long week; long couple of months, actually. I suggest you do the same. Thanks for your help, Lotte. I appreciate it.'

'Thank you, Steve. Unfortunately, I've got a class this afternoon, but I certainly intend to relax this weekend.'

Lotte sat in her office, looking out at the fast moving clouds. The wind had got up. Maybe it was the VC's intervention that put Lucy Marten's on edge? Did the VC have a go at Lucy Martens? But maybe the car accident had a completely different explanation? The circumstances of the accident will emerge; in time. Lotte's mind wandered further, to an image of Lucy Martens sitting up in bed in the hospital explaining to the police the background to the accident. I'll be implicated in some way, for sure, or maybe she will implicate the VC? Either way, what an arse-licking creep.

A trip into town sounded like a good idea. She glanced across at her seminar notes. She would have time to check them before her class in the afternoon. She took the path by the river, and thought about the last time she had walked there with Jack. Was that really before Christmas? She hoped that Jack would invite her back to his place later. In expectation, she bought some new underwear, a couple of blouses and a skirt. And some more toiletries. It was just possible that the sports bag in the back of the car might be seeing more action in the coming weeks. She made a mental note to phone Carol. She smiled to herself: what would Carol make of everything that's happened this week?

The seminar finished at four o'clock. Several of the students hung back because they wanted to hear more from Lotte about how the review had gone. She thanked them all for the kind words they had said. She explained they only lost one mark, which meant that the Department was excellent. She couldn't resist adding that the Department was excellent '...*in the eyes of the QAA.*' The emphasis was not lost on the students.

'But we knew it was excellent before they came, though, didn't we?' Lotte posed the question while leaning forward towards them. Everybody laughed, and Lotte wished them all a wonderful weekend. She walked quickly back to the office hoping that Jack would ring. It was like old times, she thought. He always used to ring around this time; in the old days. Perhaps he had sent an email. She was about look at her emails when she thought better of it. What if there was one from the VC, or one from the police, or anyone else she didn't want to hear from. The phone rang. She picked it up instantly: 'Hello, Lotte Rudolph,' she said, faster than normal.

'Hi Lotte, it's Jack.'

'Thank goodness it's you. I've missed you.'

'Missed you too. I know you might want to get home, but I was just wondering...'   Before he could finish, she blurted out: 'Love to see you, Jack.'

'Great. So, what happened with Steve Jackman. I've been phoning all day and I sent an email.'

'Sorry, I've been in and out all day and I haven't had a chance to look at my emails. Everything is fine. He thanked me for my efforts.'

'Is that it? That doesn't sound that urgent.'

'I'll tell you about it later. When shall we meet?'

'How about now. I've got the car with me today. Shall we meet back at my place at five o'clock?'

Lotte pulled up at Jack's flat at ten past five. *Led Zeppelin IV* still had some life in it when she turned the engine off. She decided to leave the new clothes and her toiletries in the boot, just in case it looked presumptuous. One pair of bright red knickers were missing from the pack. She had put them on before her seminar. Now was the time to display them, she thought. She looked up the street, and thought about the time her husband's car had been there. What the hell must Jack have thought of her? No wonder he had stopped seeing her.

They embraced and kissed, even before Jack had closed the front door, and for much longer than they had in the past. Jack held her hand and escorted her to the front room.

'How about we go out for dinner?' Jack said.

'Sure. You realise we've never done that.'

'We haven't done a lot of things, have we? I was thinking earlier, why don't we make that trip to the V and A?'

'Are you sure, Jack? Hasn't that place become a jinx for us?'

'Precisely. We need to change that. Come on, let's do it tomorrow. Why not?'

'Okay, if you say so. Does that mean…'

'Yep. I want you to stay over. And I've got another shirt for you. I love seeing you in my clothes.'

She pulled open her jacket to reveal Jack's shirt. I've enjoyed wearing it. I suppose you found my knickers? What did you do with them?'

'Now, that's for you to find out.' As he said it, he looked down at its crotch.

'Are you wearing them?'

'Yep. I put them on this morning and then wore to them work. I was hoping to see you at lunchtime and show you.'

'Sorry, I had to go into town.'

'Here's the funny thing, though. I was on my way to give a lecture to the first years on crime and deviance and I suddenly thought how appropriate it was; having your knickers on.'

'I love you. Oops, sorry, I shouldn't have said that.'

'Don't apologise. Come into the bedroom and retrieve your knickers.'

Chapter 17

Lotte and Jack arrived at Paddington Station just after 10.30 on Saturday morning. There were a few clouds in the sky, but the air felt warm.

'Why don't we walk it?' Jack asked.

'That'll take forever.'

'It'll be nice. We can walk through Hyde Park, have a coffee and hold hands.'

'What's come over *you*?'

'I'm just happy that we're doing this. It's only around a mile.'

'Are you sure?'

They entered Hyde Park and walked south on the Carriage Path. After crossing the Serpentine they stopped for coffee.

'Nice', Jack said.

'Does this mean we are finally a couple?'

'An unconventional one, let's call it that. I'm a sociologist, it wouldn't be right to be normal, would it?

'I can't get it out of my head that I'm probably going to be sacked.'

'What, sacked for being a brilliant teacher?'

'For telling Lucy Martens to fuck off.'

'When? That's brilliant. I thought you had an argument. I didn't realise it included *that* terse injunction. But you only said what everyone else wanted to say. That makes you a hero.'

'Anti-hero, maybe.'

They looked across the water in silence. Lotte spoke first: 'Well, it's official, we are an excellent department, but something you said before stuck with me. We are badged as having quality without defining it. Basically, we just did as we were told. Is that it?'

'What's a good pupil? Answer, one who pleases teacher. We're just being cajoled into doing things in a particular way, which can then be monitored by prison officers. It's a panopticon, where everything is visible. That's what transparency really means; not transparency to students but transparency to our wardens.'

'A panopticon. That's what Jos, my colleague, called it.'

'Jeremy Bentham, the perfect prison design. You know he's stuffed in the entrance to UCL. Little did they know that University College London would become one of his panopticons.' Jack laughed at his own joke.

'But we still don't really have a definition of quality, do we? Unless it *is* all to do with transparency. So long as you follow the rules and make what you do transparent, then you will be badged as being of high quality.'

They walked further south through the park.

'What makes a work of art have quality?' Jack asked.

'Do you want me to answer?'

'It's a genuine question.'

'It's aesthetics; yes? Great art does something to you. It raises your spirits. It engulfs you in some way, because of the skill of the artist, along with the talent, and imagination. How's that off the top of my head.'

'Yep, I get that. But if I'm enveloped by something, what is *that stuff?* Is it some kind of force? Is it some kind of assault on the senses? But if that's the case why do art critics always sound so erudite and posh?'

'I suppose they're trying to articulate what it is that people feel. They try to convey what is being invoked by a great piece of work.'

'So, is great teaching the same sort of thing?'

'I suppose you're trying to invoke in students the same love of a subject that you have?'

'That would demand more than comprehensive knowledge. I'm thinking about the nutty professor. He, or she, could have the greatest command of a subject but not be able to convey it. It's a communication issue; it requires not just a pedagogic device…sorry, been reading Basil Bernstein lately…but also being confident in its use.'

'But that would make a teacher *good*, not necessarily great or exceptional.'

'Yeah, but does a university teacher need to be that great, otherwise won't the students become dependent on them? The Carl Rogers problem, if you like.'

'I've been thinking about that. If the job of a university teacher is to produce an autonomous learner…an independent student…the student will need to *stop* seeing the teacher as the font of all wisdom. It was you who started me on that train of thought. Do you remember that time in your flat when we talked about my lectures?'

An image of that bright blue estate car flashed across Jack's mind: 'Okay, hold that thought. Let's get across the road.'

They left Hyde Park and crossed Kensington Road, continuing south, down Exhibition Road.

'So,' Jack continued, 'it's definitely not the knowledge of a subject that's the key; it's partly the ability to communicate it, but the key thing is, surely, the ability to convey to students their need to take responsibility for their own learning. It's kind of like doing yourself out of a job. A great teacher is a teacher that a student no longer needs.'

'I am not a teacher; I'm a facilitator of other people's learning.'

'Carl Rogers again.'

'Thanks for lending me that *Carl Rogers Reader*.'

'It's our colleague Roger Fergusson we both need to thank, I think. You'd like him.'

'I certainly liked the book. It helped me get through that inspection. And Nietzsche, of course.'

'The misogynist and Nazi.'

'A misreading Jack. How many more times. You're in detention for being facetious'

'Will you spank me?'

'I'll do more than that.'

They arrived at the side entrance to the Victoria and Albert Museum on Exhibition Road, just before midday.

'That was more than a mile, Jack Lowell.'

'Well, we did have coffee and we walked slowly...a bit like lovers might do.'

'A bit like Dave Stewart and Annie Lennox might do?'

'Yep. Hey, let's not mess this up this time.'

'Lunch first?'

'Good idea. Lead on. I'm disorientated.'

Lotte led them to the restaurant. The large round room where they sat before was almost completely full.

'I'll get some things for us. See if there's any space in the Morris Room,' Lotte said, as she pointed to the small room to the left.

'William Morris', Jack whispered to himself, as he sat waiting for Lotte. Have nothing in you home which is not either functional or aesthetically pleasing. The Morris mantra, or something like that, he thought. But what if you replaced the 'or' in that sentence with 'and'; wouldn't that make it more powerful? Things should be functional *and* aesthetically pleasing. As he looked at the walls and ceiling, his mind started to wander: A good teacher is a competent one; is a functional one, but there should also be something aesthetically pleasing about that person. They're like a great work of art. They should affect the senses in some way.

'Okay,' Lotte said, as she approached the table with a full tray. 'Here we are...it's all veggie...It's really busy here today.'

'Great, thanks. I was just thinking, this is the Morris Room. I like that thought.'

'Let me guess...because he was a socialist?'

'Well, there is that, but I was thinking about him in relation to our conversation about being a great teacher?'

'Did he write about that as well?'

'Dunno, but this question about being functional and aesthetic.'

'I see. He is controversial though, because some people thought he had *conflated* the arts with crafts: can an aesthetic sensibility be extended to simpler crafts?'

'That's a good thing, I would say. It's only those snobs who would want to maintain a distinction between high art and the rest.'

'You're such a Marxist, Jack.'

'Is that wrong these days?'

'No, but we're only one step away from the postmodern again here. If there's beauty in everything, there's beauty in nothing. Is Tracy Emmin's unmade bed beautiful?'

'I'd love to know what William Morris would have made of that?'

'One thing I can guarantee is that her bed will not make it to the V and A. I think it's in The Tate Modern. To be serious, though, I think her bed *is* art, but I wouldn't call it great art. It's shocking, and moving it to an art gallery does help bring new perspectives to everyday objects.'

'Like a soup can?'

'I'm not sure that Warhol's work is great, either. It's certainly interesting.'

'But I do like that idea of an art factory; churning out art, and downplaying the role of the artist, as a special person.'

'I can see why...because it then becomes people's art, by the people, for the people and reflecting the world they live in? Socialist Art.'

'Are you taking the piss?'

'Yep, and you love me for it.'

Jack became aroused by her smile.

'But you *are* dangerously close to the postmodern here; you realise that, Jack Lowell?'

'Yeah. I suppose I want to say whatever art we have, it will be a reflection of the material circumstances we inhabit.'

'If that's the case, then how do we explain that assault on the senses. Every human being has the same senses and the same mental framework so there has to be something universal there, surely?'

'I suppose I want to say that the predisposition is there, but what and how the senses experience something will vary from historical period and culture. And you do *learn* how to appreciate forms of greatness, don't you?'

'But that means your posh critic does have something to teach us. They know the rules?'

'I suppose I am with Morris though; that a beautifully crafted chair or table can be just as great...as aesthetically pleasing...as a Turner painting or the Mona Lisa. Call me a philistine, but I'd rather have a beautiful table in my front room.'

'Wouldn't be worth as much though.'

'There is that...Hey, let's eat and then you take me on an educational tour... please.'

They wandered around the museum, pausing to ask whether an exhibit had quality. They went into the landscape photography exhibition.

'Is photography a skill or an art?' Jack asked.

'There's a leap of imagination which places a painting of a landscape in a different order, I would say,' Lotte replied.

'But what if we see the teacher more like a photographer: very skilful and very talented. That's enough, surely?'

'Okay, in which case students don't really need to be moved by a great teacher. The search for serious quality is perhaps a false one. There isn't really any need for teachers to be that great. Maybe the QAA are just pointing out how teachers could be more skilful in what they do.'

'But there is something special about a great performance. I was thinking about an old lecturer of mine the other day. I remember being in awe of him. There was something magical about the way he brought all the ingredients together to bake a beautiful cake. Sorry, that's a bonkers analogy, but you know what I mean. It all seemed so smooth, not really controlled. It was beyond that. His love of the subject had somehow spilled over into how he was communicating it. He was a connoisseur, I suppose. He held concepts in his hands; it was as if they were real. It was an artistic performance. It was like he embodied his work, somehow. I often think about that guy. It's what made me want to be a teacher.'

'But there's a problem of bad faith here. What if the teacher acts like Sartre's waiter; becomes so engrossed in what they are doing, they actually come to believe that they were somehow destined to be like this? They would be expressing a false essence.'

'If I understand Sartre correctly, the waiter is actually expressing his existence, not his essence. That's sociological enough for me; he is still a constructed being.'

'Made, not found.'

'That's neat.'

'Not me, Richard Rorty. Postmodern again. I warned you.'

'Damn! Is that right? But there is something wonderful about a great teaching performance.'

'Yes, if it's genuine; authentic; honest. You know I had my teaching observed the other day? It wasn't any of those things. It was an inauthentic performance for the QAA.'

'But students know, don't they? That's the great thing.'

'So we're back to some universal feeling, again?'

'Well, it's certainly more than cognitive. It is emotional in some way, I suppose.'

'In your case, it sounds like you were enraptured. Did you love him?'

'In a funny kind of way I suppose I did. I certainly couldn't wait for the next performance. But I didn't fancy him, if that's what you're thinking.'

'Are you sure?' She put both her arms behind Jack's back and kissed him slowly on the neck.

'Do you remember that we promised ourselves some more elicit sex?'

'Of course, I do. At the moment we just sound like a sad couple of academics.'

'Let's say intellectuals. Academic does sound a bit sad.'

'Amounts to the same thing, doesn't it? But hey…where shall we go?'

'Certainly out of here.'

'We could claim that our senses were overwhelmed by all the art, and it overtook us.'

'What, on the way to the police station. Or we could just go to the museum shop and then get another coffee.'

'Ever Cautious Jack making an appearance again?'

'On the contrary, I want you…badly. Let's get back to my flat.'

'Okay, shop first?'

Lotte scanned the postcards before deciding on half a dozen. It was warm enough to sit outside with a coffee.

'I always collect postcards when I travel,' Jack said, 'but then forget to post them.'

'I put quotations on the back of mine. Kind of like a postcard to myself.'

'Hey, why don't we have dinner before we go back? We still haven't done that.'

***

They arrived back at Jack's flat just before 9pm.

'Glass of wine?' Jack asked.

'That would be nice.'

They sat back on the sofa in silence for several minutes.

'You know what,' Jack said, 'I don't think I want to be a great teacher. I think Carl Rogers was right. I think my job *is* to make myself redundant. That's the honourable thing to do.'

'Don't remind me of redundancy.'

A few more minutes past before they both fell asleep on the sofa. An hour or so later they took it in terms to use the bathroom.

'I think I've got one more pair of knickers left for the morning,' Lotte said.

'Good, can you leave the old ones behind?'

A few minutes later they were both asleep in Jack's bed.

Chapter 18

Rays of sunlight had broken through the gaps in the curtains and Jack watched the patterns they were leaving on his bedroom wall. It was just after 7.30am on Monday morning. He looked across at Lotte's pillow. She had gone home to Carol's the previous afternoon. He smelt the pillow. Three nights, he thought. They hadn't ever spent one night together, but now, like buses, three together. He went to the bathroom, but before putting the kettle on, he went into the front room to put on some music: B.B.King and Eric Clapton seemed right.

Jack had a class in the afternoon and then a tutorial with one of his PhD students, but he wanted to get to the office reasonably early to catch up on the fall-out from the Philosophy QAA review. If Marion Barton was in her office there would be no need to go to the senior common room; she would have the most definitive information.

***

'Morning Jack,' Marion said, as he opened her office door.

'Thanks for your phone call the other evening. I told Lotte and she had a chat with Steve Jackman. Do you have any updates?'

'The VC has just sent an email to everyone.'

'Sorry, I haven't turned my computer on yet.'

'Lucy Martens is in an induced coma. The doctors thought this was the best thing. It turns out she left the road close to the house she's just moved into. Didn't know the road very well, maybe? And it was getting dark. Apparently, it's more of a country lane than a road. It seems to have happened around 8pm; no other cars involved. Which begs the question of where she'd been. The VC told me that she'd left his office around 6.15, so she didn't go straight home. I'm saying more than is in the VC's email, so mum's the word, please. It'll all come out shortly, I'm sure.'

'Wow! Do you think she will survive?'

'No idea, I'm afraid.'

'Anything on the Philosophy review?'

'Well, it's official, they did get 23 out of 24. It was the mismatch between departmental data and central data which lost them a mark, but a great result for them, really. Would be great if they do well in the RAE again, as well. Maybe, going it alone is the way to do it.'

'Yep. Surely a local department must know much more about how to present itself than a centrally located quality team?'

'Well, in our case, definitely yes. I think Sociology got 21 because we relied too much on the Staff Development and Quality offices. It still annoys me that you weren't even allowed a look in. You took that very magnanimously, Jack.'

'On the surface maybe, but inside I was really annoyed.'

'I don't think that would happen again.'

'Not if you'd have been Head of Department, maybe?'

'Not something I ever wanted, Jack.'

He thought about how different things might have been had she been the Head of Department. He always enjoyed talking with her and being in her confidence; maybe that was enough. He also liked the way she appeared to flirt with him, but because it wasn't obvious, he hadn't ever, overtly, reciprocated. Her divorce had obviously affected her, but, just recently, she seemed to have a new-found confidence. She was only just over five feet tall, but she'd always had a real presence. He looked at her curly blonde hair, which was getting longer, and her large necklace, which he'd never seen before.

'You're like my own Greek Oracle, Marion. That's a far better role.'

There was a knock at the door. It was Thomas Minot: 'Sorry, am I disturbing you? Your administrator said she thought you were in with Marion.'

'Come in, come in, Thomas,' Marion said. 'Lovely to see you. How are you?'

'Very good, thanks.'

'Sit down,' Marion said, 'we were just talking about the Philosophy review.'

'Kind of fits with what I wanted to talk about. My Head of Department is keen to move things on. He was disappointed with our recent 21, and thinks we need to up our game. He was particularly disappointed about losing a mark for management... we are a business school.. bit ironic...but he feels that it was more to do with the lack of a clear teaching and learning strategy. I said that you might be able to help us, Jack. He jumped at the idea because the last thing he wants is that quality person telling him what to do. She's due to visit the Department next week.'

'I don't think that will be happening, Thomas.' Jack said.

'Some good news? She's left?' Thomas smiled at his questions.

'Actually, she's in hospital. The VC has sent an email round,' Marion said.

'Oh boy, sorry, I didn't know. I've come in here blabbing about myself, haven't I? What's happened?'

'Car accident. On Friday. She isn't going to be making any visits for quite some time, if at all.'

'I was in London on Friday. What happened with the philosophers?'

'They got 23,' Jack said.

'Good on 'em,' Thomas said. 'Where did they lose the mark?'

'On student welfare. Data issue,' Marion said.

'That old chestnut. Seems to be universal. Why do we keep being blamed for things that are nothing to do with us?' Thomas asked.

'I think that's a key outcome of these reviews,' Marion began, 'everything needs to be joined up. It's a paper chase really, to see that everything in those boxes all ties up.'

'Like a wiring diagram,' said Thomas. 'But my Head of Department says that our teaching observations didn't go very well.'

'That's an interesting issue,' Marion said. 'I think the QAA has realised that the subjectivity that's involved in a teaching observation simply can't be compared with the objectivity that's involved in the paper chase. That's why they gave up grading the teaching observations. They just didn't stand up to scrutiny. The criteria wasn't clear in the way that Ofsted criteria is, in schools.'

'Objectivity only in the sense of being more reliable. Not necessarily more valid as a measure of quality,' Jack said.

'Indeed,' Marion said. 'But the point I was trying to make was that observation criteria and box-file criteria are not of the same order...like comparing apples with oranges...so more weight was inevitably going to be given to the documents that were in the boxes. I'm sure that's the reason why Philosophy got 23 and not 22.'

'Were they going to get 22, then?' Thomas asked.

'Yes, it did look like it was on, but Steve Jackman and the VC intervened. I guess, and it's only a guess, that the chair of the review had no choice really. He would surely have known that he was on unstable ground. And he is, or was, a philosopher, after all. I trust you two, so please don't repeat all this. It will all come out soon, I'm sure.'

'You just can't trust this process,' Thomas said. 'I appreciate that we could certainly improve things...my department particularly...but this isn't the way to do it. I mean, think about the cost apart from anything else. Imagine if all that money had gone towards widening participation...increasing the participation of non-traditional students. That's what we call people like me now, isn't it, Jack?'

'Well, that's what they're called this week,' Jack said.

'I think we just have to see it for what it is,' Marion said. 'Inspection regimes just do what they are asked to do. What's dangerous is when people put misplaced faith in the process. Like assuming an Ofsted high-rated school must be better than one that isn't. It should be patently obvious that a school in a deprived area has issues that a school in a leafy suburb just doesn't have to deal with.'

'It should also be obvious by now,' Jack began, 'that the rich, ancient, universities are going to do better in this exercise, not because they care more about teaching and learning...clearly, they don't...but because they have more money and more resources. And the review teams must be more scared of them.'

'Much easier to pull up a little post-92 like us,' Thomas said.

'And, of course, some subjects are not resource heavy,' Jack began, 'so they must have an advantage. I very much doubt that the Philosophy students complained much about their resources last week. Perhaps a few more library books; that's all. It's a concept-heavy subject, but you can hold loads of them in your hands and store them in your head. You don't really need any equipment.'

'There's something else that's increasingly being overlooked,' Marion said. 'The scores on the six QAA areas shouldn't be added up. The QAA know that...another apples and oranges issue. There is no 24 out of 24. It's the universities themselves... they created the 24 out of 24. To be fair to the QAA, I don't think they ever wanted that to happened.'

'But they can't be stupid,' Thomas said. 'They must have known that would have happened. But, yes, universities certainly should have known better...showing off about their scores, when they knew full-well that the exercise was flawed.'

'Well,' Jack said, 'not Warwick University Economics Department. Did you see their scathing attack on the whole process in *The Times Higher*, even though they got 24. Sorry, Marion, 6 x 4.'

'These audits are now endemic across the public sector, though,' Marion said. 'It will take a lot to dismantle them. What we need are more people willing to expose the absurdity....More people to stop having faith in police crime statistics, for a start. It's high stakes when funding is related to performance on audit, so, of course, police stations will find creative new ways to record crime, to make things look better for them. You can't blame the individuals; it's now a systemic problem.'

'Just like we now look back on Victorian data on race and poverty...all created to defend the Empire and its rulers,' Thomas said. 'And on a more trivial note, I was thinking the other day, on my way into London: trains used to be regularly late into Paddington, but now most are on time. But it's not because they arrive any earlier, but simply because the rail company give the trains more time to get there. That's a funny kind of business efficiency. It's a poor service, but, magically, more efficient. More effort seems to go into looking good, rather than being good,. Actually improving the service seems to have gone out of the window.'

'When is a crime not a crime?' Jack asked. 'Answer: when it is recorded as something else, or not at all.'

'And when is a student not a student?' Thomas asked. 'Answer: when we record them as a non-starter.'

'We'll make a sociologist out of you yet,' Jack said. 'The job is to get rid of them quickly - that's efficiency.'

'But we shouldn't forget the negotiation involved,' Marion said. 'Just as middle-class people have always been able to negotiate their way out of arrest or a police caution, we are now seeing these skills being exercised during inspection and review. I would say that the Philosophy result was a successful negotiated settlement on behalf of Steve Jackman and the VC. Had the two of them come across as strident and difficult it could have gone the other way.'

'So much for objectivity,' Thomas said.

***

Back in his office, Jack turned on his computer, in order to send an email to Lotte, but also to check that email from the VC. Lotte replied to his email almost immediately and they agreed to meet outside her department block at 12.30. He checked over his notes for the seminar in the afternoon and then emailed his PhD student to remind her that she should bring the results of her data analysis to the tutorial, set for four o'clock. He sat with his feet up on his desk and reflected on his conversation with Marion and Thomas. There was just no need to define quality, he thought; a quality *process* is not actually about quality; it's just about understanding that process and acting accordingly. In the case of the QAA, you just had to prove that you weren't wasting public money. Maybe it *was* that simple. He who spends wisely, wins.

Perhaps quality is just one of those words: you apply it to the winners of the game, however that game is defined. It doesn't mean any more than that.

On his way to meet Lotte, Jack crossed paths with Norman Thornhill.

'Well, well, well,' Norman said. 'The plot certainly thickens. To lose one Quality Officer might be said to be careless, but to lose two…'

'The rumour mill is certainly very busy this morning,' Jack said.

'You mean, that the VC sacked Lucy Martens, which is why she crashed.'

'Where did you hear that?'

'I couldn't possibly say, unless you push me, of course. It came from the English Department, I think.'

'Makes sense. They seem to enjoy gossip.'

'Could be a good moment to go and see the VC about that teaching course, Jack. I'm coming round to it.'

'Let me think about it. I'll email you.'

As Jack approached Lotte's building, he saw her standing by the entrance. She smiled when she saw him. He wanted to kiss her, but held back.

'Still worried about us being seen?' she asked.

'Old habits, I suppose.' He lent forward and kissed her on the neck.

'You're not still seeing that Angela Salaman, are you?'

'No, it's not that. To be honest, we had a big argument and I haven't heard from her since, so I don't know what she's thinking.'

He thought about asking after Lotte's husband, but because he might not like the answer, he changed subject: 'Got an idea for you. How about a course on teaching and learning, run by academics?'

'What, here? I can't see it being allowed.'

'But your review result surely confirms that academics *can* be trusted to put their own house in order. What I fear is…if *we* don't do it…then the Quality Office will do it *to* us.'

'You're not wrong there.'

'You'd be great on it. New academics would love you.'

'Like you do? Seriously, though, they're not going to let me be part of it. I've just been sitting in my office waiting to be summoned by the VC.'

'Did you hear that Lucy Martens is now in a coma.'

'Yes, Steve Jackman told me.'

'There's no way that you can be connected with it. I'll vouch for you.'

'What, and say that we were having sex above your head, VC?'

'I wouldn't put it like that. But what a great alibi. Turns out that the crash happened around eight o'clock, so there is some missing time to be accounted for.'

'Okay, Columbo, can we change the subject?'

They took the river route. Just as they were about to branch off back onto the road, Jack saw that the sandwich stall a little further along was open: 'Why don't we sit by the river, with a sandwich?'

'That would be nice.'

'I was thinking,' Jack said, 'I haven't seen my parents for a few weeks, so what about the two of use taking a little trip to Brighton this weekend?'

'That would really make us seem like a couple. You *have* changed.'

'I just thought it would be a nice thing to do, don't you think?'

'How are they doing?'

'Good, actually. Well, they sound good on the phone. I think I'd know if something was up.'

'I'd love to come Jack but I promised I'd help Carol with some decorating this weekend. I thought it would be a nice break and I don't want to let Carol down. She's buying all the stuff tomorrow morning.'

'Are you saying that because you don't want to come?'

'No, of course not. You have a nice time with your parents…Send me a postcard.'

'But I might miss you.'

'Idiot. How about I stay over on Friday night, and you go off on Saturday morning?'

'Done.'

Chapter 19

Lotte left Jack's flat just before 10am on Saturday morning. Their conversation the previous evening had moved from the prospect of running a teaching and learning course back to the question of capturing quality in higher education. She decided to head for the coffee shop in the garden centre before going home. The decorating was not due to start until the afternoon. Jack had enthused her to think about how philosophical definitions of quality could inform the rationale for their teaching course, and she had taken the bait. If she went home she would get distracted and the prospect of making some notes with a good cup of coffee was appealing. They had exchanged CDs the previous evening, so she pushed REM's *Automatic for the People* into the slot. Not something she would normally listen to, but it sounded uplifting, particularly on a cloudy day. Well, I didn't get an email from the VC, she thought. But what the hell was Lucy Martens going to say if and when she came round. Maybe it *is* the VC who should be worried. Either way, it would be unlikely she would be allowed to teach on Jack's course. She smiled to herself that she was even thinking of teaching on such a course; how things change.

White's Coffee shop was bustling, but not so much that you wouldn't be able to find a seat. It smelt, and sounded, of coffee. She had to raise her voice while making her order because the coffee machine behind the counter was in full whirr. She took her coffee and walked to the wall with the windows, to sit at the one empty table for two. She faced the stream at the back of the garden centre, which was in full flow. Before drinking any coffee she pulled out her small notepad and pen in order to write two words: *arete*, and *zen*. She didn't want to lose them if her mind wandered somewhere else. She smelt her coffee, took a sip, and sat back. She smiled to herself: no sex last night; maybe we *are* a couple?

She thought back to the summer after her university finals, when she travelled across the United States on Greyhound buses. She had tried to read Robert Pirsig's *Zen and the Art of Motorcycle Maintenance*, but the stop-start nature of the trip made it difficult to take it all in. She had assumed the book would be light reading after her degree, but it turned out to require far more attention than she had anticipated. Not that she would want to admit that to any of her lecturers. It was clear to them that pop philosophy should not be taken seriously. But the book was most definitely about quality and perhaps it deserved a re-read. She remembered that the author had a made a big point about the distinction between static and dynamic quality, but couldn't remember exactly what that distinction entailed.

'Quality can't just be what people want it to be. There must be more to it than that.' Jack's statements the previous evening were still going round her head. She looked down at the word *a*rete and whispered a 'thank you' to Milton Townsend. The notion of *arete* fitted well with Aristotle's broader idea of virtuous behaviour, implying a disposition towards pursuing goodness. She drew lines down from the two words in her notebook and connected them with the word 'engagement'. Dynamic quality required subjective input from an individual; she was sure of that. Was human motivation the key element in claiming that an action had quality? If humans were not fully engaged in their actions it would be difficult to ascribe the word 'quality'. Here was a good starting point, and with that thought, she rewarded herself with another coffee and a slice of homemade carrot cake.

***

Jack spent Saturday afternoon and evening with his parents. Everything had gone well. His father had dug out some old family photos and they enjoyed reminiscing about family holidays and the old Volkswagen camper van his father had owned. Even having to watch *The Generation Game* on the TV turned out to be fun. After dinner, Jack thumbed through his parents' stack of LPs: mainly soundtracks from musicals - which Jack remembered listening to, endlessly, as a kid. When asked what he was going to do the following day, he said that he'd like to take a walk around town.

Jack lay awake in the spare room thinking about how nice it would have been if Lotte had come with him, even if it would have been a bit cramped in the single bed. At least it wasn't his childhood bedroom. That would have been embarrassing. His parents had swapped their larger council house for a smaller one when both sons had moved out. He turned off the bedside light. Surely Lotte wasn't seeing her husband this weekend? He dismissed the intruding thought almost immediately, turned over, and drifted off to sleep, to the sound of the tune *Jolly Holiday,* which was lodged in his head.

Jack left his parents house just after 10am on Sunday morning for the twenty-minute walk down into town. He crossed the A23 main thoroughfare just south of Victoria Gardens to get into the old lanes. There were just a few clouds and hardly any breeze as he headed further south towards the seafront. He wanted to fulfil Lotte's request for a postcard even if she was joking. He crossed the coast road and then walked down the stairs onto the boardwalk by the beach. He spun the postcard holders gently, but none seemed right. They weren't even ironically bad. He half thought to send a saucy card because one holder contained a large selection. He bought a couple in case he changed his mind. Both worth keeping, he thought. It's just possible they would be banned in future, on the grounds of being politically incorrect. He smiled to himself as he handed over the money for the cards. The top one showed two very large women talking above the head of a very short man:

'How you are getting on with your new boyfriend?'

'Fine, but he keeps looking into my business.'

Post-feminist irony, he thought, but he decided not to send it in case any of Lotte's colleagues or friends didn't see the irony. At least the women appeared to be in the commanding position; could make a good seminar discussion.

He looked across to the Palace Pier and decided to head out to the end of it. Half way along the pier, he sat with a cup of tea in a plastic cup and thought about simple pleasures. The sun was warm and glistening on the water. Was this a qualitative experience, he thought; it was certainly pleasurable; a sense of being at one with the immediate environment. The sea was calm and so was his mind, so did the former cause the latter? Do you need to empty your mind in order to experience this calmness? Somehow that didn't sound right. Surely the mind needs to be fully switched on; in a learning situation, anyway? Or maybe a good teacher needs to create an environment in which a student can feel a certain kind of serenity in order to be fully focused? Whatever it was, it certainly seemed to be a long way from the QAA subject review.

Back in his flat that evening he sat on his sofa eating a jacket potato with baked beans. Realising that he meant to put on the CD that Lotte had left him, he walked over to the stereo system. He had forgotten to take the CD to Brighton: Big Bill Broonzy. He finished his dinner, decided that he liked the CD, and thought of Lotte. The saucy postcard idea wasn't right, but he liked the idea of sending something. He went to his desk in the spare bedroom, and pulled open the draw which contained postcards from previous trips he had made. He lifted out a view of the rock face of *El Capitan* in Yosemite Valley, California. Not Brighton, but all she'd said was to send a postcard, not from where. The card evoked serenity, which fitted with his earlier thoughts. But there was also the question of focus; the focus needed to climb that sheer rock face. He picked up a pen ready to write 'wish you were here', but then decided on 'I want you.' He paused, then looked at the image again, and decided to make the words reflect the image; she'd like that. He left the card on his desk and went to the kitchen to pour a glass of wine.

Sitting back on the sofa he thought back to his cup of tea on the pier, then back to the postcard. A quote about quality on the back of the card could be way of continuing their conversation about learning and teaching. Lotte would surely know it was from him because he would be copying her idea about quotations. He went back to his office and looked at his book shelves. His books on education were all on the same shelf: Basil Bernstein, A.S. Neil, Ivan Illich, Charles Bailey. He pulled down the Charles Bailey book because he'd always liked the title, *Beyond The Present and the Particular*. That's what a good education should do, he thought. A quality education should take a student beyond their present situation; to imagine other possibilities. The idea chimed with the image. Bailey was a staunch defender of education for its own sake. You don't try to climb *El Capitan* for any instrumental reason, only for its own sake; the reward is in the undertaking. He flicked through the book, looking at his underlining, then returned to the postcard and wrote:

> "A liberal education...will be characterised by its capacity to liberate pupils from the pressures of the present and the particular...it will also embody a concern for activities, with mental and physical, that are valued ends rather than, or at least as well as, valued instruments." Charles Bailey (1984) *Beyond the Present and the Particular*

It might not be a definition of quality, he thought, but it was certainly a move in the right direction. He wanted to get it to Lotte quickly, so he decided to slip it under her office door the following morning. She had said she would be on campus sometime on Monday to return some library books.

***

Lotte didn't see Jack's card when she walked into her office on Monday morning. Not expecting a postcard to be on the floor, she had walked over it, needing to get her heavy bag on the desk. Turning to hang up her coat she spotted it. She recognised the view, having stayed in Yosemite for a couple of days on her American adventure. That's a coincidence, she thought. She had put her copy of the Pirsig book in her bag to begin her re-read. She turned the card over to read the message. That's got to be Jack, she thought, unless someone was flirting with her in some bizarre platonic way. Surely not Milton, although it would be sweet in his case. She was sure it was Jack's handwriting; it just looked much neater. She read the image description: *El Capitan*, Yosemite National Park, California. Ansel Adams (ca1945).

She instantly saw Jack's postcard as a challenge. She ought to be able to reciprocate, and decided not to contact him in order to maximise the impact. She wouldn't have to look hard to find her art postcards. She had seen a big envelope full of them in one of the brown boxes, which were still in the corner of her room at Carol's house. Before she had time to settle down there was a knock at the door.

'Good morning, Lotte, I'm glad you're in,' Steve Jackman said. 'Got a minute?'

'Of course, come in, Steve.'

'I've just been on the phone with the VC. He confirmed how pleased he was with the QAA result, and that was hoping for more good news on the Research Assessment Exercise. He made a point of acknowledging the hard work you had put in, particularly in dealing with that difficult reviewer. He was very grateful, so I said I would pass on the message.'

'Thank you, Steve, but I didn't really do much. It was Jos and Julian, and Bev and yourself, who did all the work.'

'Don't be modest, Lotte. You, and your students, were instrumental in the success.'

'Thanks, I appreciate you, and him, saying that.'

'I enquired about Lucy Martens. He said he would provide updates via email. She's still in a coma.'

After Steve Jackman left, Lotte stared out the window. What a situation, she thought. I'm a reluctant hero all the while that Lucy Martens stays in a coma. Then I become the villain. Unless the VC's acknowledgement was a coded message; that he did, indeed, know what Lucy Marten's was up to, and that he was grateful I'd stood up to her. Well, at least I won't be sacked *this* week, she thought. Her desk was in need of a tidy and it would be good to wash the QAA out of her hair. She put Julian's learning outcomes notes in her bin. There were a small handful of post-it notes on the desk, all stuck together; the ones she had removed from the box room. She had kept them because the incriminating comments on them had made her smile. She looked at the first three: 'Bev, whenever you see the word skill put the word transferable before it'; 'Check with Julian; is it construction alignment or constructive alignment?' And her favourite one, which just said: 'The Quality Officer?' She liked the question mark at the end.

***

Lotte cooked dinner for Carol and Marjorie that evening in the newly painted kitchen, but excused herself soon after. It was chilly in the kitchen because all the windows were open, in order to deal with the lingering paint smell, and she was eager to get a postcard ready for Jack. She knew he was presenting a paper in London on Wednesday and she wanted him to get it before he left. That would mean sliding it under his office door. If he didn't go to the office, so be it. She didn't want to go to his flat because the letter boxes were inside the main entrance and she'd have to speak to him to gain access, which would spoil the surprise. The Pirsig *Zen* book had to be the perfect place for a quote on quality. She flicked through the worn pages. It was the copy that had accompanied her across the United States. It fell open in the places where too much pressure had been put on the spine. On a few pages there were pencilled comments in the margin, but they seemed to be more about what was on her mind at the time.

She left the book on the bed and went to look for the envelope containing some of her postcards. She spread a selection across the bed. If Jack sends another card, anyone of these could be my reply, she thought. She kept coming back to the image of a nude Saraswati, the Hindu goddess of wisdom and learning. She had bought the card because she like its subversiveness; the fact she was naked. She looked again and liked the grey background. It looked a little like the granite face of the *El Capitan*, in Yosemite. This was definitely the right image and it would get Jack thinking. She picked up the Pirsig book again, hoping that her eyes would focus on the word quality and nothing else. After twenty minutes of searching back and forth, she settled on:

> "A person who sees Quality and feels it as he works is a person who cares. A person who cares about what he sees and does is a person who's bound to have some characteristic of quality." Robert Pirsig (1974) *Zen and the Art of Motorcycle Maintenance*

The two sentences had an enigmatic quality which seemed to match the Saraswati image. There was also an element of East meets West. Perfect, she thought, as she began copying out the quotation.

✳✳✳

Jack was in his office when Lotte delivered the card. He had come on to campus to print his conference paper. He heard a very gentle whoosh as it came under his door. He knew instantly it was Lotte when he looked down at the image, which was face up. He paused, then opened the door onto an empty corridor. She must have rushed off on purpose, he thought. The subterfuge was exciting, and arousing. He studied the image. Was he supposed to think of Lotte naked when he picked it up? He flipped it over to read the quotation. That's a beauty, he thought. And much more about quality than his own attempt. 1-0 to Lotte. He looked at the image again, then read the description: *Nude Saraswati*. M F Husain (1976). He went back to his computer to see what he could find out. Was there a hidden message? 'The Hindu Goddess of knowledge and Music'. Okay; that makes sense, he thought. But why was she naked? Perhaps that was a bit of mischief from Lotte. He was sure that the artist was a man. Was she teasing him, in the hope that he might say it was sexist for a man to depict a goddess in the nude? Either way, he needed to find something to send in return.

Cycling home that afternoon, Jack began thinking about quotations, but knowing that he didn't really have any suitable postcards; not after Lotte's effort. How many postcards of American national parks could he get away with? Answer: none. He knew he had a postcard somewhere which had *The School of Athens* on it. That might work. And there was also *The Death of Socrates*. He had seen the original hanging in the Metropolitan Museum of Art in New York, and had bought several copies of the postcard to send to friends. That had been some years ago, though. Before dinner, he rifled through all the draws under his desk, hoping to find that Socrates postcard. He found a paper bag which looked hopeful. It was stuffed with receipts and tickets from a trip to New York. There were several postcards in there, of New York landmarks, and three copies of the Socrates postcard. He placed one of the postcards on his desk and looked up at his bookshelf. 'Socrates: why didn't you write anything down?' he said out loud. But there was a copy of the book by Peter Abbs, on the Socratic method of teaching. Good, plenty of underlining, he thought. He settled on:

> "Education is not an object (a mass of knowledge or information or skills) which can be unambiguously handed from the teacher to the student. Education is rather an activity of mind, a particular emotional and critical orientation towards experience." Peter Abbs (1994) *The Educational Imperative: a defence of Socratic and aesthetic learning.*

Not directly about quality, he thought, but an important point, nonetheless. Or maybe it's the critical orientation that produces the quality. Or was it the emotional element; that quality requires human investment. It seemed to follow on naturally from the Robert Pirsig quotation on the back of Lotte's card.

Jack was sure that Lotte would respond, so he definitely need some new postcards. If he had a quick lunch in London the following day there would be enough time to pop out and find some new ones. He was due to present his slightly modified paper on Durkheim at 11.40 to an audience of sociologists. His thoughts turned to his paper and the risk he might be taking by including the Quality Assurance Agency as an example of a body engaged in the defrocking of sacred knowledge. But, if he wasn't challenged, he might then be able to work up the idea for a future article. There were also a couple of papers he wanted to listen to in the afternoon, which might produce some good connections with his own work. The day should all hang together nicely, he thought. It was definitely time for dinner. He wanted some time to relax in front of the TV and he needed to go through his conference paper one more time. If he drove to campus early the next morning he would be able to get his postcard under Lotte's office door, then leave the car at the train station. He just had to hope that Lotte was due to go onto campus.

***

Lotte drove to the campus mid-morning, to see if there was a postcard from Jack. She had put a handful of her own postcards in her handbag. She looked down as soon as her door was open. She recognised the painting. She bent down to pick it up, which made her handbag slip from her shoulder. She turned the card over and read the quotation. Very Jack, she thought. He's trying to please me; Philosophy 101. She read the image description: *The Death of Socrates* (1787) Jacques Louis David, Metropolitan Museum of Art. Or was he being very clever; deliberately picking a realist painting to hammer home his anti-post-modern position? Challenge accepted, she thought.

She laid out her own postcards on her, now, clear desk. She wanted something that would challenge his realist position but not something overtly postmodern. She kept coming back to Barbara Kruger. She had three postcards with Kruger images. She went for the image with a woman's face in a cracked mirror. Her conversation with Jos about the way that women had been put to work in the QAA review process had stuck with her. If socratic dialogue signifies the need to challenge orthodoxies, what greater orthodoxy could there be than the way that women are socially constructed. The book by Judith Butler, *Gender Trouble*, had been a key text on her master's course, and she had quoted her work several times in her PhD thesis. She went across to her bookshelf and pulled out the bound copy of her thesis. Within the first few pages there was a long quote from Butler's later work. She trimmed it to read:

"...it is by being interpellated within the terms of language that a certain social existence of the body first becomes possible...to be addressed is not merely to be recognised for what one already is, but to have the very term conferred by which the recognition of existence becomes possible." Judith Butler (1997) *Excitable speech: A politics of the performative*

Pleased that the quote and the image worked well together, Lotte walked across to Jack's office to deliver her postcard. On the way over, she reflected on whether she had drifted too much from the question of quality, but satisfied herself that an education which didn't challenge gender relations didn't even deserve to be called an education. She was also intrigued by what Jack would make of it: would he challenge it, or would he just embrace it in order to display his feminist credentials? She loved the thought of him squirming a little; good to keep him on his toes.

***

Jack picked up his car from the station car park just before 6.30pm. With luck, he should be able to get to his office before the porters locked up his building. He couldn't wait until the morning to see if there was a postcard from Lotte.

He took a deep breath when he got back in his car, postcard in hand. It was like a love letter. The image description read: Barbara Kruger *Untitled (You Are Not Yourself)*, 1982. Was she trying to out-sociologise him because he had gone for mainstream philosophy last time? The quote was good, he thought. He was familiar with Butler's work but not this book. The idea that socially constructed gender relations don't just sit on top of biological sexes was good sociology, he thought; that even the body is constituted by how it is referred to. He also liked the reference to Louis Althusser's use of the word *interpellation* - that we respond to how we are called. I could have used that in my paper, he thought; that the QAA is an ideological apparatus, designed to change the language by which higher education is constituted. If we respond, by using the same language, the job is done. He wondered what Charles Bailey would make of that. This is surely how the language of instrumentalism - that education is there to serve the economy - had managed to undermine more liberal notions - that education should be for its own sake. He slotted the letters from his pigeon hole into his shoulder bag, and checked that the small pack of postcards he had bought earlier was still there.

Back at his flat Jack ordered a Chinese meal on the phone; there was no food in the fridge and he was too tired to cook anything anyway. While he waited, he placed his postcards on the coffee table in the front room and opened the couple of items of mail, the first of which was a large envelope from the library. It was a copy of the Wilhelm von Humboldt memorandum. This is fortuitous, he thought. There has to be a good quote in there. He began reading. There were some nice sentences on the first few pages about the need to put scholarship at the centre of a university experience, not just for staff but also for students. There were also some notes from the translator about whether Humboldt meant knowledge or scholarship in some places, but the confusion seemed to cement the point that universities should be defined by their community of inquiring minds; not collecting existing knowledge, but searching for new knowledge. As he read, he loved the cementation of the idea that universities should be typified more by seminars than lectures, and thought back to that bizarre meeting, when the Philosophy Department had confronted Stephanie Leyland-Bell and Lucy Martens. He made a mental note to contact Josephine Conway, or perhaps it would be better to do that via Lotte? He then started marking out a few sentences which he might put on the back of a postcard.

After dinner he settled on:

"Only science and scholarship which come from the depths of the mind and which are cultivated only at those depths can contribute to the transformation of character." Wilheim von Humboldt (1810) *On the spirit and organisational framework of intellectual institutions in Berlin.*

He liked the reference to the need to be scholarly, but also how it was character building. *Bildung. H*e made a mental note to read more about it. This was surely how to connect Charles Bailey with von Humboldt: if education concentrated on building strong, thoughtful, character, that's got to be the best preparation for *anything*. You can train for a job on the job, but you need an education to develop a strong character. He thought about phoning Roger Fergusson, who he was sure would agree, but then realised that time was getting on. But which postcard? The image of Rodin's *The Thinker* did - kind of - convey the impression that a successful scholar needed to be a deep thinker; one who challenges what we know rather than just accepting it.

While he was carefully copying out the quote, he wondered if it was time to leave a post-it note on the card, suggesting they meet up. But there was definitely something very sexy about this exchange of off-beat love letters, and there was no denying that he was turned on each time he saw a postcard from Lotte. If she felt the same, he was sure that she would send another card. He went to bed looking forward to the erotic act of sliding his postcard under her office door.

***

'Good quote,' Lotte said out loud to herself on finding the postcard. Safe image, though. I bet he bought that in Athena while he was in London. She smiled as she thought of him combing through the postcards. He *had* got one up on her though; the quotation *was* good. She thought back to when Jos Conway had mentioned von Humboldt, but she hadn't followed up on it. She still had plenty of postcards to send Jack's way, but she was now struggling with the quotes. Jack knew far more about higher education pedagogy, so perhaps she should just stick with the concept of quality. She thought back to the Judith Butler quote and how she had unsuccessfully tried to interview her when she was in California. While at Berkeley, she had been introduced to the work of bell hooks by a fellow graduate student. *Teaching to Transgress;* that was the book. She had bought it, but had no idea where that copy was. It was probably in one of the brown boxes, which were now down in the cellar at Carol's house. She went back to her images. She had pretty much decided that Cindy Sherman's *Madonna* had to be the next postcard, which certainly fitted with the idea of transgression.

Lotte picked up the Cindy Sherman postcard and a pen and walked off to the library, hoping that the bell hooks' book would be there. It was. She sat down with it hoping to find a really challenging quotation. Most of the sentences didn't make much sense outside of their paragraphs, but towards the end she found:

"Nothing about the way I was trained as a teacher really prepared me to witness my students transforming themselves." bell hooks (1994) *Teaching to Transgress: Education as the Practice of Freedom*

It read like an antidote to Lucy Martens. There should be something magical about education; *good* education. It isn't something you can just engineer. There should be an element of wonderment about learning. Trying to capture it and bottle it is bound to belittle it. That's why that QAA review was so fucking depressing, she thought. Jack will like this, for sure. She copied out the quote, decided to borrow the book, and headed off to Jack's office. She wanted to see him, but the excitement of secreting the card under his door was a turn on.

***

Jack looked out of his front room window. He couldn't resist the temptation to go to his office to see if Lotte had left another card. It was 5.30pm. If she was going to do it today it would have been done by now. It was a warm day, so a cycle ride to campus would be pleasant, even if there was no card. His building appeared deserted, and his office key sounded louder than usual as he turned it in the lock. Immediate disappointment turned quickly to elation when he saw that the card had gone further into the room than the previous one. Looking down on the image, his first impression was that Lotte had sent a picture of herself. It was certainly arousing, and Lotte must have done that on purpose, he thought. He turned it over to read: Cindy Sherman, *Madonna* (1975). He then read the quote. He turned back to the image: it looked a little like the pop singer Madonna, but not sufficiently to make him think it was. Clearly, it was provocative - sexy and subversive - and he loved

Lotte for choosing it. He started up his computer so he could do some homework on the image. Great quote, he thought, and the book title was even better.

On the bike ride back to his flat, his mind wandered around some of the key concepts and theories in the sociology of education; that far from challenging the system, education reflects the system and helps to reproduce it. The subtitle of Paul Willis' book, *Learning to Labour*, came into his head: 'how working-class kids get working-class jobs', and he began singing snippets of the John Lennon song, *Working Class Hero*. Maybe that quote from Herbert Marcuse in *One Dimensional Man* might do the trick. He had it pinned on the cork board above his desk at home and knew it by heart: "The people recognise themselves in their commodities; they find their soul in their automobile, hi-fi set, split-level home, kitchen equipment." Yes, that bell hooks quote hits the nail on the head, but the reality is that most people are not transformed by their education, or if they are, they are transformed into consumers of capitalist commodities. People are not liberated by education, they are pacified by it. He thought back to the first article he had tried to write, but ended up aborting; on why sociology should be a compulsory subject in school, and all the reasons why that could never happen.

Back at his desk in his flat, he laid out his remaining three postcards and looked up at the post-it note with the quote from Marcuse. It wasn't really about education, he thought, only the aftermath. He looked again at the sociology of education books on his shelf: Bowles and Gintis, Pierre Bourdieu, and then he saw the slim volume by Ivan Illich, *Deschooling Society*. Full of provocative stuff, he thought. Just a few pages in, he found the perfect quote:

> "The pupil is..."schooled" to confuse teaching with learning, grade advancement with education, a diploma with competence, and fluency with the ability to say something new." Ivan Illich (1971) *Deschooling Society*

Yes, it was about school, not university, he thought, but if we speak of schooling as a verb, perhaps universities do continue to school their students. Maybe that's why the von Humboldt memo was really important, because universities are supposed to look and feel very different, but it's not easy trying to move beyond years of schooling. Maybe the task was greater than von Humboldt had thought? Or had it simply got much worse in the last two hundred years?

Jack liked the Hopper postcard he had bought: *Nighthawks*. He thought about Lotte's images and wandered if it was bit cliched; a bit safe. But he was still drawn to it, and the sense of alienation it conveyed did seem to fit with the Marcuse and Illich ideas: a sense of lost opportunities; a society that promises everything but manages to stifle creativity and imagination; a land of lost souls.

***

Lotte walked quickly to her office, mid-morning. She only had Sartre's *Existentialism and Humanism* and Russell's *Problems of Philosophy* in her bag, neither of which had enough weight to slow her down. She wanted to take some notes ahead of her first-year lectures on 20th century philosophy. She could have done that work at home but she hoped for another postcard from Jack. She was going to spend the day with her parents on Saturday and she knew she would enjoy that more if she'd had another card. She was relieved to see the Hopper image just inside her door. More realism, she thought. Is he doing that on purpose, or did Athena only have a limited number of cards? Probably the latter. She didn't know the Illich book, but the quote resonated. 1971, she thought. It could easily have been a criticism of the current higher education regime: chasing grades and seeking validation through certification. There's the sadness. You wouldn't expect Lucy Martens to understand what was going on, but those inspectors should know better. We are short-changing our students and nobody seems that bothered; the learning is just not significant.

The notion of significant learning had been in her head since coming across it in *The Carl Rogers Reader*. She checked that the book was still on her shelf, then laid out her remaining cards on the desk. Right from the beginning of the week she had wanted to send *Red Canna* by Georgia O'Keefe. It seemed to fit with that other Rogers' notion, of self-appropriated learning, and she knew that it would appeal to Jack. She remembered him saying he wanted to make himself redundant as a teacher. And O'Keefe's image did seem to convey that it was open to interpretation by the viewer - or the student. It didn't necessarily mean any *one* thing: was it a vivid portrait of nature or was it deliberately sexual? Lotte turned to the section of the Carl Rogers book where he had laid out some personal thoughts on teaching and learning. She settled on:

> "I have come to feel that the only learning which significantly influences behavior is self-discovered, self-appropriated learning." Carl Rogers (1957) *The Carl Rogers Reader*

It seemed to be the antidote to the Illich problem. Being taught things will only take you so far, but if you want to truly transform yourself you need to take charge of your own learning. She thought about Jack; how much she wanted to make love with him, but then switched to thinking about how teachers can inhibit learning and not even realise they are doing it. Something else that Lucy Martens would never understand, she thought. You can plan everything meticulously, but actually take the soul out of learning. She remembered Jack talking about the sociologist Max Weber and the need to re-enchant a disenchanted world. She thought about putting a lipstick kiss on the card, but then looked at the *Red Canna* image again and decided against it.

Lotte walked once more across to Jack's office. She thought about leaving a note for him to say that they should meet on Sunday, but then thought that she didn't want to be the person who broke the chain of postcard giving. There was definitely something elicit and exciting about this affair. Perhaps she should just mention that she was going to her parents in the morning. Arriving at Jack's door, she decided that nothing should detract from the postcard exchange. She kissed the card and slid it gently under his door.

***

Jack cycled to campus to pick up Lotte's postcard. He was confident it would be there. As he cycled, he thought about whether a phone call would now be in order, or perhaps she would phone him. If he left another card there was a possibility that she wouldn't pick it up until Monday. Maybe she would come round to his flat. He decided to leave those thoughts hanging.

She's done it again, he thought, as he picked up the card. He turned it over to read Georgia O'Keefe, *Red Canna* (1924), then read the Rogers quote. He knew the quote well because Roger Fergusson had often referred to it. Maybe she was letting him know that she was coming round to the view that being a brilliant teacher wasn't necessarily a good thing. He turned back to the image. What was the message there? He placed it on his desk and kept looking at it. The more he looked the more erotic it became. Was she playing with him again? He thought about phoning her. He had a couple of postcards left. He decided to defer the decision.

He started up his computer to check his emails. There was one from the Vice-Chancellor. It was headed 'Re: Possible Teaching Course'. It was a reply to his own email. Norman had been right. This *was* the right time to raise the question of a course on HE teaching, so long as it didn't sound disrespectful to Lucy Martens. Jack had carefully worded his email, suggesting that his aim was to support the Quality team, and new academic staff. He'd never had an email from the Vice-Chancellor or spoken to him directly:

Dear Jack,

Thank you for your email which I read with much interest. Could you liaise with my PA to arrange for us to meet some time on Monday afternoon.

That sounded promising, he thought; certainly not a 'no.' A haircut might be good idea. It was too late to phone the Vice Chancellor's personal assistant, so he sent her an email, and then closed down the computer.

He went to his pigeon hole in the corridor. There was one brown envelope with a franked stamp. Sitting at his desk he peeled open the envelope to find a large photograph inside. It looked like an anonymous street scene, but he could see Lotte's car. It was definitely her car because he could read the number plate. There was also a typed message inside the envelope: 'Thought you'd like to know what your girlfriend has been up to.'

'What the fuck,' Jack said out loud. Lotte's fucking husband again; it must be. He wants her back. Or had they been seeing each other? He looked again at the photo. It wasn't her old house and it wasn't Carol's house. Or had he moved somewhere else and taken a photo there? He looked at the frank mark on the envelope: no clue there. He looked at the photo again. This time he saw the street name. That must have been deliberate, he thought. He wants me to go there, but I'm not playing that stupid game; what a fuck-wit.

Sitting up in bed drinking his coffee the following morning, Jack pondered his options. He could just bin the photo; he could send another postcard to Lotte; or he could phone Lotte. There was no clear winner. What if Lotte knew nothing about the photo and it was just mischief-making by her husband? But why *was* Lotte's car in that street and why did it need to be photographed? After breakfast and a shower he decided to ring Lotte. Carol answered and explained that she had gone to visit her parents: 'Sorry Carol, I forgot.'

What if she *was* back with her husband and Carol was in on it? But not after all these postcards, surely? Fuck it, he thought. He looked out of the window and then decided to go on a long-distance bike ride.

Chapter 20

Jack drove to work on Monday morning. The bike ride on Saturday had take it out of him and he didn't fancy the prospect on placing his still sore backside on the saddle. Sunday had been a long day. Nothing from Lotte, and he hadn't been in the mood for writing another postcard. Even the teaching course now sounded like a bad idea, but he had committed himself to meeting with the VC. In the car park he checked the rear-view mirror to see if his hair looked tidy. Opening his office door, he looked down just in case there was something from Lotte. He then went to his pigeon hole, which was empty. Back at his desk, he saw the email from the Vice Chancellor's personal assistant asking him if a meeting at 3.30 that afternoon would be acceptable. He wrote back immediately and agreed to the meeting. He then swung round just to check again that there wasn't anything from Lotte on the floor. He had plenty of time to think about the teaching course before the meeting with the VC. This was the focus he needed so he started to compose a short course rationale, a list of the modules, and who might teach them.

The Vice-Chancellor's office suite turned out to be quite ordinary. Never having been though the entrance doors, Jack had imagined it would be somewhat palatial inside. The VC's personal assistant sat in the ante-room, acting as gatekeeper. The VC's office itself was a large room with a board-room style table to one side and a large desk, behind which the VC was sitting.

'Good to meet you face-to-face, Jack. I've heard good things from various sources about your work on encouraging teaching excellence. We need more people like you, Jack. I'm very grateful. So, tell me what you have in mind. Keep it brief, if you don't mind, I have a meeting with the governors shortly, and I wanted to have this meeting before I do that. Hence the short notice.'

Jack explained that he had discussed his ideas with several colleagues and thought it would be a good idea to bring people from across the academic disciplines together to share their approaches to enhancing teaching and learning practice. Jack couldn't bring himself to say 'best practice'; it sounded too much like business-speak. The VC listened carefully and nodded in approval as Jack continued to outline some of the key pedagogical concepts which would underpin the work. He wanted to impress on the VC that the ideas had academic credibility.

'Well, let me tell you what I have in mind,' the VC began. 'It appears that Lucy Martens could be in hospital for some time and I'm about to inform the governors that we should appoint an interim Head of Quality.'

Just for a second, Jack thought he was about to be offered the post. But the VC continued with: 'I have asked Stephanie Leyland-Bell if she would take the post, and she has agreed. At the Academic Board meeting last Friday, we also agreed to a wider restructuring: I want to combine Staff Development, Academic Standards and Student Services into one overarching Department for Quality.'

'I see,' Jack said.

'I'm telling you this because an email will be going out in the morning. But It seems to me that your idea could fit in nicely with these developments. I would consider creating 0.2 secondments for academic staff, one from each of the five faculties, who would work with Stephanie. I was glad to receive your email because I think this could be a natural extension of our quality work. And Stephanie mentioned you in my meeting with her. You will understand I can't promise you a secondment. Each faculty would have to decide who to put forward, but I will certainly expect to see you shortlisted. I will have to go back to the Academic Board with this extension, but, personally, I think it has good legs. And I'm sure the governors will be supportive.'

'Thank you for the update,' Jack said. 'I will give everything a careful consideration. And thank you for your time.'

Jack couldn't see Roger and Norman buying into all this. But what kind of clowns would end up taking the secondments if they didn't put themselves forward? It felt like a perverse version of the prisoner's dilemma, with no good outcome. And what was Lotte going to say? If an email from the VC was due to go out in the morning, he would have to say something to her.

Back in his flat, Jack lay on his sofa staring up up the ceiling. None of his options sounded appealing. He wanted to ring Roger and Norman but couldn't bring himself to make the calls. He wanted to ring Lotte but didn't know what to say. It was now too late to put another card under her door. If she'd been on campus, she would have seen that there was no postcard from him. And did she know about that fucking photograph?

Part Three

Calm

*"I think we're definitely mad,
but it takes a madman to see absurdity."*

(November 1st 2010 - July 25th 2014)

Chapter 1

Lotte Rudolph looked out of the window of her fourth floor office. It was the beginning of November and the bricks on the building opposite looked darker than normal. Rain on the way, she thought. She looked back at her computer screen and re-read the email from Jack Lowell. They had exchanged emails and text messages on and off, but they had not seen each other for three years. None of his previous emails had suggested they should meet up. Did he know she had recently finished a relationship? Unlikely, she thought. She had meetings all day which would give her time to mull over Jack's request.

Just before 6.30pm Lotte left her office. She had been in her current university post for just over three years and had become accustomed to staying in the office until at least this time; the journey across North London was less hectic the later she left it. After her recent relationship break-up she had moved in with her mother. Her father had died of a heart attack eighteen months earlier and her mother was on the brink of selling the house when Lotte's return was agreed. Even a one bedroom flat in North London was now out of her reach.

Lotte made the decision to find a new job when she split with Jack in September 2006. They had just returned from a trip around the Amalfi coast in southern Italy; the worst form of escapism, as it turned out. They drifted further and further apart over the following year. She finally stopped all communication when she started going out with Peter, a recently divorced English lecturer at her new place. He instigated arrangements for her own divorce, which she had been avoiding while with Jack. Any mention of her husband was always prone to put Jack into silent mode, particularly after they pieced together what her husband and Nigel Eames had been up to behind their backs.

Applying for the post of Director of the Post-Graduate Certificate in Learning and Teaching had been a speculative idea after failing to secure two Philosophy posts. The panel were impressed with the work that Lotte had been doing with her undergraduate students, and with the ideas she had to support new academics with their teaching. Not believing she would get the job made her relaxed about the whole thing. Once in post, it soon became clear that her new Head of Department would be taking a hands-off approach, so she settled into conducting pedagogical experiments with new academic staff and undergraduates; started systematically collecting and analysing the data; and then publishing the results in peer-reviewed journals.

Lotte reached for the book in her handbag as soon as she sat down on the train home but didn't retrieve it. Jack's email was on her mind and she let her thoughts wander. While living with Peter she had made conscious efforts not to let thoughts of Jack stir around in her head. She paused on a clear image of The Glastonbury Festival, in 2003, when Jack had appeared at their tent with two wood-bead bracelets and a promise that they shouldn't leave each other again. And then a further promise that the Husband-Eames situation was now history. A promise he couldn't keep, as it turned out.

Her thoughts jumped forward a year, when they had camped in the same small tent in a trip around Provence. She then thought back to their plans to buy a house together. She wished she had insisted that Jack sell his flat. She thought about how that might have changed the dynamic in their relationship. She remembered Jack starting his new job in south London, and the evenings where they had sat in silence; and the bickering every weekend. Moody bastard, she thought, as the train approached Elstree and Borehamwood Station.

***

Jack Lowell unfolded his Brompton bike as his train approached Victoria Station. From the station to work was a decent bike ride, apart from the usual niggles: the person with the large suitcase standing at the train door; the traffic-light that goes amber just too soon; and the unexpected rain shower. Today had been niggle-free. He went up the steps outside his building, with his Brompton now folded, and into the lift. He walked quickly to his third floor office and turned on his computer. He was hoping there would be a reply from Lotte in his inbox, but there was nothing. He went down the corridor to get a coffee and then checked his inbox again as soon as he returned to his office. Maybe it was a stupid idea to suggest they meet up, he thought. Perhaps he should have explained himself better in the email.

Jack was hoping that Lotte might be interested in accompanying him on the planned protest against the introduction of full-cost fees for university students the following Wednesday. In order to get up to speed with what was being proposed he had been reading The Browne Report, which put forward the idea. Reading that report had taken him back to his discussions with Lotte about quality in higher education. It was the title he couldn't get out of his head: *Putting Students at the Heart of the System*. That was pretty much the conclusion the two of them had come to - all those years ago now - but it bore no relation with what was in that report. He looked at his watch. He had two hours to finalise his notes for a research meeting due to take place at 12.30, in the Friend's Meeting House, opposite Euston station.

Cycling up Tottenham Court Road, Jack's mind wandered away from his research project back to the question of student fees. He was out of touch with developments in teaching and learning and a meeting with Lotte could help to kill two birds with one stone: if she wasn't interested in him personally, at least they might still be able to re-connect around the question of higher education teaching. He missed her, and he spent the last part of the journey fantasying about how they might mix talk of pedagogy with talk of sex.

Jack was happy in his present post and tried not to think back to his disastrous attempts to work with the Quality Office at the old place. Turning down the road towards the Waterstones book shop on Gower Street, he found himself thinking back to the times when he had tried to initiate some critical discussion around the political and social context of higher education. Always the same rebuttal: it was a luxury the University couldn't afford. Much more important, it appeared, was to stick to 'tips for teachers' and all the other cliched slogans which began appearing in the pages of the annual staff development brochure.

It didn't help when his colleagues Roger Fergusson and Norman Thornhill decided to retreat back to their respective disciplines, leaving Jack isolated and exposed to the philistines. Why had Lotte persevered with it all? He remembered her telling him that she felt it was her best chance of developing a research profile. She had been successful in securing two small research grants from the University and had used the money to work with students collecting data on enhancing the student experience. At first Jack had encouraged her, but, increasingly, he felt that her work was being hijacked to become little more than another slogan: 'You said, we did', or something similarly crass.

Jack had been in his current post for just over five years - Principal Lecturer in Sociology. Things had worked out well, after some initial regrets. He was now one of the leading researchers in his faculty. He had recently worked on a large trans-European project looking into youth disaffection. The bulk of the work had been in Italy, where he helped set up a small co-operative enterprise, which provided rehabilitation opportunities for ex-offenders and drug addicts. This had lead to a follow-up project and now this meeting, which was offering a chance to work with colleagues from three other UK universities, on a project aimed at reintroducing the study of civics in colleges up and down the country. His only regret was the drift away from teaching and his lack of contact with students. But he *was* now the researcher he'd always wanted to be. In a research meeting a couple of years back a colleague had said 'he who pays the piper' and the phrase had stuck with him. He had resigned himself to being pragmatic about academic work and the need to compromise. But the student fee issue kept gnawing away at him; he was finding it difficult to view it as just another compromise.

***

Hi Jack,

Lovely to hear from you. I'm fine, I hope you are well. Your new project sounds very interesting. I'm glad you are doing work you enjoy. I'm also concerned about the student fee issue. We have been discussing it on our teaching course for new academics. Most are against it, but some have said that they can't see an alternative. Yes, I'd enjoy a coffee and a chat about it. Late afternoon next Monday would be good for me.

Lotte

Lotte re-read her draft email. She decided to change the word 'lovely' to 'nice'. She was unsure about meeting up after all this time; 'lovely' made her sound a little too keen. She read it one more time, then clicked 'send'. She looked at her watch. She had a couple of hours to check her notes for the class she was teaching that day. Wednesday afternoon was her time with the new academics at the University. She was planning to get them thinking about undertaking a classroom-based project on higher education pedagogy. She had been contemplating how best to address the split in the group: some of them were very keen on working with their students, but others felt that it was a distraction from their own subject-based research. She was looking forward to the discussion, but she knew she needed a good introductory overview of the issues.

While in the queue for a sandwich, Lotte's mind drifted back to her conversations with her old mentor Milton Townsend, on how universities were tearing themselves apart, by having one group of academics concentrate on research and another group concentrate on teaching. Even though most of her colleagues undertaking the teaching course were new to academia they were well aware of the issues and knew that the research path was more likely to enhance their careers. She was looking forward to raising the question of whether they thought that researching the subject of pedagogy itself was a worthwhile occupation. She had her own career to offer up as an example. Might work better if I make it a fictitious example, she thought; then casually mention that it was in fact based on herself. She made a mental note to email Milton. She had been in regular contact with him for a while, but had let things slip when he told her he was retiring.

***

Hi Lotte,

That's great. Monday afternoon works for me. Do you know the Friend's Meeting House opposite Euston Station? There's a nice coffee place there. I would guess that's half way between us. What about 4.15?

Jack

Jack re-read his draft. It seemed a bit perfunctory, but to give any hint that he still fancied her could back-fire. Should he mention the planned student protest? Might be better just to pop that into the conversation next Monday; that way he would be better able to gauge her interest in a follow up meeting. Just as he was about to click 'send' he paused. Was this a good idea? What the heck, he thought. I miss her, and I do want to have that conversation about what is happening in universities. He clicked 'send', then sat back with his feet up on the desk. He needed to get on with some note taking, but he let his mind wander. He pictured himself on a scooter, winding around the roads of the Amalfi coast, with Lotte's arms around his waist. His mind then jumped to some of the questions which had been raised at a recent conference in Salerno.

Although he felt out of touch with developments in UK higher education, that conference had reawakened his interest in the academic-vocational divide in education, and how different European countries were seeking to bridge it. Some of the participants had been singing the praises of the, so-called, 'dual' German system, which seemed to have bridged the esteem gap between the two types of courses. Despite the attempts of the Blair government to raise the esteem of vocational courses in the UK, the gap between academic courses and vocational courses seemed to be as wide as ever. 'An English disease', one of his colleagues from Holland had called it. He scrawled the words on a post-it note, to remind himself to look up that phrase. But it was his German colleague that he really needed to check out. That colleague had written an article questioning just how good the German system really was. 'Don't believe the hype', was the phrase his colleague had used. Jack also made a mental note to email the coordinator of the co-op he had help set up in Salerno.

Cycling across London that evening, Public Enemy's refrain was on a permanent tape loop in Jack's head. That tape went to pause as he approached Victoria Station: a taxi driver yelled 'fuck you' after Jack had cut in to avoid a motorbike coming straight for him. 'And fuck you!', Jack yelled back. Jack's hackles were raised but it never lasted long: foul-mouthed exchanges with taxi drivers were par for the course; bird song for urban environments. They're just angry people, he reminded himself; and bikes were making it worse because they must be eating away at their business.

The next train to Brighton was delayed. He was used to it but it was still a nuisance. His bike rides were timed against certain train departures. He had often thought that the train from Paddington back to his old flat was a more convenient journey home, but his move to Brighton had been carefully thought through. He needed to distance himself from his old place, and being closer to his father seemed like the right thing to do. His mother had died just over a couple years ago from blood cancer, which was when he made the move. And Brighton was a nice place to be, and much cheaper than London.

The smell of the train toilet seemed stronger than normal that evening, but at least he had a seat. His mind drifted back to those postcards he had exchanged with Lotte; the ones about quality in higher education. Whenever those cards came into his head, he regretted that they hadn't properly explored their implications. Perhaps they'd be a good opener for his meeting with Lotte; and they might invoke an emotional response from her. The postcards were in an envelope in one of the drawers of his desk at home, and he looked forward to digging them out. He hoped that Lotte still had hers. His mind then wandered back to the Salerno conference. Regardless of whether a course was academic *or* vocational, or a combination of the two, there must be the same quality issue. Or would quality be manifested in different ways, in different courses? Certainly something worth pursuing. He made a mental note to look up the work of John Dewey; something he had been meaning to do for some time.

Chapter 2

Lotte Rudolph crossed The Euston Road hoping that The Friends Meeting House would be obvious. It was just after 4pm. She'd given herself plenty of time, just in case. She walked into the cafe, assuming this was where Jack meant. There were people sitting in the corridor as well as in the cafe, so she sat with a coffee in the most conspicuous place she could find. She thought back to the times when she would wait anxiously for Jack to show up. After a few minutes, a bearded guy wearing glasses and holding a Brompton bike appeared at the door. He began surveying the room. It was definitely Jack: the beard and glasses had made her unsure for a moment, and he looked very skinny. She waved at him, and he immediately reacted by walking towards her: 'Lotte, sorry, I didn't recognise you. You've gone blonde.'

'And I didn't recognise you. You've gone beardy.'

'Yeah. I should have mentioned it. It's not much of a beard, is it? I like your hair. What made you do that?'

'Oh, just fancied a change. I've had it for so long now, it seems normal. Sorry, I've already got a coffee.'

'Don't worry, I'll just plonk my bike down and get one. Do you want anything while I'm there?'

'I'm fine, thanks.'

She watched him at the counter. It looked like he had a small bald patch appearing at the back of his head. She wanted to tease him about it, but decided against it. Within a couple of minutes Jack sat down with his coffee: 'Hey, I was thinking as I cycled over. It's three years since we last saw each other. Can you believe that?'

'But you know what they say, that time speeds up as you get older. And you're a lot older than me, of course.'

'Ouch!. I don't feel much older though. I've been running half-marathons.'

'You look fit. I'm swimming whenever I can.'

'How's the job?'

'Good, actually. I really like working with the new staff. You were right about that. And I've finally managed to get some things published.'

'That's great. What are we talking about?'

'Mainly on teachers as researchers; specifically on researching pedagogy, and working with students.'

'Hey, that *is* great. And it relates to what I wanted to discuss. That Browne Review. I'm out of touch with developments but I couldn't help but think that it was written by someone who knows nothing about the true purpose of higher education.'

'I think he was drafted in from some oil company. It's just about saving money, as far as I can see. Or putting the burden of the cost on the student. I suppose that would be putting the student at the heart of the system; as he sees it, anyway.'

'Exactly. That's what made me think we should talk about this. Do you remember that day on Brighton Pier, when we got back together...'

'Which day? We got back together so many times.' Lotte smirked as she spoke, which prompted Jack to laugh.

'That time we started talking about those old postcards we exchanged.'

'The ones we didn't speak about for two years, you mean.'

Lotte smirked again. She looked at him, thinking that she might be going too far with the teasing, and it felt like flirting. Stop, she thought.

'Yes, those ones.' Jack smirked this time. 'I always thought we were on to something there, and I regret we didn't ever take it further.'

'How do you mean? Didn't we conclude that students *were* the key to everything.'

'Exactly. But did we ever spell out how that links with quality? Don't you think we dropped the ball a bit?'

'And allowed all the nonsense in higher education to continue apace, you mean?'

'Yes, exactly.'

'As if we could have stopped it.'

Lotte thought about how that discussion on the pier had been a distinct turning point; for her, at least. It had made her feel much more confident about her teaching and was the prod she needed, to get her first article published. But she didn't want to flatter him; not here, not now, so said nothing.

'Don't you think this is the right time to make a serious stand?' Jack paused for a moment, then continued: 'Higher education seems to going further away, not closer to what we concluded. It's like putting students at the heart of the system has become some kind of sick joke. Orwellian double-speak. It's now the end of 2010, and we seem to be going backwards, not forwards.'

'But, seriously, Jack, what can we do?'

'I think I will go on the protest march about student fees, planned for Wednesday week. The imposition of full-cost fees on students is bound to exacerbate the class divide between middle-class and working-class students, and it will help cement the view that the student is a mere *consumer* of education; the commodification of education. That's not a million miles from where we were on the pier. Student fees are just part of the wider problem.'

'But this would be completely lost on Browne and his report. He's a business man. Why did they choose him? *Because* he's a business man. And don't forget it was the Labour Government who commissioned the report. I think there's general agreement amongst politicians that we can't afford the higher education we have and that something has to be done. That's the priority. It's got nothing to do with student learning.'

'But it must adversely affect it, yes? If students are customers...they are buying a product...an expensive one at that, this *must* orient them to see learning in a perverse way?'

'I can see how the first *might* impinge on the second; it might encourage students to engage in particular ways. Not good ways. But it's our job, as teachers, to *re*-orientate the students, yes?'

'Good. That's why I wanted to see you. I need someone to talk this through with. I keep thinking that this report *is* a kind of nail in the coffin. I may need some convincing that it isn't. And look at how the Tories have embraced it. And the Liberals. All Clegg's lot seem to want to do now is *cap* the fees, not get rid of them, as they promised. It really makes me fucking angry.'

'But a march isn't going to do much, is it?'

'But it could be a symbolic start of a more serious stand. Do you fancy joining me?'

'I can't. Wednesdays are my key day at work. That's when I'm with the new academics on their teaching course.'

Lotte could see the disappointment on Jack's face. Does he want us to get back together, she thought.

'Couldn't you say they will learn more by being on the march rather than being in the classroom. There're going to be some angry students there, I'm sure. What time is your class?'

'Starts at 2.'

'Okay; how about we meet at 11.30 and you peel off at 1.30? That'll give you enough time to get back.'

'I suppose I could get the class ready the previous evening. Okay, let me think about it. I'll email you.'

'Where are you living now?' Jack asked.

'In Borehamwood.'

'Isn't that where your parents live?'

'Yeh. My father died, so I moved back in with my mother.'

'Oh, I'm sorry to hear that.'

'How's Brighton?'

'It's good. A long commute, but I don't go to the office that often. I work from home a lot. I don't do much teaching anymore; mainly research.'

'Do you miss not being around students?'

'Yeh, definitely, but needs must. But if you're teaching the staff, they're not really students either, are they?'

'No, you're right. But we talk about students all the time; I watch them teach students; and I also run workshops with students, encouraging them to undertake research projects about the student experience.'

'Interesting. And I like the way you've embraced the new lingo: student experience, student engagement.'

'Sorry, I shouldn't have said student experience, but that's what they decided to call the wider initiative: "enhancing the student experience". But I don't have a problem with student engagement. That's something I really got from those postcards; that student engagement is the key. Not in a simplistic sense…but in a deeper, more philosophical sense.'

'We really need to talk more about this. I'm sure there will be links to the work I'm currently doing on students as citizens for a new research project.'

Lotte looked Jack in the eyes, then looked down at her coffee. This could be a bad idea, she thought. Images of their previous life, and the bickering, flashed into her head. They were *not* good times, she told herself.

'Probably not a good idea, Jack. We've got baggage.'

'I know; sorry. But I still like you, Lotte, and I still love talking with you.'

'Let me think about it…and the march. I'll email you.'

***

'Shit! Shit! Shit!' Jack banged his fist on the handlebars of his Brompton after each exclamation. 'You really messed that up,' he said out loud as he rushed south down Gower Street. It was possible that she might still come on the march; there was that. But it didn't look like they would be getting back together. 'Fuck', he said quietly, forcing himself to think about something else. By the time he reached the end of The Mall, by the gates of Buckingham Palace, he was reconciled to email contact only. Student engagement and citizenship though; definitely worth exploring more, he thought. If that went well, it might lead to another meeting. But was it worth going on the march anymore?

***

Lotte sat across the dinner table from her mother.

'You're quiet. Something on your mind,' her mother said.

'Sorry, just something from work I need to think through.'

'Anything I can help with?'

'No, no…Mum…did you ever consider leaving Dad?'

'*Where did that come from?*'

'Sorry…just been thinking lately.'

'About what, exactly?'

'You know, relationships and all that.'

'Still thinking about Peter?'

'I'm over that, Mum. I don't think there's any chance of us getting back together. I thought he was right for me. He *was* right for me, at the time…but not long term.'

'I *did* think about leaving your father, but it was more like a fantasy, not reality. I knew it wasn't going to happen.'

Worried that her mother might go on to say something she didn't want to hear, she jumped in quickly: 'Sorry, Mum, we shouldn't be talking like this at the dinner table. It was just something that someone said at work. It's nothing.'

Chapter 3

Jack looked at his emails one more time. Just maybe, she will change her mind and come on the march, he thought. Unlikely, given that she had sent apologies two days earlier. And it was now 11.15 on the morning of the march. At least she had said that they should continue their conversation about developments in higher education. Maybe she was only saying that to be kind. He had not replied to the email, but now wished he had. He looked out of his office window to see there were still no clouds in the sky. Walking down his corridor, he hoped he wouldn't see any of his colleagues. He didn't want to speak to anyone and certainly didn't want to be joined by anyone on the march. He didn't consider it safe to leave his Brompton bike anywhere in London, so he made his way to Westminster by underground train, emerging into bright sunshine, just by the Houses of Parliament. Instead of heading to the gates of Parliament, he turned north to see if anything was happening around Downing Street.

'F**k Fees'; 'Stop Education Cuts'. The placards were not that witty, he thought. 'How will we afford beer?' had a nice irony, but that would probably be lost if it appeared in *The Daily Mail*. 'Don't CON-DEM students to debt' was better. The turnout *was* impressive, or at least it looked impressive. The road leading down to Parliament was packed with students and lecturers and many of the students looked like school students rather than university students. 'No ifs, no buts, no education cuts' was constantly being chanted. Good, good, Jack thought; this should make the headlines on the evening news. But how many people here were concerned about the wider implications of putting higher education into the market place? Reducing or removing student fees could turn out to be a distraction from the deeper issues.

Jack looked at the students, and thought about Robert Pirsig. He had been reading *Zen and the Art of Motorcycle Maintenance* after looking again at Lotte's postcards on quality in higher education. He'd got to the point in the book where the lead character, Phaedrus, had been considering how many students would still go to university if they didn't receive a degree certificate; how many were there for the knowledge alone? Or was it all just for the passport: to a job with good money and prospects? He thought about how many people dropped out of American higher education in the late sixties, only to drop back in again, to become lawyers and bank managers.

Time to go, he thought. He peeled off south of Parliament, on Millbank and made his way towards Lambeth Bridge. Maybe it was time to forget about the UK and focus instead on Europe. He thought back to that workers' co-op he had helped set up in southern Italy, and made a mental note to look into the Mondragon experiment in the Basque region of Spain. I must make contact again with Thomas Minot, he thought.

***

Just as his train was pulling into Brighton Station Jack felt his phone vibrating in his pocket.

'Hello?...is that you, Lotte?'

'Hello Jack. Can you talk?'

'I'm just getting off the train in Brighton, but yes, keep talking.'

'I was worried that you might have got caught up in the violence on the march.'

'What violence?'

'I've been in my class, but my colleagues told me that the march turned violent and the police were breaking up the crowd. They said people had been injured.'

'News to me. It sounds like media spin. The march I was on was all very jolly.'

'So long as you're okay.'

'I'm fine. But I did start thinking back to our old conversations about quality. I'd love to start that up again.'

Jack was glad he had said it, but now worried about how Lotte would respond.

'Okay. Send me an email. I need to get ready to go home myself.'

'Okay. I'll email you later.'

She phoned, he thought, as he unfolded his bike. When was the last time she had done that? He smiled to himself as he rode down Queen's Street towards his flat.

While a jacket potato was browning in the oven, Jack poured a glass of red wine and sat in the dark in his front room. He wanted Lotte. He looked at his watch, realising that Channel 4 News had already started. This would be a good evening to compare the news on all the channels, he thought. Lotte was right; there did seem to be some trouble. Surely the police and the Government wouldn't concoct a story about someone throwing a fire extinguisher? Estimates of the crowd seem to vary widely; possibly up to 50,000. Who do you trust on that one, he thought, but either way, it was clear that the newspapers would be giving the event a fair amount of coverage - for better or worse. He couldn't bring himself to buy a copy of *The Sun*, but made a mental note to check all the papers in the shop around the corner in the morning. One thing was clear: if students did end up paying around £10,000 per year for their university education, it might well prompt many of them to choose degrees which led to high paying jobs, and make them much more instrumental about all aspects of higher education. Students as consumers *was* well underway. He had heard one of his colleagues use that phrase; along with 'consumer power' and 'consumer sovereignty'. And what better way to get students to think like consumers than making them pay the full cost of their education?

He sat with his feet on the coffee table, comforted by the smell of his potato coming in from the kitchen. He wondered whether he had too-rosy a view of teaching students and how he might change his mind if he went back to full-time teaching. The grass is always greener, he thought. But surely, students are only instrumental if we allow them to be. Maybe Lotte was right: we *could* address this in the classroom. He thought back to the section he had recently read in Pirsig's *Zen* book, where Phadreus had asked his students to write what they wanted to write, to think for themselves, to be creative, and not be motivated by the final grade they might receive. The problem was deep; what student isn't motivated by chasing grades? He thought about Carl Rogers and the idea of significant learning. Maybe that's the problem; if the learning is not related to personal growth then how could a student be other than instrumental? It was just a means to an end; a high mark and a good degree. I must make contact again with Roger Fergusson and Norman Thornhill, he thought. He then walked into the kitchen to warm up a tin of beans.

After eating dinner with his plate on his knees, he lay back on the sofa with his feet up on the coffee table again. Maybe it was time to be more radical about the concept of citizenship? He pictured his new research colleagues, and how his suggestion of introducing the notion of critical theory and critical pedagogy into citizenship education had sunk like a lead balloon. The link between Paulo Freire's work and Carl Rogers' work suddenly seemed obvious, though. Teaching needs to be shot through with the potential to transform lives; or perhaps better, needs to provide students with a clear sense of their own agency. Actors, not victims.

He reached across to the pen and small stack of post-it notes sitting on the coffee table, and wrote 'bell hooks, teaching to transgress' on the top of the pile. I need to order that book, he thought. He closed his eyes and pictured Lotte walking into his office at work and slipping her arms around his neck. He could smell her skin. He went across to his boxes of old vinyl LPs and selected *Led Zeppelin II*. After a few minutes of playing, his mind wandered to Mondragon University and he made a mental note to see if he could find out more about whether their degree programmes had elements of critical theory and pedagogy. I wonder what Thomas Minot is up to? He switched to thinking about composing his email to Lotte, but none of the sentences in his head sounded right. A few minutes later, he drifted off to sleep, asking himself if he was a human or a dancer, to the tune of the song by The Killers.

Chapter 4

Lotte walked quickly down her corridor towards the lifts. She was running five minutes late for the first big staff meeting of the Spring term, about quality enhancement measures at the University. It was being jointly run by her Head of Department, Dr Jayne Cushing, who was also the Director of Learning and Teaching, and Elizabeth Letts, who was the Head of Quality Enhancement. Lotte had already had a briefing meeting with Jayne and was pleased with the outcome, particularly Jayne's desire to ensure that all members of academic staff should get, at least, an introduction to learning and teaching, and that all full-timers should undertake the Post-Graduate Certificate in Learning and Teaching - the course that Lotte ran. The only exemptions would be for those colleagues who already held a certificate from a previous institution, or were already fellows of the Higher Education Academy - the State funded body now in charge of monitoring teaching qualifications for academics in UK higher education.

Lotte quietly opened the door to the meeting and silently mouthed 'sorry' in the direction of Jayne, and Elizabeth Letts, both of whom were standing at the front of the room. Elizabeth Letts was speaking and she nodded to acknowledge Lotte's apology. Lotte sat on the back row, wishing that she had bought a coffee on her way to the meeting. It was a lunchtime meeting and several people were sipping from plastic cups. She looked back towards the front of the room. She was not aware of any animosity between the two speakers, but they certainly looked a little incongruous: Jayne, with her windswept hair and jeans, and Elizabeth Letts, in her grey woollen dress suit. An image of Lucy Martens came into her head. What *did* happen to her, she thought? She was pretty sure she hadn't died. She would have heard about that, surely?

Lotte put on her newly acquired glasses to see Letts' slide which listed all the ways that UK academics might demonstrate that they held teaching credentials. She explained that the standing of the University would be greatly enhanced if it could put in a 100% return to the Higher Education Statistical Agency. She then surveyed the room before explaining what this meant; that everyone had a duty to ensure that they would be able to tick at least one of the boxes on her list. She then went down the list explaining which members of staff ought to be able to tick which box. Some hands started to go up, which Letts' acknowledged: 'What about researchers who don't do any teaching'; 'does it count if you are a qualified school teacher'; 'would it be easier to apply for a Fellowship with the Higher Education Academy, rather than going through a two year teaching course?'

The two speakers took it in turns to address the questions.

Letts: 'If someone is employed as a researcher then, no, they could be exempt, but it would be important to record them as non-academic, otherwise we won't get to the 100% figure.'

Jayne: 'Academics who mainly conduct research *could* be asked to do some teaching in the future, and they may have PhD students, so, yes, I think these people should at least undertake the introduction to learning and teaching course.'

Letts: 'If someone is qualified from another education sector then that's a tick in the box.'

Jayne: 'We should ask when and where they undertook their teaching qualifications and then make a judgement about what form of continuing professional development would be appropriate for them.'

Letts: 'We should let staff decide for themselves what is the best route for them. If one route is quicker or easier that shouldn't matter.'

Jayne: 'I will always be available to advise staff, along with my colleague, Lotte Rudolph...at the back...wave Lotte if you will...on what would be the most appropriate professional development for someone to undertake.'

Lotte started to feel a little uncomfortable. She could overhear some of the whispered comments coming from her colleagues. From the row in front of her: 'Sounds like a bit of a dog's breakfast.' But she felt confident that - in time - and particularly in workshop settings, she would be able to convince her colleagues of the merits of being more serious about their teaching. Not least, because their students would benefit from it. Surely, even the most recalcitrant academics would have a hard time - these days - resisting the call to be more accountable to students. Even if they just paid lip-service to it, at least that would make her job that little bit easier. It also meant that the senior management in the institution would be likely to leave her alone; after all, she was now one of the good guys.

'Surely, we couldn't be expected to get 100% of staff teacher-qualified straight away? What would be the run-in time? I would imagine this could take several years?' The questions came from somebody Lotte didn't know. It was a good set of questions, she thought. And a challenge she was willing to rise to. Letts addressed the question: 'Thank you for the question. It's a good one. The first thing that needs to be said is that we will be in a strong position all the time we can say that our people are working *towards* a teaching credential or other professional recognition. Although I accept that we might need to address the question in future of how long we give people to achieve that status.'

That's a good point, Lotte thought. But she could also see that it could be double-edged: the shorter the period granted, the less beneficial it could be for the person in question. Good for the data, bad for student learning. It sounded like something Jack would say, and she thought about emailing him. She made a mental note to contact Milton Townsend; I wonder if he would be up for a meeting?

***

Just after 4pm the phone rang in Lotte's office. It was Jayne Cushing: 'Hello Lotte, do you have time for a chat? I've just been with Beth Letts. I was a bit concerned about the direction of travel in the meeting earlier.'

'Of course. I'll come down now, if you like.'

Lotte put down the phone, wondering whether the two women had argued or whether it was just a discussion about strategy. Walking down the corridor, she thought back to the days of Richard McGiffen and whether he would have considered *her* a recalcitrant member of staff. But her past behaviour was now one of her trump cards; after all, she knew what it was like to have the shoe on the other foot. That image of Lucy Martens flashed across her mind again.

'Thanks for your time, Lotte. I'll get to the point. Beth and I seemed comfortable that we could move towards this 100% figure. We're not starting from zero; we're already around 50%.'

'But that will probably include all the ex-school teachers we have in the Education Faculty?'

'Exactly. I think you can see the potential problem here. Do we say to the Dean of Education that although his staff are all teacher trained, they will still need to join the PGCert programme or at least apply for a fellowship with the HEA.'

'He's not going to like that, is he? Some of his staff *have,* voluntarily, come on the PGCert. One of them let slip that it did come up at one of their staff meetings. Apparently, it caused a bit of a stir, because most of them, it seems, want to make the case that they shouldn't have to do *any* re-training. And that they shouldn't have to become Fellows of the HEA when they are already members of their own professional associations.'

'That's pretty much the same argument I've had with Debbie, the Head of Nursing. She says that her staff have to register with the Nursing and Midwifery Council, and that they already have to undertake professional development work for them. Why should they have to do two lots of professional development? It seems we have two deans here that we can't rely on to support us.'

'But I do also have some nurses on the PGCert. Again, they volunteered. I was chatting with them not that long again, and they said their decision was based on the fact that the NMC was a very different sort of organisation, and that they were benefitting hugely from joining in the discussions with colleagues from across all the faculties. They particularly liked the opportunity to do some pedagogic action research with their students. I think we just need to hold the line on this.'

Jayne Cushing sat quietly for a few seconds: 'I suppose we're in thick of it, and will just have to accept that this is a bit of a battle. So long as everyone…at heart… wants to do right by their students.'

'Agreed. I always come back to that point.'

'But, here's the thing, Lotte. Before I say this, don't get concerned; I think we have it covered. I did get worried earlier when Beth asked me about whether the PGCert programme could be reduced to one year instead of two; in order to get more people through, more quickly. I knew what your reaction would be, which is the main reason I called you along.'

'Bloody hell! I might have guessed. Another sheep in wolf's clothing?'

'Another one? Do you know of others?'

'Sorry, I was thinking back to where I used to work; where someone was more interested in looking good, for themselves, rather than doing right by the students.'

'Indeed. I hope it's not as bad as that. I don't think Beth is like that.'

'The way I see is that the institution...in the long run...will do better if the students *genuinely* praised it...because the learning environment *really was* a very positive one for them. You can't pull the wool for long. And seriously, who doesn't want their staff to be well versed in what actually enhances learning?'

'Precisely; you know we agree. But...strategy, strategy...what's the best way forward on this? Rest assured, I will resist the case for shortening the course. The problem, as I see it, is if the VC thinks that the institution would do better by just concentrating on producing positive data...whatever that takes. That's where all the attention seems to be at the moment. The stakes are high, because positive data... however collected...could result in light touch quality review in the future, and that could prove to be irresistible. Leave it with me, Lotte, I just wanted you to know where I stand on this.'

***

As her train made its way north, taking her home, Lotte allowed herself to think again about Jack Lowell. Maybe they *should* continue that conversation about quality in higher education. She thought about that time when they descended the stairs in the old gym; to see if the Quality Assurance Agency review team had left the building. She felt a small rush of adrenaline, then arousal. She remembered Jack paraphrasing Michel Foucault; how the exercise of power is at its height when people engage in self-policing. Were the QAA now redundant, not because they had done a good job in enhancing teaching quality, but because they had made everyone compliant? It's an acquiescence to a marketised system of higher education. Another thing Jack would say, she thought. Of course a university needs to look good; to produce positive data, but wouldn't it be better if a university *actually was* good, and produced *real* positive learning experiences? Damn you, Jack Lowell; I sound like a bloody sociologist. And where exactly did Jayne Cushing *really* stand on this? The doubts stirred in Lotte's head.

By the time the train had reached Borehamwood, Lotte was feeling less despondent. It wasn't her responsibility to fight with Beth Letts; that was Jayne's job. And she was sure that once her colleagues saw the merits of furthering their knowledge of higher education pedagogy, they might then become ambassadors within their own faculties. A chat with Milton would be good, though, she thought. Walking the mile to her mother's house, she found herself repeating lines from a song by The Killers; and asking herself whether you need to stop being a soldier in order to start thinking about the soul of learning.

Chapter 5

Dear Jack,

Great to hear from you, and glad that the research is going well. It seems that your move has turned out well for you.

For me, I'm glad to be out of academia. I don't think it was ever what I wanted to do. I feel much more at home helping people to set up small businesses. It's a steady income now, running workshops and offering advice.

I'm also running some classes at a new local college co-operative. You should get involved. There might be something similar in Brighton. I think this could take off.

I'd be very happy to meet up, if we can find a convenient time. Perhaps we could meet in London. I could get down there in just over a couple of hours.

Vigilance, my friend

Thomas

Good, Jack thought; sounds promising. He wished he had kept in contact with Thomas. No need for a long reply; just the need to agree a date and time. He looked in his desk diary to check when the Autumn term ended. Email sent, he thought again about all his abandoned emails to Lotte. It was now mid-September and he thought about her settling into the new term. How had another nine months gone by without seeing her, he asked himself. He'd hoped that they might have spent some time together over the summer break, but her email in June, saying that she was planning a visit to California, had made him somewhat depressed. Was there any real chance of them getting back together?

He looked at his watch. He had a couple of hours to work on a paper he hoped to publish. It was important to get the article right. He stared out of the window, across to the terrace of white town houses opposite. 'Fuck', he said out loud. He was acutely aware that getting it 'right' shouldn't just mean getting the article published, although it felt exactly like that at the moment. But, if he *could* get this paper published, it would be his third since 2008, which would set him up nicely for the new research assessment exercise. One more article after this one and he would then be free to get on with other things.

Jack thought enviously about Thomas, who had freed himself from this academic research merry-go-round. What once felt like a release from a large teaching timetable, now felt like a research treadmill. He looked across at the notebook on his desk, the one he used to jot down notes on a speculative book, about the difference between work and labour. Ever since he'd written up his PhD, he had harboured thoughts of writing about how human beings need outlets for creativity in their work: The fewer the outlets, the more the work needs to be considered as mere labouring. He wrote 'work' on a post-it note, with 'Thomas' underneath; as a reminder to raise this question again at their forthcoming meeting.

Sitting on the train up to Victoria, Jack began preparing for the Research Committee meeting at 4pm. He'd got over the irritation of coming into London just for this meeting. He liked to make a day of it if he was to come up from Brighton; at least have a couple of tutorials with his PhD students. But the meeting was important. It was to discuss the demands of the new Research Excellence Framework, which had replaced the old Research Assessment Exercise. Not that anyone in the room wouldn't already know the demands. The meeting was to ensure that everyone was *en route*. He thought about which colleagues might be struggling with their articles, and what excuses they might come up with. There was also an agenda item about the word 'impact'; the new word on the block; that research now needed to prove that it was having impact *outside* of academia. He thought again about Thomas, and then his irritation about having decided to try to get his latest article - the one he'd worked on earlier - into *The Journal of Education and Work.* Just because it might appear to be more about the application of his ideas, not just their theoretical underpinning. That's pathetic, he said to himself.

Determined not to get despondent, Jack looked down at the meeting agenda he had printed, which was now covered with his hand-written notes. He looked out of the window as the train was crossing the Thames and thought about agenda item 1: Welcome to Professor James Wadhurst. Could be interesting, he thought; I hope he says something at least mildly controversial.

The Faculty Research Committee meeting was well attended; not surprising, given what might be at stake. The Head of Research, Professor Rachel Campbell-Martin, started proceedings by repeating her desire to see the Faculty improve its research standing, and how well everything was looking, to date. She then introduced the newly appointed Professor James Wadhurst, a sports psychologist. They shared a joke about him having been poached from a rival institution in London and how the research air was of a higher quality in this part of the city. Jack thought about the football Premier League and whether Wadhurst had a dodgy agent. Rachel asked Wadhurst if he would like to say a few words, to orientate the meeting. He cleared his throat loudly, then asked everyone to forget about 'publish or perish' and instead to think about 'innovation and impact.' Professor Wadhurst then glanced at Rachel, which she acknowledged with an approving smile. Rachel invited him to interject at any point as they worked through the agenda. Bit disappointing, Jack thought, but he was sure that the 'innovation and impact' comment would have irritated a number of his colleagues; certainly, Dr Rosemary Arnold, who turned round to smile at Jack from the row in front.

The next agenda item was to take soundings from each of the research clusters - as they were called - from within the Faculty. Jack would be required to address the 'Applied Social Studies' cluster, which was made up of six colleagues, including himself and Rosie Arnold. Each colleague had already given Jack a breakdown of where they were with their publications, in response to an email he had sent round the previous week. It all looked promising, so while waiting his turn to speak he allowed his mind to drift into thinking about the brief affair he'd had with Rosie a few months back. He kept one eye on Rachel, waiting for his cue. What the other clusters had to say was of little interest: the focus was not on what people were researching, only on who had published what and where. He reminded himself to add the word 'applied' to his cluster's title when he spoke. It had only recently been added. Jack had not replied to Rachel's email when the new names were announced. Clearly, it was designed to focus the minds of his colleagues; into thinking about the impact of their research. But all it did was make them laugh when Jack announced it at their last cluster meeting. Unfortunately, it didn't look like Professor Wadhurst would see the joke.

'Agenda item 3,' Rachel announced. 'The question of impact. James, perhaps I might ask you again to say a few more words to kick us off?'

'Indeed,' James Wadhurst replied. 'The first thing to say is that I don't think we need to be concerned. Yes, there has been a lot of cynical talk in academic circles about how this will distort the research process; about the diminished status of blues skies research; and that the government clearly doesn't understand how new knowledge is actually produced; what it means to be ground-breaking, and so on.'

Wadhurst paused, to look around the room, then began again: 'But, let's re-conceptualise the problem...just a little bit. As I see it, we are simply being ask to avert our eyes away from the academy; not to look to our colleagues for affirmation of our work; that's important, yes; but to think first about the whole purpose of research...to make the *world* a better place. We need to turn our eyes outward; to remind ourselves of the importance of that. We do do this; don't we? On that basis, I don't think we are *distorting* the research process; just refocusing. Cleaning our spectacles.'

Bang on cue, he then removed his glasses, and proceeded to clean them with a cloth taken from his jacket pocket. Well, at least a dove didn't appear from the cloth, Jack thought. Wadhurst had obviously gone over the top. Probably because he was determined to make his *own* impact - on the meeting. Jack felt sorry for him, in his eagerness to impress. Perhaps he feels a little guilty about his appointment, with its, no doubt, inflated salary. Perhaps he really was poached and he was feeling uneasy about that. It must be unusual for a Russell Group university professor to move out of that group. Maybe the circumstances were suspicious. But he was right about academics needing to get out more, which made Jack feel uncomfortable. 'I really need to think this through,' he said to himself.

Jack looked around the room and noted how much more animated everyone now looked. Dissenting voices were soon to the fore: 'the outcome of the new research excellence process was hardly likely to reshuffle the elite university research pack; innovation sounds too much like product manufacture rather than new knowledge; will the intensification of research activity result in two-tier academic contracts at the University?'

Ahh, Jack thought, the dreaded teaching-only contract, confirming second class status on those who signed on the dotted line. Jack was unlikely to be affected personally by that question, but it started his mind racing about how the spirit of von Humboldt really had been broken: British universities were not about uniting research and teaching; in fact, the very opposite.

Jack's train of thought kept being disturbed by Wadhurst, who had begun advising those who were having trouble fulfilling their publication quota, by suggesting that they should try to get their PhD students to undertake more teaching, at least until the end of this round of the new Research Excellence Framework. That word excellence, Jack thought. Is it the same as quality? He made a mental note to explore the differences. He then thought about his four PhD students. They were all undertaking some teaching. Two of them were happy with that; the other two were doing it somewhat reluctantly. He made another mental note, to bring up the subject with them. He then began fumbling in his bag, to find his notebook and a pen.

Rachel Campbell-Martin called the meeting to a close at 5.30pm. Her valedictory message to carry on the good work didn't hit the right note given the controversial nature of the meeting. Jack stayed in his seat in order to jot down some reminder notes: 1 PhD students; 2 von Humboldt; 3 Excellence vs Quality; 4 Russell Jacoby; 5 Email Lotte.

Just as he finished writing, he looked up, to see Rosie Arnold coming towards him.

'Hi Jack; everything okay?'

'Hi Rosie; sorry, just making a list. Well, that was interesting, wasn't it?'

'I didn't want to bring it up in the meeting, but it's been on my mind for a while: do you think we are any closer to being judged on the amount of research funds we bring in?'

'I don't think it will happen. Not yet, anyway. I could see them doing that for those who want to apply for professorships, but not the likes of us.'

'I hardly think we're in the same category, Jack. You bring in loads of research money. I don't bring in any.'

'We're still talking in the thousands, not the millions. I hardly match my salary. That will be the criterion; *if* they bring it in.'

'You must be in line for a professorship, though?'

'I don't think they would give one to the likes of me.'

'Why not? Your work is well respected, and you've done a lot more than some of the jerks who are now professors.'

'I think some were given professorships to try to increase the status of the place. I don't want to be in that category. Do you remember when the new VC got a professorship? I think he's only ever published a couple of things and that was years ago. If he was worthy of a professorship on those grounds, why didn't his last place give him one?'

'Because he was in a Russell Group university?'

'Exactly. But I think the dumbing down is creeping in everywhere now. At least Wadhurst was a professor before he arrived. But it's interesting that both of them came from The Russell Group. Does make you a bit suspicious.'

'Perhaps the time is right to call *everyone* a professor, like the Americans do.'

'But you'll still get people creating their own status hierarchy: real professors and pretend ones. Snobbery is everywhere. Personally, I don't think I've done anything groundbreaking; that's the criterion for me.'

'I often wonder if I should even be working in a university. I can't envisage a situation where I would earn *or* be given a professorship. I feel like I'm on the periphery of everything.'

'You shouldn't think like that, Rosie. They win if you think like that.'

'Fancy a drink, or are you in a hurry?'

'Sure. Here or somewhere else?'

They sat in the Student Union bar, with half a pint of lager each.

'Well,' Rosie began, 'Professor Wadhurst certainly sounds like an odd fish.'

'Between you and me, I think that joke about poaching wasn't a joke.'

'And was that a joke, Jack?'

Jack smiled when he realised what he'd said, then continued: 'I think he *was* poached, to boost our chances in the REF. I checked his publication record. He's prolific. A lot of it looks recycled, but that just proves he knows how to play the game and, to be fair, he certainly seems to have some standing in his field. And his old place did really well in the last RAE.'

'Do you think Rachel is secretly worried that we're not going to do as well as the VC would like?'

'Possibly. She never gives much away.'

'Changing subject, I *am* working on a research bid. It's only for £10,000. Would you mind taking a look, Jack? I'd feel a lot better if I could at least win something. It's on improving counselling services for students and staff. Surely I could demonstrate impact with that? Should be bloody obvious. I might also be able to get a couple of articles out of it, before the REF deadline."

'Of course. Email me what you have or we could meet and go through it.'

'Let's meet up. When are you next around campus?'

Jack was tempted to say 'tomorrow' even though he had no plans to be on campus. He looked at her long blonde hair and lipstick: 'I could be in tomorrow afternoon, or definitely Friday. I'll email you.' Leave things open, he thought. Jack had stopped seeing her when she told him her husband was trying to get back together with her. The thought that he might be monitoring her was enough to stop him emailing and phoning her. But he was still attracted to her.

'You might still have a problem with impact, I think,' Jack said.

'How do you mean?'

'Well, if the definition of impact means *outside* of academia, your work, by definition, would be inside academia. I suppose you could emphasise the fact that you were looking for impact on students beyond your own institution; that should do it.'

'It's *such* a bloody game, which ever way you look at it. You need an interpreter these days.'

'I'll see if I can do some interpreting for you. I'll check the definitions again.'

'Thanks Jack. I appreciate it. I suppose I could always duck out of the REF altogether. I've only got one paper published so far and the stress is killing me. Perhaps I should volunteer to be on a teaching-only contract. Okay, I'll get less money, I suppose, but at least I won't have a heart attack.'

'There is that,' Jack said. 'Quality of life, and all that.'

On the train home Jack drifted off to sleep and started dreaming. He was leaving the Student Union bar with Rosemary Arnold. She suggested that they check in to a hotel for the night, but on arrival Jack was sure they were being watched from a car, parked opposite. In the night, Rosie looked out of the window and then announced that her husband was outside. At that point, Jack was jolted awake by the train stopping at Haywards Heath. He sat up and turned back to thinking about the research committee meeting. I *should* be doing more bloody teaching, not less, he thought. But it's not going to happen, not with the new professor on the block. 'Fuck', he quietly said to himself, 'I'm caught in a bloody stupid trap again'. By the time the train arrived in Brighton, Elvis Presley's voice was whirring around in his head.

Chapter 6

The first class of the Spring term on the Post-Graduate Certificate in Learning and Teaching had just finished. Lotte Rudolph packed up her things, pleased that a lively debate had taken place; about the pros and cons of the University re-introducing so-called 'electives' back into the curriculum. The new versions would be a small suite of courses that students could elect to take, which would be outside the main area of their degree subject. Unlike before, when the courses were chosen from within the traditional disciplines at the University, these new courses would be more interdisciplinary, covering subjects like environmentalism and citizenship. The debate in the class had covered the question of what makes a subject interdisciplinary - is it just a combination of traditional disciplinary ideas or something deeper and more epistemological; should they, perhaps, be considered as the foundation for new sources - and new kinds - of knowledge? The most heated part of the debate had been on the question of whether the new courses should be considered strictly academic, or whether they should contain elements of advocacy, designed to be engines of social and personal change. Walking back to her office, Lotte reflected that this was not going to be an easy curriculum reform for the University, and she was glad that everyone went away having a good idea why the courses might be considered problematic.

Leaving the lift door at the end of her corridor, Lotte could see that one of the more vocal contributors from her class was standing outside her office door: Judith Myers, from the Faculty of Health.

'Hello Judith. Can I help?'

'Yes, can I have a word, if you don't mind?'

'Of course, come in.'

Lotte unlocked the door and motioned to Judith to sit down.

'What's on your mind?'

'To be honest, I'm a little unhappy about the session we just had.'

'Well, you certainly helped enliven the debate. Thanks for that. What's the problem?'

'I think you were biased against what I was saying. As you know, I've been on the committee looking at these new electives and we were very clear on the *raison d'etre* for the courses. They're supposed to be about the duty that universities have to produce educated citizens. We've spent hours discussing this. I don't think it helped when you started talking about undermining the academic mission of universities.'

'Okay...I see that, but I was just trying to put the other side of the argument, in order to help the debate along.'

'But you believe that, don't you?'

'Believe what?'

'That universities should be strictly academic; that they have no duty to society.'

'Well, I certainly believe they have a duty to pursue truth. Society needs that; yes?'

'But my point is that I don't think you were neutral; in the room. You don't like these new electives, do you?

'What I think isn't important.'

'But it came across that you were on one side of the debate. And you're the teacher. I think you should have been more neutral.'

Lotte could feel herself getting angry. She wanted to say that if these electives were as Judith was describing them, then the teachers on those courses would, most likely, also be one side of the debate; that concern for the environment was not just about good guys and bad guys. But she didn't want the conversation to go in that direction.

'I'm sorry you saw it that way, Judith, and thanks for raising it. If you push me on this, I suppose I would argue my point from a philosophical position: that, epistemologically, universities are the prime locations for the development of knowledge. Ontologically, the type of being, or person, that a university aims to produce is one who seeks untainted, truthful, knowledge. I want students to leave with the ability to pursue knowledge; not to be *given* the knowledge. If you push me again, I suppose I would I say that it's not our duty to tell our students *what* to think, but *how* to think. How does that sound?'

'But a knowledgable person isn't necessarily a good person, are they?'

Very Nietzsche, Lotte thought. I'm in danger of being hoisted by my own petard here: 'Good point. But equally, does someone who is *told* what is good…*necessarily* act in a good way.'

'No. And I can see *that.*'

'It's a shame we didn't have more time to pursue this in the class. Perhaps we could come back to it. How about I organise a university-wide seminar on this?'

'That would be good. But I don't think it should be me who puts the case for the electives. Could you invite Professor Jenkins, from the Geography Department. He's the chair of the committee. I'll mention it to him.'

'Okay, good. I'll have a think about who could argue against. Thanks for coming along, Judith. I'm sorry you felt I was biased. You've certainly got me thinking.'

After Judith's departure, Lotte exhaled: 'Oh well, you can't please everyone,' she said out loud. She comforted herself by the thought that her job would hardly be worth doing if everything was just a technical question - how best to achieve something that everyone agreed on. Morals, not techniques, she thought. She looked at her emails, hoping for one from Milton Townsend. She had written to him a few days back. She was sure he would reply. Maybe he was away. She felt a sudden urgent need to meet up with Milton, but then satisfied herself that she could hold her own if Judith's voice got multiplied.

On the train home, Lotte began mulling over who might take part in the debate on the new electives. She was sure that no policy statement had yet been issued on them. Maybe it should be a lunchtime seminar? That option was appealing. It could be the first in a series, giving voice to controversial subjects: what does it mean to have an inclusive curriculum; the future role of technology in higher education learning; students as agents of change on campus? She took out her notebook and started to jot down the ideas, and the names of some potential speakers. She would have to agree the idea with Jayne, but she was sure she would back it. Perhaps a statistician at the University could lead a discussion on damned lies and statistics? That would certainly put the cat amongst the pigeons, she thought.

As the train approached Elstree and Borehamwood Station, she thought about her father. Would he be proud of her, for seeking to defend academia from social engineering projects, or would he have said that the barbarians should just be avoided at all costs? This was the same train journey he would have taken a thousand times. As she walked home, she wondered what sort of thing would have been on his mind. No doubt, Nietzsche would have been able to take him beyond all this mundane good and evil talk.

***

In her office the following morning, Lotte was pleased to see no emails on the subject on the new electives. Two emails stood out: one confirming that her latest article on the merits of students undertaking reviews of teaching had been accepted for publication. The reviewers had previously asked for more analytical argument on the merits of academics having their teaching observed, and whether it was desirable to grade performance. She had considered these comments to be valid criticism and was happy to rewrite the section which discussed how the review of teaching was as much about what it invokes in the reviewer as the person being observed; and how the grading of observations would actually *down*-grade the whole purpose of professional conversations. The other email was an invitation to speak at another university on the subject of working successfully with undergraduates to enhance the student experience. In the middle of writing back to confirm that she would be delighted to do this, there was a knock at the door.

'Come in, Jayne. I just got an article accepted for publication; that one on student observations of teaching.'

'Well done. I think that was a great initiative. I wish we could get more take up of the idea amongst our colleagues here, though. In time, I'm sure.'

'Bit of an uphill battle.'

'And speaking of battles, I fear we might have a new one. I just got quite a rude email from Ben Jenkins, in Geography, complaining that he has no intention of defending the new undergraduate electives, and doesn't see why it would be necessary. He names you as being the person who is demanding it.'

Well, that was quick, Lotte thought. Judith must have gone straight to him after their meeting yesterday.

'Oh dear,' Lotte said. 'I fear he may have got hold of the wrong end of the stick.'

'So, you didn't demand anything of him?'

'I'll tell you exactly what happened. One of the participants in the PGCert class complained to me that she thought the session yesterday…when we discussed these new electives…was biased against them. She was concerned, so I said I would discuss with you the merits of holding…perhaps…a lunchtime seminar on the subject. Judith, who sits on the Electives Committee, said that she would ask Ben Jenkins to make the case for...in a debate. I wasn't expecting her to go straight to him.'

'He doesn't seem best pleased about it, that's for sure.'

'He might have come to me first, I have to say.'

'Perhaps I should just say to him that there seems to be some misunderstanding, and invite him to discuss it, if he wants.'

'Okay. I *was* hoping that we might arrange a *series* of lunchtime seminars. I think they would be popular. The battle of ideas, sort of thing.'

'You know I would normally say yes to this, but I think the timing is not good. It seems I've got myself into my own battle of ideas...with Beth Letts. She's managed to get an agenda item onto the next Senior Management Team meeting, about the importance of getting this 100% return on qualified teachers. Knowing some of the SMT members, I think the subtleties and nuances could very well get lost. I can see the poster now: 'Study here, where all the staff are teacher qualified.''

'Lies, damn lies, and statistics!'

'Well, quite. But this is where we are, unfortunately. I certainly don't want our department to get sidelined.'

'Please don't tell me that the PGCert is going to get cut in half.'

'I will defend the course, Lotte; you know that. You've got some great feedback from the participants, which I will use, if necessary. I'm kind of thinking that we might be in a position where we may have to lose a few battles in order to win the wider war.'

'I see that, but it does sound a bit depressing. If we just want people with some initials after their names, I could always run the course over a weekend.'

'Leave it with me, Lotte. I will fight our corner.'

In order not to get despondent, Lotte spent the next hour producing some slides on the merits of getting undergraduates more involved in all aspects of university life. But she kept coming back to a fictitious questioner: 'So tell me, Lotte, how has your work been received in your own institution?' Like a fart in a spacesuit, she said to herself. She looked out of her window, and decided to take a walk, to clear her head, and have some lunch.

Back in the office, Lotte opened up her email inbox.

My Dear Lotte,

Sorry for being a little slow to reply to your email. I'm not a slave to my inbox anymore, and sometimes my replies only get composed in my head these days.

It was a delight to hear your latest news. I'm really glad that the new job is going well for you.

I've nearly finished my latest book, and my publisher is asking whether I would consider another one. I was wondering whether A World Without Morals might be a good title. What do you think?

Yes, I would love to meet up. I don't come up to London if I can avoid it, but you would be very welcome to come down to my new place, on Hayling Island. I love it here. A bit of gardening, sea air, and all that.

Please send my regards to your mother.

Very best wishes

Milton

And what a delight to hear from you, Milton, she said to herself. My handsome prince is coming to rescue me from the wicked ivory tower. Except, it looked like she would have to ride her own horse down to *him*. She reached across for her desk diary, checked the weekend entries, then wrote back, saying that any Saturday in the next couple of months would be fine. She then turned to the research proposals she had received from her colleagues on the PGCert course. They had been asked to plan how they would research an aspect of their pedagogic practice, with a view to enhancing it. Over half the group had submitted a proposal before the deadline. The proposals were wide ranging and interesting: the pros and cons of putting lectures on-line; handling unconscious assessment bias; do student surveys actually improve student learning? She gave a paragraph of feedback to each person, mostly on research protocols and ethical issues, rather than the topics themselves. She finished the last one just after 6pm, then took one more look at her inbox. She was hoping there wouldn't be an email from Jayne. No more bad news, please.

Chapter 7

Lotte agreed to meet Milton Townsend at Havant station. After boarding the train at Waterloo, she phoned to give Milton her arrival time. From the train window, she watched the suburbs give way to the green belt. It was a warm morning in mid-March and she took a deep breath as she settled further down into her seat. An island escape, she thought. But thoughts of work were proving difficult to dislodge. A few days ago she had received a formal email from Jayne, to confirm the results of the deliberations on the Department's work. At least the PGCert had been saved; for now, at least. But colleagues were to be encouraged to apply directly to the Higher Education Academy for fellowship status, even those with less than three years teaching experience. To date, the PGCert had been compulsory for them. Jayne also confirmed that the lunchtime seminars should be put on hold, and that the new elective courses were to begin the following September, without any further debate or discussion. *Further* debate, she said to herself, as the train pulled into Guildford; there hasn't been *any* debate. As the train pulled away, she wondered how things may have panned out had she not left her old post.

Milton Townsend was standing by his beaten up car, outside Havant Station. The car looked French, but the badge was missing. Milton looked smaller than she remembered, but he couldn't ever have been more than five and a half feet tall. They hugged before getting into the car. She wanted to kiss his bald head, but thought better of it.

'Excuse the mess,' he said. 'I did clear the seat for you while I was waiting.'

'Thanks Milton, that's fine. I would have been worried if your car was tidy. What is they say about people with tidy desks?...It proves they don't do anything.'

'Well, quite. I just hope you will have the same attitude to the house.'

'It's great to see you, Milton. To be honest, I've been having a bit of a torrid time at work lately, so I've been really looking forward to this escape.'

'You gave me the impression that everything was going well.'

'I think it was, but some of those old barbarians have been regrouping at my new place. Like those blackbirds on the climbing frame in the Hitchcock film. Do you remember that scene?'

'Indeed I do.'

Milton's house did not disappoint. It was a double-fronted cottage, with a neatly manicured front garden on opposite sides of the path that lead to the front door. Inside, it had a completely un-manicured front room and study, both of which sat on opposite sides behind the front door. It smelt like an antiquarian book shop and she breathed a little deeper, to take it in. Like an essential oil, she thought.

'I bought some things for lunch this morning,' Milton said. 'If you don't think it's too cold, perhaps we could eat on the table out the back?'

'Lovely. Can I help?'

'It's just a simple salad, some soup, and bread. It's all ready. Just need to heat up the soup.'

They walked through to the kitchen which overlooked the garden. Lotte looked through an open door to the right, into what looked like a cosy snug room: 'Love the house, Milton. What made you choose Hayling Island?'

'Childhood, I think. My father was a GP and my mother a surgeon. When they could get time off together they loved nothing more than relaxing under canvas. We often camped on the island at weekends, down from Winchester, where we lived. I have very happy memories of running around the place with my brother, while my parents read poetry to each other.'

'I didn't know you had a brother.'

'Yes; Geoffrey. He moved to Australia, in 1982, when he was offered a post out there. He hadn't yet finished his PhD, and he jumped at the chance to get away from Thatcher's Britain. He's much more political than I am.'

'Do you go out to see him?'

'Occasionally. It's a long way. Not something you can do over a weekend.'

'And is it two grandchildren you have?'

'Yes. I'm ashamed to say that they see more of their grandmother than me. But now I'm settled here, I'm hoping I will see more of them. Please, take a seat. We're all set.'

They ate lunch overlooking the rear garden.

'Now, tell me Lotte, what *has* been going on at work?'

'Oh, I don't want to bore you with the details. I need cheering up. I'm much more interested in you new book. Is it out yet? And I love the title of the next one: *A World Without Morals*. I sometimes think that's the world we live in already.'

'Quite. The idea started to germinate after finishing the last one. I should be getting some copies of that one from the publisher shortly. I will send you one. Strictly on the grounds that you will recommend it to others. I'm joking, of course.'

'But of course I will. And I hope you will sign it for me. But tell me more about what's been germinating.'

'Well, I wasn't exactly sure about how to finish the last book, other than to reiterate my main contention that goodness is not so much bestowed on things or people, but is an inherent quality, born of a desire or disposition. I got stuck because whereas that made absolute sense when it came to doing something with good intention, it didn't make the same sense when it came to doing the right thing. On that, I found myself returning to Kant's principles for establishing categorical imperatives and the need to act out of a sense of duty. Put simply, doing well should be viewed as a duty.'

As Milton finished each sentence, Lotte found herself becoming less inclined to join in. His words felt like a gentle massage. If his grandchildren don't want to visit, perhaps I could come down each weekend, she thought. Milton paused, which made Lotte conscious that she wasn't saying anything: 'Brilliant, Milton. I want to read it. So, the next book becomes part two?'

'In a way, yes, but I started to conceive it more as a dark anti-dote; more as a letter to a sceptical reader; that the slippery slope away from what I'm saying produces the kind of moral relativism we see today, where, if beauty lies in the eyes of the beholder, then everything has the potential to be good, and, equally, not good.'

'A world without morals, because everything could be equally justified.'

'Yes, exactly. That's what I'm trying to work through. My stumbling block at the moment seems to be the person who acts in good faith, who is then confronted by another person acting in good faith, but whose moral foundation is diametrically opposed. I may well have to resort to Kant again, and reiterate that another person is not the means through which someone might exert their will. Thus, either there will be situations in which one person might morally trump the other, or they will agree to live which each other's differences. But I'm ahead of myself, of course. I need to work this through.'

'I'm envious, Milton. I can't imagine ever having the space to do this kind of thinking. My world has become so mundane...pedestrian...by comparison. Maybe, *that's* my problem with work. I'm not standing on moral grounds, even questionable ones; only political ones, and sometimes very petty ones...bureaucratic ones, even.'

'I remember my PhD supervisor once saying to me that everyone needs to find a time and space in each day to think freely; uncluttered thinking; unencumbered thinking. That place should be the whole university, but we know, of course, that the space in universities to do this type of thinking has dwindled. This could be a good PhD thesis for a student: to ask the academics of today, where, exactly, does the free thinking take place. I wouldn't be surprised if many people said it was somewhere *outside* of the university.'

They cleared away the lunch things and then returned to their seats. Lotte carried a tray with a cafetière of coffee, milk, sugar, and two cups. Lotte spoke first: 'I'm wondering if *universities* have become worlds without morals. I mean, so many of the questions we ask these days have been cast as technical questions; it's all about the best way to get from A to B; without any questioning of *why* we are making the journey. The moral question of why we need to be at B has been forgotten... ignored. What do you make of this, Milton: at my place they want 100% of staff to be teacher trained, but the measure of that will be the placement of people in tick boxes; with no questioning of the effectiveness of the actions they took to get a tick in that box. That's bad faith, yes?'

'Indeed. It's also instrumentalism of the worse kind. Once it is agreed that the aim is to get things in the box, the only judgement then is how full the box is. It could be full of snake oil, but that wouldn't matter, so long as it is *full* of snake oil. For administrators, there are no moral questions, just a check on how full the box is. I'm not casting aspersions, because that's their job. But *someone*...people like you, Lotte...need to be there to do the moral check. B is the box, if you will, but the A, for activities...which go *in* the box...should never be a simple instrumental question. Somebody has to be monitoring the validity of the activity.'

'To check it's being done in good faith...'

'...And to check its worthiness, in the first place...It's deep-rooted, I think. Because surely the person who is most committed to their actions; the person who wants to act in good faith...wants to do the right thing...is most likely the person least interested in measuring any outcome. There is a sublime quality to their actions, and these are surely the things we most admire in people. There's a selflessness about their actions; a distinct lack of crude instrumentalism. I say *crude* instrumentalism, because there is still a form of instrumentalism, in the sense that the action is geared towards doing good...doing virtuous things, if you will. There *is* an *application* of wisdom there. That said, it's much more integral to the action itself.'

'Undertaking professional development because it was the right thing to do; not because it would tick a box.'

'Precisely. And there is a beauty in that; Aristotle's *kalon*.'

'Milton, I wish I could stay longer.'

'You don't need to go now, though, do you?'

I wish I could stay for the weekend; I wish I could live here, she thought: 'No. I was thinking out loud. I don't want to be too late getting back.'

'Well, how about I get you to the station around 4.30? That gives us another couple of hours together.'

'Thanks, Milton. I think what I was trying to say was that I'd like longer to talk.'

'Another coffee? You sit there. I'll bring it out.'

Lotte looked at the flower-less rose bushes which had been trained to rise over the pergola at the beginning of the garden path. It would be nice to return and see them in full bloom, she thought. She looked at Milton through the kitchen window, and dared herself to ask if she could stay overnight.

'There we are', he said, as he laid down the tray on the table between them: 'In the kitchen, I thought about a quote I like from Michael Oakeshott: "A university is not a machine for achieving a particular purpose or producing a particular result; it is a manner of human activity." It fits, yes?'

'That's wonderful Milton. Where's it from?'

'From another age, I fear. 1950, I think. His essay: *The Idea of a University*.'

***

At the train station, Lotte gave Milton a tight two armed hug and kissed him on the cheek: 'Thank you, thank you, Milton. I've had a lovely time.'

'You're welcome anytime, Lotte. I don't feel the need to go many places these days.'

'Don't say that or I might be back next week.' She said it as she began turning towards the small ticket hall. She turned back to wave as she approached the station entrance.

Once onboard the train, she settled into a window seat, and took out her notebook and a pencil from her handbag. Sublime, she thought. If something is sublime it is beyond description; it has a unique form of quality; not something you would want to measure. To say that something had a lot of sublimity was absurd; indeed, sublimity didn't even sound like a word. Her thoughts turned back to when she was in The Victoria and Albert Museum with Jack, when he quizzed her about what makes good art. Was this the same good that Milton was taking about, or was he just talking about good *behaviour*? For a moment she wished she had said more to Milton, but then thought about how his voice had been a comfort blanket.

'Sublime,' Lotte whispered to herself. There's something sensual and cerebral about a sublime experience; you do know it when you experience it, even if you can't describe it; it's immersive; it overtakes you. Isn't that how we want students to experience their education; to be enraptured by it; engulfed by it? Lotte looked down at her notebook, aware that she hadn't written anything in it. Student engagement, she thought. Isn't this what the word 'engagement' really means; to be so engrossed in something that it has a unique, special, quality? It's like jumping from a world of quantity - when you stop acquiring more of something - into another order of reality; where quantities are irrelevant. You don't have more or less quality; you either have it or you don't. This has got to be my next article, she thought. She wrote down 'the true meaning of student engagement', and then added 'and why we don't have it.' 'That works,' she said quietly to herself.

She slid down her seat a little and turned to watch the world outside the train window. After a few minutes, she wrote down another sentence: 'How can you ask staff or students to be fully engaged in something when all around them is crude instrumentalism - where everything is being done for a reason beyond the immediate action?' She then wrote down 'Kant', as a reminder to look back again at his *Critique of Pure Reason*. Milton's rose bushes then came into her mind, and she closed her eyes to think of herself laying back on a deckchair in his back garden. As she drifted off, she kept hearing snippets from *Blondie* tunes in her head.

Lotte opened her eyes to see a Clapham Junction sign outside the window. 18.10, read the clock on the board, which prompted her to phone her mother, to say that she should be home around 7.30. Her mother told her she would have a meal ready for eight o'clock. Just as she was about to pop her notebook back in her handbag, she found herself composing more sentences in her head: students should not be enraptured *by* or engulfed *by*; 'by' implies passivity; they should be active agents in the process. Determined not to lose this train of thought, she quickly scribbled down the gist of a new sentence; about students as victims or agents; an either/or.

Walking down the platform at Waterloo Station, she found herself thinking about Jack again; how he had described being enraptured by one of his teachers and how she had teased him as to whether he was in love with that teacher. Jack was enraptured *by*, she thought, but what would he have needed to do to be more of an agent in his own enrapture?

Chapter 8

'Thank fuck that's over,' Jack said to himself as his train left Manchester Piccadilly Station. He took a sip of the coffee he had bought before boarding the train. He was still wrestling with the hostile questioning from the audience for his conference paper the previous afternoon. Even during the presentation he had felt like the proverbial rabbit in the headlights, not knowing which way to turn. There was the guy from Lancaster University, demanding a stronger theoretical underpinning for his concept of citizenship, but there was also the woman from Manchester University, who was demanding more empirical evidence from student voices. Then there was the woman from Sheffield Hallam, asking what the problem was, that his research could be considered the solution. Was she being sarcastic, or was that just her normal manner? His thoughts continued to dance along a spectrum; from accepting his mauling, to asking what the fuck did they know; and all stops in between. He thought back to his restless night's sleep and his recurring dream - the one where he was desperately trying to get to his university exam, only to find, on final arrival, that he had revised for the wrong paper. Was that supposed to be a comfort or a nightmare, he asked himself.

Out of duty to his colleagues, Jack had stayed at the conference for the morning presentations, but took off before lunch, not wanting to get into any more conversations about his paper. Luckily, he'd survived breakfast by having a conversation with a PhD student, about her thesis; on the role of anecdotes in the production of knowledge. How many anecdotes does it take to change a lightbulb, he thought. But there was a serious question there, about whether universities were ready to accept a wider range of sources of knowledge. He packed up his bag, wandered around town, ate lunch in Canal Street, then wandered again, this time in the general direction of the station.

Jack was on his way to meet up with Thomas Minot, in Nottingham. They had finally managed to agree on a date. It was the end of June, the sun was shining, and the train windows were open. The air felt warm and Jack's mind wandered back to balmy evenings with Lotte. He hoped the evening in Nottingham would be warm enough to eat and drink outside. Thomas had suggested that Jack stay overnight, and he was looking forward to relaxing with a cold beer. For a brief moment he thought once again about that sarcastic comment on his paper. But once the train had pulled away from Sheffield he started thinking about how nice it would be to visit Mondragon University. He pictured himself wandering around the northern Spanish hills, or were they Basque hills, he asked himself.

***

Thomas Minot had always been a snappy dresser. He certainly didn't need to identify himself; his orange shirt and trilby hat made him easy to spot.

'Hey, Jack Lowell! Good to see you, my man!'

'And good to see you, finally.'

'Yep, it's been a while. How the hell are you?'

'Definitely better for seeing you. Just had a mauling at a conference. Really glad to be here.'

'Remember, you are now entering a bullshit-free zone.'

'How does that work, in a town with two universities?'

'Two towns. We don't recognise each other. *The City and The City*, my friend. China Mieville.'

'Something I should read, I think.' Jack made a mental note of the title, and then smiled to himself when he realised that Thomas' lyrical voice also appeared to be from another place: 'You look great, Thomas.'

'And you look weary, Jack. Let's stop for a drink before we go to my place.'

They sat outside The Bell Inn, halfway to Thomas' flat.

'So,' Thomas said, 'did you check out learning co-ops in Brighton?'

'To be honest, no, not really. I found some stuff, but not something that I could just walk into. I've been so bloody wrapped up in REF stuff lately.'

'The replacement for the Research Assessment Exercise?'

'Yep. They're now stressing the impact of research, but the stress on the researcher is much the same.'

'Still a bloody game, then. You need to break away, Jack. I couldn't go back. Once you're out, you realise what a straitjacket you were in.'

'I'm also beginning to realise that I do miss the teaching. When I was doing a lot of it I envied those who could concentrate on their research. Now I'm one of them, I wish I was back where I used to be. The grass is always greener, I suppose.'

'I'm all for impact, though. Did I make a mistake in leaving?'

'I don't think so. It's not impact as you would see it. It's still academic research, with all that that entails.'

'I do still use all the old concepts and ideas. I suppose I work from the other end these days...*towards* the concepts...from the ground up...*from* practice. People who want to build their own business, from my experience, are very focused on practical issues.'

'It's a mixed up world. We want the same thing, surely?'

'C'mon, let's get to my place.'

Thomas' flat was on the top floor of a large divided town house.

'This is a great place, Thomas. Did you buy it?'

'I was renting but the option came up to buy, so I did. Two bedrooms, and I have a *piece de resistance*.' Thomas led Jack out onto a good sized balcony, with metal railings, a roof, dinner table and a sofa.

'Wow, I'd jump at this. I had to sacrifice my second bedroom to get my flat in Brighton. But the bedroom is big, so I have my desk in there. I also like being able to run and cycle along the seafront. And I've given up my car because the train into London is very straightforward.'

'You definitely get more bang for your buck up here. I chose Nottingham so I could be close to my kids. They live with their mother in Derby, so it's all good, really.'

'Brilliant on a day like this, but cold in the winter?' Jack asked.

'You bet, but all of Britain is cold to me. Having just returned from Ghana, even today seems cool.'

'You were born in Britain, though?'

'Yeh, in London. But I go back to see family in Accra every few years. Of course, you can do that now. Back in the day, if you left Ghana on a slave ship you weren't going back. There was a door of no return, as they called it, at one of the coastal forts, but they've now changed it to be the door of return. Nice touch; just hope it doesn't become a tourist trap. Not that the locals couldn't do with the money.'

'The contradictions of capitalism'.

'Hey, I had the idea that we might eat out on the balcony. Fancy some Ghanian specialities?'

'Great. Are you happy to cook? You remember I'm vegetarian?'

'I remember. It's easy to miss out the meat: Peanut butter soup, *Jollof*, and *Foufou*.'

'I have no idea what you just said, but I'm up for it.'

'There's beer in the fridge. Make yourself at home. Dump your stuff in the bedroom; on the left down the corridor. Choose your bed…both the same, for my boys. Put some music on. I'll get things started in the kitchen.'

Jack returned from the bedroom and started casting his eye over the CDs in the front room: 'I really need to get into some of these African sounds, Thomas, but where do I start?'

'You could start with The Bhundu Boys. Infectious and uplifting…a bit African, a bit American…nice hybrid…take one of the CDs with you. There should be three albums there.'

'Thanks, I will. For now, would it be too cliched to put on a bit of Bob Marley? I fancy a listen to *Three Little Birds*.'

'Cliche and Bob shouldn't never be in the same sentence! Go for it. One Love, my friend!'

Jack pressed 'play' on a Bob Marley compilation CD and then into walked into the kitchen. They clinked their beer bottles together to the sound of *Is this Love?* coming from the front room.

'Anything I can do?' Jack asked.

'You could set up the table outside, if you don't mind. All the stuff is in the cupboard, just there. Light the candles as well, if that's okay?'

After dinner, they sat at either end of the outdoor sofa. Thomas flicked a switch by the door and some outdoor lights came on. He then went into the front room to put on some more Bob Marley. He returned to the balcony with two more cold beers and a tin.

'Fancy a smoke?'

'Just the beer, thanks. You go ahead.'

'Despite the frustrations, it does sounds like you are happy in your work, Jack.'

'What else can I do? I'll be fifty before I know it. I still have this idea that I can make a difference. This citizenship project I'm involved in does seem to have some legs, though. I can see some good connections with the work I did in Italy. I'm optimistic that there might be a big trans-European research bid to be had, if I bide my time.'

Thomas took a long drag on his cigarette, let out the smoke, then said: 'I have an idea that might interest you, if you really want to make a difference.'

'Sounds mysterious. Pray tell.'

'There's a rich donor out there. I've been following his tweets. I've kept it to myself because I'm not sure my colleagues are that united. I think he wants a serious proposition.'

'What sort of proposition?'

'It sounds like he's interested in funding some workers' co-ops. He's open to new ideas. Did you read that stuff I sent you on Mondragon?'

'Sure did. It made me want work there, if I'm honest.'

'I don't think we could replicate that, but I'm certainly interested in trying to set up a training school, aimed at helping people start their own workers' co-ops. There's a great opportunity here. How about combining forces and we approach him?'

'Who is he? You mean George Soros?'

'No. I'm sure it's not him, but somebody like him. You're right; it is mysterious. He doesn't give his name, which makes me think it can't be Soros.'

'What if he turns out to be some kind of fascist capitalist?'

'His tweets aren't like that, and what have we got to lose? We just pull out if we don't like it.'

'But why do you need me?'

'If it's to be a training school *for* co-ops, I will need help with the curriculum, the teaching and learning regime. You're my man, Jack.'

'Well, the first thing we'd have to do is change that name. Both *training* and *school* don't sound right. We need something more like *education institute,* with an emphasis on the German word *bildung.*'

'There you go, my man; straight in. This is what I need. We could be a good team. And this guy does sound like he's got intellect, not just money.'

'But what about the elephant in the room? We'd have a private institute trying to produce a public good. That's the ultimate contradiction.'

'Another reason I want you on board, Jack. You know we don't disagree on this; on the principle, at least. But...*seriously*...can we afford to keep waiting for some kind of Socialist utopia. It's not going to happen; not in our lifetimes. Can you see the current Labour Party proposing anything we could get on board with?'

'I get it, I do. But principles are important. We could get hopelessly compromised.'

'That's one of the reasons I like this guy. He sent out a tweet recently about the need to re-think the distinction between public and private. New times, new ideas.'

'But maybe the old ideas were good ideas? And if we took private funding, we could end up being lumped with Grayling College, or whatever it's called.'

'Yeh, I read about that. But why not rise to the challenge? Maybe I'm barking up the wrong tree, but surely we could easily distinguish ourselves from A C Grayling. That could be a trump card for us. Not a private Oxbridge-style college for rich kids; one for poor kids, focused on high level practical skills. That's a newspaper headline I could work with. I think this guy is on the same wave length.'

'Well, to be freed from all the government quangos and all the fake accountability does sound attractive; of course.'

'And what this guy can see, I think, is that the latest government proposals... maybe, ironically...are actually paving the way for new ideas. If the idea is to open up the market to new providers of higher education, why not take that seriously and be a new provider of high level training, or whatever we decide to call it?'

'But there's the rub. You think you're free but you're still imprisoned. Surely, if you want to be a new provider...on government terms...you're going to have to submit to all the old bullshit.'

'But it's got to be worth a shot, surely? At least we'd be able to say that we *tried* to make a difference. *Exodus*!'

'More like *Buffalo Soldier*, don't you think? What if end up being on the wrong side of the argument?'

'Speculate to accumulate, my friend! We just have to redefine what it means to accumulate.'

'A workers' co-op in a sea of capitalism is like workers exploiting themselves. That's a quote from your PhD, Thomas, or have you forgotten?'

'Yes, but...the but is that I was working within a Marxist framework for my thesis...that Socialism is about transforming the production process not just the mode of distribution. Socialism requires the removal of the profit motive in the production process. But we're not anywhere near that kind of world.'

'But would we be even moving in the right direction with this proposal?'

'Who knows. One thing I've learnt from my workshops is that I can't control what my participants do with their fledgling firms. Some do want to set up co-ops but some don't. Some say they do, but then I meet them down the line and it's all changed. Hey ho! You've got to be realistic, not idealistic.'

'But without sound principles we could produce a dog's breakfast.'

'Well, we would certainly have a sound *mission*.'

'That's true. It's not unattractive. I'm just having real trouble with the idea of a private enterprise for public good.'

'You're an unreconstructed Marxist, Jack Lowell. New times, new ideas?'

'Let me think it through a bit more.'

Chapter 9

On the train to London from Nottingham, Jack stared out of the window, his thoughts turning to how Mondragon University might have got started. He found himself repeating snippets from Monty Python's *Life of Brian* in his head; the scene about splits in radical political groups. He made a mental note to re-read Marx's *Critique of the Gotha Programme*. From each according to his ability, to each according to his need, he said to himself. Students could just pay the fee they could afford, but wouldn't it be better if it was all free, funded by the State? Could we ever get back to true public eduction, publicly funded, for public good? An image of Jack Nicholson, as R P MacMurphy, flashed into his head, gripping the water faucet and trying to rip it from the floor: 'At least I bloody tried,' he whispered to himself.

Robert Pirsig was right, Jack thought: wouldn't it be great if students just wanted to be educated…for its own sake. But could you imagine teachers giving up their time, for free, just because it was an intrinsically satisfying thing to do? Only if they were being paid for doing something else first, maybe? But if it was a true communist society, there would be no money anyway, so the problem would evaporate. Thomas was probably right, though; we do need to be practical. But some kind of socialist institute for education and training? An enlightened island in a dark sea of capitalism; it doesn't work. Hardly surprising that Marx was a grumpy old sod, he thought, as he looked out towards some old canal boats.

Jack looked at his watch. He had an hour to compose his thoughts for the last meeting of the academic year, with his colleagues on the citizenship project. After that he needed to head back to campus to hear what Professor Wadhurst was now proposing for the forthcoming Research Excellence Framework. The citizenship meeting, due to take place in the Friends Meeting House, held some promise; the Wadhurst meeting, back on campus, held very little. Still, perhaps Wadhurst might go all theatrical again. The thought of getting back to his flat definitely held the most promise.

With no Brompton bike in tow, Jack decided to walk back to the University from The Friends Meeting House on the Euston Road. He had two hours between the meetings. The first had gone well. One of his colleagues had got an agreement with two colleges, to set up focus groups with A Level students, to discuss how best to embed citizenship in the curriculum. Jack had volunteered to lead one of the focus groups; if nothing else it would address some of the questions raised at his recent conference presentation. His mind wandered to thinking about whether eighteen year olds were more interested in single-issue, direct action, than traditional parliamentary politics. And how well might that notion of citizenship go down with some of the college principals? Who knows; they might be a more radical bunch than they appear. Perhaps they should have their own focus group.

Back in his office, Jack turned on his computer, replied to a few emails, then joined the short queue in the canteen for a takeaway coffee. He had ten minutes before the extraordinary Faculty Research Committee meeting. His inbox included some humorous chatter about the word 'extraordinary'; why this meeting was even necessary; and is there going to be a big announcement? Jack was relaxed about it. It was close to the end of the summer term and it was probably just a pep talk and a chance for Wadhurst to justify his inflated salary once more.

The meeting was well attended. Perhaps the word 'extraordinary' had done it, Jack thought. He could see Rosie Arnold siting on the back row, talking to Chris Hillman. Chris' area of research was youth culture, and he was in Jack's research cluster.

'Hi guys,' Jack said, as he squeezed past to sit on the other side of Rosie.

'What's this about, Jack?' Do you have an inside steer for us?' Chris asked.

'Sorry, just got back from a conference in Manchester. I have no idea.'

'How did it go?' Rosie asked.

'So, so'.

Just as Jack was about to say more, Rachel Campbell-Martin clapped her hands at the front of the room: 'Okay everyone, thanks for coming. First of all, I apologise for the intrigue about this meeting and the lack of an agenda. Because we didn't have any more scheduled meetings this term, I agreed with James that we should have a one-off meeting to discuss some new ideas for the forthcoming REF. I stress the word *discuss*, which is why there is no agenda. I want us all to have a say in the feasibility of James' proposal. James, perhaps you could take over at this point.'

Professor James Wadhurst rose slowly from his seat, cleared his throat, then surveyed the room with his eyes. Good, Jack thought, looks like it could be a performance again. 'Friends, Romans...I come not to bury teaching and learning,' Jack said to himself.

'Yes, thanks for coming everyone,' Wadhurst began. 'As Rachel indicated, I would like to make a formal proposal to the group. Actually, it's a few proposals bunched together under the umbrella of securing our success in the REF. In the months since I joined the University I've been taking a close look at our research outputs. I think there are number of things we could do to secure a good result in the first REF exercise. The first thing to say, of course, is that the exercise is new, so there can be no guarantees. That said, it's new to everyone, and we are in a good position, as a non-Russell Group university, to really make a difference this time.'

Wadhurst switched on the projector screen, tapped away on his laptop, apologised for the delay, then revealed his slide: 'Securing our Success in the REF'. There were just two bullet-pointed headings: 'Focus on Publication' and 'Balancing Research and Teaching.' Hardly merits a slide, Jack thought; surely we can all remember two things.

Wadhurst continued: 'First, let's focus on the word focus.' Wadhurst smiled at his quip, then proceeded to tell the group that we were in a good position to do well if everyone made a concerted, strategic, effort. He explained that the effort involved everyone putting themselves in the shoes of the review panels: 'Let's target our efforts!' He paused to survey the room again, with an exaggerated-eyes gesture. He looks a bit deranged, Jack thought.

Wadhurst then spent the next five minutes explaining the importance of getting published in the esteemed journals in each discipline area; minimising the interdisciplinary nature of any research; sticking to articles with empirical data; and limiting the number of joint authors.

'There's impact and there's impact,' he said. 'We need to maximise our impact on the review panel as well as making sure that our research has impact.' He then surveyed the room again, with the same exaggerated eyes. Now beginning to look a bit creepy, Jack thought.

Jack felt Rosie Arnold's thigh push slightly against his own. She then whispered in his ear: 'Doesn't sound like a proposal, more *fait accompli*.'

Jack smiled at her as she moved away. Her voice felt sensual, and he looked down at her thigh before looking back towards James Wadhurst. Hands were being raised around the room, which Rachel Campbell-Martin acknowledged: 'Yes, Alan,' she said.

Alan Watkins, from Media Studies, then spoke: 'As you have probably worked out, a lot of the work we do in the Faculty is avowedly interdisciplinary in nature. To some extent, it's what makes the Faculty distinctive. Are you asking us to lose that and become siloed again, back into the more traditional disciplines? We are clearly *not* a Russell Group university, and we should be proud of that.'

Jack could see and hear positive nods and noises as Alan was speaking.

'It's an important question,' Wadhurst began. 'Let me put it this way. We all acknowledge that we are an aspiring university...yes? If that's the case, then let's be strategic. Look at it from a review panel's point of view. It is much more likely they will look favourable on us if our published work fits into well-established disciplinary areas. Let's not make it hard for ourselves. If we are successful, we then get more funds; are more likely to win more bids in the future; and we will then have a firmer foundation for developing more interdisciplinary work.'

Given the number of hands now firmly in the air, Rachel Campbell-Martin had to announce that she would do her best to take as many questions as possible. She suggested that she might collect a group of questions before giving James Wadhurst a chance to respond: 'Are you suggesting that we target the elite journals at the expense of other outlets for our research'; 'I collaborate with colleagues in several countries, are you asking me to go rogue on them and start publishing on my own and in places we've never published before'; 'my work is mainly theoretical in nature, without data, so what exactly are you asking me to do?'

Rachel provided Wadhurst with his cue, which he acknowledged with the now customary clearing of the throat: 'All good questions, to which I will respond with a mantra: Focus, Focus, Focus. It's not about giving up on what you do, just thinking more strategically in order to secure high esteem for the institution. We will all benefit hugely from success in this research exercise. Let's not make it hard for ourselves. If I take that last question about theory, for example. Imagine a panel trying to assess its value. It could go well for us, but it's risky. Minimise that risk by providing the panel with as few opportunities as possible to devalue the work. Imagine someone who submits work using tried and tested research techniques, publishes in a well known journal, within a clearly defined disciplinary boundary, and produces data with obvious empirical implications. Isn't that precisely the person who will score well? What I'm saying is that the more we drift from that, the more opportunities we provide a panel to mark us down. Let's focus and win!'

At which point a shout came up from across the other side of the room: 'But that's just gaming, isn't it?'

Jack couldn't see who it was, but was pleased that someone had made the point.

'Well,' Wadhurst began, 'you might then argue that any measure of quality is a game, in the sense that there will be competition to be the best. Why not learn the rules, practice them, win the game, and then reap the rewards?'

Wadhurst's last comments did not go down well. The peasants are revolting, Jack thought. Games and gaming? Knowing that something is a game is not the same as gaming, or is it? Gaming smacks of cheating. His chain of thought was interrupted by Rosie Arnold who had just banged her knee twice against his thigh. She then whispered in Jack's ear again: 'As if we will come out better than The Russell Group. The game is rigged.' She stretched out the word 'rigged'.

What she said was true, Jack thought. But because her lips had touched his ear he became slightly aroused and lost his focus.

Rachel pointed to her watch and suggested that the meeting move on to Wadhurst's second bullet point.

Wadhurst cleared his throat once more and began again: 'This brings us to my second proposal, about the relationship between research and teaching. I hope this proposal might also provide some space for re-focusing. Perhaps this is part of the problem: that we simply don't have the space to think about doing things differently or taking the necessary steps to enhance our performance. Why? Because of the heavy teaching load that many of you have.'

Where's this going, Jack asked himself. This doesn't sound like research and teaching having a better relationship, more like a break-up.

'What I am proposing,' Wadhusrt began, 'is that...in the run-up to the REF...all research active staff, wherever possible, relinquish their teaching responsibilities, in order to focus on the REF.'

Give him his due, Jack thought; he's nothing but consistent: consistently unable to understand the nature of this place.

'What this would mean, in practice,' he continued, 'is that the part-time staff who are not research-active would be asked to increase their teaching hours, and all staff with PhD students should ask them to take on more teaching responsibilities. I have been informed that there could be a potential standards issue here, over the assessment of student work, but I understand from the Quality and Standards Unit, that they would be willing to run some workshops for people who have not assessed student work before.'

This guy's mad, Jack thought, or completely insensitive; probably both.

Hands were beginning to be raised around the room again, which Rachel duly acknowledged once more: 'What if I can't find an appropriate person to do my teaching; what happens if I end up not being entered into the REF, would that mean more teaching responsibilities'; 'is this the beginning of teaching-only contracts in the University?'

Jack could feel his own annoyance turning to anger. This is a bloody nightmare, he thought. He's actually bloody said it; not research *and* teach, research *or* teach. But maybe some people will like this proposal? Time to stand up and be counted.

Wadhurst cleared his throat and began again: 'I appreciate that some people might not be able to find suitable replacements for all of their teaching. In that case perhaps an email could be sent round to all students asking them not to unnecessarily trouble their tutors in the run up to the REF. Perhaps explaining to them why the REF is so important for the status of the University.'

Blimey, Jack thought, keep digging lad. Rosie's lips approached his ear again: 'You've got to say something, Jack.'

Without waiting to be acknowledged by Rachel, Jack stood up and shouted: 'Sorry, but I really must interrupt. Of course the REF is important. We all know that. But we owe our students more than this. For goodness sake, new students are now going to be paying £9,000 per year to study here from this September. Yes, we might rise slightly up the research league table, and that would be a good thing, but at what price…shortchanging our students? This is going too far, I'm afraid.'

Jack sat back down. He felt Rosie's lips on his ear again: 'Well said. Thanks.'

Jack knew he had hit the right note, because the volume had risen in the room and he could hear people saying that he was right. He looked down again at Rosie's thigh.

Rachel Campbell-Martin raised both arms in an 'order-order' gesture: 'I can see that the cat is amongst the pigeons, which is why we wanted this meeting to be a discussion. Nothing has been decided. These are proposals; proposals I was happy to bring to the meeting.'

She turned to Wadhurst: 'Thank you, James. Change is never easy.'

And change isn't always a good thing, Jack thought.

Rachel continued: 'Clearly, we need to think carefully about how to proceed. I suggest that we call the meeting to a close and I go away to consider our next steps. Perhaps I could take some soundings via email. I'm very aware that not everyone got a chance to air their views.'

The meeting closed, and thirty minutes before the scheduled time. Jack was pleased that he had spoken out, but well aware that Rachel and Wadhurst would now be talking about him behind his back. No doubt an email would follow.

'I need to buy you a drink, Dr Lowell,' Rosie Arnold said in Jack's ear.

'I accept. I need one,' Jack replied.

***

'Looks like I will be one of the first on a teaching-only contract,' Rosie said, as they approached the Student Union bar.

'I still don't think it will come to that. But after that meeting I am now wavering, I have to admit.'

They sat down with two half pints of lager.

'Will you protect me from the wicked witch, Jack?'

'How do you mean?'

'Well, it looks like Rachel, the good witch of south London, might be turning wicked, and she might be taking names. She's bound to ask you what you think of me, as a researcher.'

'It's bloody Wizard Wadhurst we need to be concerned about, I think. Hopefully, someone will expose him…as totally the wrong person for this place.'

'I think you just did, Jack.'

'What worries me is all those people who didn't say anything. The vocal ones were all the people who were opposed. I think there might well be more than a few who would be very happy with what Wadhurst was saying.'

'They bloody well should have said something, then. Let's know who we are dealing with.'

'Not easy though, when someone like me plays the student card. Who wants to be seen to be against students?'

'Good point. So how *do* we get this stopped?'

'I have a feeling that Wadhurst will say that this is just a temporary thing; to get us through the REF. But if we are successful in the REF, that's when the real pressure might be on; to keep things as they are. Let's be honest, for the so-called successful universities, the money is not in student fees, it's in those big research contracts.'

'Which will probably suit you, Jack. You will be one of the beneficiaries.'

'Yeh, but it's not right, is it? I'd really like to be doing *more* teaching, not less. Or at least have the option.'

'And I'd like the option of doing some research. Perhaps you could take me on as a junior researcher, or something?'

'Would you take a job in a private university?'

'No, definitely not. What made you say that?'

'But what if they told you that there would be no REF; no accountability to government quangos.'

'Sign me up! What, like an American university, you mean? It would be tempting. Talking of which could I tempt you with dinner, at my place?'

'Sign me up, yes. I don't want to be late home though. I haven't been home for three nights.'

'Dirty stop out.'

'I was at a conference in Manchester, then I went to see an old friend…Thomas…in Nottingham.'

'The kids are with their dad; they'll be back around nine.'

'Okay, let's go.'

Was this serious flirting, he thought, or does she just want to keep me close, to protect her from Rachel and Wadhurst? He looked at Rosie's mouth, and thought about her tongue in his ear.

Rosie's house was to the west of Clapham Common. Jack knew it would be easy enough to get back to Brighton from there: Clapham Junction was only a ten minute walk away, and he had done it twice before. They emerged from Clapham South Underground Station, arriving at Rosie's front door shortly after. Jack followed Rosie down the corridor to the kitchen, which had washing-up sitting in the sink, and papers and books strewn across the kitchen table. Jack was pleased with the scene; the same as he remembered.

'Okay, a choice,' Rosie said. 'I could rustle up something or order a takeaway. What do you think?'

'Whatever's easiest. Why not a takeaway?'

'Okay, see if you can find a menu; over there on the wall. Just nipping to the loo.'

Jack looked at his watch: 6.35. The night is young, he thought.

'So, what did you find?' Rosie asked, as she arrived back in the kitchen.

'Sorry, I couldn't find anything.'

'How about an Indian? Vegetable biriani? I know the number.'

'Great. Go for it.'

After making the call, Rosie pushed her phone into her bag. 'Ready in thirty minutes.'

She walked towards Jack and asked him to tell her more about private universities.

'Oh, it was just a day-dream, because of a conversation with my friend, Thomas. We were just wondering whether it would be a way out of all this government-quango nonsense. He's more interested in a training school to set up workers' co-ops, if truth be told.'

'Wouldn't it be great though, to break free from all this crap?'

'Or maybe we should just stay and fight our corner?'

'But I don't have any power. I'm just a pawn.'

'But a lot of pawns can make a difference.'

'True.'

Rosie looked into Jack's eyes as she spoke. He slipped his arms round her back. She placed her nose on his neck, and rubbed her hands on his chest: 'Now, or after dinner?'

'What time is your husband coming round?'

'Not yet...later.'

'But what if he comes round earlier?'

Jack could feel his excitement waning. He kissed her on the top of her head. She moved away: 'It's okay Jack. We don't have to do anything.'

Jack's mind began racing. I really don't need a confrontation with her husband; is Rosie playing a game, getting me on side, so I protect her; what if Rachel asks me if I'm having an affair with her? I need to get home, he thought.

Chapter 10

Lotte walked back to her office. She felt her door offer some resistance. Her office window was open, and she could feel the warm breeze as soon as she walked in. It was the last Thursday in July and things were quiet on campus. She had come into the University to meet with Jayne Cushing, who wanted to confirm arrangements for the Autumn term. Jayne had confirmed Lotte's fears, that her PGCert course *was* going to be reduced in length. But also that it now needed to be aligned with the questions on the National Student Survey. So much for Jayne's previous reassurances, she thought. Or did someone get to Jayne; was she on some kind of promise; was she moving to the dark side, even?

At least the PGCert course would still be eighteen months long, rather than the original proposal of reducing it to one year. Jayne also confirmed that the course would now have to include a three month-long introduction to teaching, learning and assessment module, for all new academics. But after that they would be able choose if they wanted to continue or just submit a direct application for fellowship status with the Higher Education Academy. 'I have three months', she said out loud to herself; should be enough to persuade a good number of the participants to continue with the course. The last three months of the course provided everyone with the chance to undertake some pedagogic research, and she also remained optimistic about the merit in undertaking this work.

Lotte had intended to collect up the books and articles she would need to finish the article she was working on, but she could feel herself becoming deflated again. She comforted herself in the knowledge that she had no need to come into the office again for the next couple of weeks. After that, she was due to drive to Germany with her mother, to visit relatives, and to do some walking in the Alps. She sat quietly, feeling the warm breeze again, but her revelry didn't last. 'The National Student Survey,' she said out loud. What a joke; does anybody seriously believe that this will improve anything? She banged her fist on the desk. Why should I have to contaminate my course with this shit; why does anyone take any notice of it; and where did the bloody thing come from?

The warm breeze picked up a bit and Lotte enjoyed feeling it against her face. Maybe, just maybe, she thought, there might be an opportunity to be a little subversive here. Maybe the NSS questions *could* be mapped against the course, but without changing any of the content? And perhaps her colleagues on the course would see for themselves that the NSS questions actually have little to do with improving the quality of teaching and learning? Why not have a bit of fun with it? She'd never made the NSS a topic of conversation on the PGCert course, so perhaps this would be no bad thing. She felt confident that her own research work with students gave her credibility, and because of that she wouldn't come across as overtly cynical. Perhaps she could get some undergraduate students to do some research on the survey. Now, that could be interesting, she thought.

Lotte looked out of her window, thinking that it was a good day to take a wander, and perhaps find somewhere nice to eat a sandwich in the sunshine. As she walked, she considered the idea of writing an article with some students, on the National Student Survey. Where *did* that bloody thing come from? Maybe I won't go home early, she thought.

Back in the office, it didn't take long to find out a fair amount about the history of the National Student Survey, from a Google search. She jotted down a few notes as she went and saved some of the more interesting web pages: first survey 2007; 27 questions for students about their university experience; it's not compulsory for an institution to take part; it's a national student voice survey; it provides prospective students with a chance to compare institutions on how well they did in the survey. One web page described the survey as a measure of the quality of the teaching experience for students.

That word quality again, she thought. She had already partly composed the conclusion to her latest article, which would say that student engagement was the true measure of the quality of a learning experience for students. She thought about the contrast between teaching, on the one hand, and learning, on the other. Perhaps they were just two sides of the same coin. She thought back to the *Carl Rogers Reader*. Maybe, there's the problem, that the NSS gets students to think about the *teaching* they have been subject to, rather than asking them about their own learning. The Rogers-Humboldt connection again. She thought about Jack and those postcards. She looked up and felt the warm breeze again. Maybe the next couple of weeks *could* be fun: working on the article; looking at the NSS; revamping the PGCert course. And maybe an email to Jack.

Lotte continued with her internet search. In amongst the results she saw a link to 'The National Survey of Student Engagement'. That's a new one, she thought. Then she realised it was American. She clicked to find out more, only to find that if you wanted to look at the questions you would have to buy-in to the survey. How very American she said to herself; everything *is* a commodity. She could hear Jack Lowell saying it, and thought again about emailing him. Jack, you bastard, I could do with talking to you right now. Her mind wandered back to their conversations about quality, and that Ivan Illich quote, about students confusing a diploma for an education, and being schooled.

There was a knock at the door. It was Jayne: 'Hi again Lotte, sorry, I was going to email you, but just wanted to check if you were still here. I thought it might be better to say it, rather than email it.'

'Say what? Not more bad news.'

'Well, I don't think you will like it, but I've just heard that the senior managers have given the go ahead to develop more electives. They want one on social justice. I've just got off the phone with Beth Letts.'

'What's it got to do with her?'

'Only that I know she knows. She's a good way to find out what's going on.'

'So, am I to take it that this course will be non-academic again?'

'That's why I've come along to tell you face-to-face. They don't see it like that. Someone has been charged with writing an introduction to these courses, to say something about how they are all aimed at preparing students for the challenges of the modern world.'

'Telling them how to act, in other words. What's your honest view, Jayne?'

'Honestly, I'm not sure. Like you, I'm not on the committee that's been deciding these things. I suppose we could ask for reassurances that the courses will have the appropriate level of criticality in them. But if they get validated by the Quality team, there won't be much we can do about it. I just wanted you to hear it from me. I can't see that we can fight this. I think you've got enough on your plate defending the PGCert programme, which you know I fully support.'

'Thanks Jayne. I appreciate you telling me this. Have a good weekend. Email me if you need to. I intend to work from home the next couple of weeks, then it's off to Germany.'

'Okay. Have a great time. You deserve a break. You've worked hard this year. Thank you.'

'Thanks for saying that, Jayne. Are you going away?'

'New York, actually. Really looking forward to it. Back on the 7th September.'

'What a bloody roller-coaster,' Lotte said out loud to herself. She thought about Milton Townsend and his idea that everybody needs to find some time and space to think. At least at home she could think about the things she really wanted to think about, particularly if she turned off the email system. She started to compose an email to Jack Lowell, but then thought about him enjoying a drink in the sun; probably with a woman from his new place, or the old place, even. And what if Jayne *has* been turned; by Beth Letts, maybe? And what if more of the participants on the PGCert course started complaining about having to take the course? And do I dare put my head above the parapet on those bloody electives?

Sitting on the train as it travelled north to Borehamwood, she looked up from her book - *Freedom*, by Jonathan Franzen - and thought about a trip across to see Carol Morgan. It had been nearly two years since she had last seen her. Lotte assumed she was still living in the same house. Carol had previously said that she had no intention of moving and that she was happy living with Margie. Boy, a lot has happened since I moved out of that house, she thought. A lot of which she hadn't told Carol, or her mother. There was definitely no way she would have been able to talk with her mother about the break up with Peter. A trip to see Carol really would be nice, she thought, and it would be a good chance to discuss those bloody electives. She imagined that Carol would be able to mount a good defence of them.

Chapter 11

Lotte guessed the drive to Carol Morgan's house would take less than two hours, if the motorway was kind. She had no need to use her car during the week, so the prospect of slipping a CD into the slot and winding down the window felt like a treat. *Yellow Moon* by The Neville Brothers seemed right. She put the car in reverse and waved goodbye to her mother. It was Saturday morning in the middle of August.

In little over an hour she was close to Carol's house; the motorway *had* been kind. She had agreed to meet Carol at one o'clock and. It was only just after midday, so she decided to pull into the old garden centre, where Operation Remove Lotte had begun. It would be a good place to buy Carol a gift, and to have a coffee in the cafe, assuming it was still there.

The cafe was still there. It looked different, but still had its comforting smell of coffee in the air. There was now a new seating area outside, which she could see when queuing for her coffee. Coffee in hand, she made her way outside and sat at one of the empty small tables. She thought about what her ex-husband might be doing. When her divorce was going through she had learnt of his plans to remarry and move to Leeds. And what of mischief-making Nigel Eames; hopefully, he had moved on too. She thought back to one of those shouting matches with Jack, when it finally became clear that her husband and Nigel had been wrestling with each other to prise her away from him. In a strange way, they got what they wanted. She thought about whether she should have come clean with Jack, and told him that she *had* been with Nigel Eames several times, and that she did continue to have conversations with her husband. Were Jack's dark moods really all his fault? Jack Lowell: when things were good, they were very good; when things were bad, they were shit.

Lotte took a sip of coffee. Whose bloody stupid idea was it to ask students those NSS questions, then make the claim that the answers were a judgement on the quality of their university experience? She had spent Friday afternoon looking at the NSS questions: *Staff are good at explaining things; staff have made the subject interesting; staff are enthusiastic about what they are teaching.* She thought back to when she first started teaching, when she would have considered these to be good questions. But she had moved on. She thought back to her conversations with Milton Townsend, Jos Conway, and Jack, on what it means to be a *higher* education student. It was not about being taught *existing* knowledge, but being given the skills to develop *new* knowledge. So, of what relevance was it to ask students what they thought about their teachers? This will just keep them in a state of dependence, on those teachers; the exact opposite of what they needed.

Lotte pulled out her notebook and drew a lightbulb in the middle of the page; then draw a line from it and wrote 'in-dependence' at the end; then 'Carl Rogers' underneath. She drew another line and wrote 'what we don't know'; then wrote 'von Humboldt - check with Jos'. Then one more line, with 'engagement' at the end. She looked at the emerging mind-map and thought, that's it, that's what's wrong with the NSS questions: they are asking questions about the *consumption* of knowledge; not about how students might develop new knowledge. What we should be asking students is not how good staff have been at doing things *to* them - *for* them - but how independent have students become *from* them. Lotte smiled as she closed the notebook, drank what was left of her coffee, looked at her watch, and then headed back to the front of the garden centre, where she had seen bunches of freshly cut flowers.

***

Carol and Lotte hugged on the doorstep.

'Lovely to see you, Lotte, and still blonde, I see. And you needn't have bought me flowers, but, wow, they're beautiful. Come in, come in. Follow me into the kitchen. The lunch is ready.'

'And great to see you, Carol. How are *you*? You look well.'

'You know I'm bloody 60 this year. 60; what the hell.'

'Well, I'm nearly 40 now.'

'Let's not dwell on that. Look, I've got the table laid outside. You sit down and I'll bring things through. It's just a salad and some bread.'

'Lovely, thank you. Margie not here?'

'She apologises. Her brother has come across from Canada at short notice, so she's in Bristol with her family this weekend.'

'How is she? Everything good?'

'She's fine and so are we. We've had some ups and downs over the last year, but we're still hanging on in there, as they say.'

'That doesn't sound that great.'

'I'll tell you later. Let's eat. Glass of Prosecco? Don't say no, I got it specially.'

'Okay, go on then. But only one. Got the car with me.'

After lunch, they sat in the two deck chairs that Carol had put out on the grass.

'So, Lotte, tell me more about these courses you don't like.'

'As I was saying in the email, they're these new, so-called, interdisciplinary courses, helping students to navigate the modern world, or some such talk.'

'The very fact you said "so-called" tells me you still want to distance yourself from them.'

'It's the woman question again, I suppose. What is the knowledge *for*? Are we trying to tell people how to be...or worse...to make people feel good about themselves? Should we be *telling* people *anything*?'

'Is there such a thing as feminist knowledge, black knowledge, queer knowledge... different from white straight male knowledge?'

'Precisely. You know where I stand. We must surely still be able to speak of some knowledge that's untainted by the position of the speaker, otherwise the foundation for the university is severely weakened. Maybe I'm not a feminist?'

'Feminisms or one feminism?''

'Quite. But I think the problem here is that the rationale for these new courses hasn't included any serious epistemological debate. Take 'social justice'...the latest course proposed. Does it exist, in the sense of being detached from value judgements? What one person may see as social justice, another person may see as a restriction on freedom, or political correctness gone mad, and so on.'

'But couldn't such a course actually teach us that social justice *is* a value judgement, and all that follows from that? That legal systems reflect deeper questions about right and wrong?'

'Yes, of course, but I don't believe the aim of these courses is to do that. I haven't looked at the course outline for the social justice course...it's not been validated yet, but I did look at the one called The Environment, and its littered...excuse the pun... with statements on people's duties to clean up the environment. As if it's now a closed question; on what needs to be done.'

'Tricky, yes. But you're beginning to sound like one of those climate change deniers.'

'But that's the point, in a way. Somebody who denies that the climate is changing will probably have a vested interest...in the oil industry, for example...but similarly, what's to say that a environmentalist won't have a vested interest...in promoting vegetarianism, say...without any solid evidence that this is what *must* be done. There's no must; is there?'

'Well, you can probably guess what I'm about to say. That this is where universities are muddled. They see themselves as depositories for, so-called, universal knowledge, but they are...in reality...riddled with particularistic knowledge. That's why I never wanted to work in one. Knowledge *is* political. If it's not, what's the point of it? We want to make the world a better place. So called, academic knowledge, is precisely that...*academic*...as in, without impact.'

'"So called"...that phrase again? And nice pun there...*in reality*? Surely, there *is* something universal underneath the particularistic knowledge, otherwise we're on the slippery slope to postmodernity; no truths, just perspectives?'

'Or, a world of positions: Here is my position, which I'm not going to pretend is anymore than that, and I am asking you to respect it...Another glass of Prosecco? Or do you want some water? I'll get it; you stay there.'

On Carol's return, Lotte took a sip of water: 'I suppose one way to put it is that there are now many axes of knowledge competing in universities, but our job still remains to sort the opinions...the *doxa*...from true...*epistemic*...knowledge. Everything is a footnote to Plato, sort of thing. I suppose I do still want to sift out the knowledge that has vested interest behind it, the position knowledge, the life-affirming knowledge...important stuff, okay...but not the sort of knowledge that should be in a university.'

'Okay, well that suits me, because all the action will then be on the streets, with universities just becoming redundant places.'

'I suppose what I really don't like is students being told *what* to think; what to think *about*, maybe. Perhaps we should make it clearer that universities are about teaching people *how* to think, not what to think. The ontological position...the type of person...is drawn from the epistemological position...If I'm honest, I suppose I'm still bit angry about an argument I had with one of my colleagues...a participant on my course for new academics. I think there are some deep questions here, and I wish my place would debate them...*properly*.'

'I still think the real battle of ideas is much more likely to happen *outside* a university, these days. They *are* Ivory Towers, surely; almost by definition?'

'Well, not my place, clearly.'

They looked at each other, smiled, then sat back in the sun.

'Are you happy, Lotte?'

'Is that a philosophical question?'

'I'm just thinking about how much you said you were enjoying your new job last time you were here. And you were still with Peter, then. Do you still see him at all?'

'To be honest, I dread seeing him on campus. That was such a fucking awful break up. I can't even think about it.'

'Sorry, I didn't mean to dredge things up.'

'That's okay. I *have* got some distance now. At least, I think I have...I can certainly choose 'em, can't I? Violent Stuart; Non-committal Jack; Possessive Peter. You've been lucky with Margie. You seem happy?'

'Contented...reconciled...they would be better words. We've had our moments; good and bad. We've been able to talk things, though. I don't so much *need* her, but I do still want her. She was honest enough to say that she fancied other women and we now have that in the relationship. I don't mind; I really don't. I just say to her: Don't you dare go off with them. Come back to me. So far...so good.'

'Interesting; that's very honest, Carol....Actually, I've not told *anyone* what happened with Peter.'

'And you don't need to say anything now.'

'I do want to say something, though. I don't think I've properly processed any of it; just tried to forget it...You know he had two children with his wife? He saw them a lot and I was happy with that; just not that happy to be there with him when he saw them. Clearly, his kids didn't like me. He said he hoped we would have a child of our own, and because I didn't want to hurt his feelings, I said yes, maybe. But then I got pregnant.'

'Lotte?'

'I had an abortion. I didn't tell him. I couldn't tell my mother. I couldn't tell anyone. As the months went by I became wracked with guilt; not something I'd ever really felt before; lapsed Catholic girl, maybe. He started to become really needy; started seeing less of his kids, and asking if we could keep trying for a child. I got pregnant again; I had a miscarriage. I was in the hospital, feeling weak and I fainted when I got out of bed. I came round with the doctor explaining that I needed to rest. I asked him whether the fact I'd had an abortion might have caused the miscarriage. He then asked when I'd had the abortion. I told him, and then...right at that moment... Peter appeared at the door. Fucking hell; it was like something from a film...Time stood still...Then he disappeared. We never spoke about it...He *must* have heard. I kept telling myself that he disappeared because he could see I was talking with the doctor. Fuck, what a nightmare.'

Carol got up from her deckchair and Lotte lent forward to receive her embrace.

'That's tough, Lotte…really tough. I can see why you didn't tell anyone.'

'I wanted to tell my mother, particularly when I moved in with her. At the time, I was desperate to move in with her; a safe nest, and all that. I'd look at her across the dinner table, but never said anything. Just the thought…that I might banish *her* to hell.'

They both stood up. Lotte excused herself and went to the bathroom. She returned after a few minutes.

'Carol, don't let me near that Prosecco.'

'You can stay over, if you want.'

'Thanks. I don't have any overnight stuff with me, and I agreed to go out with Mum for dinner tonight.'

'Well, look, let me get the kettle on. Let's have some tea and cake.'

'Cake! Yes please.'

Carol returned after a few minutes, and placed the tray on the small wooden table between the deckchairs.

'Maybe Jack was the best of the three?' Lotte said. 'Maybe commitment is not for me.'

'Maybe, maybe not. *Que sera, sera*, Lotte.'

'I certainly haven't felt like having any sex lately.'

'More tea, vicar?' Pat said. They laughed, and sat back again in the sun.

Lotte left Carol's house just after 5.30, hoping that the motorway would be kind again. As she pulled away, she waved to Carol, and then glanced up at the window of her old room. She'd had no intention of telling Carol about Peter. No conscious intention, certainly. Instead of putting on the CD player again, she was happy for Doris Day to be ringing out in her head. Maybe I could squeeze in another trip to see Milton before Germany, she thought. Dear, dear Milton; he'll make sure everything turns out all right. She thought of herself on top of an Alpine mountain, and started singing lines from the Johnny Nash song *I can see clearly now.*

Chapter 12

The first Faculty Research Committee meeting of the new term was set for the 5th of October. On his computer screen Jack Lowell could see the email invitation with its agenda attachment. He was in two minds as to whether to open it because of the meeting he'd attended the previous afternoon. He had been invited to meet with Rachel Campbell-Martin, along with all the other research cluster leaders. The six of them had been told that Professor Wadhurst's REF preparation proposals had now been agreed, and, as a courtesy, they were being given the heads-up before the agenda was sent out. Agreed by whom, Jack thought. Right at the outset of that meeting, unable to bite his tongue, he had asked Rachel where exactly this had been agreed. Her claim that it came from the VC sounded like an attempt to shut down the conversation. Jack followed up by asking whether a potential decrease in the quality of teaching and learning had been raised by anyone, and what steps might be taken to monitor this. Jack could see that Rachel was visibly annoyed, and because nobody in the room had stepped up to support him, he reluctantly backed down.

'Bloody cowards,' Jack said out loud, as he walked back to his office. Unless they all thought it was a good idea. Certainly Dr Jim fucking Cripps. 'Been trying to give up teaching for years!' Cripps had made the comment to Jack a few days after Wadhurst's first mention of the idea. Every time it came back into Jack's head, he rehearsed what he should have said at the time: Have you never heard of von Humboldt; would you rather the University didn't have any students'; why do even work here, if you don't like students?

Back in his office, Jack looked at his computer screen. His eyes could only see one thing: the name 'CHARLOTTE RUDOLPH'. He clicked on the subject box: 'How are you?'

Hi Jack,

Hope this email finds you well, and that you managed to get a break over the summer. I went to Germany with my mother, to see relatives, and then on to do some walking in the Alps. I spent quite a bit of time thinking again about that question of quality in higher education, and I wondered if I might pick your brains? I appreciate that you will be very busy. Happy just to hear your news if that is the case.

Lotte

Hi Lotte,

How lovely to hear from you. Yes, definitely. A few things have happened over here recently which relate to quality. How are you fixed? I could meet this Friday afternoon or next Monday afternoon. If that's too short notice, give me some dates.

Yes, I did manage to get away. I did some cycling in France. Will tell you more when we meet.

Jack

Jack re-read his email several times. He had removed the reference to Provence, in case it brought back bad memories for Lotte, and then added a modified last sentence because, without it, the email sounded a bit perfunctory. He clicked 'send', and then sat back with his feet up on his desk. He hoped for a Friday meeting: it would be a confirmation that she really did want to meet up with him. 'Lotte, Lotte', he whispered to himself. He had spent a good deal of time on his bike in Provence thinking about getting back with her, but reconciling himself to the fact that it was unlikely to happen.

Lotte and Jack agreed to meet at The Friend's Meeting House in Euston at 4pm the following Monday.

***

Jack was relieved when he saw her walk into the cafe. He always imagined her with dark hair and was a little disappointed when he saw the blonde hair again. Slightly longer, he thought; it suits.

'Hey, Lotte', Jack said as she approached him. 'So good to see you.' He hugged her, but then wondered if he had held on a bit too long: 'Do you want to sit in the courtyard? I think it's warm enough.' Jack then pointed the way.

'Okay, good,' she said.

'You go through. I'll get the coffees. Still a black Americano?'

'Yes, please.'

A few minutes later, Jack appeared through the doors, and headed across to the wooden table, from which Lotte was waving.

'So, Lotte Rudolph.'

'So, Jack Lowell.'

'Hey, it's really good to see you. Looks like we've both got quality issues then?'

'What's happening at your place, Jack?'

'Some new bloody professor; thinks he knows everything about the REF. He's decided that everyone who is research active shouldn't be teaching.'

'Really?'

'Yes, really. He says it's just in the run up to the REF submissions, but nobody believes that. He's also got this strict view on how and where we should publish, to maximise our chances of success. Yes, you can call that quality, but that's all you're doing…just *calling* it quality. What's happening at your end?'

'They want to cut my course down to size. You know, the one for the new academics. The aim now is to get everyone teacher trained, but the actual training doesn't matter, so long as people are recorded as trained. And, get this: they want the course to be aligned with the National Student Survey questions. It's a bloody joke. The more I read about that survey the more angry I get.'

'I've heard of it, but haven't had anything to do with it.'

'It's the survey that undergraduates complete, where they comment on their whole university experience. All the questions are about what's been done *to* them... not what they've done for themselves. It's anti-HE as far as I can see. About as far from quality as you can get.'

'Well, I suppose it fits with the idea of students as consumers...look what I bought, and look what I got for the money.'

'Exactly, Jack. I was hoping you would say that. But I *have* found this American survey, the NeSSE: the National Survey of Student Engagement. It sounds good, but I can't find a copy of the actual questions.'

'Interesting. We should look into it...I'm really in the dog house at my place for speaking out about the lack of attention being given to students. And right at the point where they are being expected to pay £9,000 for the privilege; the privilege of what? Being taught by postgraduate students?'

'I think there might be a double irony there, Jack. The students *are* being short-changed, yes, but the postgraduate students at my place take their teaching really seriously. Much more seriously than some of the full-time academics. Some of the worst teachers at my place seem to be the professors. Best they are kept away from students, don't you think?'

'Like the old definition of a lecture...talking in someone else's sleep?'

'So, the same old question again...What do we do? What *can* we do?'

'Well, we could leave, I suppose.'

'Or we could start a fight back, with some articles on true quality?'

'That reminds me of the Woody Allen line, when the guy says there have been some good anti-racist articles in *The New York Times* recently, and he replies by saying that baseball bats might be more effective. I'm a hypocrite though, because I've got to get two more articles published, where I have to demonstrate the impact of my research, and in a prestigious journal.'

'What would happen if you just said no?'

'I'd end up *only* teaching, probably. Hobson's choice.'

'*I* could write something, I suppose,' Lotte began. 'I'm not under any pressure to produce something for the REF; that itself says something about the lack of quality in my place...professional development isn't considered academic enough to be even thought about in terms of the REF. Two notions of quality all the time.'

'There's something bonkers and perverse here. Much as I'd like to to write an article...maybe a joint authored one with you...what I'd actually be doing is harming my university's chances of doing well in the REF. Even if what we wrote was brilliant.'

'We're decreasing quality in the name of increasing quality.'

'Which brings us neatly *to*...' Jack hanged on the last word, then continued. 'the fact that we never *did* pin down what we meant by quality. I think we should start up that conversation again.'

'I'm up for it, definitely.'

'How about we go back to our old postcards and pick up the story from there?'

'I got them out a while back, actually...for some inspiration. Strike while the iron's hot;...what about this Friday afternoon?'

'I *am* free then. Meet here again?'

'Why not.'

Chapter 13

Lotte looked at her watch: 2.15pm. She had agreed to meet Jack in an hour's time. She tidied up her desk and sent her final emails for the week. She looked across at the envelope containing her old quality postcards from Jack. Maybe their discussion just might reignite something more between them. The last few months had helped to put things in perspective. I don't need anything from Jack, but I want him, she said to herself. If nothing happens, so be it. She took one last look at her email inbox before shutting down her computer. 'Fuck,' she said out loud. 'Not another one.' She'd now had three emails from colleagues in the same week, all excusing themselves from the PGCert course on the grounds that they had decided to apply directly to the Higher Education Academy for their teaching fellowship status. And that was on top of the four emails from colleagues in the Faculty of Education, who were claiming that they were already teacher trained by having worked in schools. Those particular emails were all in quick succession, indicating that the Dean of Education must have decided on a veto of the PGCert course for his staff. Time to get out of here, she thought.

Lotte and Jack bumped in to each other by the zebra crossing on the Euston Road, outside Euston Station. Jack had pulled up at the crossing on his Brompton, just as Lotte was about to cross the road. They hugged while Jack was still astride his bike.

'Good to see you, Lotte. I've been riding up here fucking furious.'

'Why?'

'Let's get across.'

On the other side of the road, Jack continued: 'I was called in to see my Dean of Research earlier, and she asked me if I wanted to give up my role as leader of my research cluster.'

'Cluster?'

'Just the stupid name they give to the various research groups in the Faculty. I said "no", to which she said that I might feel more comfortable just concentrating on the research. She then gave me some old guff about how I showed great promise for the REF, but I took it that she wants me out of the role, in order to put in someone who is more compliant. Someone she can manage.'

'Well, you are pretty unmanageable, Jack?'

'What do you mean?'

'No, that's a good thing; in my book, anyway.'

'Let's get inside; shall we?'

They made their way out to the courtyard, where they had sat before. It was busier this time, so they perched on the end of one of the benches, with the permission of the other two people who were at the other end.

'Here are my cards,' Jack said, as he placed them on the bench. 'I'll get the coffees.'

When he returned, he could see Lotte's cards in a pile next to his.

'Gin Rummy,' he said as he sat.

'Sorry?'

'Gin Rummy. The card game, or did I say it wrong?'

'I thought you were asking if I wanted a gin, as in the drink. I wouldn't say no to that.'

'Tough day for you as well?'

'Yeh, more shit. I've got colleagues dropping like flies from my course. How are we supposed to enhance the quality of teaching and learning if people don't engage. It's all a fucking game again.'

Lotte looked into Jack's eyes. She wanted him to hold her.

'Well, maybe it's time to start playing a different game. We could create some new rules and ask people to join *us*?'

'Or we could just say fuck the lot of you?'

'Yeh, we could do that as well.'

Lotte reached across to hold his hand. He ran his other hand over her wrist, then said: ' Do you want to go and have that gin?'

'But you don't even like gin, do you?'

'Who knows, maybe I will. New things, and all that.'

Back out on the Euston Road, Jack turned to face Lotte: 'Shoot me down if this is a bad idea, but do fancy a trip to the seaside?'

'You mean Brighton?'

'Why not? I could really do with getting out of town.'

'Okay.'

She reached across to hold his arm, feeling aroused. He moved his face so their noses touched.

'But I will need to get back.'

'Let's cross that bridge later.'

***

Jack unfolded his bike outside Brighton Station: 'It's easier to wheel it rather than carry it. Welcome to sunny Brighton; well, not so sunny at the moment. We'll be at the flat in about fifteen minutes. I have a sea view; a sideways one, anyway. We can walk down to the beach once I've dropped the bike off.'

Inside the flat, Jack pointed to the front room: 'Sit down. I'll just plonk this stuff in the bedroom.'

Lotte walked into the front room and looked out of the large bay window. She assumed that Jack was tidying up the bedroom: 'You in there tidying up!' she shouted.

'Just slipping into something more comfortable!' he shouted back.

Jack reappeared in the front room a couple of minutes later.

'Well, I certainly like the new flat, Jack. And I can see that your cleaning standards show a remarkable degree of consistency…consistently poor.'

'Glad you disapprove,' he said, while approaching her.

They hugged by the fireplace.

'Can I use the loo,' Lotte said.

'Of course, just out there.'

Lotte sat on the loo. Well, I wanted to be here, and now I am, she said to herself. She smelt the skin on her arm, hoping it smelt like it used to. She hadn't sprayed on any perfume that morning. She checked her face in the mirror, pulled some pieces of hair around, and decided not to bother with any lipstick. She walked back into the front room.

'Do you want a tour of the flat?' Jack said. 'It'll take 30 seconds.'

'Why not…Show me what you got.'

'I lost a bedroom because I couldn't afford two, but it's big and it doubles up as an office.'

Lotte looked across at the duvet. It looked like Jack had just thrown it over the bed. She turned to face him. He pushed her back slightly so her backside was against his desk, and moved his nose back and forth against hers.

'I thought we were going to the seaside,' she said.

'I thought we might have a splash around here first. What do you think?'

'I think you should fuck me, Jack.'

Chapter 14

Lotte opened her eyes to see that the room was bright. The curtains were open and the bedside clock read 8.57am. She could hear Jack in the kitchen. Their clothes were on the floor alongside the remains of the evening's Chinese takeaway. She put her head under the duvet to see if she could smell him, then put her head back down on the pillow. A couple of minutes later Jack appeared by the bed, naked, but for an apron, and carrying a tray of toast and coffee: 'For you, Madame,' he said. 'We had dinner in bed, so why not breakfast.'

'Thank you kindly, sir.'

'After breakfast, I thought we might stay in bed awhile. How do you feel about that?'

'I feel very good about that.'

The next time Lotte looked again at the bedside clock it read 10:13.

'You know what this means, Jack Lowell,' she said, as she turn to face him.

'No, what does it mean?'

'That I will be wearing some of your underwear again today.'

'Ah, Lotte. I thought you would never ask. And can I wear yours? If I promise to be good?'

'Only if you promise to be bad.'

'I was thinking, perhaps we might take a walk out along the pier this morning. What do you think?'

'Sounds lovely, but reassure me on one thing.'

'Oh yeah, what's that?'

'That I *did* phone my mother last night?'

'What, to ask her whether you were allowed out to play. Yes, you definitely rang her.'

'I just had this weird dream that my mother was in the front room, while we were in here.'

'Do you want me to check?'

'No, definitely not. If she's there, she can stay there.'

'You go in the shower first. I'll get some shirts and underwear.'

'Don't forget that you've shrunk and I've got bigger.'

'Doesn't show.'

'Idiot. Don't try to flatter; you're hopeless.'

'Thanks for your feedback. Sounds like the response I got to my latest paper.'

Lotte reappeared in the bedroom to see Jack laying out his quality postcards on the desk.

'Thought we might take a look at these *before* we go out?'

'And there was me thinking you just wanted my body.'

'Love that shirt on you and the tee-shirt underneath. What did you think of the underwear?'

'Good fit, actually.'

'Now, if we could just get your hair back to black again.'

'You don't like the blonde look, then?'

'It's not that. I just think of you with dark hair.'

'Any other requests?'

'I'll think about it while I'm having a shower.'

Jack picked out some clean clothes and went to the bathroom. Lotte looked at the postcards on the desk. One by one, she turned them over to see the images: *Nude Saraswati; (You Are Not Yourself); Madonna; Red Canna*. She smiled, thinking about how good they looked together, as four quadrants. She also liked their sensual quality, and she thought back to how she had teased Jack with them. She turned round to look at Jack's bed, and the mess which still surrounded it. Life is sweet, she thought. She then reached down to her handbag to pull out the postcards he had sent her. She thought about the order they were sent, then laid them out, one under the other, with her cards next to them; all quotation-side up. She stood back to see if anything stood out. Jack's handwriting certainly looked neat; much neater than what was scrawled on the post-it notes on his desk.

Jack came back into the bedroom, rubbing his hair with a towel. He looked at the quotations, then read out loud the one in the top left hand corner. Lotte reciprocated by reading the one next to it. They continued to the end:

> "A liberal education…will be characterised by its capacity to liberate pupils from the pressures of the present and the particular…it will also embody a concern for activities, with mental and physical, that are valued ends rather than, or at least as well as, valued instruments - Charles Bailey."

> "A person who sees Quality and feels it as he works is a person who cares. A person who cares about what he sees and does is a person who's bound to have some characteristic of quality - Robert Pirsig."

> "Education is not an object (a mass of knowledge or information or skills) which can be unambiguously handed from the teacher to the student. Education is rather an activity of mind, a particular emotional and critical orientation towards experience - Peter Abbs."

> "…it is by being interpellated within the terms of language that a certain social existence of the body first becomes possible…to be addressed is not merely to be recognised for what one already is, but to have the very

term conferred by which the recognition of existence becomes possible - Judith Butler."

"Only science and scholarship which come from the depths of the mind and which are cultivated only at those depths can contribute to the transformation of character - Wilheim Von Humboldt."

"Nothing about the way I was trained as a teacher really prepared me to witness my students transforming themselves - bell hooks."

"The pupil is…"schooled" to confuse teaching with learning, grade advancement with education, a diploma with competence, and fluency with the ability to say something new - Ivan Illich."

"I have come to feel that the only learning which significantly influences behavior is self-discovered, self-appropriated learning - Carl Rogers."

'What stands out for me,' Lotte began, 'is the transformative element every time. A good education will make you a different kind of person. I suppose you could say that this is where the quality is, in the transformation.'

'But…it's also an intrinsic experience. Effort is not expended for a purpose other than what is contained in the immediate. It's the educational experience itself which is transformational.'

Jack pointed at the Charles Bailey quote.

'That's good, Jack. There's the issue for me. Not only is the modern university not understanding *what* the quality is, but also *where* it is. It doesn't reside in the mark or grade you get for a piece of work, or what you can now *do*, but rather in your disposition…I suppose…or your orientation, as Abbs put it. That's what I don't like about these new courses at my place…they're too focused on *what* you should know or be, rather than the nurturing critical judgement. Does that make sense?'

'Certainly. And that orientation needs to be clearly owned by the student.'

Jack pointed at the Carl Rogers card: 'Self-appropriated…'

'…and with a clear sense of agency.'

Jack then pointed at the von Humboldt quote: 'And with a clear sense of a student not being *given* knowledge, but knowing how to develop it, produce it - *wissenshaft* - scholarship.'

Lotte pointed at the Ivan Illich quote: 'To be schooled means to be told things… to be educated means to undo that.'

Jack pointed at the von Humboldt quote again: 'Schools are different from universities, or they should be. I'm sure von Humboldt says that. The word *higher* in higher education should *mean* something. It's not *more* schooling; it should be a completely different type of experience.'

'It subverts,' Lotte said. 'It undoes, and redoes.' She pointed at the Judith Butler quote: 'It creates the potential to see that the world…your identity…as constructed, and which can be *re*-constructed.'

'Now you sound like a sociologist, Rudolph.'

'And you're beginning to sound more like a philosopher, Lowell.'

Jack pointed at the bell hooks quote: 'Seriously, we should be *shocked* by our students. Shocked at their new found sense of agency. That they know how to change their worlds.' He pointed at the Charles Bailey quote again: 'That they are not confined by the present and the particular.'

Lotte pointed at the Robert Pirsig quote: 'You know, the more I think about his *Zen* book, the more I think he was really on to something; something quite simple, really: that when you are truly invested in something…that's where the quality resides…that there is something of *you* in whatever you are doing; it's a distinctly human quality; a dynamic quality, as he put it.'

'I've been reading that book, because of you. I can see that, but I keep getting bogged down in the argument somewhere. Maybe, it is that simple. Or am I missing something, somewhere?'

'Let's not get distracted. It is that simple idea that's important, I think. We're not doing a doctorate on Pirsig, are we? If we were, we'd have to read the follow-up book, *Lila*; where he more fully explores the distinction between dynamic and static quality. I didn't make it very far with that one.'

'You mean there's more!'

'Yes, and an irony, I think. If we become students of Pirsig, there's a distinct danger we would start looking at his work as our bible…as a manual…which we would have to keep checking. The exact opposite of what he's arguing! That would be to arrest the dynamic quality, and make it static…a set of rules to be followed.'

'Taking us backwards…back to everything that's currently wrong in universities.'

'True quality is never learnt from a manual; it's not a set of techniques.'

'Fuck. That's profound, Rudolph. My Haynes manual will show me how to change a spark plug, but not speak to the creative spark.'

'And that's not bad from you, Lowell, or is that straight from Pirsig?…For me, I'm beginning to see the term "student engagement" as our key term. To be truly *engaged* in something does have that dynamic quality; to be invested in something; to be in that creative space…this is transformational. It's not a static stance…not students as receivers of someone else's knowledge, but as creators of their own knowledge.'

'Student as producer, rather than consumer of knowledge.'

'Hey, that's good as well, Jack.'

'Not me. Credit where credit is due. I read it in a chapter by Mike Neary and Jos Winn…where they talk about students seeing themselves as *producers* of knowledge. It's the anti-dote to student as consumer. Truly *higher* education students.'

Jack walked across to the window: 'The sun is out. Shall we take that walk? I think we're actually getting somewhere, Rudolph.'

They walked down towards the seafront, crossed the main road, then headed east towards the Palace Pier. Lotte looked back across the road: 'I think I stayed in that hotel; The Old Ship Hotel.'

'When was that?'

'Oh, years ago. My father was giving a conference paper and we came with him for the weekend. I'm sure that's where we stayed.'

'It's funny to think we could have bumped into each other back then.'

'Except I would have been about thirteen at the time, and you would have been twenty. Not a good look, even back then.'

'No, good point. And I was at university at the time, anyway. Let's go down to the beach. Do you fancy fish and chips for lunch? We could sit on the beach.'

'Nice. Should you being eating fish?'

'Probably not, but it's a simple pleasure. And as Woody Allen once said, the sea is a great big restaurant, anyway; all the fish eat each other, so why shouldn't we join in?'

'It's a good job I'm not a raving feminist, Lowell. If you keep quoting Woody Allen you'll be liable to get your balls cut off.'

'Another good point. And one of the reasons I love you.'

'What, because I'm not a feminist?'

'No, because you not a raving one.'

'Idiot.'

'Pier first, then back here for lunch?'

'Sounds good.'

They walked through the entrance and onto the pier.

'I like coming here to think.' Jack said. 'I often find myself thinking about you here.'

'Dirty thoughts, I hope.'

'Of course. But also clarity of thought. You know, those moments when you empty your mind, and creative thoughts just seem to flow...with ease.'

'Sounds a bit Buddhist, Lowell. But it does connect with engagement, doesn't it? Those moments when you are in the moment... if that doesn't sound daft.'

'What sports people call "in the zone". It's a sublime moment, yes?'

'That's a coincidence; I was thinking about the word sublime a while back. It's a good word. It implies a kind of qualitative state. It's something beyond description... beyond measurement.'

'That's good, Lotte; really good. I'm thinking about that Pirsig quote again... there's something sublime there; you *feel* quality; it's that moment when you are so connected with what you're doing...that a kind of calmness takes over...Can you imagine reading about that in a university quality manual?'

'But there's *the* problem, Jack: a quality manual; it's the ultimate oxymoron.'

'You're right; if you've got a manual, you ain't got quality. Well, not the dynamic quality we've been talking about.'

'But I also think it's one of the reasons that Pirsig was never taken seriously by the community of philosophy scholars. There's too much mysticism in there.'

'I can see the rabbit hole, and you're right: shouldn't people like us be able to resist the seduction? But on the other hand, what's so mystical about something we all kinda intuitively feel…when we're totally engrossed in something? In contrast to that undesirable need to *measure* the amount of quality. Important point; surely? The latter is a Western, logical, rational mind at work. And one apt to make you miss something fundamental about being human.'

'Bloody Hell, Lowell. Post-modern and Buddhist at the same time.'

'But there *is* something there, I think. *That's* what's wrong with the REF, and all that QAA stuff. A researcher…within a REF world…could never enter that qualitative state, because their motive for doing the work is tainted by extrinsic factors…what would make me look good in this exercise? That's not going to produce true quality, because it can't.'

'So…if we follow our logic…excuse my rational mind there, Lowell…what we *now* need to do is bring back together the student experience with the researcher experience.'

'To put back together what the QAA and the REF have pulled apart. It's scholarship…*wissenshaft*. It needs to be put back in the middle of the fulcrum. It's like we've got a see-saw which has lost its middle; there's no balance anymore; it's one or the other…research *or* teaching; not both things as two sides of one coin, operating with a single notion of dynamic quality…igniting creative sparks.'

'Careful, Lowell. You've got an army of mixed metaphors on the charge there.'

'But here's the problem, writ large at my place. The very people most equipped to instil a scholarly mindset in a student…the researchers…are the ones…currently…the most distant from the students. My place is actually the opposite of a university, from von Humboldt's perspective.'

'And that's precisely what's wrong with the National Student Survey again. The questions are perfect for a world where you are *not* encouraging scholarship. Just as the REF has created a world of research totally separate from the student experience, the NSS has done it from the other end of the see-saw, to use your metaphor. It's like higher education is currently fostering the *exact* opposite of what's on our postcards. We are currently living in a world which makes complete sense if you see the student as a *consumer* of knowledge. The National Student Survey is a *great* survey if…and only if…you persist in the belief that students are there to consume knowledge. If that's the case, then, of course, it's important to ask how good their teachers have been at doing things for them…*to* them.'

'Again, the exact opposite of what a university *should be*. We shouldn't be calling teachers to account, we should be calling students to account…to account for their progress in being scholarly.'

'But that can't happen in a consumer-oriented world. The customer is always right: I paid for this, and I have the right to make a university give me what I want.'

'It's become all rights and no responsibilities. It's now a case of what has the university done for me, not what have I done and given.'

'Sounds a bit Monty Python, Rudolph, but I know what you mean. I hesitate to offer another metaphor, but I heard this a while back and I liked it: going to a university should be considered like a gym membership…you only improve your fitness if you put the effort in…the gym provides the tools…the equipment…but it's you…the student…that has to use the equipment. The current system gives the impression that you are not fit because you got shortchanged by the gym instructors, but they're only there to facilitate your progress.'

'Not sure about the metaphor, Lowell, but it's very Carl Rogers…teachers as facilitators of student learning.'

'Hey, I forgot to tell you…I did a bit of work on that NeSSE questionnaire, that one for American students. One of my colleagues is American, Janet Schuster. She worked at an American university which used it. Apparently, you do pay to use it…to have the data analysed, I suppose…and it's voluntary. She wasn't sure how widely it was used, but I really liked the sound of it. It asks questions of students, like: *how much work do you do out of class; have you worked on a project with fellow students; do you discuss your work with your tutors?* Stuff like that. I looked at the NSS questions and you're absolutely right; they're all about what's been done *to* them, not what they've done for themselves. It's ironic; you'd think that the NSS would be the American survey…keep the customer satisfied, and all that…and the NeSSE would be the British survey…what have you done to help yourself.'

'We've got some good connections here, Jack.'

'Lunch? Then back to my place to take some notes?'

'Is that a euphemism? How *are* your etchings these days?'

***

Back at Jack's flat, they entered the bedroom.

'Smells like a Chinese restaurant in here, Lowell. You get the stuff off the floor and I'll tidy the bed.'

While Jack was in the kitchen, Lotte smelt the duvet before shaking it out.

'How do I open the window?' she shouted.

'I'll do it. It's very stiff.'

Jack re-entered the room holding a small tray with a cafetière of coffee, two cups, and biscuits: 'Let's work in bed,' he said, as he placed the tray on the bedside table.

'Okay with me,' Lotte replied.

Jack walked across to open the window, then took a pad and pen from the desk. He motioned to Lotte to get into bed.

'So,' Jack said, with his knees up under the duvet, 'how about we start with "student as producer" on a left column, and "student as consumer" on a right column?'

'Good. That fits nicely with the idea of making students accountable for their learning, not the teachers and the university.'

'Okay, so that's "student accountability" on the left column and "teacher accountability" on the right column.'

'And "active learning" on the left and "passive learning" on the right?'

'Which sounds a bit like Paulo Freire...the idea of banking knowledge; students being given someone else's knowledge rather than creating their own.'

'Okay, so we have "banking" on the right, but what on the left?'

'"Critical Pedagogy", I suppose. Knowledge which will help students transform their lives?'

'Which takes us back to Carl Rogers and "significant learning".'

'So what goes to the right of that: "inconsequential learning". Maybe "bookish learning", after John Dewey?'

'Nice.'

'We need von Humboldt in here. How about existing knowledge..."textbook knowledge"...on the right, and new knowledge..."*wissenshaft*"...on the right? Or, "what we know", versus "what we don't know".'

'Which then gives us "students as scholars" on the left, and "students as pupils" on the right. Sort of works.'

'Or how about "text-book knowledge" on the right, and "journal knowledge" on the left? To imply that what is currently in text books is being proven wrong in the journals. That's a good lesson for a higher education student, yes?'

'Okay, good.'

'We need the idea of "engaged learning" in there,' Jack said. 'But what's the opposite of that: unengaged learning?'

'How about "student engagement" on the left and "student satisfaction" on the right; to get across the idea that true higher learning is not about experiencing things, but being fully engaged?'

'And that is what opens the door into quality, yes?'

'Quality as personal investment in learning?'

'Perhaps personal investment in scholarship is better? That could then apply to students and staff, equally. But my table is now falling apart on me.'

'Good. Blokes love lists; women love to deconstruct them.'

'All right, Venus, steady on there. Shit, sorry, I didn't plunge the coffee. I'll make some more. Sit tight.'

Jack came back into the bedroom with the fresh coffee: 'You know what; I think I want to say that the REF hasn't just brought in this new idea of impact. It's always been there. The quality they are measuring has always been about impact; the impact that the research has had on the *receiver*. It says nothing about the actual experience of producing the research, because it can't. That's to do with the intrinsic motivation of the researcher; the integrity with which it was produced, if you like.'

'And there's the connection with Pirsig again. Impact measures do measure quality, but it's *static* quality; not the dynamic quality that was involved in the production or creation of the knowledge or research.'

'And ditto, students; yes? The motivation to produce a good assignment lies precisely in that motivation; the desire to do good work; for its own sake; not chasing the grade. To study with integrity? That's Pirsig, Rogers and Illich, all combined.'

'We need to look at that NeSSE in more detail, Jack. Surely that survey is much more likely to move students in the direction of producing good...true...*quality* work? NeSSE equates with dynamic quality; NSS with static quality. NeSSE propels students forwards, into the unknown; NSS takes them backwards, to check on what they were given.'

'Pushing them *beyond* the present and the particular, or keeping them *within* the present and the particular.'

'There you go, Lowell...you can now start a new table.'

'That's it, isn't it? The NeSSE questions will help students improve their learning; the questions have a kind of self-fulling prophecy about them. They will bring about more of what they are attempting to measure.'

'Would be better if we could ditch the word "measure" there, don't you think? We shouldn't really be trying to measure the amount; just try to get students to make the switch from a passive notion of consuming knowledge, into a more active, dynamic, realm of learning...of scholarship.'

'A different order of reality?'

'Very Plato, Jack. Inside every sociologist there's a philosopher trying to get out.'

'I need to read that book about the two cities.'

'What, Dickens?'

'No, Miéville. I think that's his name.'

'No white whales, I hope.'

'I'm probably not pronouncing his name correctly. Thomas Minot told me about it. You remember him? It's two sets of people occupying the same territory, but not acknowledging each other; a city within a city; something like that. I haven't read it, yet.'

'A university within a university? Two sets of people; one group trying to measure a static notion of quality with an emphasis on the consumption and receipt of knowledge, and the other group operating with a dynamic notion of quality; who are not trying to measure anything; just trying to help people make the leap. They don't recognise each other...they each speak a different language.'

'That's bloody good, Rudolph. Inside every philosopher there's a sociologist trying to get out. You know, thinking about it, there could be a variation here, on Basil Bernstein's speech code idea...where university academics, those who know there's something wrong...have got used to switching between the two languages... when they're under inspection surveillance, for example.'

'They have an inspection script? Do you remember when you mocked me for that?'

'Roger Fergusson told me to call that "disavowal": I knew you were right, but I didn't want to admit it to myself...Around that time, I also remember thinking about that Monty Python sketch on the Spanish Inquisition: sometimes you just mouth things, without really believing them...particularly when the stakes are high. I think that's what political correctness started to mean in Soviet times...if you wanted to avoid a stay in a salt mine, you just said what you thought you ought to say...the politically correct manoeuvre, if you like...Shit, shall we drink the coffee this time?'

They sat upright, drinking the coffee in silence. Lotte spoke first: 'When I was going through those NSS questions, it confirmed to me that the combined effect of them is to keep students in a state of dependence; on their teachers; on the university. The *what have they done for me, not what have I done for myself.* Students will never be free to learn with that mentality. The NSS is pointing them in the wrong direction, away from a truly qualitative experience. It's part of the new educational language...'

'...a marketised language...which you either believe in, or you mouth your way through, if the Quality Thought Police are on your back. But I suppose it does all makes sense if you inhabit that other order of reality? And, of course, the government is holding a trump card...taxpayers' money. The stakes *are* high. You can't have universities devising their own methods of accountability; that's the old days. Thatcher has a lot to answer for...and Blair, for that matter.'

'But wouldn't the taxpayer be better served by professional people acting with integrity, instead of playing fucking stupid games? And now that students are paying the full cost of their higher education, where *is* that taxpayer, exactly?'

'Slowing exiting stage left, I think...Would you work in a private university?'

'What made you say that, Lowell?'

'A conversation I had with Thomas Minot. He's trying to get some private funding to set up a training school. It got me thinking...what if *we* could get some private funding to set up something...along the lines we've been talking about?'

'In principle, yes; I'd go for it. But it would have to be on a secure footing. And wouldn't we *still* be accountable...to whoever is funding it?'

'You're right. It's just been on my mind lately. I do want State-funded universities, I suppose. I think that has to be my bottom line.'

'Because you're a Marxist, Lowell. The way I see it, the government of the day will dictate...to some extent, at least...what a university is for and how it will be made accountable. The same with a privately funded one. It's the lesser of two evils.'

'Private just doesn't sound right to me. It does sound more evil.'

'But...maybe...if it had sound principles; that might solve the problem?'

'We need to talk this through. I feel another table coming on. Do you fancy staying over, Lotte?'

'I fancy the loo, actually.'

Lotte sat on the loo. Why did he have to say that, she thought; I should have said something earlier. I need to go out with my mother; that would have to be the line. She walked back to the bedroom. Jack was sitting with his knees up and the writing pad back in place.

'Just looking over this again,' he said.

'I do need to get going shortly. This has been so lovely, but I'm due to go out to dinner with my mother this evening, and it's already four o'clock.'

'Could you cancel? *We* could go out for dinner?'

'It's tempting, but I've got a stack of work to do tomorrow.'

'Okay. If you're sure. I normally see my Dad on Sunday if I'm around. I'd like you to meet him.'

'Meet your father, Jack? That doesn't sound like you. Another time, if that's okay? I do need to get back.'

'Okay, I'll check the train times and walk you to the station. I do love you in my clothes. And those black tights you had on yesterday are really sexy. Will you wear them next time?'

'Sure. And I will expect you to have typed up our notes for next time.'

'Yes, Miss. And will I ever see you with your dark hair again?'

'Maybe. If you're naughty.'

'Definitely, Miss. And please wear your reading glasses while we're in bed.'

'Do you think the balance has maybe tipped so far that we couldn't get it back?'

'You mean us?'

'No, idiot. I mean, what is happening in universities? Don't you feel a bit like Jimmy Stewart…hanging from that gutter in *Vertigo*?'

'But doesn't vertigo imply paralysis? It's the status quo that's paralysing, surely? There's got to be a cure…that anti-dote?'

'That's true, I suppose. Now, promise me something. If I put my tights on, you won't try to take them off again.'

'How could I possibly promise that?'

Chapter 15

The rays from the sun were beginning to hit Jack's bedroom window. It was just before ten o'clock on Sunday morning. Jack sat with his coffee cup resting on his knees, wishing that Lotte had stayed over. He pictured walking along the beach with her and then up to his father's house. He put the cup down and put his head under the duvet to see if he could catch a hint of her. I need that woman in my life, he thought. He looked across to his desk, where the postcards were still laid out, then down to his notepad which was still on the floor. He made a mental note to contact Roger Fergusson and Norman Thornhill. He hadn't emailed either of them for nearly six months and all that talk of Carl Rogers and Wilheim von Humboldt made him think that a chat with either - preferably both - would be a good idea.

After breakfast, Jack turned on his computer. It was possible that Lotte had emailed him; there were no texts on his phone. But there was nothing. There was an email from Thomas Minot, though, sent yesterday:

Hey Jack,

How's tricks? There's been a very interesting development with our mystery man and I wanted to sound you out. I wrote to him to signal my interest in setting up some kind of entrepreneurial incubation unit. He wrote back saying that he would be happy to receive a formal proposal from me. He also said that he was in the process of negotiating to buy up two old college sites, one in Kent and one in the Midlands. I think he wants to get in quick before the developers. If he gets them, he says he wants to make them available, for co-operative initiatives like mine. He liked my training school idea, and he's now asking me about articulating a wider teaching and learning rationale. I could sure use your help. Let me know what you think. I'm really warming to this guy. Perhaps we could have a chat on the phone?

One Love, my friend

Thomas

Jack got up and walked across to his bedroom window, from which he could see a slice of the English Channel. Nice coincidence, he thought; maybe it would be worth trying to work up yesterday's notes into some kind of curriculum. He looked round at the bed and pictured Lotte sitting there. He then looked up at the box-files on the shelves above his desk. One of them had his notes from when he helped set up the co-op in Salerno. He remembered running a workshop there on critical theory and pedagogy, based on the work of Paulo Freire. Good starting point, he thought. He made a mental note to go through the files when he returned from his father's house. He looked at his watch; time to get moving.

After a shower, some toast and more coffee, Jack picked up his mobile phone from the bedside table. He needed to phone his father to confirm his arrival time. They normally had lunch in a pub. His father always liked to phone ahead to book a table, even though there were always plenty available. There was a text from Lotte:

Looking forward to the next time you…x

He smiled, and felt himself becoming aroused. He typed back:

And looking forward to the next time you…x

Jack had plenty of time to get to his his father's house, but he left early in order to wander along the beach for a while. There was hardly any wind and the sun was still shining. He imagined walking with Lotte, hand in hand, and looked forward to doing that the following weekend. He hoped that Lotte didn't have other plans, and that she wouldn't suddenly get cold feet. His mind wandered: he pictured himself sitting with Lotte in his father's front room, then arriving at Mondragon on a scooter, Lotte on the back seat with her arms around his waist. He found himself repeating the word 'Camelot' in his head, then saying it quietly out loud, in a Richard Burton, overly theatrical style. Why *not* try to set up something similar to Mondragon, he thought, or on similar lines, at least. This mystery man might well turn out to be an intellectual rather than just a business man; a rich philanthropist who wants to do the right thing. He started thinking through ideas for a teaching and learning regime. Quality will be everywhere, he thought, and nowhere; nowhere, because there would be no need to keep searching for it, or trying to measure it. No need at all.

As Jack approached the Palace Pier, lines from the tune *Hi Ho Silver Lining* were now spinning round in his head. Should I tell Thomas to hold back for a bit, he thought, while he and Lotte considered a more ambitious proposal? An enlightened Camelot in the heart of England; an anti-dote to A C Grayling College? It would be good to see what Roger and Norman had to say about it. Maybe the public-private issue *could* be reconciled in some way? Maybe this mystery man was some kind of champagne socialist? Would Lotte be seriously interested? Thomas could certainly get his training school, at least.

***

That evening, Jack sat with his feet on the coffee table in his front room. He wanted to call Lotte. She hadn't replied to his text from the morning. He decided to text her:

How about a repeat performance next weekend…x

He smiled to himself before sending it. It hit all the right notes, and just maybe, in the right order, he thought. A few minutes later, a reply:

Do you think you will able to rise to the occasion?…x

Jack took a deep breath and then let it go. She's definitely coming, he thought. He wanted to speak with her:

Is it okay if I ring you...x

Of course...x

'Good evening, Charlotte Rudolph. I wanted to hear your voice.'

'So, what you been up to today, Jack Lowell?'

'Just the visit to my father and some more thoughts about our postcards.'

'Yeah. I've been thinking about that too, and about your body.'

'I'm glad to hear it. Can we fix that date for next Friday? I've had an email from Thomas Minot. He's got a new proposition I think we should discuss.'

'And I've got a proposition I think we should discuss.'

'Friday at 4pm, then?'

'Okay, looking forward to it. I need to get off the phone because my mother has invited a couple of friends round for dinner and I said I would join them. It sounds like they've just arrived.'

'Okay. I'll email you some info about what Thomas has in mind.'

'And I'll text you some info about what I have in mind.'

Jack sat on his sofa, with his feet on the coffee table. A glass of red wine and some Simon and Garfunkel, he thought. The *Bridge Over Troubled Water* album. Perfect. He always kept that CD on his coffee table, along with their *Greatest Hits* and *Bookends* albums; for when he was in reflective mood. As he listened, he pictured Lotte harmonising from his bedroom, just as she had done the previous weekend.

Chapter 16

Lotte opened her eyes. The curtains in Jack's flat were still open from the previous evening. It looked grey outside, and she felt a little cold. She looked at the bedside clock: 8:08am. She could see that Jack was asleep, so she put her head down on the pillow and stared up at the ceiling. Only half-way through the term; depressing. But being with Jack again felt good. Except for that talk the previous evening about being a couple again. I want Jack, she thought, but I don't need to be a couple again. She thought about how the prospect of wild sex with Jack had kept her going throughout the week. Surely, Jack felt the same? His texts were pretty clear. But all the talk about spending Christmas and the New Year together; that didn't sound very appealing. 'Live for the moment, please, Jack Lowell,' she said to herself. She turned her head to look at him, then snuggled into his back. She kissed the back of his neck, hoping for a reaction from him. He whispered: 'Morning sexy' but didn't move. She lay still, against his warm back.

A little over an hour later, Lotte and Jack were sitting with their knees up in bed, drinking coffee.

'Were you serious last night, Jack; about trying to set up something new?'

'Sort of. I've been thinking about it all week. Pipe dream?...probably. But my place is really depressing me. It cheers me up when I think about trying do something which could really make a difference. Education, for a change.'

'That would be a good book title...I wish my place would really grasp the full implications of student engagement. Maybe that's the way forward?'

'Possibly, yes. But this split between research and teaching. The very thing that students need, surely, is to bring them back together again.'

Lotte turned to put her coffee cup on the bedside table: 'Hey, Lowell, how about we bring ourselves back together again?'

He put down his coffee cup and pulled the duvet over their heads.

The next time Lotte looked across again at the bedside clock it read 9.52am. Jack appeared to be asleep, so she tip-toed round the bed and into the bathroom. She sat on the loo, wondering if she should change her mind about going home later that afternoon. After a shower, she smiled when she saw her toilet bag and wondered about what message it might send if she left it there. Opening the bathroom door, she could hear Jack in the kitchen and could smell toast. She went back into the bedroom to get dressed. Jack appeared shortly after with a plate of toast and more coffee. 'I thought we might have a brunch in town, so, just something to keep us going.'

'Sounds good.'

'I was just thinking in the kitchen, that maybe I should contact Thomas and say that I will help him set up his training school, and we just leave it at, for now. I think it probably is a pipe dream to go any further.'

'I don't think we should dismiss the idea, Jack. I was a bit sceptical last night because it sounded just too grand. But now I've slept on it, maybe we *should* talk about it a bit more.'

'I did get a bit carried away last night. That's what you do to me. Maybe a curriculum centred on what we've been talking about might be enough. It doesn't have to be a new institution. It could work in an existing one, if we could persuade enough people.'

'I agree, but a totally new venture would be fun to *discuss*, at least.'

'But a private enterprise; that just doesn't sound right, to me.'

'But that's because you're a Marxist, Lowell. I keep telling you. You're still hung up on that public-private thing, aren't you?'

'You're right. But doesn't it worry you?'

'Not really. So long as we get the students we want, and have some more freedom. And if we have a Sugar Daddy then we could arrange that?'

'But I really don't know enough about this guy. I don't know how far we could take it. Maybe that's the problem.'

'How quick would you have to make up your mind?'

'Don't know. On the training school, probably quite soon, I would guess. I'll have to check with Thomas. Beyond that, who knows?'

'Are we just talking about helping to set something up or would we work there in some capacity?'

'Depends how we sell it, I suppose. You're right though, there's no harm in discussing ideas and seeing where they take us...I'll have a shower, and perhaps we could take a walk before brunch?'

On leaving the flat, they walked away from the sea, in the direction of town.

'There's a nice place to eat that I like, over by The Lanes,' Jack said. 'It's not a greasy spoon, more an up-market one.'

'Okay, sounds good.'

Lotte thought about the right moment to say that she needed to get home that day. She sensed that Jack would try hard to dissuade her. She *could* be dissuaded.

'I forgot to tell you, Jack, I've been invited to speak back at the old place.'

'Really? Are you going to do it?'

'At first I thought, no. But then I thought, why not? It's on student engagement and It will be a good chance to try out some ideas. Maybe include some of the things we've been talking about.'

'Could be interesting, I suppose.'

'Maybe the old place has changed?'

'I don't think so. Roger and Norman still seem pretty pissed off. You remember them? The psychologist and the historian.'

'Yes. Your old partners in crime. It always looked like the three of you were plotting something.'

'Probably because we were.'

'And Jos Conway is still there; my friend in Philosophy...And it's my birthday a few days later. But no, hang on a minute, why would you remember that?'

She turned to look Jack in the eyes.'

'All right; got me there.'

'You forgot that first year we met. And I told you just a few days before!'

'December...the...'

'18th, Lowell. The 18th!'

'Well, I certainly won't be forgetting this year. You know what this means...that we've known each other for twelve years.'

'Yeah...but we've been together for probably less than half of that.'

'Absence makes the heart grow fonder?'

'Keep trying, Lowell. Keep trying.'

Chapter 17

Jack sat at his desk in his flat. It was Wednesday afternoon and he was disappointed that he hadn't heard from Lotte. Maybe she's really busy finishing her article. He had lost interest in his own, except for the fact that he knew he needed to get it in the publication pipe line. He thought about publishing something with Lotte. He turned to his notepad to jot down a potential title for an article: 'Maximising Impact'; then a few half-sentences: 'Groundbreaking work could count for nothing if it wasn't published in a prestigious journal…How could you possibly predict an idea's impact?…It could languish in a very respectable journal; get cited; get quoted; but get nowhere…An opinion piece in *The Times Higher* might change the world…The first counts as research and the second only as penmanship…but it's still scholarly?'

Education for a change; yes, good book title, he thought; by Rudolph and Lowell. He turned to his computer and looked at his email inbox. There was an email from Thomas Minot:

Hey Jack,

Big thanks for your ideas. I put something together around building knowledge from the ground up. Thanks for that John Dewey idea of not making knowledge bookish. That's now my word of the month. And I'm all over that bildung idea. I've been reading about the German system, and the idea of character formation and professional pride. I've decided that it's not academic versus vocational, but revisiting what it means to have a sense of vocation. I'm pleased with what I put together. Couldn't have done it without you. I owe you a drink. Will let you know what I get back from the Man! If he likes it, I think we might be on for a meeting with him, if you're up for it? He has an office in Amsterdam. Could be a nice little trip for us!

Found a good book for you: The Craftsman, by Richard Sennett, one of your lot, I believe? Maybe you know it?

Get Up, Stand Up

Thomas

Maybe that should be my fourth REF article, he thought: connecting von Humboldt with the modern German vocational system? He re-read Thomas' email. He could hear Thomas' warm lyrical tone, and sensed a man loving the freedom to travel in the direction his ideas took him. He felt his own frustration and hit his fist on the desk. Where's my email from Lotte? He looked at his phone; no text either.

Jack turned to his post-it notes, and wrote 'The craftsman', as a reminder to order the book. He thought back to one of Sennett's previous books, *The Corrosion of Character*, and the idea that modern work, with its emphasis on team work, was just a sham. It doesn't build character, it corrodes it. Good connection there for Thomas, he thought. He turned back to Thomas' email again, which was still on the screen. He thought about his colleagues and wished there were a few more like Thomas and few less like James fucking Wadhurst, with his little army of student-hating arse lickers. Given that there had been no revolt at his place, Jack had concluded that most of his research colleagues either agreed with Wadhurst or were just too cowardly to say anything. At least there was Rosie. It would be good to sound her out a bit more. Except for that disastrous visit to her house recently. He decided to email Roger and Norman while it was on his mind.

Hi Guys,

Long time, no hear. Hope everything is okay with you and that you haven't been ground down too much. I'm under pressure here, because of the REF, and a new professor has been creating a bit of a stir.

I've been having some interesting conversations with Thomas Minot of late. He's doing well, and has presented me with a proposition. I would enjoy a conversation about it sometime. It's about the possibility of setting up some co-operative education initiatives. Maybe you fancy a trip down to the seaside before Christmas?

Best

Jack

After sending the email, Jack sat back, thinking about when he first got together with Lotte. He had no intention of forgetting her birthday this year. He knew it was around Christmas time, but he kept forgetting the actual date. '18th of December', he said out loud. He reached across to put the date on a post-it note, but stopped, in case Lotte saw it. He pictured himself travelling down to the old place with Lotte, then listening to her keynote. Her talk was on the last day of term, so it was definitely doable. Maybe he could suggest that to her? He looked at his watch: 2.37pm. If he worked straight through until seven o'clock, that should be enough time to get his article into some kind of shape.

***

Lotte checked her email inbox. She had just finished her slides for the keynote the following day, at the old place. That's come around fast, she thought. At the last minute she had changed the title from 'Enhancing Student Participation' to 'Rules of Engagement.' It sounded bolder; a little more aggressive. She looked back through her inbox to confirm the details for the presentation. It still had the old title; no matter; that could be explained. She wanted to check the time she was on: 2.15. She was billed as the afternoon keynote speaker, before the audience split off into smaller seminar groups. She checked the title for the whole event: Staff Development Symposium: enhancing the student experience. Good, she said to herself. It did say 'symposium' and not 'conference'. She remembered her father making great play of symposia as informal events and she wanted to emphasise that in her presentation; the idea of staff and students gathering informally to discuss pedagogical matters; more as equals rather than leaders and led. And, on the assumption there wouldn't be any students at the symposium, she could raise that question as well.

She smiled as she closed down the computer. Tomorrow was the last day of term and she had no need to come into the office the following week. She sat for a moment, thinking about what an awful term it had been. At least Jack had been something to look forward to each week, and she was glad that the two of them had finally agreed to travel down to the old place together, even though she had said no several times. She thought about him sneaking into the presentation, but knew he wouldn't dare. She then smiled again, as her thoughts turned to her upcoming trip to New York, on Sunday. It was her mother's surprise birthday present. She hadn't been to New York since graduating from university and the thought of several days there pleased her every time it popped into her head.

Lotte looked at her watch. Gone seven o'clock, already. She phoned her mother to say that she was running late. She had told Jack that she would ring him at six o'clock to confirm the arrangements for the following day but she decided to hang on until she got home.

'Hi Jack, sorry I'm so late ringing you. I got caught up in things.'

'I'm just glad to hear your voice. I was getting worried that you'd changed your mind about tomorrow.'

'Well, I will do if you start going on again about coming to my presentation. It's a definite no-no.'

'It's okay, you're safe. I've confirmed my meet-up with Roger and Norman, for two o'clock.'

'Good, I'm glad to hear it. I've also agreed to meet up with Jos Conway. I would say that I will be free around four o'clock.'

'Great. I've agreed to meet Roger and Norman off campus, so I'll walk back around that time.'

'We mustn't miss that train; I can't be late. I'll meet you at Paddington at midday.'

'I'll be there. I've agreed to meet my PhD student a bit earlier. She's flying to the States on Saturday morning so it suits her. No reason why I can't get there by 11.30, if you want.'

'No, midday is fine. I've got my ticket already. Make sure you get yours.'

Lotte put down the phone, wishing she'd already told Jack she was off to New York. Given his recent spate of suggestions for leisure pursuits for the two of them, she knew he was bound to be deflated by the news. But his suggestion that they spend Friday night in a hotel in London was one of his better ones. On the train to the old place could be the best time to tell him about New York.

Chapter 18

Lotte ran up the stairs from the Underground and onto the main concourse of Paddington Station, her overnight bag banging against her back. She looked up at the train departures board, then jogged over to the platform entrance. Jack was dutifully standing there, bag by his side.

'Sorry, Jack, I got caught up doing some things with my mother.'

'I was standing here thinking you weren't coming. Come on, we've only got a couple of minutes.'

They walked quickly down the platform and onto the train. They found seats opposite each other, dropped their bags on the floor, and caught their breaths.

'I did try to text but couldn't get a signal,' Lotte said.

'Don't worry, I'm just relieved to see you. And your hair; I'm transfixed.'

'Yeh, I decided to go back to black.'

'Glad to hear it. I love new Lotte…but I loved old Lotte…just as much.'

'You're a bad liar, Lowell.'

'Are you ready for your talk?'

'Think so. I thought I'd try out some of those ideas about student engagement and scholarship; that students being scholarly is really what it means to be engaged. I'm going to use that von Humboldt quote about staff and students needing to put themselves at the service of scholarship.'

'Like it. I'm going to sound out Roger and Norman on the co-operative initiatives. I can only think of one person at my place who I could talk to about it. I feel pretty isolated.'

'You and me both. Did I tell you that my debating HE seminars got cancelled?'

'It's Foucault at work again. People are definitely self-policing themselves these days. They're so used to toeing the line, they've forgotten they're doing it. It's like a politically correct world…not in a good way…where people have worked out what they can't talk about, so they don't. They don't even think about protesting.'

'And speaking of things we don't talk about…you haven't forgotten my birthday this time? Next Tuesday.'

'No, I haven't forgotten.'

'But which birthday is it, Lowell?'

'*Your* birthday?.'

'I know it's *my* birthday, but how old will I be? It's the big 4-0. I *knew* you didn't know.'

'That's because you don't look a day over thirty.'

'Idiot.'

'Blimey, Lotte. 40.' He lent across and whispered in her ear: 'You look as gorgeous as ever.'

'On this occasion, Lowell, flattery will get you everywhere.'

'Well, we certainly need to push the boat out. I suppose I'll have to start by cancelling that discount hotel booking I made for tonight?'

'Yes, you will.'

'I did think about booking us in to the Russell Hotel, after that conversation we had about how the Russell Group universities were opening up the split between teaching and research.'

'Is that really how they got their name?'

'It is. They had a meeting in that hotel and decided to form their club. That's it. They're excellent universities because they decided to call themselves excellent. It's very Max Weber...a mode of social closure; close off entry to others, in order to raise your own status.'

'So, do I take it that we are *not* staying there?'

'Unless we win the lottery in the next twelve hours, no. Anyway, even if I could have got a good deal there, it struck me that we needed to find our *own* hotel...be a bit subversive.'

'How about The Quality Inn, then?'

'Nice one, Lotte. I should have thought of that.'

'So where *are* we staying tonight?'

'It's supposed to be a surprise. I did think about booking a double-room in Goodenough College. Good-enough; such a brilliant name. Like an anti-dote to the Russell Group's elitism.'

'But there's no such place.'

'There is. It's also in Bloomsbury. I remember Thomas Minot telling me about, when some students came over from Ghana. They stayed there, I think.'

'So, you *thought* about it...meaning that we aren't staying there?'

'No...but we *are* staying in Bloomsbury, though. Nice little place, I think.'

'But is it excellent; does it have quality?'

'I think we're now fast entering a world where if you start attaching the word quality to something you are very likely to experience the exact opposite; a good reflection of the strange Orwellian world we currently inhabit. I was thinking recently...what we need is an organisation where, because quality is everywhere, it's also nowhere. You don't have to name it. You certainly don't need an office which keeps checking that it's still there. Of course it will be there because it's in the DNA. You can't lose it.'

'The Jeff Beck approach to quality, baby.'

'Precisely.'

'And you don't need to measure it; you've either got it or you haven't.'

'Precisely, again.'

***

'Give 'em hell,' Jack said, before kissing Lotte on the cheek.

He watched her walk off in the direction of campus, before he turned towards the town centre. He had plenty of time before meeting Norman and Roger, so he decided to take a stroll, to check out some old haunts. He tried to remember the last time he was in town; it didn't appear to have changed much. He thought about Richard McGiffen's widow and whether she had moved away. He walked past the coffee place where he used to meet up with Angela Salaman. He was pretty sure she was still working in Scotland. Across town, he was pleased to see the other coffee shop he used to go to and decided to have lunch there. It was the place he was due to meet up with Norman and Roger. Good, he thought, as he looked at his watch, plenty of time to take some more notes. He was still concerned about how they might receive his idea of setting up some kind of co-operative initiative. After buying a sandwich and coffee, he sat with his notebook, thinking over again what he might say, while he waited for his old friends to arrive.

'Hey guys,' Jack said, as Roger and Norman approached him.

He hadn't seen either of them for some time, but they hadn't changed much. Roger's beard was longer and Norman looked a little wider. Roger spoke first: 'I was just saying to Norman, do you remember that time we sat in here and tried to create that teacher education programme?'

'It sounds like you are being more ambitious this time,' Norman said.

'I think we might need a whole new bloody university,' Roger added.

'Funny you should say,' Jack began, 'because I was just thinking about that very idea a few minutes ago.'

'Coffee everyone?' Norman asked. 'There's no queue…Americanos?'

Roger picked up a chair and brought it to the table that Jack had occupied for the last hour or so: 'So, Jack, do we take it that you are back with young Charlotte Rudolph?'

'Yes. I'm hoping we're back for good this time.'

'And she's giving a talk this afternoon?'

'Yep. At the staff development event. She's going to try out some ideas we've been talking about recently.'

Norman set down the tray with three Americanos, some sugar and a small jug of milk.

'Shouldn't you guys be at the staff development event?' Jack asked.

'Do you remember, Jack,' Norman began, 'when you said it couldn't get any worse. Well, it has. The Quality Office has expanded and is now taking over other departments. I have no doubt that some of the external speakers are really good, but the very thought of those quality people, up there on the stage. It's enough to make me want to throw a shoe at them. I always imagine them as little weasels, prattling on about their latest initiative, which always seems to involve academics doing more work, and work that will take us further away from research and teaching.'

'What's *really* annoying,' Roger said, 'is that academic departments are struggling to recruit staff, but a bloody army of quality puppets keep appearing. It's like an episode of Dr Who, where an alien force is reproducing faster than the human race.'

'I know I'm going to sound like a snob,' Norman said, 'but I'm going to say it anyway. Most of them don't even seem to have a master's let alone a PhD.'

'Standards, old boy!' Roger shouted.

'So,' Norman began, 'please tell us, Guido Lowell, that you've brought gunpowder with you, and that once we've blown up the place, a new phoenix will rise from the ashes?'

'Don't tempt me,' Jack said. 'I suppose it could be a metaphorical explosion. I've been spending a lot of time with Lotte discussing what a university would look like if it were taken over by *real* quality; not just slogans and phoney inspections.'

'So, you really are a couple then,' Roger said. 'When the novelty of sex wears off, you have to sublimate.'

'Thanks, Roger,' Jack said. 'Speak for yourself. But, seriously, this just might be a good opportunity to strike a blow. We've now got students paying £9,000 for their tuition; staff getting really frustrated about the REF; quality people running amok. What about seriously proposing something different?'

'Well,' Norman said, 'there's certainly a lot of discussion going on about alternative models for universities, but how do you implement them? They're going to need huge resources.'

'Enter Thomas Minot,' Jack said. 'You know he's always been interested in helping people to set up businesses. As part of that he's been running workshops on setting up workers' co-ops. Small-scale yes, but there's something in that model that we could expand…maybe?'

'I see,' Roger said. 'Correct me if I'm wrong, but your last email sounded a bit like skill exchanges. That old Ivan Illich idea. Is that the sort of thing you have in mind, Jack?'

'Yes, yes. Spot on with the Illich reference.'

'Read it when I did my teacher training course,' Roger said.

'I'm thinking we could perhaps expand that idea. But here's the thing, and I know this might sound odd, but Thomas has struck up some kind of friendship with a George Soros-type character, who wants to *fund* some new initiatives. Giving back to the community, sort of thing.'

'Bit risky, Jack, surely,' Norman said.

'Exactly what I thought, but I've been thinking about it so much that I'm beginning to come round to it. Hence the reason why I wanted to talk to you.'

'So, let's be clear,' Roger said, 'a small-scale skill exchange, along the lines of Illich, is not going to be resource rich; hiring rooms in a college; evening classes; people giving up their time; swapping skills. So, not really that risky, surely?'

'Agreed. But what if we thought bigger…much bigger?' Jack asked.

'You mean an alternative university, Jack?' Norman asked.

'Possibly,' Jack replied.

'Are you sure you haven't fallen into some kind of *folie a deux* with that young Charlotte?' Roger asked.

'Okay,' Jack began, 'that might be way too ambitious, but we could *think* about establishing something different, as a kind of experiment...Here's the thing...This rich guy is in the process of buying up two redundant colleges, to get in before the property developers do, and he's now interested in some proposals. So, yes, if I'm honest, I *am* coming round...to seriously thinking about...maybe...something along the lines of Mondragon, in Spain, although I don't know much about it. Smaller scale, yes...It's only some thoughts at the moment. I haven't mentioned it to Thomas. All I've done is help him with a training school proposal.'

'Hmmm...Interesting,' Norman said.

'It doesn't sound like you're anti?' Jack asked. 'I thought you might be shooting me down in flames. What worries *me* is that it would come across as a private institution, and that just doesn't sit well with me.'

'I'm not too concerned about that, Jack,' Norman said. 'Private doesn't have to mean for-profit. It all depends how it's set up. If it's a proper co-op I can't see it being that problematic. But you'd have to have someone draw up some kind of legal structure for it.'

'It worries *me* though, that the press might think that this is another Grayling-type College,' Jack said.

'Well, you could call it the Fidel and Che College; that might help on that front,' Roger said.

'Seriously though,' Norman began, 'I see that Grayling has been defending himself recently by saying that his college has some Marxist principles...from each, to each, and so on.'

'Really?' Jack asked. 'But that makes it worse...we *would* be lumped together.'

'Actually, I like this idea, Jack,' Roger said. 'Like Norman, I'm not too concerned about the word private. Just because something isn't funded by the State, that doesn't make it capitalist, does it?'

'No,' Jack said, 'but without State funding, it would make it difficult to keep it going, into the future.'

'Maybe, maybe not,' Norman said. 'For goodness sake, we're now in a period of history where we can't guarantee State funding for universities anyway.'

'That's pretty much what Lotte's been saying...So, I've not lost my marbles, then?' Jack asked.

'On this, no,' Roger said, looking across at Norman.

'No, far from it,' Norman began. 'I think this could be the future. Don't forget, historically, State-funding of universities is quite a recent phenomenon. And if you look to the United States, which universities are in the most trouble? It's the public-funded ones. They are at the mercy of local political decision making.'

'But let's be honest,' Jack began, 'the elite, private, universities in the States are not the bastions of learning we really want them to be, are they? They charge huge fees and they get research funds from some very dodgy sources, as far as I can see.'

'But that's it, Jack,' Roger said. 'You *would* have to draw up some kind of constitution…a set of principles…You invite funds only from reputable…responsible…sources, and you cap fees in some way. It's certainly worth thinking through, Jack.'

'I agree,' Norman said. 'And it's not a new idea, of course. We have examples to look at from the past, and, as you say, there is Mondragon. And there are new initiatives sprouting up all over the place now. And here's someone for your reading list, Jack: Ernest Boyer. He critiqued the elite universities in the United States; for not taking the teaching function seriously, and for being out of touch. Have you heard of him?'

'No. But I'll certainly check him out. Let me just write that down,' Jack said.

'And if we had a serious benefactor, with sound principles.' Roger said. 'Maybe you should go and see this guy, Jack. It couldn't be any worse than what we've got now. I've been seriously thinking about going back to school teaching.'

'And I've been seriously thinking about asking for early retirement,' Norman said. 'You should certainly go back to Thomas and see if you can find out more about this benefactor.'

***

After Roger and Norman had peeled off back to their offices, Jack continued to walk across the old campus. A few new buildings had gone up, in the spaces between the old ones. They were glass-plated and corporate looking. Another alien force, he thought. He walked past the library building, from which he could now see the old gym building, where he was due to meet Lotte. It was now called The Peacock Building, in honour of the recently retired Vice-Chancellor. As he approached, he could see people spilling out. He went up the steps and looked into the main hall. It was almost unrecognisable from the building he remembered; even the doors looked different. He hung back because he could see Lotte talking with two people at the other end of the room.

Jack watched the two people leave before walking towards Lotte: 'How did it go?' he asked.

'Oh, not so good. Quite a few hostile questions.'

'Really, from where?'

'I don't think this place is ready for some of these ideas. Certainly not the quality team.'

'How did you know it was them? Apart from the broomsticks, of course. Is that sexist?'

'Possibly, Lowell. Although all the hostile questioning did seem to come from women. I knew they were quality people, not because of the broomsticks, but because they introduced themselves before they spoke.'

'What did they say?'

'Defensive stuff, about how seriously the University takes student feedback; how students sit on committees; how the Student Union is involved in everything. I kept trying to say it was a deeper issue. I *was* getting good nods from some people in the audience, but they didn't speak up.'

'Foucault again?'

'Those two who just left were Faculty Learning and Teaching Fellows and they wanted to keep in touch, so that was nice. And I stayed in the hall after my talk to sit in on a very interesting seminar; on using Twitter and Facebook with students.'

'I thought you were meeting with your old colleague?'

'Jos Conway. I was, and I did. She texted me to say that she had to get away after my talk, so we had a quick lunch together. She's a really interesting person. I told her about some of the things we have been talking about. She's really into critical theory. She was in Nicaragua at the time of the Sandinista movement, when she did her PhD. I told her we should talk more.'

'Interesting. I wished I'd know that when I was here. I liked her, but we never really spoke.'

'Changing the subject, when they told me my talk was in the Peacock Building, I didn't realise they meant *here*.'

'I know. I had to look ask Norman and Roger where to go. They told me it was the same building.'

Jack looked up at the ceiling.

'The good old days, eh Lowell? I looked up a couple of times during my talk.'

'Shall we take a look? For old times' sake?'

'Come on then.'

They walked up the stairs, peering into the seminar rooms, just as they had done in the past. They were all dark.

'I don't think anyone will be around,' Jack said. 'It's the last day of term.'

'Slow down, Lowell, this bloody bag is heavy.'

'Swap? Mine's very light.'

'That's because you've just got a toothbrush and a pair of pants in yours.'

'I've told you before, travelling light is an art form. Hey, if the coast is clear, how about a quick workout?'

'You've changed. Do you remember how nervous you used to be?'

'I'll take that as a yes.'

As Jack finished his sentence, they arrived opposite the door to the storage room.

'I don't remember the carpet,' Jack whispered.

'And there's no shelf anymore, and no sign on the door,' Lotte whispered back.

'That's it, on the floor over there.'

Next to the old sign was a new sign, which read: 'Peacock. Quality 3:3'.

'The door's open,' Lotte whispered.

Jack followed Lotte in and whispered: 'What's happened in here?' He fumbled for the old light switch, which they only ever used a couple of times. He could feel a small row of new switches, so he flicked a couple of them. Large lights in the ceiling began pinging, and within seconds the room became glaringly bright.

'Wow,' Jack said, as they looked across the rows of brand new desks, computers, and chairs, all set out like an open-plan office. 'It looks like the quality lunatics have really taken over the asylum. And it smells corporate; toxic glue to bind the organisation together; very Durkheim.'

'A place not for the overman, but the underman; very Nietzsche,' Lotte whispered.

They smiled at each other.

'I fear our work here is *un*done, Dr Rudolph.'

'Time *all* this was undone, don't you think, Dr Lowell?'

Suddenly, the door at the other end of the room opened: 'Can I help you?...Ah, Charlotte, sorry, I didn't recognise you for a moment. I'm Greg Marsden, the new Director of Learning and Teaching here. I came to your talk. Very interesting; thank you. Are you looking for someone?'

'Sorry, Greg,' Jack said, 'I'm Jack Lowell. I used to work here, too. I did some work with the learning and teaching team. We were just having a look around to see how things have changed.'

'Yep. There are some exciting things happening here. At this very moment I'm just putting together the new teaching and learning strategy. This is where the new quality team will be located. They will be supporting me in implementing it.'

'Great,' Lotte said. 'We'll get out of your hair. We need to get moving.'

Chapter 19

Lotte looked up at the ceiling of their hotel room. It was just after 8.30 on Saturday morning. Jack had gone out, saying that he would be back shortly. She thought about the previous evening: dinner, wine, and the jokes about being contaminated by that quality office. She lifted the quilt cover to look at the marks left on her body from Jack's teeth.

Jack appeared pleased with her suggestion that they go to the Victoria and Albert Museum for lunch. She made the suggestion just after telling him that she was off to New York on Sunday. He also appeared to accept her claim that her mother had been keeping it a secret and she'd only just found out. He'd also smiled when she told him that she would be Tom to his Jerry while she was away.

Jack returned to the room, with a red rose, and a small parcel. 'Not to be opened until Tuesday, in New York,' he said.

Good, she thought, New York had not festered in his mind.

'But you must promise me that you will send me a postcard on each of the days you're there,' Jack added.

'Okay, deal. Three postcards; Monday, Tuesday, Wednesday. We fly out Sunday and back Thursday.'

'I was thinking, why don't we have a coffee at St Pancras Station, then walk along Regent's Canal, before going to the museum?'

'Okay. But first, how about you get back into bed?'

***

After coffee, they joined Regent's Canal behind King's Cross Station.

'How long will this take, Jack? It's 10.15 already.'

'I've only cycled it before, so I'm not sure. Couple of hours, maybe. We could get on the Underground at Camden. Let's see. No luggage, at least.'

'I'm sure you won't miss your pants and toothpaste. Don't let me forgot about *my* bag, though'

'It's fine. They said they would look after them; all day, if necessary.'

'I'd like to be back home before five o'clock so I can pack for tomorrow.'

'We'll be fine. Trust me.'

'I've never trusted you, Lowell.'

Around twenty minutes later, they passed the zoo, and began taking it in turns to sing lines from Simon and Garfunkel songs. As they approached Camden, the towpath became busier.

'I'm starting to wonder whether it's possible to do anything,' Jack said. 'I think we might be stuck with this anti-quality agenda for some considerable time.'

'The turning-the-tanker-round problem.'

'Precisely.'

'Or perhaps we should see it more like these canal boats. If you know the canal, you will also know the places where you *can* turn round. We just have to find one of those places. I suppose we could organise a conference, for like-minded people?'

'Probably not the best time to be doing that, though; what with the focus on REF papers at the moment.'

'There's the problem Jack. Everyone is running so fast on their own hamster wheels they daren't slow down. Maybe we could just get together with people we already know. I'm sure Jos Conway would be interested, and your friends Roger and Norman?'

'Wouldn't we just be pissing into the wind, though?'

'A very patriarchal piss, Lowell…Well, I certainly think you should go and meet with this Sugar Daddy, to see what's actually feasible. He might be leading us up a garden path, not a tow-path.'

'I know. Half of me doesn't want to meet with him because of that. I want to live in hope, I suppose. I need to talk this through with Thomas.'

They peeled off the canal at the Edgware Road, where they got on the Underground, heading for South Kensington Station. They walked through the subway tunnel leading to the various museums and turned right into the Victoria and Albert Museum. It was just after midday.

'Blimey,' Jack said. 'Every time I come here, I feel disorientated.'

'You're safe, Lowell. We'll be in the restaurant in two minutes.'

Lotte got in the queue for the salads while Jack made his way to the William Morris Room. While he waited, Norman's 'Guido Lowell' comment popped into his head. Time for some serious plotting, he thought. Around five minutes later, Lotte slid the lunch tray onto their table and sat opposite Jack: 'There we go. My treat this time. You look very serious, Jack.'

'Thanks. Food looks great. I was just thinking, it's time we started planning our escape…some serious plotting.'

'Like Paul Simon's pigeons?'

'Certainly not his antelopes and zebras. Got way too many of them at my place. Seriously, though, we do need to hang onto this dream. I can't bear the thought of next term.'

'Perhaps we need some news from nowhere?'

'How do you mean?'

'William Morris; his utopian vision, a lucid dream. Last time we were here, I decided to do a bit of homework on Morris. *News From Nowhere* was on my father's bookshelves. I started reading it. What you just said reminded me of his idea of a dream as a vision. And I hate to admit this, Lowell, but I think you were right about those Morris tables and chairs. Well, half right. If you really invest yourself in your work, you *will* produce something of quality. But that's denied to most people who work on mass-production lines.'

'Well, well, well, Rudolph, I'll make a Marxist of you yet. What I would say though is that the former is a worker, whereas the latter is a labourer. There is no dignity in labour, but there is in work. I've been doing some homework too: *The Craftsman*, Richard Sennett. I was struck by the idea that the architect and the builder have much more in common than is commonly thought. Even when the builder is working to a strict brief, they will still invest something of themselves in their work; often only small touches, but they leave their mark, sometimes hidden, but it's there.'

'*Phronesis*.'

'Bless you.'

'Idiot. *Phronesis:* practical wisdom. The Aristotelian anti-dote to Plato's division between the abstract and the practical. Plato's theory of the forms is a knowledge of first principle; knowledge uncontaminated by experience. But the essence of work lies not in knowledge of first principles…important as that might be…but in the wisdom which is inherent in the practical application of ideas. It's a celebration of work, I suppose. I hadn't thought about it like that before.'

'This is good, Rudolph. The dignity of *labour* is really no more than opium for the people. The real dignity is in the wisdom of work. There's integrity and honesty there.'

'It's monkey-like, you mean?'

'Very good, Rudolph…but don't go all orangutan on me…What I want to say…I think…is that, in that honesty…lies the true quality of work…in the human investment.'

'Yes, yes…and that would unite students with workers. It's a philosophical Paris '68! Seriously though, that's why engagement is the key word. I'm still annoyed with myself, that I couldn't get that point across in my talk.'

'That's because you had too many elephants in the room. Paul Simon elephants, that is. On second thoughts, maybe the Michel Foucault elephant as well…the one we can't speak of…the one which silences everyone.'

'Very good, Lowell.'

'Hey, I just need to pop to the loo. Shall I get more coffees?'

'Okay, good.'

Instead of making his way to the toilets, Jack went to the museum shop, and bought a card with a William Morris print on it. He placed it in his jacket pocket, checking that it would go all the way in. He returned to their table with two coffees.

'Sorry, always long queues here…I was just thinking, one of my favourite bits from Marx's *Capital* is when he talks about humans being put to shame by bees and spiders. Yes, they build perfect structures, but the difference between them and the human architect is that the latter doesn't do it by instinct, but by design; the fact that they erect their structures in their minds before they erect them in reality.'

'But architects don't actually erect the buildings, do they? They just design them.'

'You're right…but that's the effect of capitalism again…the separation of the conception of an idea from its execution; the effect of the class structure on work. Which is what makes it alienating for both worker and capitalist.'

'I think this why *News From Nowhere* was working for me. It was a dream, yes, but one which could be grasped. In Morris' time I don't think capitalism was quite the monolithic structure it is these days. It was probably easier to conceive of alternative social structures in those days.'

'And it was much clearer then, that the proletariat did have little more than their chains to lose. Now, they've invested their soul in their cars and in their kitchens.'

'Marcuse?'

'Blimey, Rudolph. You *are* becoming a Marxist.'

'Not quite. I read it on a post-it note at your flat.'

'*But*...we do have a way in, don't we? We can't change capitalism...we probably can't even change the university system, but we could re-imagine the *concept* of higher education. That could make a difference, particularly if the idea took hold... You're doing it already, Rudolph. Student engagement is a realistic re-imagination of higher education. We can dream about that, because, as you say, it's a realistic vision.'

In reply, Lotte stretched out the word 'Okay' to make it sound like a question, then said: 'But are we now saying that student engagement is a form of *phronesis*?'

'Yes, I think we are. And therein, again, lies the true quality.'

'*But*...are we *also* now saying that university is a preparation for work? Isn't that the worst kind of instrumentalism; the very thing we're supposed to be against?'

'What you've been saying about Plato has got me thinking. *He's* the source of the academic-vocational divide in this country...the English disease. When I came back from my Italian job, I started wondering whether that was actually a false dichotomy. I couldn't put my finger on it, but I think you're right: Aristotle *has* put his finger on it.'

'Okay, Michael Caine, so what's the idea now?'

'Seriously, I think there *is* a curriculum model here; one we could sell to our mystery man; certainly Thomas Minot.'

'I remember my colleague, Milton Townsend, once saying to me that universities might be businesses, but higher education is not. If we divorce higher education, as a concept, from universities, as institutions, we could be onto something. And what you just said about false dichotomies, I think I may have another one. Knowledge for its own sake and knowledge in the service of something else; that could *actually* be a red herring. There is no quality in just knowing something; pleasure, perhaps. No, the quality is in the application of that knowledge, by human investment in something. I fear I may owe my friend Carol an apology.'

'How do you mean?'

'It's been bugging me; that she made a really good case for doing away with universities, because they are just depositories for dead knowledge. What makes them alive, of course, is the dynamism involved in the human investment, in the pursuit of scholarship. Dynamic quality again.'

'That's good, Rudolph; that's very good. Which reminds me of something from my conversation with Roger and Norman. I need to check out this guy Ernest Boyer.'

'Who he?'

'An American guy, who critiqued the elite American universities, for being out of touch; *dis*-engaged, I suppose we might say. Norman gave me the reference. I've got it on a post-it note. I will check it out over Christmas.'

'Sounds interesting.'

Jack looked into Lotte's eyes: 'We're not faking it…are we?

'What, us?'

'No, our vision!'

Lotte looked into Jack's eyes: 'We're good together, Jack Lowell.'

Chapter 20

The train began pulling out of Amsterdam Central Station just as Jack Lowell and Thomas Minot found their seats. They sat opposite each other and placed their small paper bags of food and drink on the table between them.

'You were right about taking the train, Jack. This *is* a better way to take stock.'

'Hold on,' said Jack, 'my phone's vibrating. It'll be Lotte.'

'Go ahead, I need to eat something,' said Thomas.

'Well, how did it go, stranger?' On hearing Lotte's voice, Thomas smiled knowingly at Jack.

'Sorry, we've only just got on the train. The meeting went on longer than expected and we ended up rushing to get to the station. The line's not good; I'll ring you later; it went very well; we're on…You were dead right about the need to meet the mystery man.'

With that, the line cut out.

'We certainly are on, thanks to you, my friend.' Thomas lifted his plastic coffee cup in the manner of a toast.

'And thanks to you,' said Jack. 'If you hadn't recovered the situation yesterday, I don't think we would have had the meeting this morning.'

'I seriously think he was just teasing you. He wouldn't have done that if he hadn't liked what you sent him. But your face, Jack, when he asked you if you were against quality in higher education; that was priceless. I woke up this morning still laughing about it.'

'I liked that hotel…very trendy. I could imagine staying there with Lotte. Maybe he will organise another all-expenses paid trip.'

'I think he chose it just because it was close to his office. But hey, don't push your luck.'

'I think *you* could push yours. He clearly really likes you.'

'You think so?'

'Well, he certainly trusts you, and that's the important thing. I meant to ask him, why Amsterdam? With his money, he could locate himself anywhere.'

'He did tell me that he still spends a lot of time at his home, in Finland, but he likes Amsterdam, and it's more convenient for meetings. And the coffee houses, of course.'

'Another reason he likes you, I think. I did warm to him this morning. His knowledge of the Finnish education system *was* impressive. And he's certainly well read…Steiner, A.S. Neil, Freire. He's a radical, all right. I'm still a bit uneasy about the money, though.'

'Just *a bit* uneasy? On the way over, you were very uneasy. That's progress.'

'Maybe it's best I don't know too much. If it's true that it all came from currency movements during the banking crash, I suppose I should applaud him...for taking money out of the capitalist system and doing some good with it.'

'I think it is all true, Jack. I know he has a degree in Economics and a master's in Business Finance. When I first wrote to him, he was really interested in my background and what I used to teach.'

'Another reason he really likes you. Where did he study?'

'I'm pretty sure his undergraduate degree was in Finland. I know his master's came from Madrid. That's where he came across the Mondragon experiment. He wrote his dissertation on financing third-sector projects.'

'You never mentioned this before.'

'While you were doing *your* homework, I started doing my own. When I was setting up the meeting I also told him about our PhDs. Hope you don't mind; I should have told you.'

'That's okay. It explains a lot. And there was me thinking it was our charm that impressed him.'

'But c'mon, Jack, what you said about scholarship this morning, even *I* was impressed with that.'

'Yeah, it did come out well, didn't it? I surprised myself. Amazing what you can do under pressure.'

The two of them sat back in silence as they watched the countryside of northern France turn from green to black. It was mid-February and the sun had already set as they approached the Channel Tunnel. The slight change in pitch when the train entered the tunnel prompted Jack to move forward in his seat: 'If he gets both of those sites, you could end up with your own campus, you know.'

'I do know. But I'm not sure that's what I need. You will have noticed I didn't say much when it came up this morning. I think he will get them, though. He's got the money and the people to secure them. It would be brilliant for you, Jack.'

'Yeah. That site in the Midlands sounds quite big. But I don't think he was clear what he wants to do with them.'

'I really think it's up to us...to come up with ideas. We could set up an institute, or, as you said before, some kind of skill exchange, or just places to set up some workshops.'

'But we can't be the only people he's talking to.'

'We're not. I know he's got educational projects all over Europe, and he's talking to Brussels about funding trans-European projects. That's another trump card you've got, Jack; you've already worked on the kind of project he likes. I get the impression he just wants to work with a few people he trusts in each country...and see what comes of it.'

'Yeah, that *was* coming across, particularly this morning.'

'And he's really interested in the UK at the moment, because of this new legislation on opening up the HE market, to new providers. That was brilliant what you said about further education colleges.'

'I kind of just ran with it, because of what I've been reading lately; that some FE colleges are now seeking degree-awarding powers...because of that new legislation.'

'It was sweet, Jack. I think it's what swung it this morning. He was impressed with what *you* knew. I think he saw it as a twist on the German vocational system. You were smokin' there, my man.'

'I'm glad he didn't push me.'

'And that bit about the difference between universities as buildings and higher education as learning; cooking on gas with that one.'

'Yeah. I felt safer there. I've been speaking a lot with Lotte about that.'

'Shame it's dark; we might have been able to see that Kent site.'

'I really need to get that curriculum rationale firmed up first...before we start talking about moving in somewhere. We're just day-dreaming until we do that. '

Chapter 21

Jack turned his head away from his desk to watch the last of the day's light through his bedroom window. He walked across to the window and looked towards the English Channel. The sea was a carpet of calm water. After a few minutes he returned to his desk and looked down at his notepad, which had a full-page pencil drawing with one horizontal line and one vertical one, to produce four quadrants. He had written 'Ernest Boyer: four scholarships' at the top, and labelled each quadrant: Discovery; Application; Integration; Teaching. Under 'Teaching' he had written 'pedagogic research' and under 'Application' he had written 'employer engagement'. He had hoped that each quadrant would be full of other words and phrases by now, but he had spent a lot of the afternoon thinking about the article he had just submitted for publication. And how he would love to slam his resignation letter down on his Head of Department's desk. In his head he could see, Patrick McGoohan, in *The Prisoner*, storming down that corridor.

Time was getting on; he was due to meet Lotte at Brighton Station within the hour. He turned his head again, this time to check that the duvet looked presentable, and then realised he still hadn't done anything about the sinkful of washing-up in the kitchen. He pushed his notepad to one side and looked at the three postcards he had now disturbed. He placed them side by side in front of him, picture-side up. The one on the left was a photo of John Lennon standing underneath the Statue of Liberty; the one in the middle was bell hooks standing underneath a 137th Street Subway sign; and the one on the right was Frank Lloyd-Wright leaning against a wall outside the Guggenheim Museum. He turned each one over, from left to right, and looked at the messages:

> "*Working Class Hero.*" (John Lennon)

> "*...any theory that cannot be shared in everyday conversation cannot be used to educate the public.*" (bell hooks - Teaching to Transgress)

> "*You have to go wholeheartedly into anything in order to achieve anything worth having.*" (Frank Lloyd-Wright - His Living Voice)

The quotations heightened his unease about his article, but also confirmed his resolve to make a stand, even if it wasn't clear what form that might take. He had kept the postcards on his desk to help stiffen that resolve and fight off the despondency which occasionally overtook him. 'Lotte, Lotte, Lotte', he said out loud. He loosened his neck muscles, a ritual he had adopted every time he looked at the postcards. He then looked at his watch, stood up, and walked quickly to the kitchen. He added some washing-up liquid to the cold water and ran the abrasive side of the sponge against his breakfast things and lunch plate, placing each item on the rack to dry. After slipping on his jacket, he returned to the kitchen to take a look. He ran the sponge around the sink, then pushed the kettle back a few inches.

Almost immediately after entering Brighton Station, Jack could see Lotte standing underneath the destination boards; arms folded and right foot tapping on the floor.

'Old habits die hard, Lowell?'

'Sorry. You got my text?'

'Did you send that while you were tidying the flat?'

'I wanted to finish that work I've been doing on Ernest Boyer…lost track of time.'

'Well, to apologise, you get to wheel my suitcase.'

Jack smiled to himself: the suitcase was on the large side: 'A pleasure,' he said.

They left the station and began the walk down Queen Street, towards the seafront. Lotte had to raise her voice above the sound of the suitcase wheels on the pavement: 'I've also been taking some notes on Boyer. I *had* heard of him; I knew the name rang a bell. His name came up the BCUR conference I attended. When I checked my notes, it reminded me to get a copy of an article he wrote.'

'Beaker?'

'British Conference on Undergraduate Research. It showcases research undertaken by students. One of the really good things happening in HE. It's not all doom and gloom, thank goodness.'

'Yeah. I felt the same when I was reading Boyer. It's good stuff. I wished I'd known about it years ago. The book was written in 1991, I think. I was talking with Norman Thornhill the other day. He gave me some of the background.'

'Is that *Scholarship Reconsidered*?'

'Yep.'

'I think you'll like the article by him; got a copy with me. It looks like it was the last thing he published. He talks about the scholarship of engagement. That joined the dots for me.'

'We've got to pull this all together and get it sent off to our man in Amsterdam.'

'Not Havana?'

Jack looked at Lotte and smiled: 'I think the word scholarship is definitely our key.'

'And there was me thinking you just wanted my body this weekend.'

Once inside his flat, Jack hauled Lotte's suitcase onto the bed and suggested they go to dinner at a vegetarian restaurant, which had recently opened.

'Sounds good,' said Lotte. 'Both mum and I haven't eaten meat for two months now.'

'I've got some cold beers in the fridge; fancy one?'

'Please. That would be nice.'

'Take a look at my Boyer diagram on the desk. Back in a mo.'

Lotte walked over to the desk and smiled when she saw the three postcards, then looked at the four quadrants in the diagram. She shouted out to Jack: 'I thought you said you were working on this diagram; there's nothing here!'

Jack appeared at the door, with an opened beer in each hand: 'Cheers,' he said, as he handed a beer to Lotte: 'Yeah, I know. I did a lot of thinking, but didn't get much down on paper. As you can see.'

'Well, we shouldn't have too much trouble with the scholarship of teaching. We want to create a culture where university teachers are talking about their teaching; challenging assumptions about it...'

'Problematising it...'

'If you must, Lowell...certainly looking to collect evidence on what works and what doesn't work; and conducting research not just *on* their students, but *with* their students.'

'That's good, Rudolph. I needed you here earlier.'

'As well as that Boyer article, I've been reading some stuff by Healey and Jenkins. Really good; about putting students in research mode; undergraduate students, not just postgraduates. And what teachers need to do to enact that.'

'And *what* do they need to do?'

'Well, one way to put it, I suppose, is to take every opportunity to turn the notion of criticality into enquiry; turn the critical orientation to knowledge into an enquiring mind; put students in research mode; enhance their research capability; don't just talk about research, get them doing some. There's a nice quote from Alan Jenkins I came across, where he talks about students having the same attitude to knowledge production as their teachers; students and teachers as researchers; in joint endeavour.'

'That's very von Humboldt; both in the service of scholarship.'

'And the other thing I liked was when he said that lectures should be banned; or at least have lecture-free weeks. What's the thing least likely to encourage a scholarly mind amongst students? Answer: have them sitting passively in a lecture.'

'Flipping the classroom; get students to go away and discover things for themselves, then come back and report to their peers, in the classroom. Roger Fergusson sent me an article on it. I didn't connect it with Boyer...'

'FOFO.'

'Sorry?'

'FOFO; fuck off and find out; an old teacher training adage. Fits nicely with Carl Rogers as well, yes? Do you remember that time, in your old flat, when you said to me that I should give fewer answers in lectures and ask more questions. It pains me to say it, Lowell, but that really stuck with me. I started to see lectures very differently after that.'

An image of the large bright blue estate car flashed across Jack's mind: 'Yeah, I do remember that day...Look, we've got to get all this down in this diagram.'

'We only need a few words and phrases...as prompts...students as researchers; action research...the idea of professionals researching their own practice.'

'You know, Rudolph, you've just hit on something there. I've been sitting here this afternoon, looking for examples in Boyer's book of what he meant by Discovery, Application, Integration and Teaching. But I was doing it from the academic *teacher's* point of view. We could now flip all that and think about it from a student's point of view. Yes, academics conduct research to discover new things, but so could students.'

'Okay, Mr Logical, do what you do best…start creating those lists.'

'Are you taking the piss, Rudolph.'

'Yes I am; most definitely. Speaking of which, I need the loo.'

***

Lotte sat on the loo, wondering about the best time to tell Jack she intended to stay for the whole of the week. It was half-term and she only needed to go into the University on Wednesday, and possibly Thursday, and she could do that from Brighton. She thought about travelling up with Jack, and hoped he might enjoy that too.

She looked at herself in the mirror, and then down at the toothpaste marks in the sink. She smiled to herself, plumped up her hair, then held up her arm to smell her skin. She turned towards the door, but as she turned she caught sight of herself in the mirror. She returned to the sink, put her hands down on either side of it, and looked at her face again in the mirror. She thought about the meeting she had arranged with her Deputy Vice-Chancellor, on Monday week, to argue her case for paying undergraduates a nominal sum to undertake research on the student experience. She had read about how this had been successful in other universities. But her thoughts started to jump: between thinking that the prospects were good, to then feeling really alone and without support from her colleagues.

As she turned to face the bathroom door, she was comforted by the thought of spending a week with Jack. Discussing pedagogical ideas with him had always been fun. And the intrigue surrounding Jack's Sugar-Daddy had become irresistible, even if nothing came of it. Just for a moment she thought about how moody Jack might become if nothing came of it, but she quickly dismissed the thought in favour of savouring Jack's current child-like enthusiasm. She could hear the short version of the *Bookends Theme* playing in her head, which made her smile.

'Hey, Rudolph, I'm on a roll here,' said Jack, as Lotte re-entered the bedroom. 'The scholarship of application: staff and students working on projects with companies; problem-solving with businesses, using research tools. And the scholarship of integration: students using knowledge from across their modules, in inter-disciplinary ways. How does that sound?'

'Good, keep going. I can see you're getting off on those lists.'

'You always turn me on, Rudolph. I love it when you rubbish me.'

'Idiot. But hey, look, those four Boyer quadrants, we should link them with a similar diagram that Mick Healey uses. He's got this diagram where a curriculum can be geared towards students being more like an audience or more like participants. Give me the notepad. See how you get off on this.'

Lotte drew two lines on a fresh sheet of paper, in order to produce four new quadrants: 'So,' she said, 'we've got "researched-tutored" at top left; "research-based" at top right; "research-led" at bottom left; and "research-oriented" at bottom right. It's neat because the top two quadrants have students as participants and the bottom two have students as an audience…passive, if you like. Finally, on the left side we can see that there is an emphasis on research *content*…talking about the outcomes of research...and on the right side we have the emphasis on the processes involved...students actually *doing* some research.'

'Love that, Rudolph. So, we want to be top-right, really.'

'I'm pretty sure that Healey says that all options are valid to some degree; they all have their place.'

'But, surely, we want to push students towards that top right quadrant?'

'Well, certainly a curriculum that's moving in that direction.'

'And teachers who are able to do that. Wouldn't it be neat if we could sit one diagram on top of the other.'

'Diagram on diagram action, Lowell. Knock yourself out.'

'Doesn't work, though, does it? The diagrams lose their meaning if they sit on top of each other'

'The key thing we need to hang onto, I think, is this idea of an overarching scholarship of engagement; that all four scholarships require the kind of engagement we've been talking about. That was the point that Boyer was making in that article.'

'I think you're right, and I like that, but we shouldn't forget his attack on the elite US universities. If we're going to convince our mystery man to back us, we've got to show *why* we are trying to do something different, and *then* say what it is.'

'But isn't that where the co-operative bit comes in? That's your bit, Jack. I'm on much safer ground just talking about student engagement.'

'You're right again; I've dropped that ball somewhere in all this. I need to go back to Thomas on that.'

'But do we really need any of that? I appreciate that Sugar-Daddy needs to hear that, but does a curriculum centred on student engagement really need all that stuff?'

'Maybe not. But aren't we saying that marketised universities wouldn't be able to deliver what we want? Knowledge has been commodified; research has been commodified; students as consumers. Whichever way we turn, it's like being between a rock and a hard place.'

'I get that. But where exactly is *our* rock? I kind of want to take some comfort in what I feel comfortable with, if that doesn't sound daft.'

'Well, let's stick with Boyer for a moment. As I see it, the essence of his argument is that *academic* research has distorted the purpose of higher education. That, for most academics, securing a big research grant and writing academic articles has become the only game in town; that's where the money and kudos is...at the expense of everything else. We could say that it's got to a point where these universities might be better off without students altogether. They just get in the way. In the language of von Humboldt, or John Newman even, they're not really universities anymore... they're just research centres...and worse, they're chasing the dollar in the process.'

'Okay, that's good. That will certainly help in arguing that we are trying to do something different...putting students at the heart of system...or putting them *back* at the heart of the system.'

'We're not really dreaming up anything radical here; just returning universities to what they once were. The radicals are those who are trying to turn universities into something else...purveyors of commodified knowledge.'

'I need a break, Jack. I've now lost sight of the quality dimension; isn't *that* supposed to be the essence of what're trying to do here...restore quality to its rightful place?'

'Yeah. You're right. This is our task for the weekend; to pull this all together, although I think we might need more than a weekend.'

'Bloody right there, Lowell! Or is this your wheeze to keep me here longer?'

'Rumbled.'

'Well, good news. How about I stay for the week?'

'Really? You do love me after all.'

'I will do if we can have something to eat. How about I put something in the oven?'

'I'll do it.'

'No, you stay clear. Not beans on toast again. What have you got; apart from Heinz beans?'

'Definitely got those. How about jacket potatoes? Got those too. I could go out and get some wine.'

'Go on, then. While you're out, get some peanuts. Have you got any apples and cheese?'

'Yep, got those.'

'Okay. We'll have stuffed potatoes. Off you go then, lad...While you're there, get us something nice for breakfast tomorrow.'

Chapter 22

When Jack awoke the following morning the bedroom seemed lighter than normal. As he turned to look at the bedside clock - 9.47am - he realised that he hadn't closed the curtains. They had fallen asleep on his sofa in the front room, and hadn't made it to the bed until 2.30am. He turned his head towards Lotte, who looked peaceful. Lines from Supertramp songs started spinning around in his head. After a few minutes, he gently rolled out of the bed and tip-toed to the loo. When he returned to the bedroom, Lotte was looking up at the ceiling.

'I'm going to make a coffee,' said Jack. 'Want one?'

'Yes please.'

They sat up in bed, their coffee cups resting on their knees.

'I just had a really weird dream,' said Lotte. 'We were both laying in bed, in a very bright little room, which had wall-to-wall bookshelves, completely covered in poetry books. The door then opens and our teenage son walks in, and announces that he's not interested in going to university. It was really vivid.'

'Probably because you only just dreamt it. Perhaps you want to marry me?'

'It wasn't a nightmare, Lowell.'

Jack took the cup from Lotte's hand and put both cups on the bedside table. He turned back towards her, pulled the duvet over her head, then slid down under it and nestled against her. Lotte spoke first: 'So...what's for breakfast, Jack?'

'Kippers...no, not really. I bought some croissants. I'll warm them up in a minute. Then, how about we stay here for a bit and then go out for some brunch?'

'Sounds good.'

***

The brunch idea turned into lunch, after which they strolled down from The Lanes in the direction of The Palace Pier. On the pier, they lent forward against the railings and looked west in the direction of Jack's flat. The sun was shining on their faces, but the wind was strong enough to remove any warming effect.

'Not a bad day for February,' said Jack.

'Bit bracing.'

'You know, you *were* right about what you said yesterday, about quality. I've been banging on too much about Boyer, haven't I?'

'Not really. What you just said at lunch about that Jacoby book; that's important; the need for more public-facing intellectuals...community engaged intellectuals... and it's clear from that final article by Boyer that he *was* influenced by Jacoby.'

'Yeah. That was a neat coincidence. Academics drink their coffee in the senior common room; intellectuals drink their coffee in the cafe in town.'

'I remember being in Vienna as a child, and my father talking about the cultural significance of the Viennese coffee shop. Bit lost on me at the time, but the cakes were lovely.'

'There's something important here, about what it means to disseminate ideas. Academics write journal articles; intellectuals talk on the radio, the TV, and in public.'

'Ever since I started working in higher education I've resisted calling myself an academic; that word has never sat comfortably with me. If I'm understanding Boyer correctly, I'm much more interested in the idea of the scholarship of integration; putting ideas together in order to produce an interesting learning environment for students. That *is* a form of scholarship; a really important one. It's just not recognised as such.'

'Much more like the Victorian notion of a scholar; not a researcher; but a well-read polymath? Norman Thornhill is good on this stuff. Come to think of it, he's also a bit of a polymath himself.'

'I don't think I'd ever call myself that *either*, but I certainly don't think of myself as someone churning out erudite journal articles. I was thinking earlier about my old mentor, Milton Townsend. He's academic, yes, but he's much more than that; another true scholar.'

'That's why I like Boyer; that notion of the well-rounded scholar; someone who does a bit of everything...'

'...and is supported by their institution to do so...and recognises their duty to students, rather than running away from them.'

'Norman's good on that, as well. I like it when he quotes Cardinal Newman: if a university was just about producing knowledge, with no thought to its dissemination, what's the point of having students there.'

'It's that word "engagement" again, though. It's becoming a really rich word, I think. Human investment...creative sparks...making a mark...community engagement.'

'I don't know whether Boyer did it on purpose...but I think it's important that he calls discovery...doing traditional research...a form of scholarship. It shouldn't sit above, as a higher order activity; it should sit equally, with all the other forms of scholarship, and should operate with the same notion of engagement.'

'Maybe we *should* be making more of Boyer?'

'But what if that *does* take us away from the quality dimension?'

'When we finally made it to bed last night I started wondering if the words engagement and quality were actually interchangeable; two sides of the same coin, maybe?'

'That's bloody good, Lotte. That could just be our missing link. One big problem, though.'

'How so?'

'Do you remember when you used to have different thoughts when we got into bed?'

'You're such an idiot, Jack Lowell.'

'But you love me for it, don't you?'

***

The sun slowly emerged from behind a cloud and began to light up Jack Lowell's front room.

'I think I've got another diagram,' said Jack. 'Kind of like a three dimensional chess set; with Boyer on the bottom; student engagement sitting above that; and then quality on the top. All connected…I need my notepad.'

'Hold on a minute, Tyger. I'm sitting here thinking…if I'm going to be here for the week…what we really need to do is a deep clean of this flat. The state of this place is starting to impede my thought processes.'

'It's not that bad…is it?'

'Maybe you didn't notice, but when the sun just hit the coffee table, it lit up the dust.'

'Okay, but can I just quickly have a go at that diagram?'

'Go on then…Where do you keep your cleaning products?'

'In the supermarket.'

Chapter 23

Hey Jack,

The Man from Del Monte, he says yes!

He loved that scholarship of engagement stuff and he's agreed to put up some money to set up a skill exchange and fund my workshops on setting up co-ops.

He's got the Kent site and his people are still working on the other one. It's actually just outside Oxford.

But look, he now wants a formal proposal from you, to produce a full degree programme for a potential new co-operative learning institute, based at one of the sites. His people want to submit a proposal to get degree awarding powers.

He wants to see us again. We need to meet. How are you fixed?

Sun is Shining, my friend.

Thomas

Jack read the email twice, then pushed his chair back from his desk. The force he applied made the wheels turn slightly and he ended up in the middle of his office. He looked at his watch: he had a supervision with one of his PhD students in fifteen minutes, followed by three more in the afternoon. He thought about whether there would time to meet up with Lotte for lunch. It was unlikely that she would be able to make it and the travel time would hardly make it worthwhile. But he didn't want to tell her the news by email or phone. He was sure she would be in the office, so maybe they could meet up after work. She was bloody right, he thought; using the scholarship of engagement as the axis had been the right way to go. And maybe she was also right about co-ops. He could hear her voice in his head: 'co-operative learning, yes, but do we really need a whole new institution?' His train of thought was abruptly halted by a loud knock on the door.

Between supervisions, Jack sent a quick email to Lotte suggesting that they meet up for a drink after work. He then began composing an email to Thomas:

Hi Thomas,

That's fantastic news. I was hoping he would like what I put together, but I wasn't expecting much to come of it. Yes, we definitely need to meet. I'm pretty much stuck here until the end of term. Any chance we could meet up one weekend?

Jack

As he was re-reading it, there was another knock on the door. He clicked 'send', then span his chair towards the door and shouted: 'Come in'.

The final supervision ran over time. The conversation had been tricky; his PhD student didn't want to inform her proposed interviewees of the precise nature of her research. She had been adamant that this would unnaturally affect what they said, which prompted a long discussion about whether, and how, interviewees can be harmed by the research process. Jack was relieved to hear the door close. it had been a busy and draining day, and he sat quietly for several minutes before looking at his email inbox. Lotte had replied to say that she would be tied up this evening and would prefer to meet later in the week, and Thomas had replied to say that he would be with his kids the following weekend, so he would prefer it they could meet this week. Jack decided to tell Lotte about the good news via email, and then wrote to Thomas to ask whether a meet-up in London on Saturday would work for him. Maybe Lotte would come with him; they had planned to spend the weekend together. He decided to send her a PS email, in case the meeting with Thomas went ahead.

***

The train pulled out of Preston Park Station, in the direction of Brighton. Jack had just finished reading the last chapter of *News From Nowhere*. He put the book down on the small table in front of him and then started tapping his fingers on it. He looked out of the train window at the lights of Brighton. He then pictured himself looking out from an office window onto a bustling campus of students. Maybe just setting up a small skill-exchange in Brighton would be enough, he thought. He switched to a picture himself sitting at a reception desk just off The Lanes, with a steady stream of people coming in from the cold. In his head, he began singing lines from the song *Dream a Little Dream of Me*. Perhaps Lotte would move to Brighton. Maybe he could keep his PhD students and just work part-time, travelling into London twice a week. Now that his citizenship project had finished, maybe he could persuade his new-found philanthropic friend to sponsor a new research project. As the train entered Brighton Station, the tune in his head had switched to Buddy Holly, *Maybe, Baby*.

***

Lotte and her mother walked into the front room together. The washing-up was done and it was time to relax. Lotte poured the wine and her mother turned on the TV. Louis Theroux was engaging enough, but Lotte's mind kept mulling over Jack's email. Here was that chance to make a real difference, she thought. She glanced across at her mother and thought about how she would still love to write to those school inspectors - the ones who had made her mother cry - and tell them what true quality looks like. She imagined saying to one of them: 'You wouldn't know quality if it slapped you in the face'. Her mind then wandered back to Lucy Martens, that so-called Quality Officer, and what she might now be doing; surely she hasn't resurfaced at another university?

Laying in bed that night, Lotte found herself thinking about whether engagement and quality were, *really*, interchangeable terms. But isn't it up to me to make the case, she asked herself. Isn't that what the QAA did; just decide what they understood by quality, and then stuck with it? Her mind wandered to thinking about what was happening at work. *Was* this the moment? The thought of having to lead a watered-down course for another year was just too depressing to contemplate; and with no allies. She thought about what Jos Conway might be up to and made a mental note to email her. She then turned sideways to rest her face against the pillow and thought about drinking coffee with Milton amongst his rose bushes. She was glad that she had checked her emails earlier in the evening: Milton had agreed to meet her at the weekend.

She thought again about Jack's decision, that they shouldn't discuss the Sugar Daddy with anyone until a firm proposal and some funding were secure. But, on the other hand, perhaps this *was* the right moment to have a wider discussion. Perhaps Milton *and* Jos would be able to join them in London. Old friends, she thought. But it was unlikely that Jos would be able to make it, and Jack was probably right: there was nothing on the table. She stretched across to turn off the bedside lamp, but paused first to look at the William Morris card which lay next to it. She smiled, then returned her head to the pillow.

Chapter 24

It was a bright, but cold, Saturday morning. Lotte walked briskly from Paddington Station along the tow-path of the Regent's Canal towards a cafe in Little Venice that Milton Townsend had chosen for their meeting. She looked down at her phone; there was a text message from Milton to say that he was standing by the cafe entrance. Lotte replied, saying that she would be there in a few minutes. She looked at her watch - 11.06. She hated the fact that she would be late and that Milton was probably shivering.

'So sorry, Milton. It took longer than I thought to walk up from Paddington.'

'It was a spur of the moment choice. I couldn't think of anywhere else and the station didn't sound that attractive. I came here on a warm summer's evening a few years ago. Bit different today, I'm afraid.'

'Don't apologise. It's lovely to see you, and thanks for fitting me in. It must be exciting, meeting up with your brother.'

'He's on a kind of European tour; his son has been working in Spain for over a year now.'

'How much time do we have?'

'We're fine. His flight from Barcelona doesn't come in until late afternoon. If I get the Express from Paddington, I'll be there in good time. Let's get some something to eat, and then you must tell me more about what you are plotting.'

While studying the menu, Lotte could hear Jack's voice in her head: 'Don't mention the man from Del Monte.' She smiled to herself: that name was better than Sugar Daddy. She had reassured Jack that she was only going to discuss the concept of quality with Milton; nothing beyond that.

They both ordered the vegetarian breakfast.

'I didn't know you were vegetarian, Lotte. I'm trying hard to go in that direction.'

'Me too. It's new for me as well.'

While they waited for their food, Milton spoke first: 'I've enjoyed thinking through what you sent me. I hadn't thought about student engagement in the way you described it. Thank you. I think you are right about the link with intrinsic motivation, and how this has got lost in the discussions about quality in higher education. What I would add, I think, is how this might be further linked with the concept of virtue.'

'Yes, and *arete?* I was very taken by the connotations. I think I may have let that take a back seat in my thinking, though.'

'Well, logically, that would make sense if your starting point is learning. I can't see that it matters from which end you start, though. I suppose I would start from the moral imperative behind any act of education, and then make my links from there.'

'I'm glad you mentioned that. To be honest, that's maybe why I have been starting from the other end, as you say. When I hear the word "moral" I always have a kind of negative Pavlovian reaction; that education is about directing behaviour rather than the search for a more detached truth.'

'I understand that. Yes, it's a danger. But the concept of truth is multi-faceted, of course.'

'Whenever I speak with you I always feel like I've become yet another footnote to Plato. I think I need to find my inner Aristotle. When I teach Aristotle to the first years I tend to stick rigidity to the Doctrine of the Mean.'

'I would too, of course, but in the end it all connects; that reasoning involves practice; learning to steer a path between extremes is what creates harmony and beauty; part of the *arete* and the *kalon*. Because of that I tend to use the word wisdom rather than knowledge; to remind me of the Aristotelian corrective, for want of a better phrase.'

Before Lotte could reply, their breakfast arrived: 'That was quick,' she said.

'It would have taken a lot longer if it was 25 degrees outside. I think the temperature has kept a lot of people indoors today, or in the shops, maybe. But tell me, Lotte, I'm intrigued about how you intend to embed these notions of quality in your teaching. No, hold on, let's eat first.'

Lotte drank the final dregs of her coffee, waiting for Milton's knife and fork to rest on his plate before she spoke: 'To be honest, *again*...sorry, I sound like I'm unburdening myself, don't I? I suppose I am, really. I've got this possibility...of working on a new project...setting up a new kind of institution, where these ideas are the axis around which everything will revolve.'

As she spoke, she could hear Jack's warning again: 'It's just Milton', she said to herself.

'A research project. That's great,' said Milton.

'Well, it's research at the moment, but I think it has the potential to become something real.'

'Well, well, well. Now I *am* intrigued.'

'Do you remember when you said to me that universities were businesses, but higher education is not? Well, that stuck with me, so I suppose that's the real starting point...I suppose what I'm grappling with is whether I could enact my ideas on student engagement within the current university structures.'

'Well, certainly not within the current quality structures. But I understand that things are now changing; light touch and all that. But, in general, I can see that there's still a lot of dangerous instrumentalism at work. As I've said before, I think, I wouldn't want to set that up in opposition to a notion of education for its own sake, because I think education *should* serve a purpose: the pursuit of the good, guided by wisdom. Wisdom is instrumental to some extent. It's turning knowledge towards the good. But, if we operate with the notions of *arete* and *kalon*, it's also integral... it implies an action, within itself, if that makes sense...I'm intrigued Lotte, because I think this is too powerful a notion not to make a return. Once the barbarians have been driven from the temple, of course.'

'I'm glad you said that, because when I was sitting on the train this morning...I was thinking that, maybe, I'm just day-dreaming: maybe things have gone so far that they couldn't be turned around?'

'Well, let's be logical about this. What exactly do we want to turn around? Maybe I'm out of touch now, but, when I think back, one of the great things about a university classroom was its freedom. The freedom to engage your students in the ways that you want. One step back from that is the assessment regime; to think of ways to assess your students in line with your learning regime. That's still possible, I think?'

'Yes, I think it is. And that's where I was until a few months ago. Do you remember when you spoke to me about encroachment; those red lines. Here's an example: a little while back I was working with some undergraduates on a project...they were interviewing their peers on the student experience...and I suggested that we write it up, as a joint-authored article. When I told my Head of Department, she told me to be careful. Because she had aspirations for me to be entered into the next REF exercise. She suggested that I write it up as a single-authored piece because it would have greater standing. I walked away, really furious.'

'Well, it's a really good example, Lotte; of bad instrumentalism, if I could put it that way.'

'Apart from anything else, it's not fair on the students.'

'Indeed. That kind of instrumentalism is extraneous, rather than integral. Your students are being cast as a constraint on the research process, whereas, in reality, they were a crucial part of it. Even worse, your university is viewing the students as instruments through which *your* esteem, and by extension, the University's esteem, will be enhanced...at their expense. That *has* crossed a Kantian red line for me.'

'*I'm* seeing their work as an example of student scholarship, and something I really want to promote. I've been talking to a colleague a lot about this; trying to unite scholarship, engagement and quality. Based on the work of Wilheim von Humbodt and Ernest Boyer.'

'Yes, I remember Jos Conway being very impressive on this notion of scholarship.'

'I'm hoping to get her involved in some way. But here's what I came up with the other day; that a corporate university demands allegiance to its corporate principles, not scholarship. I never thought I'd ever say something like that, but I'm beginning to believe that it's true. That's bad instrumentalism, yes?'

'I suppose I would say that the two *can* sit side-by-side. As an employee I have to have allegiance to the corporation, but as an academic I must have allegiance to truth; or scholarship, as you would say. I fear that I may have got out of academia at the right moment. In my day I could pretty much feign allegiance to the institution. It never really impinged on my work. Maybe today, it does.'

'My colleague uses a Marxist framework; that knowledge has become commodified; something to be traded; which is what happens when a university becomes a corporation; it's just another word for a capitalist enterprise.'

'Well, if I understand Marx correctly, a commodity has a use-value and an exchange-value. Yes, it is for sale, but that shouldn't be its prime aim, not when it is being produced, at least.'

'So, if a piece of human understanding gets traded, it might still be untainted… in its production? It could be produced outside that constraint, but *subsequently* get exchanged.'

'Nicely put, Lotte. We might say, therefore, that higher education is under constant threat of having the use-values undermined by the exchange-values. This can only be exacerbated the more that universities become corporate in their affairs. Tricky then, for academics to hold the line.'

'There's my dilemma, in a nutshell. I'm not sure that I *am* able to hold that line anymore; not in my place, certainly. I'm also beginning to wonder if the senior management team have ever actually done any proper scholarly work, or if they have, they've clearly forgotten what it was like, or even what it's for.'

'Maybe that's the problem, Lotte: they are no longer leaders of the academic production process. They are, instead, managers of commodified resources.'

***

Jack sat drinking a coffee on a wooden bench seat inside St Pancras Station. He had agreed to meet Thomas Minot at around 2.00pm. The text message from Thomas said that he should be at St Pancras around 2.15. His train was running slightly late.

'Hey, my man,' said Thomas, as he approached Jack. 'Sorry I'm late.'

'Don't worry, it's really good to see you; if only briefly.'

'I really wanted a face-to-face, and turns out that my impromptu workshop this morning could be very useful for us.'

'How's that? Hey, coffee first?'

'Yes, thanks. And some of that good looking cake there.'

'Coming right up,' said Jack, as he turned to face the till. 'Hold the table.'

Jack returned to their table with two slices of cake on plastic plates. 'I'll just get the coffees and some forks. Sugar; yes?'

'Thanks,' said Thomas.

Jack returned to the table once more, with the coffees, and before sitting down he pulled out two plastic forks and two sachets of sugar from the breast pocket of his donkey jacket: 'So, tell me about this morning,' he said, as he sat down.

'Hmmm, good cake,' said Thomas, after savouring his first mouthful.

At which, Jack looked down and watched his own slice of cake crumble under pressure from his plastic fork.

'Look,' said Thomas, 'I really think we're on to something, if you agree. I got a consensus this morning…that a kind of co-operative learning institute could offer on-going support to people running co-ops. A sort of incubator for a whole range of ideas.'

Jack pulled out his notepad from the shoulder bag which was still around his neck: 'I need to get this down on paper,' he said. 'This has been on my mind for a while. Follow me: We've got "co-operative businesses"; we've got a "co-operative learning institute"; and we've got "co-operative learning".'

He wrote down the three terms in such a way that he could form a pencil-lined triangle between them: 'So, the key question becomes whether the three points of the triangle amount to the same thing, or whether they could be connected in some way.'

'And...*can* they be connected?' Thomas asked his question, then picked up his cardboard plate, folded it to form a channel, and proceeded to pour the crumbs of his cake into his mouth.

'Well, that's the challenge. Lotte keeps telling me that co-operative learning doesn't necessarily need a co-op. The more she says it, the more I think she might be right.'

'But she *is* still on board? The last time we spoke you said she was definitely in.'

'Oh, she's in, all right...What we're talking about here is the conceptual underpinning. I need this to be tight. I want our man to know that we've really thought this through.'

'We've got a lot to think about, Jack.' Thomas looked Jack in the eyes as he spoke: 'I needed to say this face-to-face. Our man wants to see us, as soon as possible. I know that's going to be difficult for you, in term-time.'

'Yes, it will be. Can we not wait until the Easter break?'

'I could try, but I get the distinct feeling that he wants to move quickly. I've been in email communication with him all week. Look, he's my proposition: I go on my own, but you supply me with as much as you can.'

'Won't he think that I'm not committed?'

'He knows you work full-time. I can explain it. But look, the other thing we really need to sort out is that work-related dimension; in the curriculum offer. All his emails have spoken about this; he's on some kind of roll with it.'

'Why didn't you tell me?'

'I thought it could wait until today. I think it's good news. I spent all day yesterday on it.'

'On what? It sounds a bit ominous.'

'You remember when we had that conversation about that A C Grayling place - the one for the poncy public-school boys.'

'I don't think he would quite see it like that, but, yes.'

'Well, our man has been following developments on that front; to monitor the feasibility of that place being granted degree-awarding powers.'

'Has that happened?

'Dunno. But that's not the point...for us, at least. He's now really keen on pump-priming us to set up something which is much more squarely aimed at working-class students, and is much more work-related.'

'Fucking hell, Thomas. This is a serious development.'

'I know, but a good one, I think. And a lot more money, I think.'

'I can see why you wanted to wait until we were face-to-face.'

'He sent me a copy of a document: *Putting Knowledge to Work*. Do you know it?'

'No, I don't.'

'I spent yesterday afternoon on it. It's available on the web. David Gullie seems to be the main guy.'

'Hold on, Thomas. Let me get that down on one of my post-it notes.'

'I think you'll like it. The key concept is recontextualisation; about how knowledge gets transferred...translated...when it moves between contexts.'

'It sounds very Bernstein; how knowledge in a classroom is not the same as the originally produced knowledge. And that's not the same as its application in a work place.'

'You got it. But why did our man send it?'

'And why *did* he send it?'

'He just asked us to look at it. But I think it might also be because it kind of reads like a counter to the overemphasis on the abstract knowledge contained in most university courses. One of the reasons I left, of course. I think this is his direction of thinking.'

'What some people are now calling Mode 2 knowledge; Mode 1, the more theoretical knowledge, and Mode 2, the more applied. Gibbons and colleagues, I think.'

'*I* think it's really good news. We can work with this, surely?'

'Big task again. I used to talk about these issues with Roger Fergusson and Norman Thornhill. What Bernstein called "regional knowledge".'

'You see, my man. I knew you'd be all over it.'

Jack picked up his notepad, which was still on the table: 'I feel another diagram coming on,' he said. 'So...we have the "student body" in one corner...our working-class students. Did he use that term?'

'No, I think he said "under-represented students"; but we know what he means.'

'Okay...so, in the second corner, we have the idea of "applied knowledge", and in the third corner we have "co-operative learning". And we need to connect them.'

Jack drew the pencil lines to produce a new triangle.

'So, Jack, can you now produce some kind of rationale to go along with that? That I can take to our man?'

'In the next month, probably not.'

'Come on, Jack. I don't think he's looking for anything grand. So long as we can show him that we are on the same wave length. How about a few pages for now, and I tell him this is what you are working on?'

'Okay, leave it with me.'

'I'm excited about this, Jack. I was beginning to think that my anti-theory stand was becoming a bit prejudiced, if you know what I mean. I'm also starting to get really angry about the widening participation agenda. Yes, government policy is *increasing* participation, but it's not really widening it; is it? And all this talk of skills...the magical panacea. We're short-changing working-class kids, and everyone knows it.'

'You know we agree. I'm fired up. Okay; let's do this.'

At which, Thomas held out his palm, which Jack promptly slapped.

Jack continued: 'I remember the sociologist A. H. Halsey, summarising his own social mobility data...something like, if you want to get on in this world, you need to choose your parents wisely. I don't think it's changed. I think it's getting worse. You're right. We need to stand up and be counted.'

'And summarising our previous conversations, yes, we know we can't change the world, but we can at least *try* to make a difference.'

'Education cannot compensate for society...Basil Bernstein again...but, you've persuaded me. We can try. It's too good an opportunity.'

Thomas grinned, paused, then said: 'And there was me thinking that maybe you would say it's a hopeless task...Look, even those working-class kids who *are* getting degrees these days are not getting the jobs they deserve. Everyone who's honest knows that, as well. And you're right; it is worse than in our day. We can't just sit back. We've got a chance here...to turn restricted training opportunities into some kind of real education, and help people set up their own businesses.' Thomas pointed at Jack's diagram, which was sitting between them. 'We need to make these connections, Jack.'

'I'm on it.'

'The other thing I wanted to discuss was that Sennett book, *The Craftsman*. Did you read it? I've been using it a lot in my workshops. Can we get it into that conceptual underpinning, for our man?'

'Yeah, I really enjoyed it. You're right, there's something important there for us.'

'I've been busy making some of my own connections...with that German notion of *bildung*, and I've now come across the word *beruf*. No wonder the German vocational education system works. It seems to me they are not training people for jobs, but helping students to understand all the dimensions behind having an occupation...a sense of calling, belonging, ownership, pride...not just collecting a bunch of atomistic skills.'

'I can see the connection with Sennett...that builders and architects have far more in common than is usually understood.'

'Exactly...Exactly, my man. *Everything* comes from the hand first...something is theorised because it generalises from a practical problem. Theory without application is merely academic. Keep it embodied. If we could create a place where all this is at the core, we'd have something really exciting.'

'Yeah. And I really liked the contrast between the machine and the worker. Reminded me of Marx's bees and spiders. Yes, there's perfection in what the machine produces, but the true quality is in the imperfection, because it's there you see the human hand. It really fits with what I've been discussing with Lotte.'

'Could we say that the character of the worker and the character of the piece are both forged in this way?'

'Indeed. And I loved Sennet's talk of honest brick walls and modest buildings; demonstrating the human qualities again. There seems to an ethical dimension there as well; that word dignity. I need to discuss this more with Lotte.'

'And you've been dead right about the language thing, Jack...I can see that much more clearly now...the difference between an education and training.'

'Training locates you within the present and the particular and education takes you beyond it. Charles Bailey.'

'Exactly again, my man. Being an active member of an occupation opens up so many more possibilities.'

'But are you *sure* our man is on board with all this?'

'He made a comment in one of his emails about whether I thought it was true that young people with limited opportunities were still being sold the neo-liberal myth; that it was their own fault if they hadn't found a job...that they needed to market themselves better. It confirmed to me that he *is* our man.'

'Well, it certainly confirms he likes you. That sounds like friends talking to each other.'

'And someone we can work with, yes?'

'Yes; but an ironic neo-liberal statement there.'

'Ouch! You mean Thatcher and Gorbochov?...But look, I think it was what you said about FE colleges that started that ball rolling for him.'

'How do you mean?'

'I get the distinct impression that our man saw a light bulb going off there. He became interested in the colleges because he saw them claiming degree-awarding powers...and he wanted to know more about how they were doing that...but I think he's now much more interested in them because of *what* they do, and the type of students they have.'

'Yep, I can see that.'

'How about we sell him the idea of vocationally-orientated students going to our institute - or whatever we call it...not a training centre; I get that now....Or, what if students joined our institute then went off to the colleges armed with all the entrepreneurial skills and knowledge they would now have? Or, we just bypass the colleges altogether, and we create our own whole programme of study?'

'Bloody Hell, Thomas! And I've got a month to put this all together?'

'No. We just put enough together to secure our funding and then we get together with everyone who's interested in helping us.'

'Okay, I'm persuaded. If nothing else, at least *you* get some funding to put *your* work on a safe footing.'

'Yes. But think big, my man.'

'Well, I'm due to meet up with Lotte shortly. I'll mull things over with her and get back to you...And something else, I'm now thinking about...maybe...we shouldn't say "vocationally-oriented" anymore.'

'Blimey, Jack. I'll have no words left soon.'

'I just mean...perhaps it plays into that old divide between academic and vocational. Maybe, we need some more new words and phrases. I've been talking with Lotte about this recently. Not *bridge* the gap, but actually have something in the middle...something like...professional and technical learning, perhaps? Join the architects with the builders, in some kind of authentic, applied, learning curriculum. Some of the recent academic literature seems to be pointing in this direction.'

'It ain't new though, is it? I've been reading some of the old non-bookish literature.'

'Dewey?'

'Your recommendation, if you remember.'

***

Jack and Lotte embraced on the steps up from Regent's Canal, behind King's Cross Station.'How was the walk? You look gorgeous,' said Jack.

'Very good. I was very tempted to get on the Underground, but I had plenty of time.'

'How was your meeting?'

'Really good. The cafe was really nice. We'll have to go there. But how was *your* meeting. Your text was mysterious.'

'Yeah, sorry. The meeting was quite explosive. With hindsight, it was a good idea for me to see Thomas on my own.'

'So, what happened?'

'Let's walk; it's a bit nippy.'

They crossed the road and walked back down towards King's Cross and St Pancras stations.

'Well, the good news first,' said Jack. 'It looks like we probably *will* be getting a good load of money, with the possibility of even more, if we can develop a serious curriculum rationale.'

'Fantastic...and the bad news?'

'Well...it looks like the Man from Del Monte wants more of a vocational learning centre.'

'I thought we'd agreed not to use the word vocational anymore?'

'Yeah, sorry...short-hand. I've just been thinking that this could be the opportunity...to meld the academic with the vocational, in the way we've started talking, and to create a new conceptual space. But here's the thing, it looks like he wants to set up some kind of rival to that Grayling college place, but concentrating on under-represented students...in which case we need to conceptualise a new space in a new place.'

'Well, that must be music to your Marxist ears, surely?'

'Normally, it would be. But where do we begin?...And I was worried that you might think this was a step too far. That's the bad news.'

'Not my area, no. But I trust you on this.'

'Could you just say that again?'

'Say what?'

'That you trust me...You do love me, Rudolph.'

'I will do, if we can get somewhere warm.'

'Let's go into King's Cross; up on the mezzanine?'

'I need another coffee, I think.'

'I've had too much caffeine today. Just a water for me.'

On the mezzanine, they sat looking down on the long line of departure boards.

'Bloody hell,' said Jack, looking at his receipt. 'I think I just paid more for this water than your coffee.'

'It is a lot nicer around here than it used to be, though. It was all used needles and condoms a while back.'

'*They've* probably gone up in price around here as well...But, look, I was a bit worried earlier...about what Thomas was saying. I thought it might give you cold feet.'

'They're certainly cold right now. But I actually think this might be good news, you know. When I was walking along the canal I was thinking about Aristotle.'

'I love it when you talk dirty.'

'Idiot. No, seriously, connecting the idea of *phronesis* with student engagement could really work. The human investment in the practical application of ideas; that sort of thing.'

'Brilliant. That's exactly what I've been talking to Thomas about. I suppose I would say the unity of conception and execution; the unity of the mental and the manual.'

'I've just started reading a book by Chris Winch; really good. I can see some good connections coming through. That vocational education is conceptualised very poorly in the UK, unlike in Germany. Part of the academic-vocational divide seems to be a persistent belief that practical knowledge is just about "knowing how", with no "knowing that"...the latter is just for academic knowledge.'

'When you put it like that, it sounds like the words academic and vocational are both impoverished notions. And based on what I've just been talking to Thomas about, there seems to more than a hint of social class prejudice there.'

'Maybe. But that Gilbert Ryle work on the concept of mind could be really helpful.'

'Out of my depth, I'm afraid.'

'Well, let's put it this way: know-how is much more than simply knowing how. Know how always requires some conceptual mastery. It's just not always clear.'

'And perhaps deliberately muddied by UK government policy on skills-based education?'

'Out of *my* depth, I'm afraid. But, look, what I really got from Winch was a clear sense that a vocational calling has epistemic and moral components. It made me think about how important that notion of *wissenshaft* really is. It's one of those really rich German words…'

'…like *bildung* and *beruf*, which Thomas seems to be all over at the moment.'

'As my father was always keen on telling me, German words are able to contain much more than their English counterparts…in their meanings…even holding some contradictory elements. In English, it seems much easier to strip a word down, to get a very basic meaning out of it.'

'Or hollow it out even. Like "skill" which seems to have no richness left in it at all.'

'And what's becoming much clearer to me now, is that words like "skill", in the UK at least, have lost any moral sense…Same with *wissenshaft*…in German, it's a very rich word…there's know-how in there; there's judgement in there; there's the application of science to practical ideas.'

'Fuck, Lotte. We've got to get all this into this curriculum rationale.'

'Well, *you* have, my lad.'

'Please help me! I'll pay you!'

'Let me do a bit more reading, first…The other thing I was thinking about was whether we *do* need to change the structure of universities. I think the idea of higher education, as we have been conceiving it, *is* out of kilter with the current structure of universities.'

'Bloody hell, Rudolph. You should take a walk along the canal more often.'

'Talking to Milton, it started to become much clearer to me, that my place isn't really interested in the concept of higher education anymore. Yes, a university is a place where the process of higher education is enacted, but *it can't be* when it is forcibly occupied…with business principles and corporate actors.'

'When knowledge is traded; owned, bought and sold.'

'I hate to say it Lowell, but I think you're right about that. I was kind of hoping, I suppose, that I could just get on with my student engagement work, inside that structure, but I'm not sure I can anymore.'

'I'm at a point now where I work *at* my university, but not really *for* it…They pay me…but everything that interests me takes place outside its walls. I've been reading Ron Barnett lately. I liked it when he said that an academic is more likely to have closer links with academics from the same subject on the other side of the world than colleagues in the next building. Something like that, anyway. Disciple-allegiance will also be stronger than any phoney corporate-allegiance.'

'Until the corporate agents start making their way down your corridor and breaking into your office…'

'…Sounds like a second-rate zombie-movie.'

'Well, the Man from Del Monte might just be our man, then? Let me write down that Barnett reference.'

'Here, have one of my post-it notes. Barnett: *Being a University*.'

'Thanks. Never leave home without a post-it note. That should be your motto, Lowell.'

'Shall we get something to eat?' asked Jack. 'And how about coming back to my place tonight? I need to get started on that curriculum rationale, for our man. Next year, we could be millionaires!'

'What, with somebody else's money? You plonker, Rodney.'

'Seriously, though, I could really do with extending this conversation, and I don't want to go home on my own.'

'You're getting soft in your old age, Lowell. I've got some work to do tomorrow. How about you coming back to my place tonight?'

'Really? I was beginning to think your mother was a figment of your imagination.'

'She really wants to meet you, actually. I think she thinks you're a figment of *my* imagination. I'll ring her in a minute.'

'But I don't have anything with me.'

'What, your toothpaste and a clean pair of pants? To quote you…and Marx… aren't we surrounded by a vast accumulation by commodities? Now, open that wallet again and go and buy some overpriced underwear.'

'Or I could wear some of *your* underwear tomorrow?'

'You're such a pervert, Jack.'

'And I thought you loved me for it?'

'Not at breakfast…with my mother sitting opposite…Shit, I just remembered, she's going to the theatre tonight…Okay, you win, I'll come back with you tonight. We'll do some plotting in the morning, and then I need to get back home.'

'And we are gonna need to do some more reading as well, I think.'

'Okay, let's have a good go at everything in the morning. Now, get that wallet out and we'll buy *me* some underwear.'

'You have got stuff at my place, remember.'

'Yeah, but you've probably been wearing it, haven't you?'

'Rumbled!…I *will* get to come to your place, though?'

'Here's a plan. I'll arrange for us to have dinner with my mother next Saturday and you stay over for the night.'

'And perhaps we could do some of that reading in the week and then discuss it at your place.'

'Very romantic, Lowell.'

Chapter 25

At breakfast the following Sunday morning, Lotte's mother announced that she was due to meet an old colleague in St John's Wood in a couple of hours' time. Lotte and Jack agreed to tag along, and peel off at the underground station.

Some clouds were forming by the time they entered Regent's Park. They sat down on a bench seat overlooking the boating lake, with sandwiches and coffee.

'Bit nippy,' said Jack. 'Is it ever going to warm up?'

'I'm okay...for now.'

'Someone over there with just a tee-shirt on.'

'Most be from Newcastle.'

'Don't be so northist, Rudolph.'

'And don't be so stupid, Lowell. It's Sunday, and you're not at work now.'

'Don't remind me. I really don't want to go back in tomorrow.'

'Well, you could just leave *now* if you really can't stand it anymore.'

'I really do feel like saying "fuck the lot of you" and just walking out.'

'Don't do *that*. But you do have Del Monte's money now, so you haven't got much to lose.'

'Well, we've got *some* money. We need that strong curriculum rationale if we're going to get a really big amount.'

'You can do that. It's coming together nicely now, surely?'

'I need you with me, Lotte. If we *could* start something at one of those sites...You would come with me, wouldn't you?'

'What's this, Lowell; stage fright? We could go part-time; that might work. But, first things first, we do need to start thinking seriously about getting a team of people together.'

'Yeh. Thomas is keen on that, as well. Perhaps the time is right.'

'And, personally, I'm also concerned about how the hell you'll manage all that money?'

'It's been on my mind ever since you first mentioned it. I did speak to Thomas about it. He said that Del Monte's accountants will manage the money. We just have to put in a case for what we need.'

'What, each time?'

'I don't know. That would have to be sorted. Thomas didn't seem concerned about it. He thinks Del Boy will cough up.'

'But what if he doesn't?'

'Thomas seems to have struck up a really good relationship with him. He's very buoyed up.'

'But isn't that his nature? Every time you mention Thomas, he sounds excited about something.'

'True. A man happy in his work…If it does come to nothing, I suppose I could become a builder's mate. My brother's always busy. Honest work, and all that.'

'Very Wittgenstein, Lowell…And now you've met my mother, can I ask if I will ever get to meet this elusive brother of yours?'

'I don't see him much of him these days, what with the work, and he's got three kids. I did show him a photo of you last time I saw him. He said you looked like a posh bird.'

'Well, that's because I am. And far too good for the likes of you, you little oik.'

'You're too kind, Lady Muck.'

They sat in silence looking across the water. Jack spoke first: 'There's still that question about the link with the further education colleges. We need to tighten-up that argument a bit more, I think.'

'I've been thinking about that. Maybe we've got this upside down.'

'Very Marx and Hegel, Rudolph.'

'Seriously though, why don't the students do a kind of apprenticeship, in the colleges, and *then* come to us? Like a top-up honours degree?'

'I did originally think that. It just doesn't sound that radical, though. Just like a Foundation Degree top-up, you mean? They've not had a great press, have they?'

'But why not follow the American 2+2 model; two years in the community colleges, for an associates degree, then two years with us. That would give us more time with the students, and that *would* be different.'

'I think you may have something there. We're not re-inventing the wheel, after all, and you're right, *that* would look different from what we have in the UK at the moment.'

'It's the general idea I'm thinking about. Let's be honest, qualifications come and go. There might not be Foundation Degrees in a few years' time…And, Lowell, you get your under-represented students directly from the colleges. We wouldn't have to recruit them first. That's what I was thinking.'

'Right again. You're always bloody well right these days.'

'And that's why you love me.'

'And you may have solved something else that's been bugging me. I think Thomas rather liked the idea of bypassing the traditional routes altogether, and I get that. And I get his frustration with academic knowledge, and how much happier he is working on a more practical level…*But*…if we start with the Foundation Degree…focus on the practical skills…and then increasingly introduce the idea of theorisation…I think he might go for that…particularly if we demonstrate to Thomas why its important for students…'

'…I can see where you're going, I think…'

'…the need to give students not just *access* to theoretical knowledge…but for them to understand its role in society and in the professions…'

'...understanding the will to power...'

'...but also the role of knowledge in binding communities...its sacred role...'

'...Durkheim *and* Nietzsche...'

'...a marriage made in heaven...'

'...or an analysis of how heaven got made.'

'Very good, Rudolph. Very good, indeed...And this could become an important part of the conceptual underpinning for Del Boy...My reading this week was to look at some articles by people like Michael Young, Johan Muller, David Gullie... which then made me go back to Bernstein and look again at his idea of the role of horizontal knowledge...the tacit, experiential knowledge of the workplace...and vertical knowledge...the transformation of that knowledge into the type of powerful, explanatory knowledge...the knowledge which commands societal authority. We definitely need to give our students access to this knowledge, and to understand its role.'

'Knock yourself out, Lowell...I can definitely see some nice links here with Paulo Freire and critical theory and pedagogy...turning students from victims of schooling into agents of education.'

'That word "agency" is really important, I think. All students should have an education which provides them with a sound agentic...is that a word?...orientation to work.'

'The exercise of skill involves intentionality within a normative context.'

'That's bloody good, Rudolph.'

'Not me, unfortunately. It's a quote I wrote down from that Winch book, which I've now finished. And this does all connect up nicely with our old friend Pirsig.'

'How so?'

'The technician; the static manual; how to get from A to B. It's dis-embodied knowledge. From what you said yesterday, Thomas will love that. That's just static quality. If we *are* going to use the word skill, we would have to say that it should always be viewed as more than technique. If nothing else, it has to involve judgement. And there's that moral component coming back.'

'Yes, yes. I can also see a connection with Max Weber here, as well. How to enchant a disenchanted world. It's humans that give everything meaning. No work is just about techniques. Even if it was, humans would compel themselves, somehow, to leave their mark. I just thought of the sociologist Donald Roy. I think that was his name. He wrote about how people, even in the face of the most mind-numbing labour, still look to leave their mark. And the builder who signs his name somewhere. Sennett provides some great examples of that, I seem to remember.'

'Very Hitchcock...always leaving his mark...Seriously, though, everything *is* a human project, not just following a manual. And that would connect us back to *wissenshaft*...always pushing that old envelope.'

'Great...Could we then say that all occupations...utilising those rich German words...should have three key components: a degree of autonomy for the worker; a degree of scholarship; and a moral, perhaps, civic responsibility? And that education should seek to inculcate those...as values.'

'Yes. I think we could definitely say that. And don't forget about the need to make judgements. Something else I got from that Winch book: all meaningful work involves that kind of intelligent action...action guided by the widest notion of skill.'

'Brilliant. And back to Sennett again. Architects and builders...in practice...are not that different...professions and technical occupations all involve the exercise of judgement.'

'There is a virtue in work which has quality; a moral intelligence at work.'

'Well, I think we deserve another coffee after that.'

'Go on then.'

Jack returned to the table and spoke before he sat down: 'I've just been thinking... about that old book *Learning to Labour*, by Paul Willis. You know, we *have* got a big task on our hands here...There's a long tradition of anti-authoritarianism amongst the working-class in this country...their anti-middle-class stance...their symbolic power grabs...it makes sense...'

'...because academic knowledge *is* over-theorised...and education reflects bourgeois values and interests...'

'...and they're not stupid...they know what's going on...powerful knowledge and the knowledge of the powerful...nice distinction from Michael Young, I think...You *would* want to make a stand against that...if your were powerless...but, ironically, aren't working-class kids actually shooting themselves in their own foot?'

'Feet, even...Standards, Lowell.'

'And precisely why they hate middle-class teachers, Rudolph.'

'But, let's go back to Judith Butler for a minute...gender roles are performances... repeated endlessly...and so are social class roles. What happens when working-class kids are taught by working-class teachers...people from technical trades...'

'...they collude...and confirm the anti-intellectualism?'

'Exactly...a pedagogic device...isn't that what you'd call it?'

'Embedding a slave mentality...isn't that what you'd call it?'

'Either way, we're definitely in the game of de-constructing constructed identities.'

'The appellation problem...if you respond as you are called, you embed the status quo...and working-class kids keep getting working-class jobs...'

'And the master and the slave are both reproduced.'

'Fuck. We can't change this. It's way too big.'

'No; that's defeatist, Lowell. The first step is to know this...knowledge *is* power... if enough of us know this, we can at least make some inroads...'

'...and from speaking to Thomas, I think Del Boy knows this.'

'There you go, my lad...and all the more reason not to trust the State...not for now, at least.'

'You're bloody well right again, Rudolph…We do have to give this a go…I'm up and down like a yo-yo at the moment.'

'Let's be practical, and start by finding some more like-minded people. We need to thrash out the ideas. It's time to turn this dream into a reality, Jack.'

'But maybe we *should* just stick with people we know; to start with, anyway?'

'Look, let's have a meeting…with friends…I'm in email communication with Jos Conway at the moment. She's still in the Philosophy Department at the old place. I think she would be keen, and a good asset. She's a real expert on critical pedagogy, and will see all the links instantly.'

'Norman and Roger would definitely come. That gives us a philosopher, an historian, and a psychologist. How about you friend, Milton Townsend?'

'He would certainly help us. I don't know if he would come to a meeting, though.'

'And we've got Thomas, and Del Boy.'

'And I'd come just to see that this guy is real. Still a small meeting though.'

'Anybody from your place?'

'No one I really trust, no. Didn't you mention someone at your place?'

'Yeah. She would be good. She gets it.'

'I *could* ask Julian Ashwood. Do you remember him? In my old department. He helped in that QAA review?'

'I remember the name.'

'He emails me from time to time. He's worked at several places and has now done some work for the QAA, I think. He's really into the concept of quality.'

'A good example of why we need to be cautious. You never told me that you had some sympathy for the devil.'

'I enjoy the arguments. He does seem to have the inside line on developments in policing recalcitrant academics. That could be useful to us?'

'What, so we then do the exact opposite?'

'Possibly. But things have moved on, I think. They talk about quality enhancement now, not quality assurance.'

'Sounds like weasel words for the same thing.'

'Maybe. But pays to know what the Devil is up to.'

'Keep your enemies close…Well, if you trust him.'

'I think he's harmless. And he does know a lot of people.'

'Norman will give him short shrift, if necessary.'

'He may not be interested, of course.'

'Hey, I just thought…Marion…do you remember her? She had the office next to me at the old place. She's so level-headed, and she'd be really good on the legal side of things.'

'That's a scary thought.'

'What, Marion?'

'No, you idiot. The legal stuff.'

'I know. Thomas says Del Boy's people will sort that side of things. We're the educators…apparently. But Marion…yes. She'll keep an eye on them. She'll make sure we're not being led up a garden path.'

'And who keeps an eye on us?'

'Who educates the educators, you mean?'

'I suppose the students could do that. If we had our own institution. We could have a student body…with power.'

'And cut out the middle-man. What the QAA was *supposed* to be doing, I think.'

'Another reason for having Julian there?'

'Definitely Marion, though. If I can track her down. She retired, but she did send me a forwarding email address. I'll run all this past Thomas. He liked Marion. Perhaps we could put everything we have into some kind of paper. Like a pre-read, and send it round to everyone? It's not as if we would be starting from scratch. Assuming Del Boy likes what we put together, there's our starting point.'

'Some mood music. But let's not make it all theoretical. That would be ironic.'

'Don't you mean paradoxical?'

'Watch it, Lowell. I could always change my mind about you.'

Chapter 26

The Windsor Station platform was busy, mainly with several clumps of schoolchildren. It was a hot Friday afternoon in early July, and Jack Lowell was irritated by the heat, the kids, and not having any space to unfold his Brompton bike. Although he had checked the directions while on the train from London, he took another look at his map before he left the station. There was no rush. He was due to meet up with Lotte in three hours time, but had decided to set off early, to take a bike-ride around Windsor Great Park, large parts of which appeared to be open to the public.

Thomas Minot had booked a small conference suite for the weekend. Everyone who had been invited to their 'Co-operative Learning Scoping Meeting' had accepted, but most were due to arrive the following morning. Jack had persuaded Lotte to come over on the Friday, so they could run through everything, but the real reason was because he wanted her company. He cycled directly to the conference suite, in order to check-in, to look at the meeting rooms, and to drop off his bag, which was weighing down his bike. As he walked up the stairs to his bedroom, he became irritated again, this time by his own polite deference to the well-spoken person at reception. Why do I do that, he asked himself.

***

Lotte approached Windsor in her car just before 7.10pm. Only ten minutes late, she thought. Her mind was on the telephone conversation she'd had with Carol Morgan the previous evening. The phone call had come out of the blue; a catch up call to see how Lotte was getting on. Lotte spoke about how well things were now going with Jack, and his ideas for this new project. She was aware that she was calling it 'Jack's project', even though she was probably now more enthusiastic about it than he was. She also knew the reason - a bit of distance, in case it all went belly up. She then smiled at the recurring thought that here was a privately-educated school girl enthusiastically embracing a project at the opposite end of the social spectrum. Had Jack worked out where she was educated? He'd never mentioned it, but she'd rehearsed her defence: you can't help your background; it was her German grandmother who had put up the money; wasn't Karl Marx very middle-class? And the trump card: wasn't she now being ultra-subversive?

As she turned into the road which led to the conference suite, she found herself repeating a sentence from Carol: '*How* we think *is* probably more important than what we think, but to what use we put our thinking is the real question.' It chimed with a lot of what Milton Townsend had been saying. It would have been good to have invited Carol to the meeting, she thought. She was looking forward to seeing Jos Conway again, and she smiled as she thought about Julian Ashwood, and what he might look like these days. Although she had been excited by the prospect of Milton addressing the meeting, some doubts had begun to surface. She was aware that she didn't like the idea of sharing Milton with everyone, but also that she didn't want to let him down. What if he thought the project was daft? Still, he hadn't said anything about the paper that Jack had circulated, so, hopefully, that was a good sign.

As she pulled into the car park she could see Jack standing on the front entrance steps. He's such a puppy dog these days, she thought; more like a Labrador though, rather than the Whippet he used to be. She liked his weight gain, but knew he wouldn't like it if she joked about it.

'Come on, Rudolph!' shouted Jack, as Lotte's head appeared over the top of her car. 'We've got dinner in fifteen minutes.'

'Sorry, traffic was horrendous. I thought I'd just plough on rather than keep sending text messages. This looks very nice. Who's here?'

'Thomas and Roger. Everyone else is coming in the morning.'

'Okay, good. Here, take my bag, darling.'

'Don't you darling me, darling.'

***

After re-introducing Lotte to Roger and Thomas, Jack could see that the person on reception was keen to usher them towards the dining room. As they shuffled to take their places, Lotte looked at Thomas: 'How did you find this place?'

'I didn't. It was all arranged by our benefactor. I think he had a meeting here. When I explained where everyone would be travelling from, he suggested it. A bit of a trek for me, though.'

'He's footing the bill for everything?' asked Roger.

'Including the alcohol?' added Jack.

'Apparently so, but best we go easy on that, I would suggest,' replied Thomas.

'Good point,' said Jack. 'Perhaps we could agree with everyone that they pay for their own drinks.'

'Sensible,' said Roger. 'I'll order a bottle of red for the table, to get us going. Heads down everyone, here comes the waiter.'

Meals ordered, Roger poured a glass of wine for everyone, then said: 'So, I understand that the benefactor is not gracing us with his presence.'

'Afraid not,' said Thomas. 'He's got meetings elsewhere…Romania and Bulgaria. He just wants us to get on with it, I think. He did say to me once that he likes to be hands- off, for fear of putting people on their guard. Once he has trust…and Jack, hats off to you, my friend, on that front.'

'Well, a lot of that paper was Lotte, and if you hadn't paved the way, we wouldn't be sitting here.'

'I liked what you sent round, Jack,' said Roger. 'I spent a whole evening on the phone discussing it with Norman. It's exciting. I'm looking forward to tomorrow. Our main concern was that work-related element, the 2+2 American model. That looked a bit rushed.'

'You're right, Roger,' said Jack. 'It looked rushed because it was. I had originally thought that students might start with us, before they go off to the FE colleges.'

'That was me, Roger,' said Lotte. 'I just thought it made more sense to start in the colleges. Apart from anything else, we then don't have to recruit the students… from scratch, so to speak…But, yes, we need to thrash this out. Hopefully, tomorrow? Personally speaking, I feel much safer on the student engagement and quality side of things.'

'Yes, that's strong,' said Roger. 'I really liked what you had there, and it sets up the teacher training challenge really well…the professional development challenge, as you called it.'

'That reminds me,' said Thomas. 'I wrote down this quote from Richard Sennett the other day.' Thomas stretched down to his shoulder bag, which was resting against his chair legs, and began shuffling the paper inside it.

'Thomas always has his Mary Poppins bag with him,' said Jack.

'Here we are,' said Thomas, as he placed a small note-book size piece of paper on the table. The writing was facing Jack, so he read it aloud:

"Craftsmanship names an enduring, basic human impulse, the desire to do a job well for its own sake." Sennett, R. *The Craftsman*, 2010, page 9.

'Glad you haven't forgotten how to produce a proper academic reference, Thomas,' said Jack.

'That's really good,' said Lotte. 'A nice linchpin.'

'I did my homework,' said Thomas, 'like a good student. I read your paper, and I suddenly saw it. That's the link with quality. I'll be honest, I was struggling a bit before that.'

'But,' said Roger, 'here's our problem again: do we want students to *begin* their course knowing this, or could it come later?'

'A dialectical relationship?' asked Jack, aware that Lotte was smirking at him as he spoke, but without making it obvious.

'Personally,' began Thomas. 'I would still prefer it if we went it alone, and have nothing to do with the mainstream…but…I have a suggestion…here comes the dinner. Let's discuss this tomorrow. Shall I order another bottle of wine while the waiter's here?'

Chapter 27

After breakfast at the conference centre, Lotte and Jack made their excuses and went upstairs to check out the room which had been hired for them. They pushed the chairs around to create a half circle, and then walked towards the window which looked out over the garden. Lotte looked back into the room, then asked: 'That's enough chairs?'

'Think so. I counted ten of us. How about a wander in the garden?'

'Sounds good.'

'I doubt anyone will arrive much before 10.30.'

'So, we're going from eleven until one, and then two until four?'

'Or later, if necessary.'

'Are you still happy to chair the meeting, Jack? You didn't seem so sure again this morning?'

'Well, I'm definitely happy to take some notes. Will you do the same; I don't want to miss anything. Thomas did agree to kick us off. I really don't want it to look like I'm leading this, and he can give the background info on Del Boy.'

'Okay, let's go,' said Lotte, as she began turning away from the window. 'It's a lovely room.'

They stepped out into the garden at the back of the conference centre, and instantly felt the warmth of the sun.

'Perhaps we could ask that we have this morning's coffee out here,' said Jack.

'Good idea. 10.30? Jos, Julian and Milton all said they would be able to get here by then.'

'Marion said that she might be a little late; she's driving over from South Wales. I didn't hear anything from Norman, but he will be on time, I'm sure. I didn't hear back from Rosie Arnold either, but I'm sure she'll come. I didn't tell her we all knew each other.'

'Why not?'

'I didn't want her to feel intimidated.'

'Well, *we* don't know each very well, do we? I haven't seen Jos or Julian for ages.'

'You're right. And I don't know them at all, really. And Thomas probably won't remember everyone…You'll like Rosie. She's into women's rights.'

'Aren't we all?'

'You know what I mean. Perhaps we could all come out here later this afternoon; sort of plenary? Windsor Great Park is over the back there. Perhaps we could hire some guns and take pot shots at defenceless members of the Royal Family, as they wander through the grounds…Sort of group bonding exercise.'

'After which, the surviving members could then drive you straight to The Tower.'

'Where I could make a stand and die as a principled martyr.'

'My man for all seasons. In reality, you'd be crucified by the right wing press.'

'Lotte the Royalist; doesn't suit you.'

'You do have to admire their will to power, though. Do you think *they* have faith in what they are doing?'

'What, their ability to sponge off the nation, while pretending they're serving the nation?'

'Well, a lot of people still seem have faith in them.'

'I look forward to the day when they're all de-frocked and their sacred status is reduced to the profanity it always was.'

'Until we're all super-men, people will always feel the need to have faith in *something* bigger than themselves.'

'And that's all we have time for on today's Opium for the People programme.'

'You're such an idiot, Lowell. We'd better get ready for some meet and greet.'

After coffee and the necessary introductions, everyone followed Thomas up to the conference room: 'Please, sit where you wish,' he said.

After a few moments of shuffling around, Thomas then turned to Jack: 'Two empty places, Jack?'

'Yeah, looks like Marion and Rosie are running late. Marion said she might be a bit late. I expect they'll arrive shortly. I suggest we make a start.'

Thomas read the fire regulations from a sheet of paper, explained that there would no more coffee until lunch, but there was water by the window behind them, and reminded everyone where the toilets were. He announced that he had no slides; that they would use Jack and Lotte's paper as their guide; and that this should be a roundtable discussion, to raise issues. He then reminded everyone of the purpose of the three sessions: this morning to raise any broad issues; this afternoon to look at more specific curriculum issues; and tomorrow morning, to consider the next steps. He then smiled broadly and reminded everyone that lunch and dinner would be provided today, and there would be breakfast and lunch tomorrow. He forgot to mention their agreement over alcohol, but Roger reminded him, which everybody nodded in agreement with.

Thomas asked the group whether they would like some background on how this project had come together, which everyone unanimously agreed to. He explained how his original undergraduate course on entrepreneurship had morphed into his workshops on setting up workers' co-ops, and how he had come across the project's benefactor, who wished to remain anonymous, as much as possible. He smiled at Jack when he explained that the benefactor was now interested in funding a project which sought links between workers' co-ops, co-operative learning, and the idea of a co-operative learning institute. He emphasised that nothing was set in stone, just that the benefactor had been impressed with the ideas that Jack and Lotte had put together. He then held up Jack and Lotte's paper, and said that this was the position they were currently in, and that here was the opportunity to see where this might now be taken.

Jack raised his hand and explained to the group that they took the decision to keep the discussion amongst friends, and that everyone had been hand-picked. He laughed as he said 'hand-picked', which was greeted with smiles and mocking nods of agreement. Jack then asked Thomas if he might say something about his recent reading of Richard Sennett and the importance of work-related learning in their discussions with the benefactor.

'Yes,' said Thomas. 'That's an important point. As most of you know, I think, I left the university sector somewhat dismayed with how the practical questions around setting up a business were always being sidelined...by the more academic considerations, shall we say...oh, and, of course, the lack of trust in professionals, brought on by the quality police.'

'Amen to that, brother!' exclaimed Roger. 'I mean the quality police...And maybe the other...Sorry Thomas, carry on.'

'Well, Lotte and Jack connected both dimensions really well, I thought, so perhaps we could come back to that later. But, on Sennett...Jack got me thinking when he spoke about bridging the academic-vocational divide in education, and I started digging around the German system...I really got into the thinking behind words like *beruf* and *bildung*...started thinking more about vocation as an old-fashioned calling...To cut a long story short, the people at my workshops started to see the connections...a sense of belonging and ownership, and how that links with the ideas behind a workers' co-op. Does that make sense?'

Norman raised his hand, and said: 'Sorry, do we need to raise our hands?' At which, Thomas turned to Jack: 'Jack? What's our protocol?'

'No, I don't think so,' said Jack. 'I think the group is small enough that we all chip in when we see fit. I'm desperate not to see myself as a chair, or leader of this group...'

'Just like a workers' co-op!' shouted Roger, then laughed at his own comment.

'Why not,' said Jack. 'What were you going to say, Norman?'

'Yes, it does make sense, Thomas. But I'm not familiar with Sennett. Could you outline the connections a bit more?'

'Sorry, Norman. What I should have said was that I really liked Sennett's discussion of the craftsman's embedded practice...I think that's what he called it...and the distinction between the *erlebnis*...the sense of having experienced something... and the *erfahrung*...the meaning of it, to the craftsman...I remember Jack making a distinction between a job and real work. It seems to me that the English way to develop competence amongst a workforce is very much related to seeing work as merely a job...and to see a skill as simply something to be acquired. Rather than an ongoing relationship with tasks...one which requires constant active engagement... to craft something, I suppose. I'm not being very clear, am I?'

Milton Townsend raise his hand, then spoke: 'Very clear, actually, Thomas. Speaking strictly as a philosopher, I think this takes us to the heart of something really important. I, too, am not familiar with Sennett's work, but this distinction in German, *I* think, opens up the moral quality that's in any form of work...work is very rarely just a technique...something to be mastered, which can then be repeated, without thought...but something which, yes, requires constant reflection. It's what gives work its aesthetic quality, and its purpose and meaning. We might even say it's what makes us human.'

'Yes,' said Thomas. 'And much better put than my mumblings. At one point I think Sennett says that getting something right, when you are a craftsman, is not just about following the rules. It's clearly not a technical question. It's far more than that.'

'Thank you,' said Milton. 'I must read that book. What I really liked about the paper, which I enjoyed enormously, was the very earnest attempt to make everything link with a much richer notion of quality. I will try to be concise: what we've had in UK universities for the last twenty years or so is a notion of quality which is very much about following the rules, which *does* make it a technical question. Something is deemed to be of high quality because the rules were followed; no deviation means high quality; it's a compliance regime; assured by people who are checking that the rules *were* followed. But true human quality is not like that; not like that at all. I'm not familiar with the Robert Pirsig book either, but I liked the way the paper used the idea of static quality, to refer to compliance, and contrasted that with the idea of dynamic quality, to refer to the *human* project; the human investment in something. I don't know if I would use the words static and dynamic but the conceptual distinction is a good one, I think.'

Julian Ashwood raised his hand, then spoke: 'Hello everyone, and I'm glad that some of you remember me. I'd like to formally thank Lotte for inviting me to this meeting. I too, really enjoyed the paper. As I explained to a couple of you over coffee earlier, I've been doing some work evaluating and reviewing university departments up and down the country. I've also been following developments at the QAA very carefully. I appreciate, of course, that this might sound out of kilter with the thinking in this group...but I do like the shift that's taken place in their discussions about quality...more towards quality enhancement and away from quality assurance. The way I see it...with the benefit of hindsight, or perhaps *in*-sight...is that universities needed to go through an assurance phase, in order to get to an enhancement phase. That quality is now much more about universities reflecting, *themselves*, on what they are doing. In that sense, I do see a move more in the direction of that notion of dynamic quality.'

'I'm not convinced,' interjected Jack quickly. 'Yes, I see what you're driving at, but I wouldn't say that the quality agenda has crossed that line. I would say that we now have, perhaps, a more progressive static quality regime, but I wouldn't call it dynamic, in any way.'

Julian motioned to reply, but gave way to Milton, who had his hand raised: 'Somebody please correct me if I'm wrong, but what I took from the paper was an attempt to rescue the concept of quality from its extrinsic, quantitative, straitjacket. As I see it, turning things into quantities, which can be measured, must affect quality negatively, because true quality is a substance which doesn't lend itself to measurement. It's a process...something much more akin to a state of mind...than an outcome.'

'And, could I add to that,' said Norman. 'In an age where *everything* seems to be a skill...a competence...that perhaps we should be seeking to restore the idea of a disposition. A much wider, richer notion; a moral, decision making capacity; something able to convey a very human capacity. Connecting this with the idea of quality is crucial, I believe. And yes, thank you Lotte and Jack for a great paper, and the way you spelt that out.'

'Thank you,' said Jack. 'And that reminds me of a quote that Lotte and I spent a lot of time discussing. It came from Peter Abbs, about education being a critical orientation of mind. I think this is why that word "employability" bugs me so much. While I can accept that the emphasis *has* shifted, away from viewing education as a crude job training exercise, we still seem to be in a rather unsatisfactory instrumental world…it's still about *collecting* skills and competencies. They are just a little less crude. Certainly not that deep, critical, orientation of mind. That's a true education, and also the place to find true quality.'

'Sorry, Jack,' interrupted Thomas, 'but I think I've just had a light-bulb moment… that the same should apply to work, as well as education…*work* as a critical orientation of mind…not just that ever-expanding collection of atomistic skills.'

'Sorry everyone,' said Julian, 'but could I just come back to what is playing on my mind. I do get where you are coming from, but I also see the case for transparency; intrinsic qualities are somewhat amorphous, particularly in an age of value for money. I'm not disagreeing; just trying to recognise the reality of higher education provision in the 21st century.'

Jack was about to jump in, but gave way to Milton: 'But could I add something important, I think. An intrinsic quality is, in reality, always facing outwards; it is in that sense always an orientation to action. The problem, I think, is profound, because the reality you speak of, Julian, *is* preoccupied with measurement, with quantities, whereas the type of quality I…we…are interested in just isn't like that. It's amorphous, only in that language of measurement.'

'I think this also gets us to the heart of the related matter,' said Norman. 'The need for transparency exists precisely because of the breakdown in the trust we have for professional people. There's an irony, here, of course; that our desire to inculcate the value of pride in workmanship in our students, is happening at the same time this pride has been eroded in the life of the professional academic.'

'Quality *is* an internal matter, I think,' said Jack. 'External evidence, the kind used in inspection regimes, is like a trace. It points in the direction of what came before it. In which case, to place faith in the latter must, surely, obscure the true nature of quality. It's an obscuration, or masquerade, if you like.'

'I see that too,' said Julian. 'There's been some good work done by Graham Gibbs on this. He's published a couple of really good monographs on quality; does anybody know them?…What is it that enhances the learning of students?…It's academics talking with each other about teaching and learning; it's low teacher-student ratios; it's students understanding assessment criteria; it's engagement in learning tasks… that sort of thing. Unfortunately, the proxies we have to measure the amount of those things are poor: the QAA, the NSS…They don't actually measure these things very well, if at all. To use your word, Jack, they are traces; clues, about where we need to look.'

'I think it's even worse than that,' said Jack. 'Let's be honest, students from elite universities get elite jobs, but not because they are clever. What I mean is that these proxies, as you called them, are also distorted by the snob factor. It's not the quality of the learning and teaching regime which decides student choices...is it? As Max Weber pointed out a hundred years ago, the middle-class enthusiasm for education has very little to do with a new-found thirst for knowledge, and much more to do with perpetuating modes of social closure for their offspring. Public school, Oxbridge...they exist to perpetuate social inequality...to keep the plebs out. These new proxies, no matter how good they are, cannot override the wider *social* function that education performs.'

'Well, thank you, Professor Lowell,' began Lotte, with a big smile on her face, 'for delivering this year's Reith lecture on radical thinking in the twentieth century... But seriously...I was only looking at Graham Gibbs' work the other day...*Dimensions of Quality*; yes, Julian? And, without all the socialist trappings, I'm inclined to think that he would probably agree with you, Jack. The current measures of quality do distort and obscure...But what *I* got from his work was a confirmation that student engagement actually *is* the key. Furthermore, I would say that students on task, as he calls it, could easily be linked with the kind of pride in one's work that Sennett is talking about. Which I think connects with your light-bulb moment, Thomas. And I would link *that* with Alan Jenkins' idea that we want students to experience *their* learning in the same way that their teachers do...when *they* undertake research...To put themselves in research mode...to take a scholarly approach. Because of that, I would agree that the QAA haven't fully grasped these wider and deeper implications behind the notion of quality.'

'And thank *you*, Professor Rudolph,' said Jack. 'I'm wondering if this might be the point to say, in time honoured fashioned, that I think we should come back to Lotte's point after lunch, when we get stuck into curriculum matters a bit more. And also, just to say, that my phone has been vibrating in my pocket...I wasn't being rude by looking at it...but I have a message from Rosie Arnold, my colleague, who says she should be with us by lunchtime, and another message from Marion, who said she had just entered the outskirts of Windsor. That sounds a bit ominous, doesn't it?' Jack laughed at his own comment, which encouraged others to smile and pass comment to each other.

Roger Fergusson moved forward on his chair: 'Not like me, I know, but I've been sitting here quietly, thinking that maybe there is some kind of middle ground here, where, if any external judgement *is* going to be made, then it should be on whether the ingredients for good learning are in place...are the ingredients most likely to produce quality in full view...You can take a horse to water, but you can't make it drink, sort of thing. If Gibbs is right, and I see nothing wrong with what you said, Julian and Lotte, then to pass judgement is to check that everything *is* in place... that's actually a judgement on the ingredients, not any outcomes, or intentions...If the students don't actually drink...'

'...then it's their own fault,' Jack added.

At that, the door opened. It took a moment for Jack to realise that it was Marion; her hair was longer and curlier than he remembered, and she appeared shorter. Her flat shoes, thought Jack: 'Marion!' he exclaimed. 'So good to see you. Please come and join us. Thanks for coming.'

'So sorry everyone, I completely messed up the timings. Is anyone as old as me and remembers Reggie Perrin...leaves on the line; signal failure at Waterloo? In my case: brain malfunction on leaving the M4.'

Everybody either smiled or laughed at Marion's comment. Jack then pointed to the two empty chairs, which were next to each other, and said: 'Well, so far, we've been in debate about the nature of quality and how it relates to the world of work.'

'Good to hear,' said Marion. 'Yes, the paper you sent round was really enjoyable, if a little challenging, given the amount of time I've been spending in the garden recently. I'm not sure I have much to offer...But look at me, I've disturbed everything; really sorry.'

'Nonsense, Marion,' said Jack. 'I think you remember everyone. Look, I have an idea: how about we take a formal break now. Perhaps take a wander in the garden and continue the conversation in smaller groups. Then have some lunch, and take stock afterwards?'

Everyone agreed it was a good idea, and started to make their way to the door. Lotte had been sitting next to Jos. She placed her arm on her thigh, to indicate that she should sit still. As the door closed behind everyone, she whispered to Jos: 'Sorry, Jos, it didn't look like you could get a word in edgeways.'

'Just like old times, Lotte. Some things never change; imposters in the male temple, again.'

'Yes, exactly,' said Lotte. 'I'm so glad you could come.'

'You know me, I would have spoken up if I really needed to. What I really want to say relates more to the curriculum. I'm happy to leave that until after lunch. I really liked all those connections with Ernest Boyer in the paper. Was that you, Lotte?'

'No. Actually it was you. As I started to piece things together with Jack, it took me back to a lot of things you said at the time of that hideous QAA inspection.'

'Don't remind me of that...Although, looking back, it was quite funny, wasn't it?'

'I know. Do you remember that reviewer; the one who observed me teach; who kept coming up with problems?'

'How could I forget. But the real problem was surely that bloody quality officer. I'm not sure *he* was actually that bad.'

'Just a bit sad...Actually, I think he was probably right on some things. Looking back again, I don't think we were as transparent as maybe we should have been. Maybe we were too much on the defensive...digging in a bit too much.'

'Rutting stags, maybe...on both sides?...Or is that too patriarchal a metaphor?'

'Maybe it's what that system did to us all?'

'For sure...But the chief reviewer would surely have put that guy in his place, if he *was* out of line. Which is ironic, of course, because there wasn't ever much transparency from their side.'

'I think the real problem is now much clearer, though...that underneath the politics of us wanting to defend our professional autonomy...was that deeper epistemological problem we are now exploring: that both sides were operating with different notions of quality; two orders of reality.'

'Nicely put, Lotte...Do you know what happened to that quality officer, after that accident. It all went very quiet?'

'She does cross my mind from time to time; usually when I'm angry about something. She just seemed to disappear. Maybe the VC put *her* in her place.'

'Maybe she was just out of her depth...I think Steve Jackman handled everything pretty well. Much better than I would have.'

'Was it that bad being Head of Department?'

'When Steve left, it seemed like a good move, but I hated pretty much every minute of it. All glorified admin...a good administrator could probably have done most of it. It was such a relief when I gave it up. The VC was kind. It was his idea that I apply for the Research Director for the Humanities post.'

'From your email, it sounds like you are enjoying that.'

'To be honest, I was happiest when I was just a straightforward academic; in the classroom; doing some research.'

'That's the dream, these days, I suppose. I'm an academic, get me out of here!'

'Quite right! Anyway, forget all of that. You must tell me more about Jack. Are you and he walking out together these days?'

'Yes, we are. He's always on probation, though.'

'Looks like he's got you well trained, though. I notice you were the note-taker this morning. Women's work is never done.'

'Funny you should mention that. We were supposed to be doing that together. You're right. He didn't write down a bloody thing, did he? I need to have a word.'

***

Just before one o'clock, the person from reception walked into the garden area, to announce that lunch was ready. Behind him stood Rosie Arnold. Jack broke away from his conversation with Marion and walked towards the steps. She looks like she's just come through one of the bushes rather than the car park, he thought, but he liked her tee-shirt, beads and bangles, which glistened in the sun: 'Rosie! So glad you're here. I'll introduce you to everyone over lunch.'

Rosie curtsied to everyone: 'I made it...Sorry to be so late...I'm a bit flustered.'

Each small group then started to make its way towards the dining room. One large table was laid for lunch and everyone sat in their same groups. At one end, Lotte sat next to Milton and opposite Julian. Over lunch they continued their conversation about who is best placed to make a judgement over whether something, or someone, has quality. In the middle of the table, Norman and Roger sat next to each other, opposite Jos and Thomas. They continued their conversation about what constitutes a workers' co-op. And at the other end of the table, Jack sat opposite Rosie and Marion, where Marion opened up a conversation about whether the main outcome of this project was to establish a co-operative university, and what that might look like.

After lunch, everyone spilled out into the garden again. It was now a very hot afternoon and the conversation turned to whether they might stay there for the afternoon session. Thomas suggested a compromise, that they should go back to the room, where Lotte would outline some key curriculum ideas, but then they should return to the garden for some plenary thoughts. There were no dissenting voices, and shortly after 2pm everyone was back in the room, in their same seats. Rosie was last in the room, and Jack offered her the remaining seat, by moving his arms in an exaggerated and mocking chivalrous gesture.

At Thomas's request, Lotte made her way to the front, turned on the projector, and put her pen drive into the side of the laptop which had been provided by the conference centre: 'While that's warming up,' she began, 'could I also formally thank everyone for coming. The conversations this morning and over lunch have been invaluable. As you know, everything is rather speculative at the moment, but we have a chance here to try to make a difference...somehow...in the direction that higher education in the UK might take over the next few years. Maybe nothing will come of it...perhaps just a few academic papers or articles.' She smiled at her comment. 'Or perhaps we might be able to do something much more practical, and I'm sure we'll discuss that tomorrow.'

At that point, Thomas interjected: 'Yes, sorry everyone. I know you all have questions about whether we are trying to open up a new institution, but I think it best to hold that over until the morning. Good way to keep you all here.' He laughed loudly at his last comment. 'Sorry, Lotte, please continue.'

'No; thank *you*, Thomas. That's given me the chance to find my couple of slides.' She pointed up at the screen, at a diagram in the form of a triangle, which was now in clear view: 'You will recognise this triangle from the paper. I just wanted to spend a few moments talking to it, by way of introduction to our discussion this afternoon. You can see that we have "student engagement" at one point; "quality" at the second point; and "Boyer's four scholarships" at the third point. I deliberately skewed the triangle so it looked off-centre...not an easy task for someone like me, with limited IT skills...in order not to privilege any of three points; they're all equally important. We made it one of the key challenges in the paper to connect the three points in a meaningful way.'

She then moved to the second slide, which had the same three headings, but this time within three Venn diagram circles, which were overlapped to produce a shaded middle area: 'So...here we see how the three ideas now need to intersect, so that each partakes of the other two. Of course, as in all Venn diagrams, there will be parts of each circle which do not overlap...either at all, or just for two of the circles. That's in order to recognise that, for instance, some notions of quality cannot...or perhaps better, should not...overlap with, say, student engagement. And some notions of student engagement may have little connection with Boyer's work...and so on. So... our curriculum challenge becomes to ensure that our shaded area in the middle is at the core of what we intend to do. I hope that's clear...and...over to you. Any comments?' As she was finishing, she began making her way back to her seat.

Jack was first to speak: 'It took me a while to get there, but I increasingly began to see the three headings in the diagram as three sides of the same coin...if that doesn't sound daft...at least within the shaded area. So, yes, student engagement could, for example, include wider aspects of the student experience...a sense of general well-being, maybe...and nothing wrong with that...but the fundamental core would need to be a form of student engagement which overlaps with the dynamic quality we outlined in the paper, and Boyer's notion of the four scholarships of engagement. In a nutshell, I suppose we might say that a fully engaged student would be one who is engaged in a form of scholarly endeavour...because you have to be fully immersed... invested...in such an endeavour.' He then looked across to Lotte, who nodded in agreement.

Jos came in quickly: 'Yes; thanks Jack. That notion of being in the service of scholarship as a kind of noble endeavour came across very strongly. And I really liked it; very Wilheim von Humboldt. But the bit I was most impressed with was this idea of having students making their way around Boyer's four scholarships, not just staff; really liked that.'

'And,' began Lotte, 'it fits nicely, to my mind, with the Alan Jenkins idea of students thinking about their work in the same way that a member of staff might think about their work. Indeed, perhaps in joint endeavour; staff and students working together in scholarly mode.'

'Lovely. Really good,' said Jos.

Rosie Arnold had her hand raised. 'Rosie?' asked Jack.

'Sorry, wasn't sure if I should raise my hand or not,' said Rosie.

'We agreed not to bother with that this morning,' said Jack. 'What were you going to say?'

'Yes, I see that, and I like it, but I don't think we should forget how radical Boyer *is*, in the context of *staff*. Here we are in the middle of 2013, nearly twenty-five years after Boyer's book on scholarship, and we still have staff fixated on what he called the scholarship of discovery. And even worse, staff doing research with the sole aim of writing it up as a journal article...is that *really* a scholarship of engagement? Here's my confession...I'm actually hopeless in that area, but I do want to be scholarly.' At that point she turned to look at Jack: 'If it wasn't for Jack, I think I might have left my university by now. He saved me, by pointing out that there's more to scholarship than writing journal articles, particularly when it comes to making an impact. It's just that it isn't valued at the moment...but by whom exactly?...I really wanted to come today, to learn some more about these wider Boyer-type possibilities, so thank you, Jack...There's got to be a better way of doing things.'

Milton and Norman were both poised to speak, but gave way to Marion, who had moved forward on her chair: 'Here's *my* confession...just within these walls, you understand...Before I retired a year ago, I was asked my advice at my old place... where some of you still work...on how to implement new contracts for staff...where everybody would be asked to sign a new one...which would include definitions of what it meant to be "research active". I said...based on the definitions I was provided with...that it would be *very* difficult, and not very conducive to a healthy academic environment. If I hadn't already handed in my notice, I doubt I would have added my final comment there.'

'Blimey!' shouted Roger. 'Exactly what everyone thought they were up to! The bastards!'

'Well,' said Marion, 'the fact that it *didn't* happen...I assume it hasn't happened since I left...means that the Senior Management Team must have realised how divisive it would have been.'

'But the very fact they wanted to do it; speaks volumes, surely,' said Roger.

'Well,' began Marion, 'the thing that most struck *me* in the paper was the linking of these wider ideas on scholarship with student engagement. The student experience is everything these days; you said, we jumped, and all that. The number of times I was consulted on how to deal with a student complaint. What I'm driving at is that...*if* these wider ideas on scholarship can be embedded *in the curriculum*... in the student offer...then the University...all universities...would *have* to rethink... *seriously*...about the reuniting of research with teaching...for staff *and* students. A nice win-win for us, I think. Well, not for me, of course. I'll be back in my garden on The Gower Peninsula.'

'That's good, Marion,' said Roger. 'Not the bit about you being in your garden; that's good too, of course. But the idea, that, for a university to do otherwise, would make it look like it was against students, and you can't do that, can you?...But tell me more about what the SMT were up to...'

Thomas interjected: 'Probably best that we leave that conversation for later, Roger. Maybe you need to buy Marion a few glasses of wine?'

'Before I forget,' said Norman. 'I've been sitting here thinking about something I read in article by Lewis Elton: a research-rich institutional environment is not the same as research-rich learning environment, for students. Perhaps we should keep that at the forefront of our minds?'

Julian had his arm raised, which Thomas acknowledged: 'I can't disagree with that, Norman, but I've been sitting here thinking that maybe there is an elephant in the room. It's clear to me that everyone here really cares about learning and teaching; we are united on that...and everyone wants to be scholarly, but not narrowly focused on academic research.' Julian cast his eyes along the group, to the right and then the left. 'But, we do still have a quality issue, I think. Whether we like the process or not, research does have a national quality check, as does teaching. So what would be the quality check on these wider notions of scholarship. Forgive me, but some student scholarship might *actually* be quite poor.'

Jack launched in quickly: 'But...only if we don't grasp the full implications of the idea of quality we are working with here.' Jack pointed to the Venn diagram, which was still on the screen: 'If the scholarship we are talking about is dynamic... intrinsically motivated...requiring full investment...*there's* the quality. Any attempt to measure the extrinsic impact has to be very secondary. For example, if staff and students work on a community engagement project and then publicise it through the media...on the TV or radio, maybe...there's the dynamic quality; in their full investment in wanting to do good...'

'The motivation to do a job well,' said Thomas. 'That's key for me, because I can see there the connection with *bildung* and *beruf*. Those two German words I've become really interested in lately. It all connects for me.'

'Yes! Yes!' exclaimed Roger. 'In which case, we need a curriculum centred on the self-development of the student. We really ought to be able to produce more self-motivated students...much earlier in their courses.'

While Roger was speaking, Norman had placed his hand on Roger's shoulder, which he acknowledged by turning to face him. Norman took his cue: 'But I *can* see a few more elephants...What I liked in the paper was the moral foundation in our thinking...I like the idea of student engagement, yes, but I also like the need to fully acknowledge the moral foundation, which must surely lay at the heart of any... *good*...human endeavour.'

Norman then turned to Milton, who was sitting to the other side of him. Norman gave a knowing smile, then continued: 'But, we do have to accept...don't we?...that we are all from the humanities and social sciences...and yet, we are proposing... correct me if I'm wrong...to establish a curriculum aimed at professional and technical subjects. That's a big challenge, surely?'

'Yes,' said Milton. 'But I do like the general direction of this conversation. What we are acknowledging is the need to be very clear about what we understand by the very idea of there being a *higher* education. I was particularly taken by a conversation I had with Lotte a while back, after which I could see that the word scholarship... *wissenshaft*...should be at the core of the experience of a *higher* education. Just because something happens in a university...that doesn't, of necessity...make it higher education. The university, after all, is just a collection of buildings; whereas, higher education is a concept.'

'Thank you, Milton,' said Norman. 'Which brings me to another elephant...'

'Steady on, Norman,' said Roger. 'We'll have a herd of elephants in this room before long.'

'Thank you for that, Roger. But seriously, I'm still unclear as to whether we are trying to put a curriculum rationale together, which could be used in any *existing* university, or whether we are actually trying to create a new institution.'

'To borrow from Jack again,' said Thomas, 'we will definitely come back to that tomorrow morning. Certainly, *I* would like a new institution, and I think our benefactor wants that, but we really need to talk this through.' He turned to Julian, who seemed keen to contribute: 'Julian?'

'Yes. I'd like to come back to this idea of higher education. In my review work over the last few years, I've been very much guided by the QAA HE level descriptors, and the clear movement one should should see in an undergraduate student, as they go from year-one to year-three: an enhanced ability to be systematic in the organisation of one's understanding and then apply that to new contexts; an enhanced ability to recognise the limits of a discipline's knowledge; and a greater appreciation of the conditions under which knowledge is discovered.'

'Or manufactured,' interjected Jack. 'Getting students to recognise the increasingly contested nature of knowledge as one moves away from what is known to what is not known.'

'I've just finished reading Stefan Collini's book, *What are Universities For?*' said Norman. 'Based on what Milton just said, it might have been better if he'd have called it: *What is higher education for?* I mention this because it relates back to one of my elephants, Roger, and why I introduced the question of us being humanities-based people. It seems to me that one of our challenges is, precisely...as Collini outlines... to make the case for the role of the humanities. They are under attack, and have been...let's be honest...since Thatcherism. So, whilst I agree that Boyer was really on to something when he spoke of the the all-round scholar...which I agree, Lotte, would be wonderful to reproduce with students...but what we shouldn't forget, is the need to bring back together, not just teaching and research, but also C. P. Snow's "two cultures". Collini's reminder of what the humanities have to offer...illumination, insight, understanding...all things we value in this room...*also* need to be reconciled with scientific discovery...and the vexing that is at the heart of all good scholarship. As he reminds us, sometimes just looking at something differently is itself a form of discovery.'

'Two sides of a coin?' asked Thomas.

'Indeed,' said Norman. 'If you will allow me, I'd like to finish with this quotation from Collini. I have the book with me.' He reached down to his old leather briefcase to retrieve the book, then waved it in the air, before removing the bookmark from one of its pages: 'On page 85 Collini says:

> "Very little that is of any interest or significance in our lives is like a crossword puzzle or a chess problem. The kinds of understanding and judgement exercised in the humanities are of a piece with the kinds of understanding and judgment involved in living a life."

'Wise words,' said Milton. 'In every meaning of that word.'

Roger moved forward in his chair and said: 'Yes. I always liked it when Freud spoke about *his* new discipline, *psycho...analysis*: a combination of insights from the humanities *and* scientific discoveries. That would fit, I think.'

Lotte put her hand on Jos' thigh again, along with a short wry smile as their faces met. She then rose from her seat and strode purposefully to the front: 'Thanks everyone. I wonder if this is the point where we might take stock. It looks like we have some kind of consensus here.' She looked down at her notebook, which she was holding in her left hand: 'From my notes, I see that we have a lot of elephants and a couple of coins.' At which, she looked up and smiled at everyone. She was greeted with nods and laughter. 'But, essentially, we do seem to have some agreement about the implications of the diagram.' She turned to point up at the diagram on the screen, then turned to look at Jos: 'Jos, you reminded me earlier, in the garden, of Paulo Freire's notion of the banking principle; of schooling, as a verb; meaning to deposit things in students' heads.'

'Yes,' said Jos. 'It was because your paper reminded me of the idea that a true education should be the opposite of that: give students the opportunity to be agents in their education, not victims of it. It struck me that this might be a core curriculum principle for us.'

'And,' said Marion, 'because of that, I'm sitting here wondering if we are now in a position to try to formulate a *set* of core principles...now that...as Lotte said...we do seem to have our broad consensus in place?'

Everyone nodded in agreement.

'Okay,' said Lotte, 'so, I'm now thinking...with everyone's agreement...we perhaps might spill out into the garden again, have some coffee, and discuss amongst ourselves what some of these core principles should be. And then we kick off tomorrow morning with them?'

'Good,' said Thomas. 'I, for one, am in full agreement with that. I was beginning to get worried about how I might summarise everything. Shall we go into the garden?'

***

After around twenty minutes in the garden, Lotte began watching Jack intently out of the corner of her eye. He was in conversation with Rosie and Julian. She was aware that Thomas and Marion might notice what she was doing, so she moved herself slightly, to be out of Jack's eye-line. Thomas was explaining how important he felt it was to produce a curriculum which united the academic and the vocational, and that this should be a core principle. Marion suggested that perhaps they were two sides of the same coin, which Thomas laughed loudly at. Lotte then outlined some key Aristotelian ideas, and asked Thomas whether he thought that *phronesis* could become a key term in the curriculum. He agreed, which prompted Marion to suggest that perhaps some kind of student charter should be produced, which outlined, from the start of the course, what students should expect from the curriculum.

Lotte could see that Jack was now heading towards her group: 'Sorry to interrupt,' he said, 'but Rosie has just made a good suggestion; that we should gather up some key points from the conversations, and produce a slide we could use in the morning.'

'Good idea,' said Thomas. 'Are you and Lotte happy to do that?'

Lotte and Jack flashed a glance at each other, which prompted Marion to say: 'Come on, Thomas, let's leave the two of them, so they can think that through. I want to learn more about your workshops.'

Once Marion and Thomas were a few feet away, Lotte addressed Jack: 'Enjoying your conversation with Julian and Rosie, were you?'

'Yes, I was. I've been unsure about Julian all day. Really not sure he gets it. Do you think it was a good idea to invite him?'

'He's harmless. You *were* giving him a hard time earlier.'

'Was I?'

'What? You didn't even notice? I wouldn't be surprised if he doesn't want to be part of this group anymore.'

'I think we've been getting on just fine. We just had this funny conversation about football.'

'What, while we're supposed to be talking about the curriculum? I suppose Rosie was riveted by that as well.'

'Actually, Ms Philosopher, he was talking about Albert Camus, and his view that everything that's important in life can be learnt from football...particularly morals. Good connection, yes?'

'Bit tenuous.'

'But hey, here's a funny thing. I told him that my Dad was really into football and after England won the World Cup, he started calling me Jackie, after Jack Charlton. I was christened John, but he kept saying Jackie, much to my Mum's annoyance, apparently.'

'And why exactly is that funny? Is that what Rosie the Rivetted was laughing at?'

'Well, it turns out that Julian was named after The Beatles' song *Hey Jude*. His real name is Jude, but when he went to university he changed it to Julian because he thought it sounded better. I did the same. I was John at school, but when I went to university I thought Jack sounded better. That's a funny coincidence.'

'Could be the start of a nice little bromance for the two of you.'

'What's wrong, Lotte? You're sounding way too sarcastic. Should we not have invited Julian and Rosie? I think Rosie's been great today.'

'Ooooh Jack...or whatever your bloody name is...my saviour; you've been so helpful and lovely.' As she said it, Lotte did a quick curtsy and tilted her head, Princess Diana-style: 'It looks to everyone like you've been fucking her. *Have* you been fucking her?'

'No, of course not.'

'Have you ever fucked her?'

'What, in the past?'

'Well, not in the fucking future, obviously.'

'Have you been fucking Julian? Is that why you invited *him*?'

'Okay. You have, then. And no, I haven't been *fucking* Julian...Jude, or whatever *his* fucking name is. Although I admit, yes, I did used to fancy him.'

'Lotte, please....please keep your voice down. Everyone will hear us. What's going on here?'

'Just forget it, Jack.'

'How can I? Look, we can wrap things up here. Why don't we take a wander?'

Jack walked across the garden, from the corner where he had been arguing with Lotte, and up the steps which led into the conference centre. He clapped his hands, and then shouted: 'Sorry to disturb the conversations. Please carry on. I just thought that perhaps we should now call a formal close to the day.' He looked down at his watch: 'It's now ten past four, so why don't we enjoy the sunshine for a few hours. Dinner is at 7.30. And, just to say, Rosie had a good idea; that Lotte and I gather up some of your thoughts about curriculum principles, and we present them on a slide at the beginning of our final session in the morning. So, with that in mind, perhaps we could all jot down some comments at the bar, before dinner. And one more thing: big, big thanks for coming today. I hope you've enjoyed it as much as I have; thought-provoking; thank you.'

With that, a small round of applause spontaneously started up, along with a few shouts of 'thank you'. Jack watched Lotte make her way to the steps, then into the conference centre. He decided not to follow her. He walked across to Milton and Norman, who were sitting on one of the benches. He perched at the end of the bench, then quietly said that he didn't want to disturb them; he just needed to sit for a while. 'Lotte, Lotte,' he said to himself. He then tuned in and out of a conversation about the differences between Cardinal Newman and Stefan Collini, on the role of universities.

***

Jack found Lotte lying on the bed in their room. She agreed to a walk. They wandered out of the conference centre car park and in the direction of Windsor Great Park. They walked in silence, until Lotte suddenly turned to face Jack. She wrapped her arms behind his back, and whispered 'sorry' into his ear. He felt her tongue caress his ear lobe and became instantly aroused.

'I'm sorry too,' he said.

'What for, you fool.' She sniffled as she spoke, and Jack could see a tear slowly making its way down her cheek. He lent across and licked it.

'I'm sorry,' she said again. 'Things just got on top of me.'

'That's okay,' said Jack. 'There's a lot happening. It's stressful.'

'I know it sounds daft…I just got wound up by the way that the men in the group were dominating everything this morning…I just thought, here we are trying to do something different, but it's all…somehow…all the same. I'd always looked up to Milton, and then, suddenly there he was…just another one of the guys…and bloody Rosie the Riveted…' She sniffled again. They looked at each other and laughed.

'And Julian Lennon…Jude Camus..or whatever *his* bloody name is,' said Jack. They laughed again and hugged each other tightly.

'I fucking love you, Lowell,' said Lotte, after a long pause.

'And I fucking love *you*, Rudolph.'

'We can make this work, can't we?'

'It's already working, isn't it? Look at us.'

'Not us, you idiot, the project. *We're* definitely a lost cause.'

They laughed again. After another tight hug, and another long pause, Lotte said: 'Look, I do need to have a serious word with you…'

'…What have I done *now*?'

'Before we speak to everyone at the bar, we should exchange our notes from the day…how did you get on with yours?' She looked at him with a wry smile.

Jack looked straight back at her, and said: 'Have I ever told you that you look really sexy when you do that.'

'Yes, you have. All the time.'

Chapter 28

Lotte and Jack sat drinking tea in bed. The window in their conference suite bedroom was open and a warm breeze was making the bottom of the net curtain gently curl into the room.

'I had some wild, weird dreams last night,' said Lotte.

'So did I. I was standing by the projector in that room, completely naked.'

'Really?'

'No, not really. But that's the dream you're supposed to have, isn't it?'

'I'm sure Rosie would have enjoyed it.'

'What *do* I have to do to apologise, Charlotte Rudolph?'

'Nothing. I'm just teasing. It really doesn't matter, Jack. It really doesn't matter. It's a beautiful Sunday morning; we got that slide together; and we've got a chance to make a difference. Even this tea is quite nice.'

'I just couldn't face the prospect of that instant coffee. Look at those two sachets over there, just staring at us.'

'Are you becoming a snob, Lowell?'

***

After breakfast, Jack and Lotte made their excuses, about needing to prepare for the day, and then walked up the stairs to the conference room.

'Everyone seems on good form, this morning,' said Jack.

'That could be the nice weather, of course. But, you're right, it does seem to be going well. I'm sorry again about that wobble yesterday; anxiety getting the better of me.'

'No more on that, Rudolph. I arrived here very nervous, but, if nothing else, we've proved to ourselves that we *have* got something here. Still not quite sure what it is, yet…but, we're not mad, at least.'

'I think we're definitely mad, but it takes a madman to see absurdity. And what's happening in universities is increasingly absurd.'

'I will admit, there were a few moments yesterday where I thought we might be falling down the proverbial rabbit hole.'

'Well, that would be better than the toilet pan, I suppose.'

'You don't think it all sounds a bit self-congratulatory, though…everybody being very polite…and then they all go home thinking that it *is* all a bit bonkers?'

'No, I don't think that. Yes, more polite than normal, but it takes time to gel, and don't forget, we've chosen people who are: one, pissed off with the way things are; and two, are already on our side.'

'Good point. Now it's *me* having a wobble.'

Lotte walked towards the projector, while Jack walked towards the rear window: 'Do you think The Royal Family see the absurdity of *their* position?'

'They're too invested in it...'

'Like senior managers in universities?'

'Good research project for you there, Lowell.'

'Certainly a good research *methods* dilemma. Could you get them to be honest?'

'Not if there's no integrity in the first place...or they live in a world without morals.'

'Good point.'

Jack turned to look at the screen, which was just beginning to reveal the slide they had prepared for the session.

'Looks good,' said Lotte, as she stepped back. 'Can you see it all okay? Ten sentences on one slide does make it all look a bit small.'

'It's fine,' said Jack. 'That was a good idea to force everyone to write down just one short phrase. Good teacher, Rudolph.'

'Well, easy to write up; there was that. I woke up this morning, though, still smiling about how a simple task became so difficult...a sentence or a couple of words; who's got a pen; what, on these scraps of paper?'

'Once a student, always a student.'

'And that *was* ridiculous...that some of them couldn't even remember to write their names down. I'm still wondering if we should add their names; we've got time.'

'No. Let's leave it. We could play another game...where they have to guess who wrote what?'

'Except some of them have probably forgotten what they wrote.'

'Bit ageist, Rudolph.'

'One last check, please. We *were* a bit drunk when I finished typing, remember.'

They stood next to each other, looking at the slide in front of them:

Some Curriculum Principles

Process driven, not content driven

Student engagement as the scholarship of engagement

Problem solving and character building

Active seminars, not passive lectures

Students monitoring their own progress

Staff and students in the service of scholarship

One culture of criticality

Quality as a form of virtue

The all-round scholar (students and staff)

Independent learning as quality enhancement

Jack walked back to the window, and looked down on their group, who had spilled out into the garden: 'Come and look at this. I think the group *are* beginning to gel.'

They heard a roar of laughter from Thomas, who was standing with Roger and Rosie.

'I was a bit worried about Thomas,' said Jack. 'I thought he might think that this would be like an academic conference.'

'He's certainly got a new found love of the German language. Good job my father's not here. Lost in translation, and all that.'

'For goodness sake, don't tell him that. We really need him...to secure those funds, if nothing else...Like you said before, let's just say German words are very rich.'

'Hey, I thought we *had* the money?'

'We do...I think...that's *my* anxiety creeping in. I need to *see* the money, I suppose.'

'Maybe we should employ Tom Cruise, then?'

'Very good, Rudolph...Hey, look busy. Thomas is gathering everyone together.'

'Give me a kiss first, Johnny Boy.'

***

'Spot the phrase!' exclaimed Roger as he made his way to his seat.

'Funny you should mention that, Roger,' said Lotte. 'We we wondering if everyone would know who said what.'

'On second thoughts, don't do that,' said Roger. 'Mine looks a bit tepid.'

'Don't worry,' said Jack. 'It's the overall look of the phrases that's important; to see if we've captured enough of what we were talking about yesterday.'

'Okay!' announced Lotte. 'I think we're all in our places. The same as yesterday, I see.' She smiled as she said it, which prompted the group to smile in return, and then look around at each other.

'Always good to create a safe learning environment' said Roger.

'Very Maslow, Roger,' replied Lotte. She clapped her hands together: 'Well, now we've had our basic needs met, could I echo what Jack just said, and ask us to consider whether we've captured some core principles here.' She turned to look at the slide, and then made her way back to her seat.

'I really like this,' said Rosie. 'I'd be very happy to work somewhere where these were the priorities. Certainly very different from where I work now...I have two questions...if that's okay?'

'Of course,' said Jack.

'I take it that the "one culture" reference means to try to unite the sciences with the humanities? And could someone say a bit more about a process-driven curriculum?'

'I'm happy to address the process-driven bit,' replied Jack. 'Who wants to take the one culture question; Norman?'

'Yes, that was me. How *did* you guess, Jack?'

'Because you were one of the few to put their name to their phrase,' said Jack, in a pointed, mocking style.

'I was concerned,' continued Norman, 'to try to get across the idea that, yes, it would be good to see everyone in the service of scholarship.' He pointed at the slide, then proceeded: 'But equally important to see everyone working in the service of making the world a better place; if that doesn't sound too crassly virtuous. Indeed, Milton reminded me yesterday of the importance of virtue, in both scientific discovery and human understanding. There are more similarities than differences between the sciences and humanities would be one way to put it. I think it would be great if we had a curriculum which emphasised to students the unity of endeavour in pursuing the good.'

'Thanks Norman,' said Jack. 'Which relates really nicely to our idea of quality. How does that sound, Rosie?'

Before she could say anything, Milton jumped in: 'More than that, Jack, I think; that quality and virtue are coterminous concepts. Sorry, Rosie.'

'And perhaps another coin for you there, Lotte,' interjected Roger. 'Sorry, Rosie.'

'Yes, very happy with all that,' said Rosie. 'Apart from your joke, Roger, of course. And I suppose that does relate to the process-driven notion; that *what* we are teaching is not as important as the attributes we are trying to instil in students? Is that right? Not sure that attributes there is the right word.'

'Yes. I think so,' said Jack. 'That works for me. That was me who put the process-driven phrase up there; to get across the idea, that once students are disposed to a certain orientation to knowledge production, then our work, as teachers, is pretty much done. The *process* of learning is more important...'

'Very Carl Rogers,' said Roger. 'Glad you remembered what I taught you, Jack. And I think this brings us to an important practical point. I'm thinking about that seminar and lecture phrase, which I wished I'd said. If we want students to see the discursive seminar as the thing around which everything revolves, we will have to think carefully about the architecture of a learning institution. Would we even need any lecture theatres? Perhaps all lectures could just become podcasts, which students listen to, in their own time? This is the way things are going, I think. Which brings me to *my* elephant. Well, we all need to adopt an elephant, don't we? What I mean is that, not only do we not have any science people in the room...although I would say that Psychology probably does qualify...but we also don't have any IT people in the room. They *are* becoming key these days.'

'But should they drive the curriculum?' asked Jack. 'I take your point, Roger, but we shouldn't put the cart before the horse; IT should facilitate the pedagogical principles, not direct them.'

'I see that, Jack,' said Roger. 'But it's still an elephant, I think. Maybe a baby one. But baby elephants are still quite big. Flipped classrooms could be the solution, I suppose. Sorry, I'm thinking out loud: encourage students to direct their own learning; bring that knowledge back to the seminar room; and have IT people who can support that model of learning? Certainly needs thinking through. Sorry, I've started to ramble.' Roger could see that Jos was waving her hand in the air: 'Save me, Jos...please.'

'I don't know if I'm up to that,' said Jos. 'But in a funny kind of way, it does relate to what I want to say...that we do need to get across the view that teachers are not saviours; they are not the font of all wisdom. As I was saying to some of you at dinner last night, I got interested in the educative act via my research into liberation theology. Ever since I got my first job in higher education, I've always thought that the whole Western project of education has been very much one of telling people what you think they need to know. It's long overdue, that we go back to basics, and try to fully grasp how subversive a true education should be. I really like Monica McLean's book on critical theory and the classroom, which I recommend to everyone.'

'Thanks, Jos.' said Lotte. 'I'd like to echo that; great book. Thanks for reminding us.'

Jack quickly scribbled 'Monica McLean' on a post-it note from his shoulder bag.

'Could I come in?' asked Thomas.

'Of course, Thomas,' said Lotte.

'I haven't got any elephants, or coins for that matter. But I've just been sitting here, trying to piece some things together. I'm really taken by this problem-solving curriculum idea. I was reading recently that a lot of MBAs in the USA...indeed, I think that the Harvard Law School...now do everything via a problem-solving curriculum; scenarios that students have to grapple with, and come up with solutions to. Indeed, I think some them now call it a "solutions focused curriculum", just in case the word "problem" sounds a bit negative, I suppose...a bit PC over there, I think...Anyway, what I'm driving at is the need to make higher education more authentic...flipped classrooms; solutions-focused seminars; forms of critical pedagogy...it is coming together for me. It all sounds like a more valid and valuable educational experience. I have to be honest, I was a bit worried about this weekend...that my time out of the university system might have made us poles apart...but I'm actually getting really buoyed up here.'

'Thanks Thomas,' said Jack. 'I have to say that I was worried on your behalf. Look, I have another suggestion...I'm aware that time is getting on...unless anyone wants to say anything more about the slide, could I suggest that I ask Thomas to say something about our next steps. We had a quick chat after dinner, aware that some of you...including me...have some questions about our benefactor and where all this might be going. After that, perhaps we might congregate in the garden again, before lunch and continue our conversations there? Oh yes, and a reminder, that we need to get our bags out of our rooms before we go to lunch, which is at one o'clock.'

Everyone nodded in agreement, which prompted Thomas to move to the front of the room.

'Well, just to repeat, I've got so much from this weekend. I hope you've enjoyed it and the hospitality, which was laid on by our benefactor. Loads of questions, yes, so let me try to answer *some* of them, at least. First, the very good news, that, indeed, we do have considerable funding coming our way. As I've been saying to many of you, our benefactor is rich...very rich...making his money on the stock market...but he wants to do good by it. He wants to remain anonymous, as much as possible, and our job...Jack and I...was to convince him...I think...that we are on the same wave length, and that we can be trusted. Jack...Jack, take a bow...has done a fantastic job, as you can see from the paper...along with Lotte, of course...Lotte, take a bow...and we are now in the envious position...*if* we choose...to work up what we have into some kind of curriculum offer, possibly with real students. Much to be decided, yet, of course, but this weekend was very much a suck-it-and-see event, I think...to see if what we have on paper actually does have some real practical legs. I may have some mixed metaphors there; sorry.'

'Well,' shouted Roger, 'we've got plenty of elephants and coins, so a few mixed metaphors won't hurt, surely.'

'Indeed. So, in no particular order, let me try to address the questions you've all been asking me. The first really important thing to say is that we *will* have two campuses...one in Kent and one just outside Oxford. They are both old agricultural colleges, so lots of land and outbuildings, hopefully. These can be our bases. The Kent one is secure and I'm waiting to hear about the other one. Our benefactor has snatched them away from property developers.'

'One in the eye!' shouted Jos.

'Yes,' said Thomas. 'If all else fails at least there is that. But seriously, what I would like to do...as some of you know...is use...maybe the Oxford site,...as a workers' co-op training site, maybe with a few pop-up businesses and skill exchanges, if you're familiar with that term, from Ivan Illich's work...where people exchange skills without payment for services. I'm saying this because *if* all else *does* fails then at least we will have this socialist-style business park...for want of a better phrase. But...we also have the prospect now of extending that to include a co-operative style higher education institute...' Thomas then paused, to acknowledge Rosie's hand, which was waving in the air.

'Maybe a polytechnic would be a good title; that term seems to have disappeared...speaking as someone who got a degree from a polytechnic, before it became a university.'

'That's interesting,' replied Thomas. 'Thanks Rosie. Jack and I have had many discussions about what we should name things. He's also told me off for using the wrong words...like training school...and the like...Sorry, Julian, you wanted to say something.'

'Yes,' said Julian. 'Thanks. We may encounter a big problem; another elephant, maybe...'

'No room for anymore large elephants, I'm afraid!' shouted Roger.

'Thank you, Roger,' said Julian. 'What I'm driving at is that the QAA do have a tight rein on what you can and can't call things.'

'Blimey,' exclaimed Roger. 'An elephant with reins on!'

'Quite,' said Julian. 'But there is a serious point here, that if you want to accredit the academic programmes then you will need to make sure you are following the QAA guidelines...very strictly, I would say. Somebody correct me if I'm wrong, but I think that the word "polytechnic", for example, is now moribund. Probably why you haven't heard the term lately, Rosie.'

'Yes,' said Marion. 'I *think* Julian is quite right there. Nothing to stop you using it, but you couldn't use it to validate a suite of academic courses. I think that's right.'

'So,' said Jack, 'we might well have a large *white* elephant here...Sorry, Roger...So, let me get this straight...if we want to run an institution separate altogether from the QAA, then we can, more or less, do as we please...but to validate would mean to align with the QAA...yes? But outside of that we could validate and name as we please. Have I got that right?'

'The Jack Lowell Institute for Wayward Boys and Girls,' said Roger.

'Here's the situation as I see it,' said Marion. 'Correct me if *I'm* wrong, Julian. An institute of learning *could* call itself what it wants, and do what it wants, so long as it doesn't break the law of the land...fraud, and all that goes along with that. But, I think this is the key...if you want access to the Student Loan Book, then we must seek accreditation with the Quality Assurance Agency. And if we seek accreditation, then we must abide by the rules for gaining degree-awarding powers.'

'The student loan book?' asked Rosie.

'Yes, sorry. It's a reference to the right of an institution to grant its students access to government-backed student loans.'

'And that, I think, is is what our benefactor has in mind,' said Thomas. 'The reason he is attracted to the UK is because he wants a radical curriculum offer, but also to have it accredited, validated...to be *in* the system, if not completely *part* of it. I'm not sure that he full understands some of these implications, though. Maybe he does.'

'But this does sound like the QAA has a mechanism to stop us being too radical,' said Jack.

'Maybe, maybe not,' said Marion. 'We could be creative...dare I say it, a bit subversive...and kill two birds with one stone...validate legally, but operate radically.'

'That could be the college motto, Jack', said Norman. 'Probably should be in Latin, though. Let me work on that.'

'Would look good on a hoodie, Jack,' said Roger.

'Thanks guys. I like the idea, but we do seem to have some serious implications here. So, what happens if we don't want to access to the Student Loan Book? I assume that means that students couldn't be funded to come on our courses?'

'The associate degrees, maybe,' said Marion. 'One of things we haven't properly discussed, which I rather liked in the paper, was this idea of the 2+2 model. *If* the students undertook a UK-style Foundation Degree first...for two years...Those courses *are* nationally recognised and validated, so the students would be in the existing system, for that part, at least...*If* we were willing to stick with the title of Foundation Degree...That could be half of our problem solved?'

'Yes,' said Julian. 'I'm pretty sure that's correct. If we used the term "Foundation Degree", then students could achieve that, through a further education college, and *then* come to a separate institute, or whatever you decide to call it. But no public funding for the latter.'

'Thanks Julian,' said Jack. 'We did, kind of, tag on the bit about 2+2. It was the last thing we were discussing before writing up the paper. Obviously, this will need quite a bit more thought, particularly after what you and Marion have just said.'

'And,' began Norman, 'this seems to take us into the territory of public versus private funding and all that goes with that. *If* you could get the benefactor to set up scholarships...sorry, that sounds like a pun...I mean scholarships as in grants for students...for those who want to go beyond the Foundation Degree...then I could see that this could work. That way, for some of the programme, at least, you would be bypassing the public purse, and, therefore, we wouldn't be accountable to the State, the QAA, or any other public body. And, let's be honest, State funding for students these days is only a not-so-cheap loan, anyway. Personally, I'm not too concerned about seeking private funding...if it's principled...but you would be very dependent on having built a credible institution. Otherwise, would our offer be that attractive to students?'

'Well,' said Jos, 'there would certainly be *some* degree of credibility for students, if they knew they didn't have to pay back the fee. It could be a grant, rather than a loan. Remember those days, anyone? So long as we had an alternative source of funding.'

'Okay,' said Thomas. 'How about this: a Foundation Degree, funded by the State, then onto our institute, with partial funding via our benefactor, matched by private funding from co-operative enterprises?'

'There's a lot to get our heads around, here,' said Jack. 'Personally, I'm still not comfortable with the idea of private funding, but I *can* see real merit in an army of co-ops passing on a percentage of their earnings, to fund an education institute.'

'You know, Jack,' said Norman, 'I appreciate your desire to separate us from the A C Grayling initiative...The New College of the Humanities, to give it its correct title...we've spoken about this on several occasions...but...logically...we *are* sitting on the same plain. We *do* occupy the same territory, and maybe that's no bad thing... Hear me out...what I've learnt from this weekend...one of the many things...is that professional and technical degrees might be more than enough...*already*...to distinguish us from Grayling. And, certainly our curriculum offer...even in its present fledgling state...is already quite a radical departure from the norm. I may need to check this out, but it looks to me that Grayling has quite a conservative curriculum structure...traditional lectures and tutorials...and nothing wrong with that, if that's what you want...but we have something quite different here, I think. More than enough to distinguish us.'

'Thanks Norman,' said Jack. 'Yes, Norman and I have argued about this many times in the past. If I'm honest...I do have a serious hang-up about the funding situation. I suppose I could live with a socialist benefactor, and I do really like the co-op tithe idea, but is this really sustainable...into the future?'

'It just might be more sustainable than relying on the State, you know,' said Norman. 'Yes, we could get a Labour government, next time round, but all of this might not be high up on their agenda. And what would happen if that government collapsed? I'm afraid to say that public funding could be far more precarious than private funding. That's the state of the nation, and a sign of times, I'm afraid.'

'Well, that's brought us down to earth with a bump,' said Roger. 'Nothing like a dose of reality.'

'Well, look,' said Thomas, 'this is surely why we are all here. I'm still optimistic that we have something. I appreciate what you are saying, Jack, but I'm coming round to the view, based very much on being practical...that maybe...maybe...the public-private funding issue *is* a bit of a red-herring...an unnecessary ideological barrier, perhaps. Maybe the future lies in a radical reimagining of how things might be funded? I think Norman could be right...relying on the State could be precarious. A co-operative movement, in the long run, could be the way to go...if we could get things on a firm footing. I think this is what our benefactor has in mind. He just acts as a pump-primer, to get things moving.'

'I'm way out of my depth, here,' said Milton. 'I'm just a humble philosopher, which is what I took A C Grayling to be. I haven't been following his attempts to set up a new college, but I do like his philosophical work. He's been a big influence on my own work, and his discussion of the concept of the good could be really useful to us, I think. But, in terms of where *we* are at the moment, we do seem to have a sound conceptual framework emerging here; for the curriculum, at least. It seems to me that if our concepts are sound...they sit on a firm structure...then the funding streams could be viewed as secondary. At the risk of bringing more metaphorical animals into the room...sorry Roger...maybe there's another horse and cart here: If we can keep the funding cart firmly behind our curriculum horse then...maybe, just maybe...we really do have something solid here. We shouldn't let the secondary considerations of funding knock us off course...Would it be silly of me to speculate, that, if we could get a firm curriculum structure in place...and I do think we are close...then, perhaps we could ask Julian if he might be willing to act as a kind of QAA guide...in an unofficial capacity, of course...to see how closely, or not, we *are* aligned with the QAA guidelines. Is that a sensible suggestion, or not, I wonder?'

'Yes, I could do that,' said Julian. 'It would have to be very unofficial, and maybe Marion and Jos might be willing to work with me on this?'

Marion and Jos looked at each other, and then nodded in agreement.

'Sorry everyone,' interrupted Thomas, 'but I'm looking at my watch and thinking that maybe it would be a good idea to spill out into the garden shortly and continue these conversations in smaller groups. That worked well, yesterday, I thought. So, with your agreement, of course, maybe I could just say a few more final words about our benefactor and the next steps, as I see them. I've been making some notes.'

Everyone looked at each other and nodded in agreement.

'So, began Thomas, let me try to summarise where I think we are, and what the next steps should be. First, thanks everyone. This has been brilliant.'

Thomas turned to face the slide, which was still on the screen. I think we have some good principles here. Jack and Lotte, could you integrate these into your paper, which I will then send off to our man, as an updated version?'

Jack and Lotte looked around at everyone, and, based on the approving nods, they agreed to Thomas' suggestion.

'Good,' said Thomas. 'I will also ask our man to confirm that we do indeed have these two campuses, particularly the Oxford one. I had in my head that it was further north than that. And if and when we do have them, perhaps, in a few months we might hold a follow up meeting at one of them.'

'Thomas, sorry to interrupt your flow,' said Roger, 'but what do we actually know about these campuses? Can we just use the buildings, as they are?'

'It's a good question, Roger. What I *do* know is that our man is willing to make the buildings fit for our purposes. As I said to a couple of you last night, I believe that most of the rooms won't need a great deal of work, and those outbuildings...should be great for little co-operative enterprises.'

'Okay, that sounds good,' said Norman. 'I know I keep raising this with you, Thomas, but I really would like more clarity on whether it is the intention that we will be working on these campuses, and, crucially, in what capacity?'

'Yes, sorry, Norman,' said Thomas. 'I'm aware that I keep sidestepping this question. I think it really is up to us what we do on these campuses, so long as our man has seen the plan. But maybe I should now be more forthcoming with him, and ask what he is, and isn't, willing to fund.'

'Sorry if I sound selfish,' said Norman, 'but it would be a big commitment, I think, even if we only committed ourselves to a few hours a week. I, for one, have just put in my application for a professorship.'

'Thanks for being so honest, Norman,' said Jos. 'I'll be honest too, and say that I would be willingly to hand in my notice if I thought I would have a new, secure, post to go to.'

'Yes,' said Thomas. 'I appreciate that I need to bite the bullet on this, and just ask...outright...how far the funding might stretch. You understand, I hope, that I've been a little nervous, in case I overstep the mark. But, you're right, of course. And, *I'll* be honest as well, I would love to get some kind of job security, for myself. I will definitely raise this and get back to you all. As a matter of interest, who might be looking for some kind of post, if it could be arranged?'

'Difficult to say, I think, Thomas,' said Marion. 'Personally, I'm retired, as you all know, so, no, I don't need a post, but if I did, I think I would want to know about my pension rights, my national insurance contributions, and things like that.'

'Yes, sorry,' said Thomas. 'Bit of a daft question. I need to find out more, obviously.'

'I would definitely consider a post,' said Rosie.

'And let's be honest about something else,' said Jos. 'None of us are spring chickens...sorry, Roger...more animals...which means we would surely have to consider posts for some new kids on the block...and some learning technologists... and others.'

'And,' said Marion, 'if you consider for a moment what it costs to run an educational institution...if that's what happens...we could be talking about millions and millions of pounds.'

'Okay,' said Thomas. 'I can see where I need to go with this. Thanks everyone. I will put all this in writing...possible jobs for us...jobs for others...IT people... tutors...Of course, all this could be made a bit easier if we took our students straight from existing Foundation Degrees...but I also appreciate this could be considered a practical solution rather than a deeper philosophical...or wider educational... one. So much there still to think about. Which brings me to the last thing I want to say, about a prospective timetable, which I can now see may have to be extended, somewhat. What I do know is that our man *is* serious, and he did mention that it may take at least three years to get things moving. On the basis of that, I took it that he is willing to commit a lot of funds. How about I suggest to him that we try to get things in place over the next year, ready to launch something...whatever that is...in September 2014?'

'Sounds good to me,' said Jack. 'Anyone else?'

'That sounds like a good timeline,' said Milton. 'I'm also retired, as you know, but I'm willing to commit a good deal of my time to this project. I only need my expenses paid, if I need to travel.'

'How about this,' said Jos. 'We plan to meet in the new year, to give Jack, Lotte, and Thomas the time and space to work things through. At that meeting we produce something concrete, which would then give us around a six month period to launch something the following September.'

The group began nodding and looking at each other.

'Okay, great,' said Thomas. 'You've done my work for me. With your agreement then, we are talking about trying to get ready to launch *something* for September 2014.'

'I think that's too tight a timeline to get the QAA onboard,' said Julian. 'But if you are thinking about launching your own initiative, then...perhaps...an application for degree- awarding powers might come later?'

'I think that's how Grayling has proceeded,' said Norman. 'I would be happy to see that as my homework, and get back to you all on that.'

'That's great. Thanks Norman,' said Thomas.

'And I would be happy to look further into the legal situation,' said Marion.

'Okay, sounds like we have a plan,' said Thomas. 'I'll confirm all of this in an email to everyone, and if anything is missing, maybe some others might volunteer to fill in the gaps?'

Everyone nodded in agreement once more.

'Great,' said Thomas. 'On that positive note, shall we now retire to the garden?'

'One more thing,' said Norman. '*Constitutio legalis, radicalis operatio*. Roger, I nominate you to be the person who looks into merchandising, and the design of mottos and logos.'

'At last!' exclaimed Roger. 'I'm being trusted to do something!'

***

After lunch, Jack and Lotte waved everybody goodbye from the steps to the main reception. Arms were fully extended from the opened windows of the cars as the tyres crunched their way across the pea shingle to the exit.

'Well, our work here is done, I think,' said Jack, as he began turning to face the entrance doors.

'Let's clear up that room and get out of here,' replied Lotte.

'You were very quiet this morning,' said Jack, as they entered the meeting room.

'I know. I was happy just to listen to everyone. To be honest, I think I did want to confirm to myself that all this *is* worth pursuing.'

'And what did you conclude?'

'That it definitely is, you idiot. I would have said something to you, otherwise. It was really good to get Milton's backing over lunch.'

'Yes. I really like him. He's a bit like the Greek Oracle.'

'One thing I *did* like, was that the women have become more outspoken, and the men seemed more willing to back down.'

'Yes. I did have a word about that.'

'What!'

'Don't worry. I just said to some of the guys that *I* was concerned about my *own* behaviour, not theirs.'

'That was sensitive, Lowell. Are you discovering your feminine side? But, before you decide you want me to call you Lorreta, I *do* think it would be good to get a few more women on board.'

'Okay. I'm happy with that. Do you have anyone in mind? We need to think carefully. It's clear to me that trust *is* important. We do seem to have bonded really well. I'm still worried about Julian, if *I'm* being honest. Did you notice that he kept distancing himself, when he spoke. I hope he hasn't planted any seeds of doubt… Certainly nothing rotten there, but I just have a feeling that he could just scupper things.'

'Are you sure it's not because I said I fancied him?'

'You don't still fancy him, do you?'

'Hey Johnny Rotten; drop it, please. And there was me thinking that the two of you were getting on so well. I *do* know what you mean, though. I think it's just him. He's always kept his cards close to his chest. He's difficult to gauge.'

'Jude the Obscure?'

'Not bad for you, Lowell. Keep working on your act.'

'Just sensing that something is not quite right there. Maybe it was because everybody else seemed so buoyed up.'

'Yeh, it *was* great to see everyone getting on so well. I don't think Julian, on his own, *could* sow any serious seeds of doubt. And Roger! I didn't know he was such a clown.'

'Yeah. A good sign that he was relaxed. I think he's been under quite a bit of pressure lately. This project is good for him. Between you and me, I think Norman's professorship application got to him a bit. He did say to me a while back that he was getting a bit annoyed…that he felt he was being overlooked. He knows about my experience. He wasn't that interested in the past. He was a school teacher. Did you know that?'

'Makes sense now that you say it. But *you* must still be on course to get that professorship. You've been quiet about that, lately.'

'I think I've seriously blotted my copybook on that front. Fucking Wadhurst and co.'

'You're so easy to read, Lowell. Always the working-class hero. Please don't end up as a rebel without a cause, and certainly not an angry old man; not a good look.... But seriously, based on what we now have, do you feel more confident about leaving your place and working for Del Boy?'

'We need to discuss this, Rudolph. If you can read me so well, you'll know I've been avoiding this question, lately. Let's get this room tidied up and we'll talk in the car.'

'The boy doth protest too much, methinks.'

***

Lotte turned left from the M4, to join the M25, on the way to her mother's house.

'Well, Lowell, now *you've* been very quiet. You do still want to come back to my place?'

'Of course. It's not that. It's just starting to get a bit too real, I think. I *would* leave my place, but only if you would. We haven't spoken about it since that day in the park, so I've started thinking that maybe you've changed *your* mind. You would still do it?'

'What is this? Some kind of suicide pact. I'll do it if, you will?'

'I need you, Lotte.'

'Bloody hell, Jack! You *have* become sensitive. We should go to conference centres more often. *Yes*, I would consider leaving, you know that; perhaps part-time, like I said before. But Marion is right; we do need more reassurances. I hadn't thought about pensions, holidays, and all that.'

'That's another thing I've been meaning to discuss...we *are* going on that trip to France next month? I've been avoiding that as well, because I didn't want to hear you say no.'

'I just don't want to go in a tent again. *Now*...if we were to stay in some nice hotels, or *gites*...'

'Are you blackmailing me, Rudolph? Anything, anything you want; it's yours.'

'Okay, ease up there, Johnny Holiday! Yes, France, here we come!'

'Very funny, Rudolph...Actually, very good.'

'There is one more thing...'

'Anything...anything you want!'

'When we get to my mother's house, please don't start talking about culling members of the Royal Family. Just say we had a nice time in Windsor. What time did you say you wanted to be at work tomorrow?'

'Eleven o'clock. I'll cycle to the station, get the underground, and cycle again from there.'

'I could come with you. I don't need to go in tomorrow, but I could work in the office, and then we meet up later and plan the French trip.'

'You *do* love me, Rudolph.'

'Always conditional, Lowell. Always conditional…*Now*,…Johnny be good.'

'Which reminds me…I have a message for you…You keep calling me Johnny and I start calling you Rudi.'

Chapter 29

Jack and Lotte looked out of the train window, at the Oxfordshire countryside.

'It all looks a bit bleak out there,' said Jack.

'Not bad for a Saturday morning in the middle of January, though. Soon be Spring; new shoots and all that, and we've waited a long time to get to see this place.'

'You're in a good mood. I hope Thomas is. He sounded a bit low last night.'

'The thought of a cold night in an Oxford hotel, perhaps?'

'Well, not if he chose the Premier Inn…A beer and a laugh with Lenny Henry.'

'There *is* that. You know he's starting a PhD.'

'He did his doctorate years ago, on workers' co-ops.'

'I wasn't talking about Thomas; I meant Lenny Henry, you idiot.'

'That's a cheery thought, and more power to his elbow on that. This project has certainly cheered up Thomas. His real interest *is* in workers' co-ops. He's coming full circle, so to speak.'

'This *could* really work for us as well, though, particularly if we go part-time; to hedge our bets. And it would be really easy to get to this place. We're nearly in Oxford already.'

'Let's take a good look first. If it looks good on a grey day in January, that could bode well.'

***

Thomas, Jack and Lotte walked up the path to the main entrance of the abandoned college just outside Oxford. Thomas removed a ring of large keys from his coat pocket and proceeded to work his way through them.

'Are they joke keys?' asked Lotte. 'This is like a scene from a Harry Potter film.'

'Each one has got a little tag on it. I checked earlier. The green tag is for the gates and the red tag is the front door.'

They walked along the shingled driveway towards the main entrance.

'Dream big, my friends,' said Thomas, as they approached the large oak door.'

'I hope it creaks as we go in,' said Jack.

'So long as a flock of bats doesn't fly out in our faces,' said Lotte. '*Is* it a flock?'

'Don't know,' said Jack. 'Pretend we're Americans; a *bunch* of bats.'

'Well, here we go,' said Thomas, as he turned the key in the lock.

Once inside, they walked slowly down the corridor, looking up and around, opening each door they each came to.

'Blimey,' said Lotte. 'It's bloody cold in here.'

'Yeah,' said Thomas. 'Our man warned me it would be cold. What he didn't say is that it would be colder inside than outside.'

'Hey, Hermione, I found that loo you said you wanted,' said Jack, as he reappeared in the corridor.

'The water's on,' said Thomas. 'And the electricity. And our man says his people will bring in some heaters, in time for our forthcoming meeting.'

'There's a huge room here,' said Jack, as he reappeared in the corridor once again. 'Would be good for our meeting, I think.'

'And there's a kind of kitchen room over here,' said Thomas.

'The loos are surprisingly clean,' said Lotte, when she reappeared in the corridor.

'This is great,' said Jack. 'I even like the smell of this place…like an old church.'

'And more good news,' said Thomas. 'I got an email from our man yesterday. His people will be going into the Kent site next week. Near Ashford.'

'It's all good,' said Jack. 'Do we agree?'

'Absolutely,' said Thomas.

'*When* did you say those heaters were coming?' asked Lotte.

***

They made their way back to Oxford, where Thomas suggested they get a late lunch at the place he had eaten the previous evening.

'I think you could be right, Thomas,' said Jack, as they were being shown to their table. 'There's so much potential in that place…good transport links…some accommodation for students…if we go in that direction.'

They shuffled into their places around the table.

'And nearer a lot more FE colleges, compared to the Kent site,' said Thomas. 'If we go in *that* direction, of course.'

'Nice little place, this,' said Lotte.

'Yeah. I chose it because I fancied a pizza last night,' said Thomas, as he started to remove his shoulder bag. 'Not sure I'm ready to take off my coat yet. But look, I've got some ideas for our meeting. Shall we order, first? Here comes the waiter.'

'So, when are we going to *have* this meeting?' asked Lotte.

'Well, first thing to confirm: are we sure we want the meeting *at* the college? It *was* bloody cold,' said Thomas. 'The hotel I was in last night looked like it had some conference rooms.'

'What, the Premier Inn?' asked Jack.

'No,' said Thomas. I was in some huge hotel by a ring road.'

'Ignore my friend,' said Lotte. 'Please continue, Thomas. *I'm* all ears, at least.'

'So,' began Thomas, 'let's assume that the heaters are on and working, then it would make sense, I think, to have the meeting there. It was a bit of a trek into town last night from my hotel. So no real gain on that front.'

Lotte and Jack nodded in agreement.

'But, whether it would be a good idea to use that site as our main site…still early days on that,' said Thomas.

'Yeah,' said Jack. 'I think that probably hangs on the when, why, and how of having students on campus.'

'We can discuss that at the meeting,' said Thomas. 'We do now need to make some big decisions. I suggest we have the meeting in the week of half-term, so that people don't lose their weekend, like last time. Remind me, who's got kids?'

'I think it will be tricky, both ways,' said Lotte. 'Why don't we just ask them what day they want? It's not as if we have to book the place.'

'I agree,' said Jack. 'How about we suggest the Friday of half-term, with a possible spill-over into Saturday morning. An evening in Oxford, somewhere like this, could be good for bonding.'

'Okay,' said Thomas. 'Why don't I just send round an email with some suggestions for mid-February. Not the 28th, though; my birthday. Going out with the kids after school...And I'll send the revised paper at the same time, with the curriculum model...That's bloody good, that paper, you two. Our man clearly loved it.'

Thomas held up his hand in order to receive two high-fives, which were reciprocated. 'And Happy Birthday for the 28th,' said Lotte.

'Thanks,' said Thomas. 'But, here's the thing, I also want everyone to take a look at this report by Dan Cook.' He lent down in order to pull out a copy of the report from his shoulder bag: 'I think this is really good. It spells out the core principles needed for a co-operative university. I know some of us might still think this is a step too far, including me, if I'm really honest. *But*, if they read your paper *and* this document, I think they might see the links better. I'm certainly becoming more persuaded...If not, so be it.'

'Sounds good to me,' said Jack. Let me write that reference down...But what does the man from Del Monte think about this?'

'I don't know whether he knows the Cook work...I didn't mention it to him...but, what I thought, is...*if* people like it...it might make us all a bit more committed to the idea of a learning institute...do a bit more reading around the subject...then we send off another revision to your paper. I'm sure he will be on board. He does know a lot about, so-called, third-sector organisations. And, remember, his long term aim is to unite various similar initiatives around Europe...and secure some more money, from Brussels.'

'But what happens if we're out of kilter?' asked Jack.

'We're not,' replied Thomas. 'We're definitely not. He would have said something. If anything, I would say we might even be ahead of the curve...on the curriculum, work-related elements, and on the quality front, at least. But, that's for a European conference, surely? If he invites everyone to speak, including us, then we move on from there.'

Half way though Thomas' last comments the pasta meals arrived. So as not to disturb Thomas' flow, Jack pointed at each person, to show where the bowls should go: 'And could we have some more water?' asked Jack of the waiter, once Thomas had stopped speaking. 'Looks lovely, thank you.'

'On expenses?' asked Lotte.

'*Bien sûr*,' said Thomas. 'Sorry, that should have been in Italian.'

Lotte twisted her fork around the spaghetti in her bowl, and, before taking a mouthful, asked the question: 'Are you sure you're both okay about my friend Carol joining the group?'

'Definitely,' said Thomas. 'From what you told me, I think she'll be a real asset.'

'Yes,' said Jack. 'You've persuaded me. I was just a bit concerned about the trust... group-bonding thing. But I think you're right. She will get on well with Roger, I'm sure...on the self-development side of things. And her legal knowledge...Marion will appreciate that.'

'I know I shouldn't say that I owe her,' began Lotte, 'but you know what I mean. She's really helped me on the idea of knowledge in service, so to speak. We could make more of that, I suppose...knowledge for its own sake versus instrumental knowledge...another one of those false dichotomies we've spoken about. Knowledge in service of the good, as Milton put it once, is not really instrumental; it's integral to knowledge production, or wisdom, as he likes to say.'

'Amen to that, brothers,' said Thomas. 'And sisters, of course.'

'All constructed beings, Thomas,' said Lotte.

'And all sociologists now, I see,' said Jack.

Thomas raised his glass of water to invite a toast, which was reciprocated with a three-way clink.

Chapter 30

Jack opened the large dark-oak door to the room which had been chosen for the meeting. The sun was shining through the large floor-to-ceiling windows, and the sun-exposed parts of the varnished wooden floor had taken on an orange hue.

'I'm so glad we got here early, Jack. Those heaters are only just beginning to kick in. That sun doesn't seem to be making much difference.'

'I think we'll be fine,' said Jack. He looked at his watch: 'It's not even 9.30; we've got over an hour for the place to warm up a bit. Let's make sure we can get this projector to work. I'll feel a lot better when I can see our slides on the screen.'

Jack turned on the projector and laptop, which were sitting on a small table, but then noticed that the screen had not been erected. He walked towards the unassembled screen - which was leaning up against the wall - and began to put it together. After some wrestling with the contraption, accompanied by some swear words, he said: 'There,' and then stepped back to see how it looked.

Lotte turned away from the window: 'It looks a bit flimsy, Jack. Are you sure you've got those legs right?'

'Nope. It's a bloody nuisance. You do it, while I get the slides up.'

'Certainly, sir. And would you like a cup of tea to go with your attitude?'

'Fuck this thing,' said Jack, as he wrestled, once more, with the three-pronged leg arrangement.

'Hey, calm down Johnny Strabler, you're acting like a bloody wild thing.'

'Sorry, Rudi...but I need today to go well...Come here, and give me a big kiss.'

They hugged in front of the projector, before breaking away to look at the screen, which was tilted to one side, facing the windows.

'Perfect,' said Lotte, '...if we put the seats out in the grounds.'

'We're going to run out of time if we're not careful. Thomas said there should be a new coffee maker in the kitchen, and some biscuits. We need to check it's all working.'

'Let's do that first,' said Lotte, eager not to see him lose his temper again: 'I'll have a go at the legs in a minute.'

They walked across the corridor to the kitchen.

'It was nice having breakfast with Marion and Thomas this morning,' said Jack, as he plugged in the coffee maker. 'They both seemed on good form.'

'I know. And that hotel was a lot warmer than this place. Maybe we *should* have set up shop there?'

'Too late, now, Rudolph. I think everyone will enjoy this place, though.'

'It's all good, Lowell.'

***

The first people to arrive were Thomas and Marion, who walked through the front door just after 10.15. Everybody else arrived within the next forty minutes. Thomas had pinned a note on the front door, with the invitation to open the door, then immediately close the door, then walk all the way down the corridor to the last room on the right. By 10.55, everybody was standing in the large room, drinking coffee and tea, and eating biscuits. Ten minutes later, Thomas clapped his hands and invited everyone to take a seat in the large semi-circle of chairs.

'Well,' began Thomas, 'welcome to our very own Hogwarts. I wish I could magic up a bit more heat, but it certainly seems warmer than when I arrived. I really feel the cold, so maybe it's just me.'

'Perhaps a game of Quidditch in the grounds to warm us up,' said Roger.

'I'm sure we could find some bats, if we looked,' replied Thomas.

'Cricket bats or real bats?' asked Roger.

'Very good, Roger,' said Thomas. 'We had a variation on that joke when we first came here.' Thomas looked across at Lotte, who took a quick bow.

'But, look,' began Thomas, 'we should certainly take a wander later. First things first, though. Let me formally introduce Carol to our group of jokers.' Thomas looked across to Carol, who was sitting next to Lotte. She followed suit, with a quick bow.

'Thank you, everyone,' said Carol. 'I know Lotte, of course, who has brought me up to speed on everything. Very interesting. And I think I've said hello to everyone already.'

'Do you want me to go round the group, Carol?' asked Thomas.

'No, no, don't do that,' replied Carol. 'I'm old, and it would be embarrassing if I forget everyone's names.'

'We're all getting on a bit,' said Roger.

'I'm not going to forget *your* name, Roger,' said Carol. 'You've already made quite an impression on me.'

'Too kind,' said Roger, after which he also took a short bow.

'Not the impression you were hoping, I think,' said Norman, who was sitting next to Roger.

Thomas clapped his hands again, and invited everyone to view the slide, which was being projected behind him.

'We thought this would be a good way to kick off, so, while you're re-familiarising yourselves with it...it's the same as in the paper we circulated...could I just say that we have a sandwich lunch, due to arrive just before one o'clock. We have tea and coffee in the kitchen opposite, where you'll also find the toilets. I'm determined that we should formally finish by 4.00, to give everyone the chance to have a wander, and then go back to the hotel, before dinner, which is all booked. I think we have enough cars between us. And, before I hand over to Jack, could I just say a big thanks to everyone, for agreeing to stay overnight. It should mean that we can get a lot done; check over this place; and have some fun together. Jack, over to you.'

'Thanks everyone,' said Jack, as he moved towards the projector and laptop: 'Blimey, it's getting real, isn't it? So, based on our email communications, what I'm suggesting is that we spend the time before lunch on our revised paper, looking specifically at the connections...if any...between co-operative learning and co-operative institutions. I hope you all got a chance to take a good look at the Dan Cook consultancy report. I wasn't familiar with it, but I found it fascinating. Lots of questions, I'm sure. And, then, after lunch, perhaps we could address some of the more practical concerns...around funding, jobs, and so on. How does that all sound?'

Everyone looked around at each other, and nodded in agreement.

'Okay, so...if we take a look at the diagram,' said Jack.

It was a more polished version of the triangle diagram that Jack had sketched out for Thomas, when they had met at St Pancras Station, with "Co-Operative Learning" at one point, "Co-Operative University" at the second point, and "Co-Operative Enterprises" at the third point. The triangle was off-centre in appearance so as not to privilege any of the points.

'As we outlined in the paper,' he continued, 'the challenge was to...meaningfully... connect the three terms. Naturally, the idea of something being co-operative doesn't mean any one thing, in which case the definition at each of the three points might vary, but there *is*...hopefully...an underlying set of ideas: that, to be co-operative implies a much more horizontal notion of power, in opposition to the traditional vertical one...where only people at the top make the key decisions. In co-operative learning, for example, we would expect to see students being partners in learning... *with* members of staff...which could include negotiated learning outcomes; shared responsibility for teaching, learning, and assessment strategies; and a stake in the overall management and mission of the institution. As we said in the paper, I think we could argue that the other two points in the triangle might have variations on these ideas, but...fundamentally...the underlying principles would be the same... Now...the problem, as I see it...or perhaps better, as Lotte saw it...we argued about this a lot...is whether all three points of the triangle *need* the other two, or whether they could happily exist autonomously.'

Jack moved on to the second slide, which was a Venn diagram version of the previous triangle, with the same terms, this time sitting in three overlapping circles.

'I'm a creature of habit,' he said. 'You will remember how we turned the triangle at the Windsor meeting into a Venn diagram. Call it a lack of imagination, but we've done the same here. I managed to convince myself...perhaps nobody else...that the sweet spot in the middle...the shaded area...is, indeed, a sweet spot; that, when each of three ideas come together, they enrich each other...strengthen each other. So, for example...yes, co-operative learning could exist without a co-operative university... but it would be strengthened if it *did* operate within that structure...and so on. I've said enough. You will have read in the paper how the argument was pursued. Over to you. I know this has already stimulated quite a bit of discussion via email.'

'Thanks Jack, said Norman. 'Very clear, as usual. I'm happy to lay my cards on the table straightaway. You already know my position, but for everyone else: I am convinced that the three points of the previous triangle *should* be united in this project, but I don't think that...*necessarily*...the three need each other. I don't think they are *integral* to each other, if you will. I see it more as a practical relationship, rather than a necessary relationship. If I'm completely honest, I would just *like* to work somewhere which was more co-operative in its constitution; it's a matter of *like* rather than logic. Lotte, forgive me if I'm wrong, but I get the impression that this is, maybe, how you see it?'

'Astute as ever, Norman,' said Lotte. 'Yes, you're right; that's a good way to put it, but I'll be honest too...I've always been more motivated by the idea of students as partners in learning, not organisational structures. I'm motivated by the philosophy, not the political economy. And yes, Jack and I have certainly argued a lot about this, as I think you all know.'

'What say you, Citizen Smith?' asked Roger, in the form of a statement. He continued: 'But seriously, Jack, I think the *practical* argument has a lot of merit...as a funding stream. Let's assume for a minute that the benefactor pulls out, or he funds us for a short period only...In that case it makes complete practical sense to me that co-operative enterprises could be a key...if not *the* key funding stream. It makes sense to me to make that connection a tight one, even if it is only a practical one.'

'If I could come in there,' said Carol.

'Of course, Carol,' said Jack. 'And apologies for making those references to the previous meeting.'

'That's okay, Jack. Lotte has filled me in on everything. I feel up to speed, and I like everything I'm hearing. I was saying to a couple of you earlier that I've spend a good deal of my time over the last few years providing advice to women who want to set up women's refuges, and other similar support centres. There's no end to the amount of good will out there. *But,* to make these organisations stable...sound... economically viable...that's another matter.'

'Thanks Carol; that's crucial,' said Thomas.'I'm Thomas...we've had some email communication...the token black guy in the project...Your experience is going to be invaluable, I'm absolutely sure.'

'Yes,' said Carol. 'Loved your ideas, Thomas, and I've heard all about you from Lotte. I'm really keen to get involved in any way I can.'

'Don't worry, Thomas,' said Lotte. 'I only told her the good things.'

Milton raised his hand, which Lotte acknowledged: 'Milton, please go ahead.'

'Yes, thank you Lotte,' said Milton. 'I'm sitting here, listening carefully to everyone, and I see the merit in what's been said so far. And I do want to support this idea of a sweet-spot. I've been mulling this over for some time...I'm not a political animal, either...just the same old, stable...not so sound, these days...philosopher. And this notion of commodification...which was well outlined in the paper...*is* really important, I feel. It's been my conviction for some time that Philosophy, as a university subject, has been under attack. Perhaps not intentionally, but as the result of recent policies and practices, which have had the effect of undermining it. For example, my experience of the research evaluation exercises in universities, have, indeed, somewhat commodified, not just Philosophy, but other similar subjects. I do think this term is a good one. We have had an increasing sense that knowledge is, literally, a product, or series of products, which can be bought and sold; that universities will chase projects which have large funds attached to them; and students have increasingly been asked to think about their degree certificate as a marketable product. This is really not good for the humanities…and, thank you, Norman, I have now read the Collini book…and I'm now convinced that it isn't good for *any* subject, actually…if it wants to be a true, honest, university discipline. My conclusion, I hope, is obvious…briefly, that the organisation of the institution *is* integral to how it treats knowledge. Marketised forms of research will dilute and distort authentic research. And marketised degrees will dilute and distort authentic learning.'

'Thanks Milton, said Jack. 'Brilliantly incisive, as always.'

'No,' replied Milton. 'Thank you Jack…and Lotte…for such an incisive paper.'

'Could I come in, Jack?' asked Thomas.

'Of course,' said Jack. 'You don't need to ask.'

'I'm sitting here, thinking back to that public-private question, which has come up a lot. I now feel pretty secure in *my* thinking, that it *is* a bit of a red-herring. Sorry, can't remember who first said that…Norman, I think…but my point is that we really shouldn't be concerned about *where* the money comes from…from the State, private capital…but the *use* to which it is put. If the people who provide the funds know and understand the context in which the money will be used, then I don't think we need to be too concerned where it comes from. We should be able to make it clear that the mission of our institution…or institutions…is to see the knowledge as serving a public good…even if the funds came from private sources.'

'But there must be limits,' said Rosie. 'For example, speaking as someone who supports animal rights, I wouldn't be happy to have funds from a organisation that has a track record of abusing animals.'

'Yes,' said Thomas. 'You're quite right. I thought I was on some solid ground there, but I feel I'm sinking fast already…'

'Except,' said Marion, '…if we had a governing board, which included students, of course…then we ought to be able to come to democratic decisions about what sources of funding are acceptable, and which ones are not.'

'And,' added Jos, 'to make it clear…in a mission statement, or some such document…that this what our institution does…and stands for. In which case, I would have thought that some organisations…reading that mission statement… wouldn't want to fund us anyway.'

'Perhaps,' began Jack, 'we might say that we would be re-appropriating the funds; transforming them from inappropriate exchange-value into appropriate use-value?'

'But let's not get too principled,' said Marion. 'All organisations get compromised from time to time, and make mistakes. To use the old cliche: it's what you learn from the experience that's important. I was often asked my advice about how to get my institution out of a tricky situation.'

'An example, just one, Marion!' shouted Roger.

'How many times do I have to tell you, Roger. Mum's the word.'

Marion's comment had the effect of lightening the mood amongst the group. Several furrowed brows had turned to smiles, which Jack acknowledged: 'Thanks for putting Roger back in his box, Marion. Perhaps this is the moment to break into smaller groups. But first, let me see if I've got this right.'

Jack went to the laptop, to return to the triangle diagram.

'So, if we go back to this first diagram, could we say that the line which connects "Co-operative Learning" with "Co-operative University" *is* an integral...necessary... connection. But the one between "Co-operative-University" and "Co-operative Enterprises" is more of a practical line, born not of a definitional necessity, but a practical necessity...as a means to put us on a firmer footing...economically, if not philosophically?'

'And,' said Thomas, 'just in case it wasn't obvious from the paper, I've always taken the view, that the line between "Co-operative Learning" and "Co-operative Enterprises" can only ever be expressed as a hope more than an expectation...the idea of students and staff working collaboratively in a college setting *might* lead to the desire to want to extend that into the world of work. I have a lot of experience of that happening, going right back to my course on entrepreneurship, *but* I have to accept that, once outside of a learning workshop context, people do go onto to work in a wide range of contexts. It would be hard to control that. I agree with you there, Marion.'

'Thanks Thomas,' said Jack. 'I think that sets us up nicely. So, I do want to say a little more about our emerging curriculum model, but, given that there seems to be general agreement about that, let's leave that until after lunch. Okay, we have the sandwiches coming just before one o'clock, so let's carry on talking until they arrive, and then reconvene at two. I appreciate that although the sun is shining, it's probably not outdoor weather, but please feel free to wander around the building. If you find that a door is locked, then it's because some work is going on behind it... health and safety, and all. That's right, Thomas?'

'Yes, that's right,' confirmed Thomas. 'And, just to follow on from Jack, we agreed earlier that I would do another "next steps" piece this afternoon, picking up on the questions you've been asking me. That should then set us up for the morning. And, as per my email last week, I'd like to finish tomorrow, by agreeing on who will be assigned to which bit of homework, post-meeting. I will mingle over lunch to try to confirm some of those tasks. That should then leave us free from any work this evening.'

***

Jack and Lotte ate their sandwich lunches looking out through one of the large windows.

'It's going well again,' said Lotte. 'Carol, Thomas and Jos look engrossed. Good team.'

'I know. You were right about Jos; her knowledge of critical theory and pedagogy is really impressive, and Carol's really got Thomas fired up. Still worried about Julian; he hasn't said much to anyone since he's been here.'

'I think he's just taking it all in. He seems very animated at the moment, over in the corner, with Milton and Rosie. If we *are* going to try for degree-awarding powers we will need him, I think.'

'I know, but at what cost? Are you *sure* he's on board?'

'Not *sure*, no. I'll have a word with him. We've still got another half an hour.'

'Okay, good. I just want to have a word with Norman and Roger, and then I need to take a quick wander outside, to rehearse what I'm going to say this afternoon. Think I'll just say it quickly, and then let Thomas give us the update on where we are with everything.'

'And we need to check out that flat on the top floor, don't forget.'

'I know. I'm excited about that. Thomas kept that quiet, didn't he? Between you and me, I think he might have been eyeing it up for himself.'

'So what changed his mind?'

'He said something about it not being practical. He likes spending time with his boys, and it's very small, apparently.'

'It would be nice for *us*, knowing that we could stay there whenever we wanted.'

'Yep. Sleeping over the shop does sound like fun.'

***

Once everyone had reassembled after lunch, Jack pointed to the screen, which was now showing a new slide:

Student Curriculum Journey - Potential Modules

Introductory - year-one
Principles and Values.......
The Nature of the Good......
Citizenship

Intermediate - year-two
Solutions Incubator......
The Nature of Work and Identity......
Entrepreneurship

Capstone - year-three
Professional Formation......
The Nature of Knowledge......
Engaged Scholarship

'So,' began Jack, 'here are the modules or courses we decided were essential. And thank you to everyone who came up with the titles. Lotte and I enjoyed playing around them, and their implications. We put them in this order to reflect the traditional journey of a three-year degree student, although we still need to agree the length of our whole programme...or degree, if that's what we go for...one-year, two-year, three-year...four-year, even...We are still just talking about the core ideas at the moment.'

'Sorry Jack,' interrupted Julian, 'but would this be a good time to raise that alignment issue I've been emailing about?'

'Yes, of course, go ahead.'

'As you all know,' began Julian, 'I've been tasked with looking at how well what we have could be aligned with the national regulatory frameworks for higher education qualifications. With that in mind, I would suggest that each of these modules is given the nominal length of 60 credits...amounting to 180 credits per year, over three years. That would then amount to 360 credits in total...the same as a traditional degree. That way, if we chose alignment with the QAA, we would have the same structure.'

'Except,' said Thomas, 'if we assume that the students would already have accumulated 240 credits through an HE in FE Foundation Degree, we would then be looking to accredit only 120 credits...amounting to six modules of 20 credits each, which could be taken over one or two years, perhaps? That could be much more manageable for us?'

'But what about the other three modules?' asked Roger.

'Yes, sorry,' said Thomas. 'I was thinking that perhaps the first three introductory modules could be incorporated within the second year of the Foundation Degree; as part of the deal we strike with each of the FE colleges, and their validating universities.'

'You're right, Thomas,' replied Julian. 'There are many possible permutations here. I did start laying out some of these the other day. I'd be happy to send them round to everyone...and add a few more. I'm just working with the basic *principle* of alignment at the moment, the mapping across, if you like. It's obviously up to us which of the credit structures we actually end up operating with.'

'I suppose,' began Lotte, 'we could adopt the American semester approach, and just have two long terms, with the modules finishing at the end of each semester, rather than stretching them across the whole year?'

'I like that idea,' said Milton. 'I have the feeling that the British adoption of the American model is somewhat confused. Courses or modules should be more self-contained and finish at the end of each semester...if we are to be true to that system. Personally, I think Thomas is right...that the first three modules should be basic and introductory and perhaps *would* be better contained in the Foundation Degree...a distinct pathway for those students who have opted for the top-up, or whatever we decide to call our honours component. That would also follow the American model... that only certain students, not necessarily the brightest, would be on the honours track. You could then have the remaining six modules being studied over three semesters...two per semester...leaving the final semester as a capstone research project.'

'With its own student negotiated learning outcomes,' added Lotte.

'Yes,' said Jack. 'It's taken me a while to get to this point, but this 2+2 model does seem to work, conceptually. That we start with the more everyday world of work - what Bernstein calls horizontal knowledge...the tacit skills-based knowledge of the workplace...and we slowly introduce the role and significance of what Bernstein calls vertical knowledge...explaining to students its importance in occupational formation.'

'And that's why the first three modules should be in the Foundation Degree,' said Milton, 'to avoid a mismatch between the foundation and the later modules.'

'That's beautiful,' said Thomas. 'This our moment, I think. From Richard Sennett, we keep the learning embodied to start with. We then generalise from practical situations. We demonstrate throughout the modules that a true craftsmen is always in dialogue...with the different sources of his or her knowledge. There is no academic-vocational divide. We don't even speak of it, only the unity of hand and head.'

'And heart,' added Roger.

'Yes, yes,' said Thomas. 'That sense of pride in one's work...that sense of civic responsibility that comes from being an active member of an occupational group. I thought the latest paper from Jack and Lotte put this really well. And I can now see much more clearly how this could be an important thread running throughout all our modules.' Thomas looked up at the screen, which still had the module titles displayed: 'Brilliant.'

'Could I add to that,' began Milton, 'I thought the updated paper was very concise on the philosophical distinction between "knowing how" and "knowing that", and... actually...how unhelpful it can be. In reality, the two are always in dialogue with each other, to use that word again. It's another one of those unhelpful dichotomies. I think you were right not to dwell on Gilbert Ryle's original discussion, only to make the point that a mind-body distinction is not a helpful one when it comes to professional learning. As I've said before, I think, this seems to be in accord with an outward focus for ideas. Regardless of where ideas are actually stored...in a metaphorical mind, shall we say...how often do they just sit there? Solving a problem is rarely just a mental operation. Problems come from practical situations, and solutions are usually turned back towards them.'

'And could I add to *that*,' began Rosie, 'that I'm now much clearer that the distinction between professional and *technical* learning...and their occupations...is also a very unhelpful distinction...What all occupational groups need is the same type of holistic learning...and I think our modules could produce this....I don't know the first thing about engineering or any of the science and technology subjects, but if we could combine the specialists' knowledge in the FE colleges with our modules on the *concept* of work...and identity...and community...this could all fit together really well...Exciting.'

'Especially if they were also to produce a clear notion of student *agency* as well as occupational ownership,' added Jos. 'I agree; this *is* exciting. We need our modules to operate with a clear notion of critical pedagogy; with a deep sense of the transformational possibilities for students; the liberatory potential. I would like to think, that once students have been through such a programme, my guess is that they *would* see the link with democracy and empowerment, and might, naturally, gravitate towards co-operative working practices.'

'And,' began Rosie, 'if we can get that strong sense of the wider implications behind the notion of scholarship...following on from Boyer...then, yes, really, really exciting.'

'Yes, said Jos. 'Perhaps another thread should be that continuous reference to the *wissenshaft*...that, along with occupational ownership, comes a responsibility to nurture the occupation, to move it forward...to develop it, through scholarship.

That sense of agency again. Echoing something that Jack said me at dinner, this is what makes a worker, rather than a labourer. Unfortunately, something that the UK education system doesn't seem to have grasped.'

'And one more thread,' added Milton, 'if those first three modules could also really emphasise this notion of doing a job well...the notion of quality as an intrinsic attribute...then, yes, I agree, too. This *is* very exciting.'

'This is great,' said Jack. 'It looks like we do have the agreement I thought we had. I think we might just have reached, not Nirvana perhaps, but at least got to a point where we have a clear vision. So, if we could leave it there for now.' He looked up at the slide, then continued. 'These then, are our modules, but with no final decision on their length or their credit rating or how they will sit within a programme of study. That can come later. Just that they should all operate within our emerging teaching and learning regime, and those important threads. In which case, with your agreement, perhaps this should be the point where I hand over to Thomas to bring us up to speed with developments concerning our benefactor?'

Heads began nodding, accompanied by other affirmative gestures. Jack and Thomas then exchanged places at the front.

'Thanks Jack,' said Thomas. 'Let's leave that slide up in case we want to refer to it again. I'll try to make this brief, so that we can continue our conversations in smaller groups. In no particular order...but let me confirm first, that our benefactor is really pleased with the progress we have been making and he has confirmed that he is willing to back us. I wouldn't say that the funds are unlimited...that's not what he said...but he has confirmed that he will provide what we need, if the case is clear, and within the boundaries of what has been laid out in Jack and Lotte's revised paper.'

'Well done, you two,' said Roger. 'We all owe you a drink this evening, I think. And you, of course, Thomas.'

'Good all-round team work, I would say, Roger,' replied Thomas, then continued: 'So, to confirm again, we have *this* site, which has huge potential, I feel. Our benefactor also likes it, and will commit the funds to get it ship-shape. We also have that site in Kent, which we might take a look at sometime. But...some big news...He *is* willing to fund some posts...part-time or full-time and to pay stipends to those who wish to contribute, but don't need a post. I asked him how many posts, and he said he would look at it on a case-by-case basis. He is assuming that our group, here assembled, will become an initial governing body, and he will certainly stump up the money needed for *us*.'

'And the on-costs, Thomas?' asked Marion.

'Yes, I'm very happy to confirm that he has agreed to draw up contracts for those who need them, to ensure that everyone will be on the same pay and conditions as they are now. And including any additional payments to ensure that there is no shortfall in pension contributions.'

'That's brilliant,' said Jos. 'Well done, that man.'

'And what about the life-line for the project, Thomas?' asked Norman.

'Thanks Norman. So, what we have on the table is a three-year fully funded project, to start from September 2014. With the first year as a kind of reconnaissance period, where we try out out ideas, set things up, *et cetera*. And then things will kick in properly from September 2015, for a further two years. After that, he would expect to see some future funding streams being established, so that *his* funding could be withdrawn, over a further two years. In which case, what we have here is a five-year funded project, with funding reduced in the last two years, as we move towards self-sufficiency.'

'I think that's excellent, Thomas,' said Marion. 'What do others think?'

'Yes, I agree,' said Jack. 'Much more than I was expecting. You kept this quiet, Thomas.'

'I only got the confirmation yesterday, and I liked the drama of waiting for this moment.' He smiled as he completed his sentence.

The group exchanged glances and smiles, and congratulated Thomas.

'The other thing to confirm,' said Thomas, 'is that our benefactor has been in communication with a few Labour MPs. Apparently, they are very keen to monitor the project, with a view to looking at future policy, should they win the next General Election.'

'Wow,' said Norman. 'That's a *very* interesting development. I hope we get the chance to meet these MPs…to orientate them towards relevant literature and ideas. Wouldn't it be great if we had some evidence-driven politics, instead of the usual politics-driven evidence.'

'Yes,' said Milton, 'that would be very refreshing, if a little too optimistic, perhaps? Forgive me, I'm very long in the tooth on this, or perhaps I'm just another footnote to Plato: the country will never proposer until the philosophers take over from the politicians. Forgive me *again*. I'm starting to sound a little flippant, I fear.'

'Not really, Milton,' said Jack. 'Your general sentiment is surely a sound one. And a warning…to be on our guard. But, perhaps we do have a real opportunity here, to put the future direction of higher education on a firmer footing. That way, it wouldn't be so easy to hi-jack it again.'

'Before I forget,' said Thomas, 'our man is hoping to put together a multi-national bid to Brussels, in 2016, so that similar efforts around all the EU nations could be co-ordinated in some way.'

'Really exciting,' said Jos. 'I have to say that I was thinking about going part-time, but having heard this, I might be willing to leave my present post and go full-time with this. If we manage to get the kind of backing you are talking about here, Thomas, I think we could really be onto something big.'

'And let's not forget,' said Norman, 'about the other similar initiatives sprouting up…just in the UK. It's been on my mind to contact the Co-operative College, in Manchester. They've been beavering away on these issues for nearly a hundred years, and there are others. The more I read about them, the more I think there *is* some kind of movement here. I'm certainly not seeing this project as a risk anymore. That said, personally, I think I would be more comfortable with a part-time post… for now, at least.'

'Well,' said Thomas, 'perhaps this is the point to continue our conversations in smaller groups; take a proper tour of the place, to see what you think; and then reconvene here, at five o'clock. I think we have enough cars to get us all back to the hotel. Dinner is booked for 7.30.'

'Thanks Thomas,' said Jack, at which point a spontaneous round of applause broke out.

'And, just to say,' continued Thomas, 'I will try to complete that list of tasks for everyone. Maybe you won't be be applauding after you see *that*. Seriously though, I will put them on a slide for tomorrow, leaving the rest of the time to see if we can make some headway on those other practical matters: do we have a name for our project; a name for this institution…and so on? And anything else I may have forgotten!'

Chapter 31

The cars arrived back at the abandoned agricultural college just after 9.40am on Saturday morning.

'And to think this place could have been knocked down,' said Rosie to Thomas, as they approached the old college in the back of Marion's car.

'Worse than that,' began Thomas. 'we could have ended up with a load of unnecessary second homes for rich people.'

Everyone made their way back along the corridor towards the room they had used the previous day. Everything was as they left it, and by 9.55 they were all back in the seats they had occupied before. Thomas looked up at the screen, waiting for the projector to warm up. He turned round and said: 'Okay, everyone, thanks for a great night last night, and I hope nobody left anything at the hotel. Let's get down to business, shall we? I'd like to wrap everything up by midday, when a sandwich lunch will arrive. If you're in a rush to get away…and why shouldn't you be…I hope we can arrange between us to get everyone back to the station for those who need to get a train…I'll just get the slides up. I'm glad I prepared these before dinner; I got a little drunk last night.'

'Didn't we all!' exclaimed Roger.

'Drunk on all the good ideas, my friend,' replied Thomas, after which he turned to face the screen: 'Here's the agenda I prepared, just so we keep to some order. I know there's still a lot of work to do before September, so, let's try to be clear about who is going to work on what, and then take stock on where we are at the moment:

To Do List
1 Homework Assignments
2 Our Vision and Governance
3 Dimensions of Quality and Pedagogy
4 Programme Modules
6 Titles and Names

'I think the headings are clear,' continued Thomas, 'so could I move straight onto the second slide, the homework list, and thank you, everyone, for agreeing to undertake these tasks. Jack, are we agreed that you and Lotte will incorporate the results of all this into a further revised paper?'

'Yes,' said Jack. 'I don't think we agreed that, but it makes sense to keep everything in one document, which, I suppose will now need a name itself…it's looking more like a handbook.'

Everyone agreed that this was a good idea.

'With that in mind,' said Lotte, 'I wonder if we might have a deadline of the 31st July, to give us a couple of weeks to put it all together?'

'Maybe 15th June would be better,' said Marion. 'Looking at the slide, it looks like you two will have a lot to incorporate.'

Everyone agreed once more. Thomas then read out loud what was on his second slide:

Homework Assignments

Thomas - to look into Mondragon and co-operative initiatives in the UK

Marion - to look into the legal dimensions

Carol - to look into finance models

Julian - to look at government quangos and current policy documents

Norman - to look into Grayling developments and alternative HE providers in the UK

Milton - to look into values and principles of education as a public good

Rosie - to look into student charters and the work of student bodies

Jack - to look into models of community and commercial partnership working

Lotte - to look into literature on co-operative learning and students as partners

Jos - to look into worldwide perspectives on the role of critical pedagogy

Roger - to look into literature on models of professional development

---

As he went down the list, each named person either nodded or spoke in the affirmative. Once complete, Thomas added: 'Right, great. As I said last night, I don't think we should set a word limit; each person should present their findings as they see fit, and then send them to Lotte and Jack on or before the 15th June...Okay, if we are happy with that, let's move more into discussion mode, and start looking to outline our vision and governance ideas. As there's quite a bit of work still to be done here, would it be okay if I record this session, to help me with note taking?'

Everyone agreed, and after Thomas tested his recording sound levels, he began again: 'If I may, I would like to to say...as I see it...that our ultimate vision is to produce a model for self-perpetuating workers' co-ops, incorporating an educational institute, or hub, based here, at this site.'

'And, could I add,' said Jack, 'that the project part...the first three to five years... should be viewed as a series of experiments, centred around the notion of the creation of non-commodified knowledge, education and learning.'

'Okay, Jack,' said Thomas. 'I think I now have my head around that concept, but, first things first, we do need an agreement on what a co-operative initiative actually *is*, while recognising that it doesn't necessarily mean one thing. We certainly don't need to re-invent the wheel; there are are several documents out there, with good statements on what co-ops should look like, and I regularly use them. The key thing, of course, would be a notion of democratic member control. So, with that in mind, I've prepared this list, to guide our conversation. All based on my knowledge and experience, but I appreciate, of course, that it will need some moulding and tweaking for our purposes.'

Our Vision and Governance

1. Interlocking Co-operative Organisations
2. Democratic and Participatory Values
3. Rotating Governing Body
4. Social Justice Model of Finance
5. A Scholarship of Engagement

'Thanks Thomas and Jack,' said Norman. 'I think we should state...right up front... that we will operate with a public-spirited governing body. That way, we could make it clear that the source of any income will be subservient to that spirit.'

'And,' began Marion, 'we should make it clear that whatever income is generated from private sources, a pool of money must be made available to support poor students and community-oriented research, which will not be subject to external control or constraint.'

'Yes,' said Milton, 'and we must make it clear that the research we undertake, or scholarship - which I do now agree, is a better word - is unencumbered. It must be freely undertaken, in a spirit of the pursuit of the truth and the good. Furthermore, we need to make it clear, that we are all acting in the service of scholarship. Indeed, that the very definition of higher education *is* unencumbered scholarship. I use the word unencumbered carefully, because I wouldn't want to imply that the scholarship should operate in a vacuum. It should be undertaken with clear purpose: it should be virtuous, and not constrained by extraneous factors.'

'Yes, yes, Milton,' said Jos. 'In the spirit of von Humboldt.'

'And in partnership with students,' added Lotte.

'Yes, Lotte,' said Jos. 'And, to go back to the funding issue, perhaps we might look at the Steiner model for schools; that the rich students subsidise the poor ones. You pay what you can afford. Assuming, of course, they still do that.'

'Happy to look into that, Jos,' said Carol.

'And could I add,' said Thomas, 'that we should be promoting the idea of the free exchange of skills and ideas, wherever possible. I try to encourage that in my workshops. *This* place, for instance, could easily house any number of workshops, where people could freely exchange skills...including students...who might then be able to earn credit-money against their fees.'

'Yes,' said Norman, 'I think that principle is well established in some other places. I believe that Mondragon has a principle that students pay what they can, while others get endowments. And, of course, in the case of staff, acting as public intellectuals, they might do consultancy work, the proceeds from which could be ploughed back into the institute. We'd certainly need someone to co-ordinate all of this, but, first, we need to get the principle established.'

'Happy to look into all of that,' said Carol.

'We should get together on that,' added Thomas.

'I'd be happy to help,' added Marion. 'I think we should be able to produce a pretty robust model of means-tested fees, student funding through scholarships, endowments, sponsorship by co-ops, *et cetera, et cetera*.'

'And,' added Lotte, 'we could use the American model, where jobs around the institute could be done by students. I remember when I was at the University of California, that many of the people working in the canteen, the library, and so on, were students. They could offset some of their fees with this kind of work, and the poorer students could be given the pick of the jobs.'

'Yes,' said Jos. 'Students could forgo income in order to pay for fees or do a 50/50 split.'

'And, if you remember,' said Thomas, 'one of the ideas behind the incubator module was to have staff and students sitting down with people from co-operative enterprises, working on solving commercial problems...forms of scholarship based on co-operative partnerships...where the co-ops could pay the students for their time, or similar arrangement.'

'And,' added Lotte, 'we could always use some of the endowment money to fund students to undertake projects in and around the institute. Pretty much like the scheme I already run.'

'I suppose,' began Thomas, 'we could always try to enshrine some kind of principle, that students would be able to defer any fees into the future, and pay, as and when...possibly in kind...particularly if they help to set up a co-op themselves. This is exciting.'

'Yes, I agree,' said Jos. 'We've got the makings of a great common-wealth model here...with everyone having a stake in the movement.'

'Yes,' said Milton. 'I'm happy to work on enshrining that idea into our values and principles. But I do have to ask the question about how far we could go with the idea of a jointly owned and democratically controlled organisation. To cut to the chase, would students want to *own* the institute? They will be much more transient...if that doesn't sound too rude...when compared with the majority of staff.'

'If I understand you correctly, Milton,' said Lotte, 'students could be stake-holders in the sense that they adhere to the key principles, but they wouldn't necessarily have a long-term financial stake in the institute?'

'These are important points, you two,' said Thomas, 'but students might well want a stake in the *movement*, the collective. Certainly, we would need to think that through very carefully.'

'Yes, certainly,' said Marion. 'I would be happy to look into that.'

'Which,' began Thomas, 'brings us to the question of what it actually means to *have* a stake; a financial stake; an investment in the enterprise. This is normal, in traditional co-ops, so would we be expecting the teaching staff to have a similar financial stake in the *learning institute*? I would be happy to work with Carol, Marion and Jos on this. This could be key, I think.'

The three of them looked at each other, then nodded affirmatively.

'But,' said Jack, 'let's not forget that our benefactor may well have ideas on this, and, with his pump-priming approach, it should buy us some time to try out some ideas.'

'Could I come in there?' asked Norman. 'The governing body will, naturally, have extra responsibilities. So, if that is *us*...to begin with, at least...how would we invite anyone else to join? How would the rotation work, exactly, Thomas?'

'Yes, you're right, Norman,' said Thomas. 'My understanding is that our man does expect us to be the initial governing body, from which we would then slowly add representatives from the student body, and from other co-ops. We have to set a limit, but we could start with, say, twenty-four people?'

'As I see it,' said Jack, 'yes, I think that's right...to kick us off. But, in time, hopefully, it should naturally...organically...grow. I can see a situation where we quickly start to recruit new co-operative members this way, who we invite onto the governing board from time to time...particularly as *we* get older, and start to take a back seat. We could, of course, set a limit on how long anyone can sit on the governing board... four years, five years...Thomas?'

'Yes. I'll take a look at what happens elsewhere...Mondragon, for example. Important, though, to establish the principle that you must have a financial stake in our initiative, in order to become a member of the governing body. But, in the case of students, we could recruit, say, half a dozen, so long as they are studying with us. Any others...those, for example, who go on to work somewhere in the movement...could be considered like any other stake-holder. I'll work on this, as part of *my* homework.

'Which brings us neatly to pay, I think,' said Jack. 'Do we pay everyone more or less the same money? I'm thinking about staff at the institute; people working in the wider co-ops; and what about the students?'

'Well,' began Thomas, 'on a matter of principle, I would suggest that it is pretty well established in the wider co-operative movement, that it's not just about equal stakes and equal say, but also equal pay. Or at least some kind of principle that the highest earner shouldn't be paid more than an agreed percentage above the lowest paid. But, being practical, could I suggest that, Jack, you look into that with regard to the learning institute; I will look into that with regard to the co-operative enterprises;

and, maybe Lotte, you could look into that with regard to paying students for any work they do...Just trying to be practical.'

Affirmative nods came from around the group.

'Question, please,' said Norman. 'My mind has started to wander to the people who might work at the learning institute...beyond us...I'm thinking about other teaching staff and administrators. Where are we with that?'

'Not very far would be the honest answer, I think,' said Thomas. 'Being practical again, maybe we should now move on to Dimensions of Pedagogy and Quality. I'm not ducking the question, Norman, but maybe we should look at that first, because this is where we will, most likely, need these people, and I'm aware that time is getting on. I'm anxious that we don't spill over, beyond midday'

Norman nodded in agreement.

Thomas continued: 'Julian, I wonder if I could ask you to kick us off on this topic? I have the list you gave me on a slide. Let me just find it.'

As Julian made his way to the front, everyone looked up at the new slide:

National Framework Compliance

1 Mission statement

2 Programme specification, benchmarked against the national Quality Code.

3 Module outlines with learning outcomes

4 Governance model

5 Students as Partners guidelines

6 Equal opportunities and inclusion statements

7 Research and Scholarship policy

8 Quality enhancement policy

'Thank you, Thomas,' began Julian. 'What I've produced here is a standard list of things that the Quality Assurance Agency would expect to see if we were seeking degree-awarding powers. Naturally, we would need to produce a wider rationale for our teaching, learning and assessment regime, but these are the sort of things which need very explicit articulations. I think we are all clear that this might be an *aspiration* on our part, and certainly not something we could achieve immediately. For a start, we would need 1,000 students. Of course, we might decide to go in a completely different direction. But new qualifications and initiatives do keep coming, and we might want to align with them in future, so I think it would be wise to be mindful of this list in whatever we do.'

'Well,' said Jack, 'could I kick off by saying that, yes, we would certainly have a position on quality, but it might well be quite different from the norm. I think our key principle there should be to ask the question whether...whatever has been created or produced...has been done with integrity, with the desire to do well, with full engagement....which would go for student work as well as staff...The dynamic quality comes from the intention of the performer.'

'Yes, absolutely, Jack,' said Milton. 'On the subject of staff research...scholarship... the only true measure of quality should be that type of engagement. To make a further judgement about how its has been received is not really a judgement about its quality, but its impact. Poor quality work can have an impact and good quality work can have little impact. If you wish to call impact a quality measure, that is all you are doing - *calling it* that. I think you did a fine job of making that clear in the paper, and yes, I agree, it should be our starting point on all matters to do with quality. Personally, I would go further, and make it very clear to the current regulatory bodies that we are operating here with a different order of quality: not a counting of quantities; the number of citations; the number of first class degrees; the number of students with jobs, *et cetera*. Those things say nothing about the process of learning or knowledge creation, because they can't. Someone earning more money is not a better person; far from it.'

'Hear this man, hear this man!' exclaimed Roger. 'And let's be clear...professionals will never be motivated by external audit; it's anathema to the very identity of being professional, and certainly a point which should be emphasised on the module about professional formation.'

'Yes,' said Marion. 'Being professional requires trust, and the return for that trust is likely to be huge. We seriously need to rediscover this...as a principle, maybe? Personally, I don't see much of a risk. I think this is a key part of what we are trying to do here: restoring trust in the beleaguered professional. Doing a job well is a form of duty, which any approach to professional formation should seek to embed.'

'One of the things I've really learnt from being amongst you all,' began Thomas, 'is to rediscover that true sense of vocation; that sense of someone having a calling; and the responsibilities that go with that. I used to believe that I was really on to something when I started talking about rescuing the notion of enterprise from its capitalistic interpretations. Yes, being entrepreneurial should have connotations of being creative and developing new ideas. But I can now see more clearly that it should also have connotations of *character* formation, which is a form of integrity, I suppose.'

'Thanks Thomas,' said Jack. 'And one thing I'm very clear on is a distinction between having a job...which has connotations of time serving and labouring - and being fully engaged in work...from conception of an idea and seeing it through to the execution of a creative task. I'm trying not to sound overdramatic here, but I think this kind of work *is* what it means to be human...it's a lifeblood. I certainly agree with Milton on that. I also think Herbert Marcuse was really on to something when he talked about the distinction between consumption and production...Capitalism has an inbuilt need to turn active producers into passive consumers...and because labouring is shit it makes it easier for people to see their identity being forged by what they consume. I think it would be fantastic to get these ideas discussed in our modules.'

'If work was enjoyable and fulfilling there would be no need for leisure,' said Jos.

'Hold that thought, Jos,' said Norman. 'That could be our college motto.'

'And wouldn't it be great,' said Thomas, 'if we could then take those ideas from the Work and Identity module, and embed them into the Incubator module...

bringing people together as a model of professional learning - employer, FE staff, Institute staff, students...all learning from each other...all focused on problem-solving...turning a problem into its solution through a business plan and the use of research tools. I can also see how this unit could naturally spill over into a wider co-operative hub...linking the institute with co-operative enterprises...to create a wider nurturing environment. Our benefactor called it an organic ecosystem, I think, which would have the potential to attract venture capital from like-minded individuals. I'm getting ahead of myself, sorry.'

'I just love your enthusiasm, Thomas,' said Rosie. 'It's infectious. Thank you. And to link that with the four scholarships...*Putting knowledge to work*, as that great document outlined. Thanks for that reference. I could see a clear connection there with Boyer...discovery knowledge being put to work...in the service of enhancing the community, for example...rather than sitting gathering dust on university library shelves.'

'Thank you, Rosie,' said Milton. 'And could I echo that by emphasising how important I think it is to rediscover this idea of a public intellectual, rather than a cloistered academic...someone looking outward to the community, rather than inward to the university quadrangle. And thank you, Jack, for recommending Jacoby to me. And I noted that Boyer does refer to him, as well. I can also now see how the scholarship of integration does seem to come closest to what I understand by wisdom. That is, having the ability to integrate knowledge from various sources, and to put it to work in the service of the good.'

'Thank you, Milton,' said Lotte. 'And if our modules could emphasise how important it is for staff *and* students to see themselves working *in partnership*... jointly in the service of scholarship.'

'And wouldn't it be great,' added Rosie, 'if our governing body could enshrine and monitor the idea that staff...and students...all got the chance to regularly experience all four of the scholarships...rather than the ridiculous situation we now have, where if you're good at research, you only get to do that, and if you're good at teaching, you only get to do that.'

'The all-round scholar,' said Jack. 'You're right, Rosie; not only should that be a feature of the modules, it should also be part of our values and principles.'

'Completely agree,' said Milton.

'Rotating scholars...staff *and* students...and a rotating governing body...staff *and* students,' added Norman.

'A right old merry-go-round,' said Roger. 'Boing! One for the oldies in the room, there. Maybe I could fashion a logo out of that? Or a hoodie, with Zebedee on it?'

'Thank you, Roger,' said Lotte. 'I'm far too young to know what the hell you're talking about. But, if I may, I'd like to take us closer to some of the key pedagogical questions I think we need to consider...For example, should the teaching rooms be laid out as seminar rooms; should lecturing be recorded on podcasts, which students can listen to, whenever they want; should students be encouraged to teach their peers, with the staff acting as facilitators; should all the modules operate with a problem-based learning approach, where students are encouraged to use a range of research tools, to help put their knowledge to work? And, wherever possible, should students be encouraged to present their findings and solutions as scholarly pieces of work...in some kind of public domain?'

'Brilliant,' said Roger. 'That's a yes from me...an active use of the notion of a flipped classroom. And I've just reminded myself of an old book by Malcolm Knowles, where he distinguished a pedagogic classroom from an andragogic one - the latter being a more democratic, participatory one...not dominated by didactic teachers.'

'Thanks Roger.' said Lotte, 'And I wonder if we might experiment with some kind of scholarship journal, in the spirit of Boyer, which encourages staff and students to present their work in a range of ways...perhaps the journal could be in an on-line format, so that videos and other ways of presenting ideas could feature? And with students on the editorial board. Is that an example of andragogy, Roger?'

'Speaking literally, students as men, not boys,' interrupted Norman.

'Or as adults, not children, speaking feminist...ally,' replied Lotte, smiling at Norman.

'Either way, that's a great idea, Lotte,' said Rosie. 'Perhaps we could devote a future meeting to the idea of an on-line journal?'

'It would certainly be great to get our student progress files completely electronic,' said Jos. 'And I'd love to see us using the American National Survey of Student Engagement in this way. So that students could use the questions to monitor their own engagement.'

'And,' began Lotte, 'could I say at this point how unfortunate I think it really was to link the question of quality in teaching and learning with idea of the student as a consumer, not as a *partner* in the learning process; casting the student as one who consumes the teaching, rather than being part of the process of learning. I think this is why the UK started speaking about students being *satisfied.* In that context, all those NSS questions make sense: as questions about what has been *done to* the student, rather than what they, themselves, have actively taken part in.'

'Well said, Lotte,' replied Jos. 'Perhaps we could form a small sub-group to look into this. I think this is an exciting opportunity for us. To make a stand; help push the envelope, as that say in the States; and improve student learning. A triple whammy.'

'Indeed,' said Milton. 'Particularly if we could bring it all together under our quality umbrella.'

'Maybe we could call the student progress files *Arete*; give it a brand?' asked Roger.

'Certainly worth considering, Roger,' replied Milton. 'I will have to defer, though, to those who know more about branding and the electronic world.'

'And,' began Julian, pointing at his slide, which was still on the screen, 'although I can see a lot of radical thinking here, in this group, I really don't see why it couldn't be aligned with the QAA, particularly if there was a clear rationale.'

'At the risk of blowing my own trumpet,' said Jack. 'Maybe that sub-group could start from that quality triangle...and the need to link our notion of quality with student engagement and Boyer's four scholarships?'

'Julian, could I ask a question,' began Marion. 'I'm rather taken by that NeSSE survey. The more I look at it, the more I like it, and the more I dislike the UK National Student Survey. My understanding remains that the latter is still not compulsory. Are you able to confirm that?'

'Yes, you *are* right, but it would be a big risk not to take part,' replied Julian.

'If you want to be a good boy, you mean?' asked Roger.

'Well, being practical,' said Jos, 'we could develop our own engagement approach, and then, in addition, just administer the NSS because we have to. But, to repeat, wouldn't it be nice to think that *our* approach, based around student engagement, might, in the end, be seen as the way forward?'

'Student satisfaction is just not the same as student engagement,' began Lotte, 'and a university scoring well on the first is not necessarily one which would score well on the second, and it's the second which correlates better with student learning gains. We should be in a position to prove that. And I think it would be in accord with the work of Graham Gibbs. And wouldn't it also be great if our approach to *assessment* was fully integrated into our progress file, and for that to become a sector norm in the future, as well: *ipsative*, formative, self-assessment by students themselves; students monitoring their own progress; no exams, no grades; complete intrinsic motivation...by the end of the course, at least.'

'Carl Rogers would be proud of us,' said Roger.

'And, hopefully, Graham Gibbs again,' replied Lotte. 'All underpinned by our dynamic notion of quality.'

'I'm in full agreement,' said Norman. 'But, I think this does put pressure on us, to make sure that all staff and students fully understand the implications, inferences, and nuances here.'

'Thanks Norman,' said Lotte. 'I've been thinking about this a lot lately. I certainly think we should tell students, up front, what the expectations will be, and what their responsibilities will be. I'm thinking that perhaps we should have a short course, for both staff and students...a joint induction course...that everyone attends before the start of each academic year...maybe just a few days...including new and old staff and new and old students. And that we make this part of the on-going professional development offer, which I'm now thinking should *always* include students as well as staff.'

'Yes,' said Jack. 'Just a reminder, that the professional development idea was outlined in one of the appendices to our paper...sorry, I can't remember which one it was now...If you remember, we were proposing that we put on teaching and learning seminars each Wednesday afternoon, during term-time, where we discuss on-going professional development needs and invite outside speakers to discuss wider issues in higher education.'

'I think that's another great idea,' said Rosie. 'I think the students would really benefit from this...and the staff would surely benefit from the students being there.'

'Maybe,' began Norman, 'this is the point where I reintroduce that question of who, exactly, are the staff at the institute...being practical, we have a lot to co-ordinate here...do we need an Office for this? Would the subject specialists in the FE colleges take part in our staff development offer...and what about learning technologists? We might well need an army of them.'

'Thanks Norman,' said Thomas. 'I probably need to arrange a meeting with our benefactor to discuss all of this. But, on the subject of learning technologists, he *has* spoken to me about this. I know he wants to kit out the place with some state of the art computing equipment, and he said that he wants to recruit some good people. He's really into this side of things.'

'And in terms of professional development,' began Lotte, 'I'm pretty clear that *everyone*, from top to bottom...sorry, that didn't sound very democratic, did it?...that everyone, no matter where they work...should *all* be part of the same workshops and events.'

'I'd certainly like to see a full-time coordinator role,' said Norman. 'Someone really on top of recruitment, induction, timetables...as well as monitoring the completion of the courses or modules'

'And student placements in commercial settings will certainly need careful planning,' said Marion. 'There may well be some important legal implications there.'

'And we will also need to coordinate our small army of subject-based tutors,' said Rosie. 'And how will *they* be paid? Or are they the full-time FE subject specialists? Sorry if I missed this from a previous conversation.'

'No,' said Thomas. 'You're right, Rosie. I think we've been skirting around this subject. That's probably my fault because I've been waiting to see how our man might want to handle this.'

'Many years ago,' began Marion, 'I did some work for the Open University. If they still use the same model for tutors, perhaps we could learn from that?'

'Yes,' said Norman, 'I was thinking the same.'

'Norman, I wonder,' began Thomas, 'if we could add the Open University to your list of alternative providers, and you report back on ideas for recruiting and paying our subject specialists? If the majority will be our FE colleagues, we could pay them extra for any tutorial work they do. But, yes, in that case, it will be *vital* that they are part of our professional development programme...And...just thinking out loud... they should certainly be considered as potential stake-holders in the movement... should they so choose.'

'So, just to be clear,' said Rosie, 'if we can solve the payment problem, we are looking at our subject specialists being the people who will help monitor student progress...linking the ideas from our modules with their subject specialisms? But is it only *us* who teaches on our new modules?'

'In the beginning, yes, I think so,' said Jack. 'But the nice thing about having a project...to kick us off...is that we can experiment...discuss and evaluate, as we go... As I see it, particularly as we come towards the end of the project...if everything is going well...we would then start to actively look for new tutors, teachers, even new roles. By then, hopefully, we might be mentoring new people...Which reminds me... given that we do have a *project* here...for the first three years, at least...we probably should also establish a Steering Group, who could act as advisors and evaluators; those, precisely, *without* a stake.'

'Good point, Jack,' said Thomas. 'Maybe we could invite some of the authors and academics who have influenced our thinking?'

'Nothing to lose there,' replied Jack. 'I'll send round some emails and see what comes back.'

'I'm looking at my watch again,' said Thomas. 'Perhaps this is the moment to put up the final slide, to look at who has volunteered to help develop our modules. If we're happy with that, perhaps we could then just have a quick ten minutes on some of the naming issues?'

Everyone nodded in agreement and looked up at the screen which was now showing Thomas' final slide:

Developing the Modules

Principles and Values - Thomas and Norman
The Nature of the Good - Milton and Lotte
Citizenship - Jack and Milton

Solutions Incubator - Thomas and Rosie
The Nature of Work and Identity - Jack and Roger
Entrepreneurship - Thomas and Jos

Professional Formation - Roger and Lotte
The Nature of Knowledge - Jos and Norman
Engaged Scholarship - Rosie and Lotte

'So,' said Thomas, 'are we all happy with this? And thank you, those of you who agreed to work on these. And, just to be clear, we are still just *thinking about* how these modules might feature in an actual programme...not dealing, yet, with their actual credit ratings. It's just the ideas we are concentrating on at the moment.'

'Deadlines, Thomas?' asked Norman.

'Jack and Lotte, I'm looking to you,' said Thomas.

'Well,' said Lotte, 'there's a lot to do, and we wouldn't be looking to run any modules until September 2015, so why don't we say...end of this October? At that point, we could then take another look at the credit ratings, and the semester structure, if that's the route we take.'

'That sounds good to me,' said Norman.

Everyone nodded in agreement.

'Maybe we could organise a meeting for the beginning of October to discuss progress, and then we all go off to do some further polishing?' suggested Jack.

Again, everyone nodded in agreement.

'So, said Thomas, 'we have that lunch coming shortly, so could we end with a quick discussion around titles and names. Clearly, we don't need to agree anything now, and there are legal questions here, as Marion and Julian have pointed out. I will also check with our man, because he may have a view on this. But no harm in us having a few suggestions ready.'

'Could I kick off,' said Jack, 'with perhaps the least controversial title; the one for the project. I would like to suggest that we call it: The Quality and Co-Operative Learning Project. I think that does what it says on the tin.'

'Sounds good to me,' said Thomas. 'Anyone else?'

Everyone looked around at each other, then made affirmative noises.

'Okay,' said Thomas, 'that was easy. Unless, of course, everyone just wants to get out of here now, and will agree to anything.' He laughed at has own comment, which prompted some merriment.

'I've been thinking about the name for *this* place, the learning institute,' said Roger. 'What about The Free UK University?'

'I like the use of the word "Free", Roger,' said Marion, 'but, as we've discussed before, I don't think we are entitled to use the word "university", not without permission certainly, and this could complicate any future claim for charitable status, if we don't seek permission.'

'I think,' began Norman, 'that my friend is making a little joke, Marion. The acronym.'

'Sorry, Marion,' said Roger. 'My friend is correct in his thinking. I was hoping it wouldn't be so noticeable.'

'Bloody good idea, though,' said Thomas. 'A two-fingered approach. But seriously, are we in agreement that the word "free" should be in there?'

'How about The Humboldt Free Polytechnic?' said Jack.

'Except,' began Julian, 'we still have that problem with "Polytechnic". I did check, and it does seem to be a non-word. As Marion said, we don't want any unnecessary complications, particularly if, in future, we want to officially register ourselves...for State support and degree-awarding powers.'

'But,' said Rosie, 'if we like the word "Polytechnic", why don't we mount a campaign to bring it back? We could use "Institute" for the time being, knowing that it was really code for "Polytechnic".'

'I agree,' said Jos. 'Why don't we subversively push on several fronts...the use of something like a NeSSE, instead of the NSS..."Polytechnic" instead of "University"... wider notions of scholarship?...I'm optimistic that people *would* see the sense in what we are arguing for...particularly once they saw what we were actually doing.'

'I haven't got a name suggestion,' said Milton, 'but I do rather like the idea that "Higher Education" should feature in any titles; to cement the idea that this is the key concept. Just because an organisation is allowed to call itself a university, that doesn't mean it is *really* delivering higher education.'

'That reminds me,' said Thomas. 'I was reading recently, about how some Canadian colleges are able to access ring-fenced government funding...on the grounds that they are specialists in applied research. I think they *are* allowed to call themselves polytechnics, because of that, although most have decided to keep their original names…Their brand, I suppose…or worried about new acronyms, perhaps?' Thomas smiled at Roger and Norman as he finished speaking.

'Very interesting,' said Jos. 'I will check that out. And, one more thing, do we have a name for our course…diploma, certificate, degree, or whatever we decide?'

'Sorry,' interrupted Norman. 'Perhaps I should be the official acronym checker? Just in case?'

'I was thinking,' said Rosie, 'that we might take the title of the Foundation Degree…Engineering, for example…and then add "and Co-operative Learning" to it, when they finish with us.'

'Engineering and Co-operative Learning,' said Thomas. 'I like that. It's simple.'

'Yep,' said Jack. 'Whatever the subject, just add that on the end, or something similar, if we change our minds.'

Everyone looked around and then nodded in agreement.

'On that note,' said Thomas, 'I think I can hear the sandwiches arriving. So, shall we agree that we will continue to think about names, and I will ask our man about it. I'm now turning off the recorder, and I will use everything we've just discussed in my write-up for Jack and Lotte. *But*, it does look like we are in agreement about the project's title, which is really all we need to decide right now. So…here's to The Quality and Co-operative Learning Project. I think that's a safe acronym, Norman?'

'Indeed, indeed,' said Norman. 'And could I leave you all with a proposed new motto: *Honorabile Opus, Minuit Otium*.'

'I'm all for inclusion, Norman, as you know, but you might like to take a look at your own acronym, there,' said Roger.

Laughter began to erupt amongst the group.

'*Touché*, Roger; t*ouché*,' said Norman.

***

Jack and Lotte agreed with the group that they would stay behind after lunch and tidy everything up. After cleaning the kitchen, they made a start on the room where their meeting had taken place.

'Best you leave that screen alone, Lowell,' said Lotte. 'You put the chairs away.'

'Do you think that flat upstairs will work for us? It *is* small?' asked Jack, as he picked up the first chair.

'I think it's rather cosy. It's not as if we won't have your flat and my mother's place. Assuming you don't annoy her, of course.'

'She loves me, you know that.'

'I really have no idea why.'

'Because I'm witty and intelligent?'

'In your dreams, Lowell; *in…your…dreams*. We will definitely need to get a new sofa, a new mattress, fridge, and cooker.'

'I know the cooker looked a bit rough, but it did seem to be working. I think we'll be just fine; don't you?'

'In terms of cleanliness, it's no worse than your flat, I suppose.'

'You're too kind…Hey, I certainly think Norman was right about a co-ordinator role. I can see that you and Jos will work well on monitoring student progress, but… even though it pains me to say it…there's definitely some administrative support needed there, and I'm not sure that's really an academic role.'

'I'll have a word with Carol.'

'She was quiet this morning.'

'I think I know what it is. Margie's having a bit of a hard time at the moment. They spoke to each other on the phone last night. I think she just wanted to sit and listen this morning. She's completely on board.'

'Okay, good. Yes, do have a word with her. I like her. I wish I'd got to know her better when you were living with her.'

'And there was me thinking you were scared of her.'

'She was great at dinner last night on that false dichotomy between knowledge for its own sake and knowledge in service of something else. All knowledge must be in service of something, otherwise it *is* just dead knowledge.'

'Yep. She can hold her own with anyone. And Milton is surely right, we do need a really tight link between the idea of knowledge in service to the good and our idea of quality. We need to check our never-ending paper to make sure we've spelt that out.'

'Do you think that everyone's still being a bit self-congratulatory?'

'A little bit, perhaps, but I'm sure it will get more heated as things become more real. Just have to hope we can hold it all together.'

'We can't even hold ourselves together, Lowell.'

'Good point…You know, as I was listening to Milton it started me thinking, that knowledge produced outside of our quality context is no better than commodities being produced simply because they make money. The meaning context is lost. I need to go back to Max Weber and check that: the notion of *science as a vocation*. That could help bring things together nicely; for me anyway…It's the wisdom that provides the meaning.'

'Part of the false dichotomy problem? Not just armies of metaphors, but also armies of dichotomies. Which turn out to be metaphors themselves, I suppose.'

'Everything needs deconstructing: Theory-practice; academic-vocational; mind-body…How about we say this…that the dichotomies seem to make sense at their extremes…on a spectrum…but all the real action is in the middle, where they meet… in the interplay.'

'Hmmm…so it's the extremes that create the conceptual metaphors, maybe? There is a logic in seeing "a mind" as a kind of storage place, but I take your point, that the creative spark, as you put it once, wherever that comes from, is always in conversation with the practical skills. Detaching those skills is a purely analytic exercise. The two-sided coin again.'

'That also seems to fit neatly with the Pirsig subject-object unity. It's in the relationship between the two that we become truly human. If that's metaphysical, then so be it.'

'But dangerously post-modern for you, again, Lowell.'

'Maybe that's another false dichotomy. I've been reading about the concept of late-modernity recently...maybe the era of the Enlightenment is just running its course.'

'Bloody hell, Lowell. I told you there was a philosopher trying to get out of you... Actually, I've been seriously wondering whether the distinction between middle-class and working-class is also running its course.'

'How do you mean?'

'That, conceptually, it's really becoming a hinderance. If knowledge and skill are always in dialogue with each other, it makes little sense to distinguish between jobs which are middle-class and working-class. That's just a divide and rule thing: Give the working- class a different type of education...a practical one...and the middle-class an academic one. It's ideologically driven, not epistemologically driven.'

'Elevating propositional knowledge and closing it off from the working-class. A pernicious footnote to Plato, maybe?...'

'...and that pernicious metaphor of gold, silver, and bronze...in the soul of each social class...And talking to Roger and Norman over dinner, I can see that a lot of middle-class professionals...the silvers, maybe...*have* lost their power base, and their working conditions are now much more working-class...bronze...in nature. And Thomas is surely right, that working-class kids really do need...and deserve...a much more expansive education. I feel really fired up about that, now.'

'There you go, Rudolph. The sociologist in *you*, again...But fired up enough, to forge some new metals?'

'Very good for you, Lowell.'

'You just reminded me of that great book by Harry Braverman, about the degradation of work in the twentieth century. De-skilling the working-class in order to control them. Is that now the fate of the middle-classes?'

'But that's the point about our project, surely. If you strip people of control over their work, they end up as labourers...as you would say...and the quality will surely suffer...whether you're middle-class or working-class.'

'Proletarianisation and the loss of quality.'

'There you go, Lowell. Your bestseller in the making.'

'But there *is* something that's been bugging me. I didn't want to raise it in the meetings because it's definitely a bum note. I think Julian hit on it, and I tried to steer away from it.'

'What are you driving at?'

'*Can* you trust professionals? If you give them too much autonomy won't they exploit that? There's a lot of sociological literature on this. Weberian modes of social closure. People using their knowledge to raise their social status, at the expense of their clients.'

'There's a will to power there, definitely. It's always double-edged, I suppose. I can live with that...the world is messy...the desire to make good, is just a desire. It lives alongside other, less savoury desires...Aristotle has always bugged me a bit, if I'm honest. Yes, he's a champion of *phronesis*...but also a villain of the peace, because he saw the leisured-classes as the only ones who could be motivated by the *arete*...because the instrumentality in artisan work would always be problematic... as he saw it. That's elitist, but there might also be a lesson there. Things *are* messy. Another two-sided coin?'

'Sounds more like a double-headed snake...I suppose we could rationalise the issue by distinguishing between professionalisation...the attempt to increase social status...the will to power, as you would say...and professionalism...the type of virtuousness we are interested in.'

'They might just have to live alongside each other...like a Greek tragedy.'

'Political motivations, masquerading as sound epistemological ones. Of course, you'd want to keep the philistines from your discipline or professional door...when they come knocking...when the chips are down...you'll do whatever it takes to keep your power base.'

'That's better Lowell...search for the Nietzsche inside yourself.'

'Which reminds me, am I right, that Julian still seems to be hanging onto the idea that the QAA's notion of quality can somehow be reconciled with what we are proposing?'

'Reconciliation is a good word there, Jack. I think he likes the idea that things can be brought together. His own false dichotomy, maybe? Or maybe he just finds it hard to commit himself to anything.'

'Easily led, as my mother used to say.'

'I think he's always been like that. I don't think he really sees the alternative epistemological order we are proposing. *But*...he does have a role for us, I think. Certainly if we do go down the line of seeking degree-awarding powers.'

'I just don't trust him; never have, really.'

'I didn't trust Rosie, but I feel okay about her now, unless you fuck things up, of course.'

'I think Rosie and Jos spoke well about our campaigning role. Yes, we want to change things, but we need to be clever.'

'I could give you some quotes by Nietzsche on that...Don't worry...let's stick with Plato for this one. If everything really is a footnote to Plato, I suppose we could say that a lot of people in universities these days have become so accustomed to what is in front of them, that they have forgotten to look up and realise that universities have become mere shadows of what they should be.'

'That there's a real university somewhere, and a true quality behind the facade?'

'Something like that. We should get together with Milton on this; perhaps over the summer?'

Jack finished loading the chairs against the side wall, and then walked across the room, towards the windows: 'I suppose...particularly when the stakes are high...

people *will* just perform, as required. As Althusser said, appellation works when you respond to how you are called. And VCs earn a lot of money, so the stakes *are* high for them…in so many ways.'

'And the same goes for students, of course. As we've said many times, If you cast students as customers they will act like customers…and blame those they bought things from when they get something they don't like.'

'You just reminded me of something that's been bugging me…everyone performs, as in, they go through the motions, particularly when the stakes are high…'

'…but everyone also performs by having a constructed social identity in the first place.'

'Blimey, Rudolph, we're finishing each other's sentences. That's got to stop.'

Lotte walked towards Jack. They held hands, and looked out onto the grounds, through one of the large windows.

'So, Lowell…in summary…what have we got?: Dynamic quality comes from human agency; true quality does not lie in the beholder…the consumer…but the producer…'

'…and measuring the impact of that on the consumer is a form of static quality… at best, a trace left by true quality, at worst, a distraction…'

'…intrinsic…sublime…invested…*versus*…extrinsic…measured…instrumental…'

'I feel another table coming on.'

'Not another one…*please*.'

'Okay…But what you just said reminds me of something I forgot to cement this morning…the idea that work, as we are conceiving it, is not just the end of leisure, but also of art. That Morris-Ruskin idea we started talking about at the V and A. Blimey, that seems like years ago now.'

'Because it was?'

'That idea that everyone has the potential to be an artist, in the conception and execution of meaningful work…'

'..and the virtue and beauty therein.'

'…and the more that students and workers have control over what they produce, the higher those qualities will be…'

'…and the greater the sensuous pleasure…'

'…Work as the expression of what it mean to be human.'

'You know, Lowell, you really are becoming quite the romantic as well as the philosopher in your old age. I thought *everything* was supposed to be a social construct?'

'It is…but, as Durkheim said, there is truth and objectivity in understanding the social function that knowledge performs.'

'But, as Nietzsche said, prevailing interpretations are a function of power, not truth.'

'And, as Norman Thornhill said: *Touché,* Lotte; *touché.*'

'Quite...But that marriage between Nietzsche and Durkheim...no serious grounds for divorce...yet.'

'Speaking of marriages, I think it was really important to cement those links between co-operative learning, and the need for a co-operative university to seriously enact that...for staff *and* students...and for workers' co-ops to be the key funding stream.'

'Sounds more like a *ménage à trois.*'

'Let's get out of here, shall we?'

'You know, we may be out of sync with a lot of what's going in the sector at the moment, but I like where we are. As the great Mama Cass sang...'

'*...California Dreamin?*'

'That's not a bad shout, looking out on this grey winter's day. But I was thinking more, *Make your own kind of music.*'

'Time for a singalong in the car, methinks. If I can get M People out of my head.'

Chapter 32

The sun was streaming through the windows of the top floor one-bedroom flat at the old agricultural college, just outside Oxford. The clock on the bedside table read 7.37am when Jack Lowell turned over to cuddle into the back of Lotte Rudolph. It was Friday 25th July, 2014, five weeks before 'The Quality and Co-operative Learning in Higher Education Project' was to be officially launched. The two of them had made several journeys up to the site over the previous couple of months, having made the decision - from September - that they would travel up to the flat each Wednesday evening, and return on Sunday evening. They had both negotiated 0.5 contracts at their universities, and agreed that those hours would be served from Monday to Wednesday. Lotte had stood down from her course leadership role, but would continue to teach on the training course for new academics, as well as facilitating undergraduate research projects on aspects of higher education pedagogy. Jack had agreed to take the lead on a new PhD student supervision course for the Faculty, as well as continuing to supervise some PhD students.

They had begun the task of furnishing the flat, after a complete rewiring of the whole campus had taken place, which included new internet routers. They had replaced the mattress on the old wooden bed which had been left behind, and they had kept the two small bed-side tables. There were no curtains on the double-sided windows, but they had both agreed this was not a priority; they had got used to the summer sun waking them up each morning. The bedroom had a fireplace which had an identical one on the other side of the wall. Behind the wall opposite the fireplace was the door to a functional bathroom, which had an old roll-top bath, with shower-head over it, and an old Victorian sink, with a bathroom cabinet above it. Stretching below each of the bath and sink taps there were dark green water marks in the shape of little streams, leading down to the plug holes. They both agreed that the streams had a certain elegance to them, and told a story about past users. But they also agreed that the streams at the back of the loo would - somehow - have to be removed.

The only other room was larger and included a set of basic kitchen units under one of the windows. Underneath the window on the other side was a beaten-up old sofa, which they had pushed closer to the fireplace, so they could introduce their only significant purchase to date: a huge, old, double-sided desk, which they had bought in a second-hand shop in Oxford. They had also bought two old dining chairs from the same place, which now sat on either side of the desk. The desk jutted out into the room from the remaining wall. There was just enough space for this arrangement not to interfere with the opening of the only door into the flat, which sat between the desk and the start of the kitchen units. There was a sink, a fridge, and a cooker against that wall; all in a poor state. A TV aerial lead dangled on the floor, but they hadn't tested it yet. Lotte had brought up an old Roberts radio from her mother's house. It used to sit on her father's desk and now sat proudly on their new desk.

Just before 8am, Lotte spoke while they were still cuddling: 'I just had this weird dream. We were next door sitting at our desk and in came this steady stream of

Oxford dons, asking about what we thought we were up to. You were sitting there… your beard was longer, thicker, and completely grey…and you were explaining to them the theory of commodity fetishism, while I started to explain the principles behind the establishment of the University of Berlin. None of which any of them knew much about. They all walked off in a huff, mumbling about new kids on the block, and what they were going to do about us. I then shouted down the stairs, that there was nothing new about what we were doing. It then switched to the next day. I was dressed as Mother Superior, as each one of them returned and approached me. I was asking them to search inside themselves for the soul of learning; only then could they begin their journey to enlightenment.'

'Well, Charlotte, perhaps you would like lay down on my *chaise longue,* while I get my pipe. How is your mother, by the way?'

'Why don't you just make the coffee?'

'I'm on it,' said Jack, as he detached himself from her.

'I really like it here, Jack.' She took a deep breath. 'I feel calm and happy. I even like that damp smell, especially when you walk through the front door.'

'I know what you mean.'

'And it's so quiet and peaceful. Did you hear those cows last night, and the cockerels again this morning?'

'It's a right old rural idyll; and that's not easy to say. But don't get too romantic, we've got work to do.' He placed his feet down on the wide dark brown, and uneven, floor boards. 'I'll get that coffee on.'

'We can still have the coffee in bed, surely?'

'Of course. Back in a mo.'

Jack returned to the bedroom a few minutes later, with two small coffee cups and a cafetière on a small round tin tray: 'I had a weird dream as well,' said Jack, as he climbed back into bed. 'We were at the recording of The Rolling Stones song *Sympathy for the Devil.* The two of us were doing backing vocals…woo, wooing… and all that, and then I suggested to Mick Jagger that he change the line about the Kennedys, to "Who killed the Quality Officers?" which he agreed to. Bit bizarre, really, because I can't see how you could sing that line, but, somehow, it worked.'

'I don't think we will need Uncle Sigmund to interpret that one. You're still smarting from that email yesterday, from Julian, about the need for a Quality Office in order to appease the QAA.'

'Fucking little weasel. Has he been listening to anything we've been saying? The very essence of this place will be quality…and certainly not one which needs measuring and policing. That's the exact *opposite* of what we're trying to do.'

'Steady on there, Buster Bloodvessel. You don't need to convince me. Drink your coffee; listen to the birds; chill.'

'Well, for *fuck's* sake.'

Lotte looked intently at Jack.

'What?' he said, slightly angry, but also slightly concerned.

'Jack. I get your anger, I do. But we've got a great chance here, to change the script, for both of us. I'm going to be really honest with you here. I know I said I didn't care about that Lucy Martens, or what happened to her, but I do kinda feel sorry for her...a bit, anyway. And I do lie awake sometimes thinking that I caused her to go off the road that night, by winding her up.'

'Well, I've got some news on that front. I was going to leave it awhile, but Marion told me that she did resurface...working in quality control for some big company. Hey, you probably did her a favour. That's where she should have been all along - PR puff, reputation management, or whatever they call it nowadays.'

'Blimey...you should have fucking told me...but I suppose that's good news.'

'And I'm going to be really honest with you...I still sometimes lie awake thinking that if I hadn't wound up Roger, he wouldn't have got so angry with Richard McGiffen, and he wouldn't have then fallen down the stairs with all those QAA boxes stuffed full of old gumph.'

'That's really what your dream is about, Jack. You know that; don't you? You knew about my hidden guilt, as well.'

'I'm a sensitive soul, aren't I?

'And a fucking arse 'ole.'

'Thank you for your feedback. I will act on it as soon as I'm able.'

'Shall we conclude that we killed off the Quality Officers, metaphorically, but only because we were motivated by the need to protect the theft of a precious object?'

'Nice defence...in the court of academia, I suppose.'

'I was thinking about that post-it note I saw on the desk in your flat: 'Who Killed Reality?'

'Yeah, because I couldn't remember the name of that book by Baudrillard.'

'Maybe we need a new post-it note, on the desk here: 'Who Stole Quality?'... Another perfect crime...'

'...because The Academy hasn't noticed what's been stolen from under their very noses?'

'And to remind us to be constantly on our guard.'

'So that's why Julian has been sent to us? Sounds like a bloody game of Whac-a-Mole. Take your eye off the prize and another Quality Officer pops up...What about: Whac-a-Quality Weasel?'

'Might need big hammers.'

'Vigilance, my friend, as Thomas likes to say.'

'I think we both need to discover our inner-Minots, and just chill a bit.'

'I know. I love that guy. He's in his element at the moment. He's really transformed one of the out-buildings. And we must go and see what he's been doing down in Kent.'

'Has he sorted out any accommodation for *himself*, yet?'

'He said he was now looking at some places in Birmingham. Easier for his boys, I think.'

'Hey, you, what do you want for your birthday? Fifty years old tomorrow; if you make it to tomorrow, that is. Besides, you need to be on your toes, my lad: I may have to trade you in for a younger model.'

'I'll give you a run for your money any day, Rudolph.'

'Seriously, is there anything you want?'

'Just for this project to be a success…oh, and a decent sofa, I suppose.'

'Okay. Let's do some work this morning, and then go into Oxford this afternoon…back to the place where we got the desk. Those guys humped that desk up the stairs, so they shouldn't have any trouble with a sofa.'

'Okay. Coffee, cuddle, to-do list…in that order.'

'Aye, aye, Captain…On second thoughts, I would like coffee, to-do list, cuddle.'

'Why?'

'Just to check you're still under my thumb, Lowell.'

Jack looked into her eyes, then pulled the duvet over her head: 'No coffee for you, Rudolph, until you repeat that we are an anarcho-syndicalist commune, and we have no leader.'

After taking it in turns to shower, they sat either side of their desk, eating muesli from two plastic bowls. Jack spoke first: 'How about we check our emails, then take the check-list with us and have a wander around the grounds again? It's such a nice morning, and I think it might cloud over later.'

'Okay. The wellies are still in the boot of the car. We can pick them up on the way out.'

Lotte watched Jack as he feverishly wrote in his notebook: 'So, what's on that bloody list, Lowell.'

'Twelve things, so far…but we don't have to cross them all off this weekend.'

'Well, thank goodness for that, otherwise it could be a very sad birthday for you, my boy. On second thoughts, you'll probably get off on it…when you see all those ticks.'

'Well, number one…which we could certainly do when we get back from town…is to look at that new classroom furniture that's turned up. We need to check it's got the wheels we asked for, and perhaps we could lay out one of the classrooms, to get an idea.'

'I thought the idea was to make it easy to reconfigure the rooms?'

'I was thinking perhaps we could have some fun with it…a kind of default arrangement…We could try to lay the furniture diagonally across the room, so that everything looks more off-centre…so there's no obvious pedagogic head to the room.'

'The disrupted classroom…a sense of pedagogic vertigo? Or do you think we should follow Roger and start saying andragogic?'

'After Roger said that, I did a bit of homework on the root of those words. Apparently, the Greek word "ped" is different from the Latin one. In Greek we are talking about "being led". In our case, leading a child to learning, I suppose. But in

Latin we are talking about "feet". In our case, being put at the feet of someone, a teacher.'

'Works both way, though; yes?'

'Perhaps we need a "no pedestal policy". Do you want to write one?'

'Not really. Just wanted a bit of fun with the classroom. We can do it anytime, I suppose.'

'No, let's do it. Before we go out to dinner?'

'Okay...I've also been thinking again about what Norman said about rotating roles...rotating leadership roles and rotating scholarship roles...Boyer's all-round scholar.'

'Or Roger's Magic Roundabout?'

'Indeed...I was thinking that there's vertigo there as well, but only because it's disruptive to the present status quo. Your dream about the Oxford dons was rather prophetic and ironic at the same time...'

'...because we've also allowed someone to walk off with the word "collegiate". In broad daylight.'

'Precisely, Rudolph. Precisely.'

'A complete collegiate approach to all things. Get that on one of your post-it notes, Lowell. I think that's another principle.'

'Bloody Hell,' said Jack, staring down at his laptop. 'Listen to this, another email from Julian, sent last night. Who sends an email at 9.47 on a Friday night?'

'Someone without a life.'

Jack read out loud: 'Dear Jack and Lotte, I've been speaking to some friends at the QAA, and I'm now becoming more than a little concerned that we might encounter a number of difficulties in seeking degree-awarding powers. Perhaps we could have a chat about this early next week? Kind Regards, *Fucking* Julian.'

'Forget it, Jack. It's just him again. It's his way of making himself important.'

'But we specifically agreed, that we would consult *documents*, not directly speak to anyone...not until we were on a firm footing.'

'It says "friends"; maybe it was just a casual conversation; nothing official. And note, that he says that it's *him* who has the concerns. I wouldn't be surprised if he doesn't know anyone at the QAA, let alone have friends there.'

'I just knew he couldn't be trusted; right from the start.'

'Calm down, Jack. We can work it out.'

'Well, thank you, Paul McCartney. I'm feeling more John Lennon at this moment, I have to say.'

'Whac-a-Mole or Search for the Inner-Minot, Jack? Which game do you want to play? Come on, let's get outside...and don't forget your list.'

'You taking the piss, Rudolph?'

'Always, darling...always.'

They lent on Lotte's car as they pulled on the cheap Wellington boots they had bought the last time they were in Oxford.

'Have I got one of yours here?' asked Jack. 'I can't get this bloody thing on.'

'I think you have…Swapsies?'

'I told you we should've got different colours.'

'And miss the chance to look like a sad couple? Matching cagoules next, Lowell.'

'Thank you, darling. That would be lovely.'

Their wellies made crunching noises as they made their way along the driveway, until they reached a metal gate, which led into a large open green space with a few tall oak trees. They began walking around the perimeter, towards the area that the morning sun had already dried out.

'One good thing,' began Jack, 'is that we now have Marjorie on board. You did well, there, Lotte.'

'Not me, really; it was Carol. Margie was being made redundant, if you remember. It was Carol who persuaded her. The three of us just sat and talked it through.'

'She's just what we needed. I was worried about how we would even begin to think about student recruitment…student placements…student welfare. I think I was a bit naive; kind of assuming that if we cared about students then it would all, somehow, slot into place.'

'I know what you mean. Do you remember when we talked about a university within a university? A kind of two tribes thing…where the bureaucrats and administrators worked alongside the academics, but they didn't recognise each other…speaking different languages…I really liked that idea.'

'Yeah; China Miéville. That's a coincidence, I finally got round to reading it. I liked his use of "unvisible" rather than "invisible"…a form of disavowal; seeing but not seeing…not *allowing* yourself to see what's really there.'

'Really like that too, because it relates to what I want to say…that it could have the effect on academics, that they start to believe they would be better off without the administrators altogether. Whereas, in fact, what's needed are administrators who speak the same language; share the same values.'

'Moving over from the dark into the light? But your dream last night told us that some academics have gone in the opposite direction. Fortunate and unfortunate border crossings, perhaps?'

'Nicely put…But, back to Margie. What I didn't tell you is that they are now looking for a place around Oxford, which means that Margie could be here, on campus, for a lot of the time.'

'You don't think their relationship will cause any problems?'

'Why should it? And anyway, you idiot, *we're* in a relationship, don't forget.'

'Yeah, sorry. I just never think about us like that…in a *relationship*.'

'Carry on thinking like that, and we won't be in any form of relationship, my lad.'

'You know what, though, Marjorie's knowledge of further education colleges will be really useful. I think it would be great if she came with me, and Thomas, each time we visit a college. And Marion said that she would set up a Memorandum of Agreement each time we get a college on board.'

'Which reminds me...we need to talk about contracts for everyone. Or is that not on your list?'

'It's number two on the list, actually.'

'So,...we have Margie on a full-time contract, along with Thomas, and we have Carol on a 0.5 contract.'

'Yep, with Jos and Rosie still to decide whether they want to be full-time. I must contact both of them. For the time being, they will be on 0.5 contracts, along with Roger and Norman.'

'Which leaves Milton and Marion, who will be paid lump sums according to the work they undertake...as and when?'

'Yep. I just need to confirm a rate for them; probably £500 per day.'

'And then there's Julian, of course.'

'And there was me trying to forget him. He *was* number three on the list, though.'

'We can just *use* Julian, surely? Use him as and when. And keep him at arm's length. I think that's what he wants, anyway. Just give him the same contract as Milton and Marion. That'll keep him sweet.'

'Sympathy for the Devil is never easy, though.'

They approached the biggest of the oak trees, then sat at its foot, as they had done once before. They could feel the warmth of the sun as they lent back on the large trunk.

'So, what else is on that list, Lowell?'

'Forget the list...for now, anyway. I just want to savour this moment...You're right, this place *is* great.'

'I'm always right. You know that...So...Jagger or Richards?'

'Got to be Richards...all the way...surely?'

'I think that song was mainly Jagger, though.'

'Two sides of the same coin again? Each needs the other?'

'Just like us, darling.' With that, Lotte began singing lines from the song *It Takes Two*: 'Come on, Marvin, join in.'

They sang loudly, while looking out across the fields towards the River Thames.

'It does all seem to have come together rather well, Charlotte Rudolph. Our dreams just might have come true. Now...let's not get married, and spoil this beautiful relationship.'

Epilogue

The Conservative Party won the General Election held in May 2015, and one year later - in June 2016 - the people of the UK voted in the Brexit Referendum to leave the European Union. Both events had serious repercussions for our story: the link with the small band of MPs in the Labour Party was lost, and Britain's role in a potential Brussel's funded project was questioned.

That said, the old agricultural college was still on course to receive its first intake of students - around fifty - in September 2015. The students were going to be fully funded by the project in exchange for working with staff on setting up a new hub for co-operative initiatives. A long-term name for the learning institute and the hub was yet to be agreed.

I left my university post and lost my job as narrator around the end of this story, which leaves open the question of how the main characters would have dealt with some of the more recent reforms in UK higher education - for example, the introduction of the Teaching Excellence Framework, The Knowledge Exchange Framework, and developments in higher technical qualifications. My feeling is that they would have considered all of them to be still operating with a static notion of quality, and thereby continuing to impoverish higher learning and the process of professional formation.

And what of our lovers? I like to think they are still working somewhere in higher education, possibly at a newly formed Humboldt Free Polytechnic or a place like it, and that they are continuing to do a good job well.

And what of that *concept* of quality? Perhaps its pursuit will always be elusive and that's the way it should be? Or perhaps we shouldn't allow ourselves to be so seduced by such a slippery abstract noun?

Charlie Rondeau

Bibliography

The following books and articles inspired this tale.

Ainley, P. (1993) *Class and Skill: Changing Divisions of Knowledge and Labour.* London: Continuum.

Abbs, P. (1994) *The Educational Imperative: a defence of Socratic and aesthetic learning.* Washington DC: Falmer Press.

Bailey, C. (1984) *Beyond the Present and the Particular: a theory of liberal education.* Boston MA: Routledge

Barnett, R. (2010) *Being a University.* London: Routledge.

Baudrillard, J. (2007) *The Perfect Crime.* London: Verso.

Beck, J., and M. Young (2005) The assault on the professions and the restructuring of academic and professional identities: A Bernsteinian analysis, *British Journal of Sociology of Education,* 26(2): 183-97.

Bernstein, B. (2000) *Pedagogy, Symbolic Control and Identity: theory, research and critique.* Lanham, MD: Rowman and Littlefield.

Boyer, E.L. (1990) *Scholarship Reconsidered: priorities for the professoriate.* Princeton, NJ: The Carnegie Foundation for the Advancement of Teaching.

Boyer, E.L. (1996) The scholarship of engagement, *Journal of Public Outreach,* 1(1): 11-20.

Butler, J. (1990) *Gender Trouble: feminism and the subversion of identity.* New York: Routledge.

Collini, S. (2012) *What are Universities For?* London: Penguin.

Cook, D. (2013) *Realising the Co-Operative University: A consultancy report for The Co-operative College.* [Available online].

Dewey, J. (1916) *Democracy and Education: an introduction to the philosophy of education.* New York: Macmillan.

Freire, P. (1970) *Pedagogy of the Oppressed.* New York: Continuum.

Garfinkel, H. (1967) Good Organizational Reasons for Bad Clinic Records, in Garfinkel, H. (1967) *Studies in Ethnomethodology,* New York: Prentice-Hall.

Gibbs, G. (2010) *Dimensions of Quality.* York: HEA.

Gibbs, G. (2012) *Implications of 'Dimensions of Quality' in a market environment.* York: HEA.

Grayling, A.C. (2003) *What is Good?: the search for the best way to live.* London: Weidenfeld and Nicolson.

Guile, D. and Evans, K. (2010) *Putting Knowledge to Work: re-contextualising knowledge through the design and implementation of work-based learning at higher education levels.* London: fdf Publications.

Healey, M. and Jenkins, A. (2009) *Developing undergraduate research and inquiry.* York: HEA.

hooks, b. (1994) *Teaching to Transgress: education as the practice of freedom.* New York: Routledge.

Humboldt, W. von [1810] (1970) On the spirit and organisational framework of intellectual institutions in Berlin, *Minerva,* 8: 242-267.

Illich, I. (1971) *Deschooling Society.* New York.: Harrow Books.

Jacoby, R. (1987) *The Last Intellectuals: American Culture In The Age Of Academe.* New York: Basic Books.

Knowles, M. (1973) *The Adult Learner: A neglected species.* New York: Gulf.

Lomas, L. (2007) Zen, motorcycle maintenance and quality in higher education, *Quality Assurance in Education*,15 (4), 402-412.

Marcuse, H. [1964] (2002) *One Dimensional Man*, New York: Routledge Classics.

McLean, M. (2006) *Pedagogy and the University: critical theory and practice.* London: Continuum.

Miéville, C. (2009) *The City and The City.* London: Pan Macmillan.

Morris, W. [1891] (1995) *News From Nowhere.* Cambridge: Cambridge University Press.

Neary, M. and Winn, J. (2009) Student as Producer: reinventing the student experience in higher education, in Bell, L., Stevenson, H. and Neary, M. (2009) *The Future of Higher Education.* London: Continuum.

Newman, J. H. [1854] (1982) *The Idea of a University.* Indiana: University of Notre Dame Press.

Pirsig, R. (1974) *Zen and the Art of Motorcycle Maintenance.* New York: William Morrow.

Pirsig, R. (1991) *Lila: an inquiry into morals.* New York: Bantam Books.

Readings, B. (1997) *The University in Ruins.* Cambridge MA: Harvard University Press.

Ritzer, G. (2000) *The McDonaldization of Society.* Thousand Oaks CA: Pine Forge Press.

Sayer, D. (2015) *Rank Hypocrisies: the insult of the REF.* London: Sage.

Rogers, C. (1957) Personal thoughts on teaching and learning, reproduced in Kischenbaum, H. and Henderson V.L. (eds) (1989) *The Carl Rogers Reader.* New York: Houghton Mifflin.

Sennett, R. (2008) *The Craftsman.* London: Penguin Books.

Winch, C. (2010) *Dimensions of Expertise: A Conceptual Exploration of Vocational Knowledge.* London: Continuum.

Young, M. and Muller, J. (eds.) (2014) *Knowledge, Expertise and the Professions.* London: Routledge.

Acknowledgements

I would like to thank all the authors who appear in the bibliography. Every text was inspirational, and not just for this tale.

I am indebted to all my colleagues and friends who read earlier drafts of the manuscript; for their ideas and for their corrections. Naturally, any errors which remain are entirely my responsibility. Thank you especially: Peter, Penny, Maria, Jo, Becky, Simon, Caroline, and Tony. And thanks to Vrinda and Ashley, for their diligent work on the book design, the typesetting, and the cover design. I would also like to thank all the colleagues I've worked with over the years, particularly those I've vehemently disagreed with. New ideas are born out of opposition to old ones.

And thank you, Emile Durkheim and Frederick Nietzsche. If Durkheim was right, the university might be considered a place to explore how the sacred gets elevated from the profane. If Nietzsche was right, it might be considered a place to explore the Apollonian desire to create order out of Dionysian chaos. The university: a place to explore the constant *interplay* between what is considered scared and profane, and the *interplay* between order and chaos. Different sides of the same coin, maybe?

For that to happen, a university needs to conceptualised more as a space rather than a place; a space for *higher* education, and a recognition that everything we currently know may turn out to be wrong. On that score, I would like to thank Bill Readings for his idea that a university might be better conceived as a place to accommodate dissensus, rather than a place to establish consensus.

About the author

Charlie Rondeau worked in a UK university throughout the period in which this story is set. Her first teaching job was in further education, where she taught both Sociology and Philosophy. Upon securing a university post, she began writing about the meaning and role of higher and further education in society, as well as supporting academics to enhance their knowledge and understanding of higher education pedagogy. She is now formally retired but continues to write and engage in the battle of ideas for the soul of higher education.

Footnote

If you have any comments or questions about this book, please feel free to email me at: charlierondeauauthor@gmail.com

Charlie Rondeau